STOLEN IN THE NIGHT

An unputdownable psychological thriller
with a breathtaking twist

PATRICIA
MACDONALD

JOFFE BOOKS

Revised edition 2022
Joffe Books, London
www.joffebooks.com

First published in Great Britain and the USA
in 2007 by Atria Books

This paperback edition was first published
in Great Britain in 2022

Cover art by Nick Castle

ISBN: 978-1-80405-674-5

To the Boggle girls:
Anne, Carmen, Craig, Harriett, Kate, and Terryl — for the pleasure of your company.

CHAPTER 1

Holding her breath, nine-year-old Tess DeGraff ascended toward the shimmering green light, sparkling strands of bubbles streaming in her wake. She broke the surface and let out a shriek that was half yelp of pain, half pure exultation.

"Tess, Phoebe, swim closer to the dock," Dawn DeGraff called out to her daughters from where she sat on a blanket on the grassy bank. Dawn was cradling her youngest, three-month-old Sean, and talking with another couple who had arrived at the lake, their toddler in tow. But her attention never wandered far from her children.

Tess looked around and caught the eye of her thirteen-year-old sister, Phoebe. Phoebe's wet blonde hair was plastered to her head. The bliss in her eyes mirrored Tess's. They exchanged a conspiratorial glance and both began to dog paddle ineffectually in the direction of the dock.

All of a sudden, Tess felt something tugging her ankle, dragging her down, and she screamed. The tug gave way, and her father surfaced beside her with a wide grin.

"Dad, you scared me!" Tessa cried, pummeling his broad chest with her small fists. Rob DeGraff laughed and caught both of his slippery, squealing daughters up in his arms. For a moment the three of them clung together, suspended in the cold waters of the peaceful lake. Tess could see gooseflesh on Phoebe's downy arms, and the pink beginnings of a sunburn across her nose. Phoebe smiled, keeping her lips together to cover her braces. But her eyes gleamed and danced.

"My beautiful fishies," Rob said.

Phoebe, too old at thirteen to linger long in a parental embrace, wriggled free and began to do the backstroke across the dark surface of the lake. Her long blonde hair floated around her like golden tentacles.

Tess redoubled her grip on her father's neck and surveyed the mirrored surface of the icy lake waters, reflecting the jagged, deep green trees of the forest on the mountainside. Above them the August sun was bright and the air as hot as it ever became in New Hampshire's White Mountains. Her gaze traveled the shoreline and came to rest on a group of teenagers, girls in bikinis and boys in swim trunks or blue jean shorts, clustered on boulders at the water's edge. They all seemed to know one another except for one, good-looking, muscular young man, Tess's sixteen-year-old brother Jake. A beautiful blonde girl in the group gasped with delight, and an overweight, red-haired kid led the jeers as Jake swung out over the lake on a rope tied to a tree branch, let go with a whoop, and pulled off an aerial somersault before plunging into the sparkling water. On the other side of the lake a few fishermen in boats floated on the placid surface. Otherwise the whole beautiful expanse of Lake Innisquam seemed to belong only to her.

"I love it here," Tess whispered in her father's ear.

"Me, too, Tess," Rob said contentedly as they hung linked together in the water, their legs treading.

They had left their apartment in Boston early that morning eager for the journey. They were a family with more energy and curiosity than money, and camping was their travel and vacation solution. Rob and Dawn had married when they were both students at Boston University. Now Rob was an assistant professor of physics at MIT. The family still lived in the sunny, book-filled, rambling apartment on Commonwealth Avenue that the couple had once shared with an assortment of roommates. Dawn had her own business making whole-grain baked goods for a university co-op, and the children were used to negotiating city life, but they were also experienced campers.

Today they had arrived at their National Forest campsite a little after noon and set up their area with an efficiency born of experience. This year Dawn was occupied with the baby but the girls were able to take up the slack. While Tess and Phoebe pumped up air mattresses and gathered wood for the campfire, Rob enlisted his grumbling sixteen-year-old son to help him set up the tents. Jake had reached a rebellious age. He showed no interest in his studies, despite the fact that academics were so important to his father, and he could hardly be persuaded to come along on this trip. He had a summer job on a constuction crew and he insisted that his boss couldn't spare him. Only Dawn's pleas that he come with them on one last camping trip had finally elicited a begrudging grunt of acquiescence.

Rob and Jake pitched two tents alongside each other.

"Why do I have to sleep with those two?" Jake had complained.

"So that Sean won't wake you kids in the night. And so that the girls will have you there to look out for them."

Jake continued to grumble, but his father did his best to ignore the mutterings.

By the time Dawn had pronounced their campsite homey and served lunch on the red cedar trestle table, everyone was tired, sweaty, and in a hurry to get to the lake. They tramped through the woods to the lakeshore together, but as soon as they arrived, Jake spotted the group of teenagers and boldly headed in their direction.

Tess looked over again at the boulder that Jake was scrambling up, wresting another turn at the rope from a pale-skinned boy with black hair. "How come Jake's over there with those kids?" Tess asked. "He doesn't even know them."

"He just wants to be with kids his own age," Rob said.

"How come he's screaming like that?" Tess asked.

"*Cherchez la femme,*" Rob said, smiling.

"What does that mean?"

"I think he's trying to impress the girls," said Rob.

Tess frowned disapprovingly at the shrieking teenagers. She glanced up at her mother on the hillside, her tanned legs extended in front of her as she chatted with the woman on a neighboring blanket while the woman's husband, looking pirate-like with long black hair, stood nearby, watching their toddler play at the water's edge. "Who are those people Mom's talking to?" Tess asked.

"I don't know. Probably some other campers. Hey, what do you say we give Mom a chance to get in the water?" Rob suggested.

Tess nodded, and she and her father pointed themselves toward shore and began to swim.

On the blanket, under the shade of a maple tree, Sean was dozing while Dawn and the other young woman, a fair-skinned blonde, chatted. Tessa and Rob came up the grassy bank to where they sat.

"Hey, you two," said Dawn, her broad smile lighting up her face. "Annette, this is my husband, Rob, and my daughter Tess. Annette and her husband, Kenneth, own that inn we passed near the entrance to the campground."

"Oh really," said Rob, reaching out to shake her hand. "You run the place yourselves?"

"I run it, mainly," said Annette. "Ken's trying to write, so when my parents left us the inn, we decided to move up here so he could have more time to work."

"I think that's everybody's fantasy, to own an inn like that," said Dawn.

"It's a lot of work," said Annette with a small sigh.

The black-haired man strode to the water's edge, swung his protesting toddler up in his arms, and climbed the grassy hill to rejoin the adults. "Kenneth Phalen," he said, setting the toddler on the ground and extending a hand to Rob.

"And Lisa," his wife reminded him, pointing to the little girl.

"Nice to meet you both," said Rob. "Your wife says you're a writer. What do you write?"

Ken shook his long hair back. "Well, I've had a couple of short pieces published in magazines. But now I'm working on a novel."

He seemed ready to launch into a long explanation but Annette interrupted, turning to Rob. "Dawn tells me you're a professor at MIT? That's impressive."

"Assistant," Rob demurred.

"Still," she said.

Bored with their grown-up conversation, Tess was watching the pink-cheeked Lisa as she began to lurch, in the toddler's side-to-side gait, across the grass. Tess wished she had her camera to take a picture of her. She was cute as a doll, her ringlets shining in the hot afternoon sun. Tess squinted up at the puffy clouds gathering in the sunny afternoon sky. Soon the beautiful day would be over. She looked over at her mother beseechingly and caught her eye.

"What is it, Tess?" she asked.

"Will you come in the water, Mom?" she pleaded.

Dawn smiled at her, bemused. "Is it cold?"

Tess shook her head, wide-eyed. "No. Really."

"Go ahead, hon," Rob said. "I'll keep an eye on Sean."

Dawn was not the sort of person who needed to be coaxed to have fun. As Rob toweled off and flopped down on the blanket beside his new son, Dawn took Tess's hand. "Okay, let's go," she said, tucking her dark brown hair behind her ear and smiling. "'Scuse us."

Tess waded back into the water, leading the way. Phoebe stood up, waist high in the lake, and began to splash.

"Honey, don't splash me," said Dawn. "It's going to take me a minute to adjust."

Phoebe shrugged but desisted. Tess slipped back into the cold lake like a seal, but her mother entered more gingerly, rubbing her arms and saying "brrr" until suddenly she inhaled a deep breath, extended her arms, and dove in, emerging a few moments later out past where Phoebe stood, laughing. Dawn waved to Rob and the other couple on the shore and they all waved back.

Tess swam to her mother's arms. Dawn glanced over at the group of teenagers. Jake was seated among them on the boulders now, loudly joining in the chatter. The pretty blonde was seated right beside him.

"Dad says he's trying to make the girls like him," Tess informed her mother.

Dawn smiled a little wistfully. "He's growing up on us."

"Well, I think he should stay with his family," Tess said.

"Oh, it won't be long till it's you over there," Dawn said.

"Not me," Tess insisted. "I'd rather be with you."

Dawn gave her a kiss on the forehead. "Hey, come on. Let's catch Phoebe. Pheebs," she cried, "we're coming to get you."

Phoebe, who was floating on her back, gazing at the brilliant blue sky and the puffy clouds, righted herself in the water. The sun flashed off the shiny surface of the "Believe" medallion, which she always wore on a silver chain around her neck. It had been a birthday gift from their godmother, and Tess had one exactly like it. She never wore hers swimming, however, for fear of losing it. "What?" Phoebe said.

"We're getting you," Tess threatened.

Phoebe's laughing eyes widened and then she screamed and began frantically to paddle away.

* * *

Jake returned to the campsite shivering as the sun was setting, and changed into dry clothes as Rob started the campfire and Dawn managed to find everyone a stick long enough to toast marshmallows after their skillet dinner had finished cooking on the camp stove. Their faces burnished by the lantern light, they ate their dinner hungrily, agreeing that the food at home never tasted this good, the same thing they said on every camping trip. After dinner they huddled around the campfire while sparks flew up like a cloud of orange bees, and the mountain evening air grew chilly. The kids sat on logs and tree stumps, their parents on folding camp chairs, and they all toasted their impaled marshmallows over the campfire.

Rob told a couple of ghost stories so familiar that the girls' screams anticipated the punch lines. Afterward, as the fire died away, there were good-night kisses all around. Phoebe and Tess wore socks, sweatpants, and fleece hoodies because of the cold night air. They ducked into their tent and crawled into sleeping bags, propping their long-handled flashlight on the ground between their air mattresses.

Tess reached into her backpack and fished around until she pulled out the camera she had begged for, and received, on her ninth birthday. She turned the lens on Phoebe, who was brushing out her tangled, golden hair.

"Pheebs," she said.

Phoebe looked up at her sister and Tess snapped the photo.

"Put that down," Phoebe commanded her. "I hate having my picture taken."

"But you look cool with that big shadow behind you," said Tess, gazing at her sister's silhouette, large and dark as a thundercloud against the tent wall.

"I don't care. Stop doing that."

In response, Tess snapped another picture and Phoebe threw her hairbrush at her younger sister, hitting her in the forehead.

"Ow," Tess yelped, lowering the camera.

"Put it away," said Phoebe.

Tess stuck out her tongue, but placed the camera carefully back into her knapsack just as Jake entered the tent. He had wide shoulders, even features, and beautiful, golden-brown hair that was curly again now that it was dry. He crouched just inside the door of the tent wearing boots, jeans, and an MIT sweatshirt.

"Hurry up and take your boots off and get in your sleeping bag," said Phoebe. "So we can turn out the light."

Jake pulled back the flap on the tent and peered out at the quiet campsite, the embers of the fire still glowing. He began to chew on his thumbnail absently. "I'm going to go out for a little while," he said.

Tess stared at him in disbelief, but Phoebe sat up and protested. "Go out? Where?"

"I'm going to walk into town. Into Stone Hill. There's a dance tonight," said Jake.

"You can't leave here," Phoebe protested. "Does Dad know about this?"

Jake glared at her. "No. And don't you tell him, you little brat. I'll be back in a couple of hours. It's no big deal."

"If it's no big deal, why don't you ask Dad if it's okay?" Phoebe insisted.

"I don't have to get his permission for everything I do," said Jake irritably.

"He'll be so mad if he finds out," Phoebe warned.

"If you two keep your mouths shut, he won't have to find out, will he?"

Tess and Phoebe exchanged a glance, Tess looking frightened, Phoebe looking angry. "You're supposed to stay here with us," said Phoebe.

"Don't be such a baby. You're two feet from Mom and Dad. I'll be back before you know it."

Phoebe was shaking her golden head.

"Besides, I'll give you each five bucks if you keep quiet," he said.

Tess's eyes lit up, thinking of the film she could buy. She was almost out. That seemed like a pretty good deal to her. Phoebe glared at her older brother. "If you don't pay up, I'll tell them. And you will get in trouble."

"I'll pay. I'll pay. Now go to sleep," said Jake disgustedly, turning his back on them and leaving the tent.

Tess clutched the stuffed dog she had brought with her and snuggled down into the warmth of her sleeping bag. She wondered if she would be able to sleep without Jake in the tent. Before she could finish the thought, she was already into her dream.

* * *

The noise that awoke her was a ripping sound and then a rush of cold air seemed to smack her in the face. Tess struggled to open her eyes, still groggy. The flashlight was still on and she could see that Phoebe was already sitting up. Suddenly Tess's eyes focused on what she was seeing and her heart gave a sickening thud.

Phoebe's blue eyes were wide with fear, a dirty hand with ragged fingernails covering her mouth. Pressed against Phoebe's neck was a knife that made a dent in her skin. There was a giant tear in the side of the tent beside Phoebe's bag and a large, ugly man in a filthy, army green jacket crouched there, filling up the hole, clutching Phoebe close to him. He had black hair pulled into a messy ponytail and big glasses with black frames.

Tess's heart pounded and she rubbed her eyes, wondering if she was really awake or in a nightmare. Phoebe made a pitiful noise and her eyes entreated Tess over the knuckles of the hand that gagged her.

Tess looked square in the face of the man who held her sister. "Hey . . ." she protested.

"Shut up," he growled. "Don't make a sound."

Tess was shuddering from head to toe.

"You listen to me, little girl. If you make one peep or tell anybody, I'll kill your sister here. Do you understand me?"

Tess felt as if a trapped bird was flying madly around her rib cage, flapping its wings.

"Do you?" he demanded, poking at Phoebe's throat with the knife. Phoebe made a plaintive gurgle in her throat.

"Yes . . ." said Tess.

"Not one sound. Don't tell anyone. I'll kill her if you do."

Tears rose to Tess's eyes and her chin trembled. "I won't," she said.

She was not prepared for what happened next. In front of her eyes, Phoebe was jerked from her sleeping bag and pulled out through the hole in the side of the tent. One minute she was there and then . . . she was gone.

Tess's mouth dropped open and she covered it with her small hands. All she could see through the jagged hole was blackness, darkness. She heard rustling sounds outside, into the woods. As if monsters were moving among the trees, able to hear if she made the smallest sound. She did not dare to move or speak. She kept thinking, Phoebe! She kept seeing the look of terror in her sister's eyes, the man's knife glinting against her pale throat.

Tess needed to pee, but she did not dare budge. Even if she wanted to go, she wouldn't know the way in the dark to the dimly lit latrine on the campground path. Besides, she knew not to go there without Phoebe. They always used the buddy system. That was the rule. And she and Phoebe were buddies. They went together or not at all. Tears began to run down Tess's cheeks at the thought of her sister alone in the woods with that man with the knife. She wept, she waited. She felt pee soaking the legs of her sweatpants but she did not move. She sat like a statue for a long time.

"Jesus Christ. What the hell . . . ?"

Jake appeared, wild-eyed, at the hole in the tent. "Tess. What the hell happened?" He looked around the tent. "Are you all right? Where's Phoebe?"

Tess stared at him, wondering if she should tell. "Where is Phoebe?" he shouted at her.

Before Tess could decide to answer, Jake withdrew from the tear in the side of the tent. "Dad!" he yelled. "Mom. Dad, help!"

In an instant, the campsite was a chaos of flashlights, lanterns, the cries of the baby. Tess's father, his eyes frantic, scrambled into the tent and grabbed her by the arms, pressing her to his chest for a moment and then squeezing her upper arms, searching her eyes. "Tess, what happened here? Tell me. What happened to Phoebe?"

Outside the tent, she could hear her mother moaning and Jake pleading in a small voice. "I'm sorry, Mom. I'm sorry."

Tess began to sob. "I can't," she said. "He said not to. He said not to tell."

"Who said that?" Rob DeGraff choked out, his voice shaking, the whites showing around his eyes. "Tell me, Tess. This instant."

Tess's small body was trembling. Her words came out in a whisper, sloppy with tears. "The man who ripped the tent with his knife. The man who took Phoebe."

"What? Rob, what happened? Is Tess all right? Where is Phoebe?" Dawn was screaming from outside the tent.

Rob gasped and doubled over, as if he had been stabbed with the ugly man's knife himself, and then he groaned. "Oh my God! Oh no."

Her father's groans made her feel sick to her stomach and gave her bad goose bumps from head to toe. She had never before heard a sound like that coming from her father. He was the one who was always laughing and saying that everything would be all right. But not this time. This time he sounded like an animal howling in pain. She wondered if he was mad at her. She couldn't bear for him to be mad at her. She had to make him understand. Her voice was pleading. "Dad, I had to do what he said. He told me to keep quiet after he left, or . . ."

"What, Tess?" he cried. "What?"

Tess hung her head. Her voice was a whisper. "Or he was going to kill her."

CHAPTER 2

Twenty Years Later

"Erny," Tess called out, standing hands on hips in the doorway of her son's room, which looked like it had been sacked and pillaged. "Answer me when I speak to you."

Erny, a wiry ten-year-old with shiny black eyes, brown skin, and uncombed, curly black hair, clambered up the stairs of the town house. "The taxi's here," he announced.

"What happened to your room?" Tess demanded.

"I was packing," he explained. "Come on, Ma, we have to go."

Tess shook her head and then closed the door on the catastrophe that was Erny's bedroom. "When we get back, you're going to have to clean that mess up."

Erny was jiggling with pent-up energy. "I will, I will. Come on, we'll miss the plane."

"We're not going to miss the plane," Tess said calmly, although she felt half-sick and her stomach was in a knot. "Where's your bag?"

"Downstairs."

"Okay, put your sweatshirt on and tell the taxi driver to wait. I'll be right there."

Erny descended the staircase two steps at a time. Tess took a last look in her bedroom. Her gaze fell on the framed photo on her bureau top. It was a snapshot of a blonde girl with braces and sweet, dreamy blue eyes, intently brushing out her long hair. Her shadow loomed large behind her in the lantern light. Tess kissed her own index finger and gently pressed her fingertip to the cheek of the girl in the photo. Then she turned away, pulled out the handle on her bag, and rolled the suitcase to the top of the stairs. She picked it up and carried it down. Erny was leaning out the front door, pleading for the taxi driver to wait for them.

Their cat, Sosa, named after one of the baseball players Erny idolized, peered out at them from under the living room sofa. "Say good-bye to Sosa," said Tess. "He's under the couch."

As Tess pulled her jacket from the hall closet, she heard Erny flopping down on the living room rug, crooning to Sosa and promising him that he would be well cared for by Erny's best friend, Jonah. Jonah was the son of Tess's best friend, Becca, and Becca's husband, Wade Maitland. The Maitlands lived three blocks away from them in their Georgetown neighborhood. Wade was an executive producer on Tess's documentary team and Tess was the one who had introduced him to her childhood friend, Rebecca. They fell in love almost at once, and ever since Tess was always credited with being a matchmaker. The two women loved the fact that their sons got along so well. It gave their old friendship a brand-new dimension. It was good, Tess thought, to have friends like that to rely on. Especially for this trip, when she felt unusually fragile and worried.

"Everything will be fine," Tess called out to Erny. She repeated those words to herself silently, like a mantra. As if by insisting on it, she could convince herself that this was just an ordinary trip to see her family. Everything will be fine.

Tess checked herself in the hallway mirror. Her shiny, brunette hair parted naturally a little off center and fell to her shoulders around her oval face and dark brown eyes. She had a creamy complexion, high, healthy color, and deep, comma-shaped dimples in each cheek that showed at the slightest hint of a smile. A friend once told her that men made monkeys of themselves trying to make Tess laugh just so they could see those dimples. Tess had denied it, but she suspected it was true. Today, as was her habit, she wore a minimum of makeup. She inspected her outfit, wondering if her silk shirt and tweed hacking jacket would be warm enough for late October in New England. Normally, on a trip to New Hampshire, she would have worn her work clothes — a roomy canvas coat with lots of pockets, jeans, and muck boots. Out in the field, she dressed for speed and comfort. She worked as a cinematographer on a team she'd joined when she'd been an intern in film school that made documentaries for cable and public television. She enjoyed everything about her team and her work, including the fact that she could buy most of her work wardrobe from Eddie Bauer. But on this particular trip, she felt as if she needed to look slightly more businesslike.

There was a crash from the direction of the living room. Tess's heart leapt.

"What was that?" she called out as she rushed to the doorway.

Erny, looking worried, was holding two ragged-edged porcelain triangles that had once been a square plate depicting an ancient map of the world. She kept the plate on display on the table behind the sofa.

Tess took the pieces from Erny and looked at them ruefully. She had bought that plate in a Paris flea market long ago and had always treasured it. But life with a child had taught her that mishaps were commonplace, and that it was a mistake to become too attached to breakable belongings. "What happened?" she asked.

"I was hugging Sosa and he ran away from me and jumped over the table," said Erny. "He didn't mean to break it, Ma."

"I know," said Tess with a sigh. She placed the pieces carefully on the mantel over the fireplace. "Maybe we can glue it back together."

"I'll get the glue," Erny cried hopefully.

"Not now. We have to go. When we get back."

"Sosa's just scared of being alone. Jonah'd better take care of him," Erny muttered, smacking his fist into his palm.

"He will. His mom will make sure he does. Come on. Grab your bag." She forced herself to adopt a lighthearted tone for Erny's sake. "We've got places to go and people to see."

Erny, rarely downcast for long, shouldered his backpack and shot the handle on his suitcase. "I'm ready."

Tess smiled back at him. "*Vámanos!*"

The driver helped them put their luggage in the trunk and they piled into the backseat of the cab. "Dulles, please," said Tess, naming the airport.

Erny pressed his nose to the window, gazing out at the familiar street. As the car pulled away from the curb, Tess looked back at their Georgetown home. It was a true city house — a two-story neo-Colonial brick town house in the middle of a block of similar attached houses with multipaned windows, buttercream trim and window boxes, wrought-iron stair rails, and marble steps. There was a tree in front, and Erny's school was only two blocks away. Tess had bought the house using her share of the proceeds from the documentary team's first sale to HBO. When she'd bought the house, she'd been twenty-three and single and had just wanted privacy and a home of her own. The house had proved to be both a good investment and later an indispensable asset when Erny came into her life.

She'd met Erny when the team was shooting a documentary about grandparents forced to become parents for their grandchildren. Erny's grandmother, Inez, had lost her single daughter to drugs and the street. The identity of Erny's father was unknown. From the first day of shooting, Erny, who'd been five at the time, showed an irrepressible interest in everything the team did. He attached himself to Tess and asked her a million questions about the camera. Erny's grandmother, though infirm and poor, adored her grandson and protected him fiercely, and the segment about them was among the most touching in the film.

Several months later, when the film was cut and ready to be aired, Tess called Inez to invite her and Erny to a screening. She learned then that Inez had died suddenly, and that Erny now was in foster care. Tess immediately arranged to visit Erny at his foster parents' run-down, chaotic home. She thought that seeing the film so soon after Inez's death might be traumatic for the five-year-old, but Erny insisted that he wanted to come to the screening, and his foster parents, who were caring for six kids at the time, seemed indifferent. Finally, full of misgivings, Tess agreed to take him with her.

Erny was ready when she came to pick him up, hair combed, wearing his best clothes. He sat without fidgeting, watching the film intently, squeezing her hand the entire time. When she brought him back to his foster parents, he clung to her silently and refused to let her go. Tess promised she would come to see him again and he watched her leave with hopelessness in his eyes. Tess returned home to her lovely, quiet house.

Over the next few days she told herself that Erny's situation was sad but couldn't be helped. She told herself it was not her problem and there was nothing she could do about it. She was young and single and couldn't take on the burden of a child, no matter how winning he was. She'd never have a boyfriend or a social life again. She tossed and turned at night and finally realized that she was not going to be able to reason her feelings away. Six months later, the adoption went through and ever since, Tess had been a single mother. Sure enough, her social life tapered off. She stayed home a lot and when she did date, she developed a tendency to judge every man she dated by his reaction to Erny. Most of them didn't want to arrange their lives around the needs of a child. Tess found, to her surprise, that she didn't regret the loss of any guy who felt that way. When her friends shook their heads and warned her that she would end up alone, she pretended not to care. But in her heart she shared their apprehension.

Adoption hadn't been an easy road, for either her or Erny. Still, she had never regretted the decision.

"Do you think Dawn will let me use Sean's bike this time?" Erny asked.

He could not yet bring himself to call Tess's mother "grandma." Tess understood. She also knew that he usually enjoyed their visits to her family. But this time could be different. For both of them. "I'm pretty sure she will," said Tess.

"Maybe this time I'll ride out to the mountain," Erny announced.

"We'll see," said Tess.

* * *

At the airport, after checking in and going through security, Tess and Erny proceeded to their gate. Tess stopped at a newsstand and bought herself a newspaper and a book of Sudoku puzzles they could do together on the plane. Erny was better at the number game than she was and never tired of seeing her reaction when he beat her to the solution. Then they walked down to the crowded waiting area at the boarding gate and found two seats. Tess walked up to the desk and asked the uniformed ticket agent if she knew what gate their connecting flight would be leaving from in Boston.

The woman tapped a few keys on her computer keyboard. "You'll arrive in Boston at gate A-seven and depart for Unionville, New Hampshire, from gate C-three."

"Have we got a lot of ground to cover there?" Tess asked.

The woman shook her head and looked at the times of the flights. "You arrive Boston at noon and leave for Unionville at one. That gives you plenty of time."

Tessa thanked her and went back to the seat where Erny was fidgeting.

"Can I watch the planes leaving?" he said, pointing to the floor-to-ceiling windows behind the ticket counter.

"Sure. Stay where I can see you," said Tess.

Erny bolted from the chair and flattened himself against the windows, peering out at the planes on the tarmac. Tess picked up the newspaper. On the fourth page of the *Washington Post* she found the article she was looking for. The dateline was Stone Hill, New Hampshire. Tess began to read.

The office of New Hampshire Governor John Putnam confirmed today that the DNA results will be announced tomorrow in the case of Lazarus Abbott, who was executed ten years ago in this state for the rape-murder of thirteen-year-old Phoebe DeGraff. Twenty years ago the girl was abducted from her family's campsite in the White Mountain National Park and her body was found two days later in a shallow roadside ditch. Based on the description of the lone eyewitness, the victim's younger sister, Police Chief Aldous Fuller arrested the 23-year-old Abbott, a convicted sexual deviant who still lived with his mother and stepfather. Semen found on the girl's underwear was a match to Abbott's blood type. Abbott's trial lasted only three days. The jury agreed on the death penalty within an hour of the conclusion of the sentencing hearing.

Although the physical evidence was scant, the eyewitness testimony was damning. The victim's sister, nine-year-old Tess DeGraff, who was present when the abduction occurred, positively identified Abbott under oath as the man who ripped open the side of their tent with a knife and warned her not to scream or he would kill Phoebe with the knife he was wielding. The child's pale, grave face and unwavering certainty sealed Abbott's fate and he was executed, after exhausting all his legal avenues of appeal, ten years ago.

Abbott insisted on his innocence right until the moment of his execution and his mother, Edith Abbott, was finally able to persuade Ben Ramsey, a local attorney, to take up her cause and have the evidence in the case tested for a DNA match. DNA evidence was not widely available at the time when the crime was committed and the courts refused to order it in the years leading up to and after Abbott's execution. But the newly elected Governor Putnam, who is a vocal opponent of the death penalty, agreed to Mr Ramsey's request to order the testing.

The evidence of semen on the clothes and skin from under the fingernails of Phoebe DeGraff was still in the possession of the Stone Hill Police Department and the tests have been carried out at the Center for Forensic Sciences in Toronto. Edith Abbott has always insisted that the results of these tests will clear her son's name. Tomorrow the announcement will be made by the governor at the offices of the Stone Hill Record, *a local newspaper that had joined Ramsey in pressing for the testing of the DNA, although the newspaper does not champion the cause of Lazarus Abbott. "The people of this town have long felt that justice was done in this case," said Channing Morris, editor and publisher of the* Stone Hill Record, *reflecting the widely held conviction in this area that Abbott was guilty. "I think the whole business is unfortunate. But we have nothing to fear from the truth. Let's get it out in the open and put this matter to rest, once and for all," the publisher said.*

"May I have your attention, please?" the ticket agent announced over the PA system. "We are now beginning to board flight Two-eighty-six to Montreal, with a stop in Boston."

Erny barreled over to where Tessa sat. "Ma, that's us. You better put the paper down."

Tess was jerked back to the present. Grim-faced, she took out their boarding passes and zipped up her bag. She forced herself to smile at her son. "You looking forward to this trip?" Tessa asked him.

Erny nodded. "You think Uncle Jake will take me for a ride in his truck?"

"Oh sure," said Tess.

"Come on, get up," Erny urged.

"Take it easy. We're not boarding with this group. Sit down a minute." Erny collapsed into a seat, jiggling his leg. Tess went back to the paper and read the final paragraph of the article:

> *Edith Abbott is waiting anxiously for tomorrow's news — the results which would prove that her son was executed for a crime he did not commit. "I'm not worried," said Edith today, sitting beside Ben Ramsey, the attorney who has worked diligently on her behalf. "This time tomorrow the world will know that my son was an innocent man."*

"Like hell," Tess muttered, folding up the paper.

"What?" said Erny, turning to his mother.

"Nothing," said Tess. "Let's go." She shouldered her bag and they joined the line to board the plane. As they passed a waste can, Tess tossed the newspaper into it.

CHAPTER 3

Tess and Erny rolled their suitcases down the jetway and came out into the arrival gate at the Unionville airport. Tess looked around for her sister-in-law, Julie, who was supposed to be meeting them. She didn't see Julie anywhere. What she saw instead were clusters of reporters with microphones and news cameramen stationed around the small waiting area of the airport. Tess had a bad feeling that they were here because of the news conference tomorrow. She knew that the case was a big deal on the Internet and on the network and cable news shows. She lowered her gaze, hoping that they had not somehow gotten wind of her arrival this afternoon and were lying in wait for her.

Gesturing for Erny to join her, she pulled her bag toward a bank of seats in an empty arrival gate, pulled out her cell phone, and dialed Julie's cell. After a few rings, Julie answered, although the reception was poor and Julie sounded exasperated.

"I'm stuck out here, trying to get into the parking lot," Julie complained. "There's about a million news vans gumming up the works because the governor is arriving. You know — for tomorrow. Sit tight. I'll be there to pick you up as soon as I can park."

"We can come out and meet you," Tess suggested, but it was too late. Julie had already ended the call.

Tess tucked her phone away. Good, she thought. The reporters were waiting for the governor. It was just anxiety that had made her think they would be looking for her. How would they recognize her anyway? she thought. After twenty years, she bore no resemblance to the child who had testified against Lazarus Abbott. "Okay, Erny," she said, "Aunt Julie is on her way. I'm going to duck into the ladies' room. You need to go to the men's room?"

Erny shook his head.

"I'm going to leave my bag, then. You wait right here for me, okay?"

"Can I get something to drink?" he asked.

Tess reached in her satchel, extracted a bill, and handed it to him. "Okay. There's a newsstand right over there. Get what you want. But keep an eye on the luggage. I'll be right out."

Tess watched him tear off for the newsstand and then she pushed open the door to the restroom and went in. After a quick stop in the toilet, she came out and checked her makeup in the mirror. She looked washed-out and tired under the unflattering lights. She swiped a lipstick across her lips and was about to turn to go when she heard a feeble cry from the stall at the end of the row. Tess hesitated and then she heard the cry again.

"Are you all right?" Tess asked, feeling awkward.

"I need some help."

Tess walked down to the handicapped stall and pushed on the door. It was not locked and it gave way. Tess saw a small-boned, delicate woman with a gamine haircut sprawled on the floor of the oversize stall.

"Oh my God. Are you okay?" she asked, crouching down and reaching under the woman's arms. The woman was wearing a cashmere tunic that was soft to the touch and her arms were thin and felt rubbery in Tess's grasp.

"If you could just help me up," said the woman.

"Sure," said Tess. "Sure." She pulled the woman to her feet.

The woman seemed more downcast than embarrassed. "I'm sorry to bother you like this. I have a . . . condition. Sometimes I . . . lose my balance. Could you just help me outside? These floors are slippery. My husband's outside. He's waiting for me."

"No problem," said Tess. She put an arm around the woman's birdlike waist and they shuffled along together. Tess could see bruises on the woman's thin forearms as her sleeves rode up. "You sure you're okay?"

"Fine," said the woman grimly. "Quite a commotion here today, isn't it?" She clearly wanted to change the subject.

"No kidding," said Tess.

"The governor's arriving. My husband and I are meeting him. He's staying with us," the woman said proudly.

"Really?" said Tess.

The woman nodded. "He and my husband went to college together. My husband publishes a newspaper." They had made their way out of the restroom and a strikingly handsome man with soft black hair that flopped across his forehead rushed up to them.

"Sally," he cried. "What happened?" The man was dressed casually and had wide, intense, gray eyes, the pupils ringed in black.

"I'm fine. I had a little episode, but this lady helped me," said Sally.

"Oh, thank you so much," he said, slipping his arm around his wife in place of Tess's arm. "I'm very grateful to you."

"Don't mention it," said Tess.

"Mom," Erny cried, rushing across the concourse with a bottle of Gatorade and a comic book.

Tess could tell that the publisher was about to introduce himself and his wife and ask her about Erny. The last thing Tess wanted was to mention her own name. A newspaperman who was meeting the governor was sure to recognize it right away and be full of questions, and that was something

Tess definitely preferred to avoid. "Come on," she said to Erny. "We'd better scoot." She gave the man and his wife a friendly smile and started to nudge Erny to gather up his bag.

All of a sudden Tess heard someone calling her name. She looked up and immediately caught sight of her sister-in-law Julie, a heavyset woman with glasses, her blonde hair cut short in a no-nonsense style. Over her nurse's uniform Julie wore a bulky sweater of variegated colors that she had most likely knitted herself, Tess thought. Knitting and church were Julie's primary interests now that her daughter was grown and out of the house. Julie's round face broke into a sweet smile and she waved enthusiastically.

Tess waved back. Though only in her late thirties, her sister-in-law looked much older. She had been a teenager when Jake first met her during their family's ill-fated camping trip to Stone Hill. Back then, Julie was a teenage beauty with long, wavy blonde hair and a curvaceous figure. She and Jake had fallen in love with adolescent intensity, quickly and completely. During the days after Phoebe's disappearance, and then later, during the trial, Julie had stayed glued to Jake's side. Tess could still remember spying on the teenage lovers, sitting nearly on top of each other in the corner of the living room at the Stone Hill Inn where the DeGraffs were given rooms for a pittance throughout the whole ordeal. A year later, when Jake was finished with high school, he moved up to Stone Hill to be with Julie, and they married shortly thereafter. Their one child, Kelli, was now in the army and Jake had a house-painting business in Stone Hill.

Julie opened her arms wide and embraced Tess and then Erny. "Look at you!" she exclaimed as she gazed admiringly at Erny. "You are really getting big."

Erny shrugged, but smiled. His aunt was always kind to him.

"Do you have any other luggage?" she asked.

"No. We're good to go," said Tess.

"Well, okay," said Julie. "I'm parked out here." Then she noticed the publisher, who was insisting that his wife sit down and rest. "Chan!" she exclaimed.

The man seemed mystified by the sight of Julie calling his name. He frowned slightly, combing his unruly hair back off his forehead with his fingers. Then suddenly recognition dawned in his pale, gray eyes. "Julie. Hi. I haven't seen you in . . ."

"A long time," Julie said. She looked pointedly at the petite woman on his arm.

"Oh, this is my wife, Sally."

"How do you do?" said Julie warmly, smiling at the delicate woman. "I've heard about you. It's nice to finally meet you. My husband's the one who painted your house this summer."

The woman's smile transformed her pained-looking features. "Oh yes. Of course. How is Jake?"

"Fine. We're both fine," said Julie, nodding enthusiastically. "What are you folks doing here?"

"We're here to pick up the governor," said Chan. "He's coming straight from a party meeting in St. Louis. We knew each other in college so I invited him to stay with us tonight."

"Oh," said Julie. "Chan, Sally, I want you both to meet my sister-in-law, Tess DeGraff. She and her son came so they could be here for the announcement tomorrow, too. Tess, this is Channing Morris. He's the owner of the *Stone Hill Record* where the press conference will take place. And this is his wife."

Tess cringed inwardly, but she smiled at them. "We've met," said Tess.

"Well, not officially," said Chan. "I didn't realize you were . . . involved in this whole thing. It must be a terrible ordeal for your family. If it's any consolation to you, most of us think Edith Abbott is kind of a crackpot. Don't quote me," he said, smiling.

"Thanks," said Tess. "Frankly, I'll be glad when it's over."

"I'm sure you will be. Hey, if you're going to be around a little while," he said eagerly, "I'd love to sit down with you and talk about all this for the paper."

Tess forced herself to smile politely. Despite his disarming smile, Chan Morris was a journalist with a newspaper to sell and hers was a meaty story. Even Wade Maitland, her dear friend and the executive producer of her crew, had tried hard to convince her that they should accompany her to New Hampshire and shoot footage for a possible documentary about the controversial death penalty case. Tess had refused in no uncertain terms. To her, it was not a story, but her family's never-ending nightmare. "Well, maybe, after it's over," said Tess. "Today we're all a little on edge."

"Of course you are," said Chan. He glanced at his watch. "The governor's flight should be arriving any minute. My wife has been so keyed-up about this visit," he said, looking indulgently at the pretty woman on his arm. "She's been fussing over the house and the food for days."

Sally colored slightly. "Well, he's an important guest," she said.

"I'm sure it'll be lovely. You have such a beautiful home," said Julie.

Sally looked confused. "Have you visited us?"

"No, no. Not for years. But everybody knows the Whitman farm . . ." said Julie.

"Julie, speaking of that," said Chan, the friendly tone of his voice turning decidedly brisker, "can you ask Jake when he's going to finish painting the trim on the third-floor windows? The house looks . . . unfinished. Frankly it's a little embarrassing with the governor coming. I've left him half a dozen messages, but . . ."

Julie's face turned pink. "He still hasn't finished the trim? I'm sorry, Chan. I don't know what he was thinking."

"Once I paid him, he seemed to disappear," said Chan.

"I'll tell him," Julie promised. "I feel terrible about this."

"Not your fault," said Chan, although he clearly wasn't saying the same about Jake. "Well, we'd better be getting to the gate. Nice to meet you, Tess. I'm sure everything will turn out . . . as we expect it to tomorrow."

"Thanks. Nice to meet you both," said Tess as the couple smiled and turned away.

Julie was shaking her head. "What am I going to do with him?" she said.

"Who?" Tess asked.

"Your brother. He never finishes his jobs. He painted their house this summer. It's the end of October and he still hasn't done all the trim. I don't know what to do. If I say anything to him, he goes ballistic and tells me to mind my own business."

"Jake," Tess shook her head.

"I tell you, Tess, he has the worst reputation around this town."

Tess knew that Julie was probably right, but she didn't want to become embroiled in a discussion of her brother's marriage and his shortcomings. She groped for a change of subject. "They seem like nice people," she said, nodding toward the newspaper publisher and his wife, who were slowly crossing over to the arrival gates.

"Chan? Oh yeah. Gosh, I've known Chan since he moved here in junior high." Julie shook her head and assumed the sort of grave expression she wore when she was about to convey tragic gossip. "He lost both his parents in one year. He had to come and live with his grandmother."

Tess glanced at Erny, hoping he wasn't listening, hoping Julie's mention of the publisher's sad childhood wouldn't remind him of his own similar fate. But Erny, like most children, was not terribly interested in the grown-ups' conversation.

"He was quite the talk of the town when he arrived, I'll tell you. He turned every head. Every girl at school had a crush on him. I even dated him for a while," Julie announced proudly.

"Really?" said Tess. She could easily imagine how Chan Morris's handsome face and large gray eyes had set teenage hearts aflutter.

Julie nodded. "My father had high hopes, I can tell you that. He was picturing me as Mrs Channing Morris, living large in that big house on the Whitman farm." Julie sighed. "But no such luck," Julie said.

It annoyed Tess to hear Julie obviously rueing the fact that she had ended up with Jake for a husband instead. Her brother had his faults, but he had worked hard and been a good father to Kelli, as far as Tess could tell. And judging from the fact that Channing Morris had failed to even recognize Julie at first, it was plain that the publisher felt no similar regrets. "His wife is really lovely," Tess said.

"Oh yeah. She seems sweet. But it's sad. She's got a muscle-wasting disease. Did you see how she was leaning on Chan? When she's by herself she has to use a cane or a wheelchair. Everyone knows about her at the hospital. Apparently there's not much they can do for her."

"That is sad," said Tess.

"It's a tragedy. For both of them. I mean, to look at them you would think they had the world on a string." Julie shook her head.

"It's true," Tess murmured. "You never know."

Tess put an arm around Erny's narrow shoulders and together they followed Julie, who was extracting her car keys from her purse as she chattered on about the publisher and his wife. Tess's thoughts returned to her own family's sorrows and to the grim mission of her visit here. Oblivious to the fact that she had lost her audience, Julie was still gossiping as she led the way to the automatic doors and out into the airport parking lot.

* * *

The Stone Hill Inn was a traditional New England white clapboard-sided house with dark green shutters. The front door was flanked by a pair of benches facing one another, shaped like church pews and painted the same green as the shutters. Behind the benches were a pair of white trellises. In summer they were covered with climbing pink roses, but now there were only brown vines crisscrossing the white wooden grids. The inn sat at the end of a quiet road, surrounded by brown fields with gray stone fences. A few trees, still wearing the last blaze of autumn, ringed the edge of the fields. Dawn opened the door as they came up the walk and rushed out to greet them, shivering in her thin cardigan, her yellow Lab, Leo, beside her.

"Mom, hi," said Tess, embracing her. "It's so good to see you."

"Oh, you look wonderful," said Dawn, releasing Tess and holding her at arm's length. "And you . . ." she said, turning to Erny.

Erny had fallen to his knees and thrown his arms around Leo's ruff. He grimaced with glee as Leo licked his face.

"Hey, I want one of those," said Dawn.

Erny scrambled to his feet and put his arms around her and Dawn held him tightly for a moment. Tess watched her mother embrace her son with a full heart. Dawn had moved from Boston to Stone Hill after the death of Rob DeGraff, from a heart attack at the age of forty-seven. Tess always suspected that the stress and the shock of Phoebe's murder had destroyed her father's health. On a visit to Jake and Julie's during a holiday, Dawn noticed an ad for an innkeeper at the Stone Hill Inn. When she questioned Jake about the Phalens, he explained to his mother that the Phalens' daughter, Lisa, had killed herself at the age of fourteen. After that, Annette began to drink and she and her husband, Kenneth, separated. They sold the inn and moved away. The new owner wanted it strictly as an investment.

To her own surprise, Dawn found herself applying for and getting the job as the innkeeper. She and Sean moved up from Boston and into the inn. Sean finished high school in Stone Hill, and then immediately left for Australia with a couple of his buddies. Dawn referred to her youngest child's decampment for Australia as Sean's "walkabout."

Tess had always admired her mother's incredible strength. Dawn had held them all together after Phoebe's murder and had stayed strong even when she lost Rob. But strength was not the same thing as happiness, or peace of mind. There was an emptiness in Dawn's eyes. She moved through her life with the same efficiency and purpose as ever, but her face was haggard and the buoyancy of her spirit seemed to have flown away on the day that Phoebe's lifeless body was found, and it had never returned. Now Dawn's hair was starting to gray and her face seemed more drawn than usual.

"Come on in. Julie, can you stay for a cup of tea? I made those thumbprint cookies you like," said Dawn.

Julie shook her head with real regret. "Oh, I do like them. But I'd better get over to the hospital. I'm filling in for a friend and my shift starts in twenty minutes. Tell my husband, when he gets back from work . . ." She hesitated and then seemed to think better of it. "Never mind. I'll tell him when I see him."

"Thank you so much for picking up Tess and Erny," said Dawn. "I hate that drive to the airport." Most people pronounced Erny's name as if he were one of the *Sesame Street* puppets, but Tess noted that her mother, with her usual sensitivity, pronounced her son's name as *Air*-knee, just as Tess did, and even tried to roll the R. Tess had once explained to Dawn that she wanted to pronounce it as Erny's grandmother, Inez, had, and Dawn had instantly understood.

"Just as well you didn't go," said Julie. "It was a madhouse out there, between the reporters and the governor's arrival . . ."

"Are you coming to the press conference tomorrow?" Tess asked.

"I'm working again. I'm sorry," said Julie. "But I'll see you afterwards."

"Do you know if Jake is coming?" Tess asked.

Julie rolled her eyes. "Oh, believe me, he wouldn't miss it. I'm going to run. I'll talk to you later."

"Come inside, you two," Dawn insisted, ushering them up the path behind the bounding Leo and through the front doorway of the inn. Inside, there was a wide vestibule that led to the main hallway. On the right of the hallway was a paneled library with a door for privacy, which usually stood open, a pair of wing chairs, and a leather sofa. On the left was a large sitting room with a fireplace. The interior of the inn was painted in subdued but lovely shades of slate blue and acanthus green, which complemented the hooked wool rugs, the comfortably upholstered furniture in Colonial-era floral patterns, and the many antique wooden tables that glowed with a waxed sheen. "I had to put you two in the same room," Dawn apologized, fishing a large key out of the pocket of her skirt. "With all the journalists in town for the governor's announcement, we are full."

"Oh no, Mom," said Tess. "Don't tell me there are reporters staying here. We won't have a minute's peace."

"No, no," said Dawn. "I think I managed to weed out anybody from a news organization. But there are still a lot of leaf peepers in town, and everything else is full."

"Okay, well, that's fine, Mom. We don't mind bunking together."

Dawn held up the key. "It's down the hall on the first floor. Erny, you want to take the bags to your room?"

Erny eagerly reached for the key.

"And open the kitchen door for Leo, would you?"

"Sure," said Erny. He started down the hall, Leo in tow.

"Come in the sitting room and get warm." A fire was already lit in the wide, age-blackened hearth. "Here, sit," said Dawn.

Tess flopped down into the sofa and gazed at her mother, who was adding a log to the fire and adjusting it with a poker.

"Are you feeling all right, Mom?" she asked.

"Fine, dear," Dawn said absently.

"You must be dreading this press conference tomorrow," Tess said.

Dawn gazed into the fire. "Actually, I'm not . . . I'm not planning on going, Tess. I can't face all that again. I think I'll wait here. I'll stay here with Erny."

Tess was taken aback. She had assumed her mother would go. "Are you sure?"

Dawn looked at her daughter and shook her head. "I don't think I can," she said.

Tess got up and put her arms around her mother, who stood stiffly, her gaze vacant. Dawn seemed numb, as if she were encased in bubble wrap, looking out at the world with detachment. Even as she held her in her arms, Tess mourned for her feisty, exuberant mother, a woman who was just a memory. "It's all right. Don't worry about it. Jake and I will do it. Leave it to us. We'll represent the family. In a strange way," she said grimly, "I'm looking forward to it."

At the sound of the front door opening, Dawn pulled away from her daughter's embrace. "Well, speak of the devil," she said.

Tess turned and saw her brother, in a worn engineer's jacket, his thick blond hair speckled with dried paint, entering the room His skin was weathered, his hair thinning, and there were lines around his mouth and eyes, but he still retained his rugged good looks.

"You just missed your wife," said Dawn.

"No such luck," said Jake. "I passed her coming up the road. She stopped long enough to tell me what a jerk I was. Hey, Tess." Brother and sister embraced briefly and Jake sat down in a spindly-looking Windsor-style armchair by the fireplace. "How was the trip?" he asked.

"Not bad," said Tess. "Erny's putting our bags in the room. He's excited to be here. He doesn't really understand what this is all about."

"He's better off," said Jake.

"Apparently, this is going to be quite a scene tomorrow."

"Asshole," Jake muttered.

Jake was angry. Nothing unusual there, Tess thought. He had been angry for years. He always had a story about what was currently infuriating him, but Tess suspected that it all stemmed from that long-ago night when his decision to go to town, and leave his sisters alone, led to catastrophe. "Who's an asshole?" Tess asked.

"Governor Putnam. This is all about politics. This is a career move for him. He thinks Lazarus Abbott is going to be exonerated and he's gonna be on the national scene as the great hero of the anti–death-penalty set. I can't wait until this backfires in his face. And that attorney that Edith Abbott hired. Ramsey." Jake shook his head.

"It said in the paper that he's a local guy," said Tess.

"Well, he's local, but he's new," said Dawn. "He just moved here a year or two ago. Didn't he, Jake?"

Jake nodded. "Yeah. He was a big-shot Philadelphia lawyer and his place here was a vacation home. Then his wife died and he moved up here full-time. I guess he decided to chuck the rat race and come live among 'the little people.'"

"Oh Jake, now, you don't know that," Dawn said.

"Anyway, he no sooner arrived than he got involved with that nut job, Edith Abbott. I guess he figures we're such hicks that we must have convicted the wrong man. Why don't people like that mind their own fucking business?"

"Jake," Dawn admonished him. "Erny's coming."

They all glanced toward the door of the sitting room and saw Erny edging into the room. Jake's face lit up. "Hey. How's my guy? Come 'ere."

Erny grinned and went over to his uncle, high-fiving him and giggling as Jake squeezed him in a bear hug. "Yeah, you and me will have a good time while you're here. We'll go honky-tonkin'. Get us a couple of tattoos. Whaddya say?"

Erny grinned, wide-eyed, at his mother. "Can I?" he asked.

"No," said Tess, bemused.

"I'm going to the kitchen. I made these cookies . . ." said Dawn. "Erny, you want to help me?"

"Okay," said Erny. He was a child with energy to spare and never minded having a job to do. It was one of many things that made Tess proud of her son.

Just then the front door opened again. "I'll go see who it is," Erny called out and ran for the front door before anyone could stop him.

Tess heard murmurs in the front hallway and Dawn went out to see if there was a prospective guest in the foyer. A minute later she returned to the parlor. "We have company," said Dawn, her eyes widened in warning.

"Who?" asked Tess.

"It's Nelson Abbott. Come in, Nelson."

Tess looked at Jake. "Abbott?" she whispered.

"Lazarus's stepfather," said Jake in a low voice.

Tess looked up warily at the man who was following her mother through the door. He removed his John Deere cap and crushed it in a large grimy hand. He was a craggy-faced man in his sixties shaped rather like a hedgehog, with a small mouth, angry black eyes, and a gray, military-style haircut. He was wearing work boots caked with mud and a fleece vest.

"Hello, Nelson," said Jake.

"This is my daughter, Tess," said Dawn. "And you've met her son, Erny. Nelson, why don't you have a seat? We were just going to get some cookies from the kitchen."

Nelson glanced from Tess to Erny, frowning with disapproval as he seemed to note the ethnic difference between them. Then he cleared his throat and shook his head. "I ain't stayin'," he said stiffly. "I just come over here to tell you all that I don't want no part of this circus tomorrow. I won't be there. My wife won't listen to reason about her son. I can't help that. But Lazarus was not right mentally. It's a well-known fact. I did the best I could with him." Nelson sighed.

Jake nodded. "Thanks, Nelson. It's good of you to come by and say that."

"Never wanted any part of this . . . crusade of hers."

"I know," said Jake.

"Can't you sit down for a while? At least have something to drink?" Dawn asked.

"Nope. I've got to get back to work. Winter's comin', you know. I got rosebushes to wrap. And the leaves don't rake themselves. I just wanted you to know my thinking."

"Thank you," said Tess. "We appreciate it."

"Are you sure you won't stay?" said Dawn. "We have plenty."

Nelson shook his head sharply. "Nope. I've said what I came to say."

"I'll walk you to the door," said Dawn.

Nelson nodded and turned away. Tess could hear their voices in the hallway and then the sound of the front door closing. She raised her eyebrows at her brother. "That was strange," said Tess.

"I thought it was decent of him," said Jake.

"I guess it was. It's just . . . he's not exactly a pleasant fellow."

Jake shrugged. "He's just been driven around the twist by that crazy wife of his. I swear, I would've strangled that woman by now."

"Jake, please," said Tess.

Jake frowned. "Oh, come on, Tess. It's just a figure of speech. And besides, it happens to be true." He shook his head. "Edith Abbott spent a fortune on attorneys trying to clear her precious Lazarus, and they don't have a dime to spare. Nelson knows as well as we do that it was money down the drain."

Tess shivered, despite the warmth of the fire. "God, I will be so glad when all of this is over tomorrow," she said.

Jake nodded grimly. "Me, too. For once and for all," he said.

CHAPTER 4

Feeling the chill, Tess fumbled for the quilt that had slipped off the bed during her restless night. She opened her eyes and instantly was jarred fully awake by the realization of what lay ahead of her today. It was not that she was worried about what the test results on the evidence would be — far from it. She had seen Lazarus Abbott take her sister. There was never a doubt in her mind. She was just a little concerned that she would not be able to maintain her composure in the face of all those news people's questions about Phoebe's murder. Tess could think about Phoebe now, after the passage of twenty years, with some equanimity, but there was a good chance that her voice would crack and her eyes would well up if she actually had to answer questions about her sister's death.

Tess's gaze traveled past the soothing flowers and vines on the gray-blue bedroom wallpaper and out the window to the bare trees' branches. Beyond the trees the brown fields, bordered by rock walls and covered with the white lace of early frost, stretched out, spiked with evergreens, to the horizon and the granite peaks of the White Mountain National Park. The day was beautiful, the sky blue, the clouds puffy, just as it had been on the last day of her sister's life. Deceptive,

Tess thought, and for a moment she saw again, in her mind's eye, Phoebe's gentle face, forever thirteen in her memory.

With a sigh, Tess turned over in the narrow bed and looked across the room. The other bed was a tumult of sheets and blankets and Erny was already gone. Probably helping Dawn with breakfast. Tess smiled at the thought of him. He had needed her desperately when his grandmother had died and left him all alone in the world. But Tess had needed him, too. It had not been easy all these years to keep doubt and depression at bay. Her childhood had been severed in two by Phoebe's murder. Before that time, all she could remember was happiness. And after, even the happiest days had a melancholy shadow. Sometimes she thought that she and Erny had been brought together by fate to save each other from those shadows.

Tess looked at the clock. She had to get up and get ready. For a moment more she lay there, avoiding the inevitable. She turned her gaze back to the window and was jolted by the sight of a gaunt man in a gray parka, standing on the nearby path that cut through the knee-deep brown grass of the field, staring in at her. Their eyes met and he held hers with his gaze until Tess averted her eyes.

For a moment Tess remained under the covers, her heart pounding, unnerved by the stranger's intruding gaze. Then her anger flared. She jumped up and pulled down the shade with a snap. It was probably one of those goddamn reporters, she thought. Couldn't they at least have the decency to stay out in front of the house? She made the bed, washed her face, and got dressed in a good pair of pants, a cashmere turtleneck, and her hacking jacket. When she pulled back the edge of the shade and peeked out, the man was gone.

She walked over to the bureau with its framed mirror, a vase of winter pansies, and her comb, brush, earrings, and makeup. She brushed her thick brunette hair back, considered putting it into a ponytail but decided against it. She put on some silver hoop earrings, some blush and lipstick. Last, she picked up the silver necklace on the linen bureau scarf. It had a rectangular pendant that read "Believe" on it and was the twin of the one that Phoebe had always worn. For some reason, it gave Tess comfort to wear it. It was a kind of promise, to always keep Phoebe's memory alive. Tess fastened the clasp on the necklace and then tucked it inside her sweater as she normally did. She liked to wear it beneath her clothes, to keep it close to her heart.

The door to the room burst open and Erny stood there grinning. "Good. You're up. Dawn says you have to come on. Uncle Jake is already here. We're all eating pancakes."

"Did you help make 'em?" Tess asked him with a smile.

"Yup," he said. "Blueberry."

"Cool," Tess said, although she had little appetite. "I'd like to try those."

"Okay, hurry up," said Erny.

"Hey, just a minute. How about this bed, buddy?"

"Dawn said I didn't have to make it," he assured her.

"I said you do."

"Aw Ma," he complained.

"Now," Tess said. "Chop, chop."

Erny went to his bed and shook the sheets into some semblance of order. Then he jerked up the bedspread, smoothed it out, and tossed the pillow on it while Tess gathered up her satchel and checked its contents.

"How come the shade's down?" he asked.

Tess thought of the man in the field outside her window. "I don't need the whole world watching while I get dressed," she said.

"There's nobody around," said Erny.

"There are a lot of reporters," she said. "They're here for this press conference."

"Can I go with you to the press conference?" he asked.

"I don't think so, honey," said Tess. "This is . . . grown-up stuff."

"Why are there so many reporters?" he asked.

Tess sat down on the edge of her bed, wondering how exactly to explain. She had promised herself that she would explain everything if he asked. But up until this moment, he had shown little curiosity about the reason for their trip.

"Well," said Tess. "You know that my sister was killed a long time ago," she said. From time to time he had been with her when she visited the grave and she had always answered his questions, minus the grim details, about Phoebe's death.

Erny nodded. "I know. Phoebe."

"Right," said Tess. "Well, a man named Lazarus Abbott was caught and convicted of the crime, but some people still think the wrong person was blamed for it. So they decided to retest the old evidence from the case. And we came here this time to hear about the results."

Erny had seen crime shows like *CSI*. He had a vague idea of what she was talking about. "So if the evidence doesn't match, they'll let the guy go," he said eagerly.

Tess blanched. "No . . . Lazarus Abbott got the death penalty for killing my sister."

"He's dead?"

"Yes," said Tess.

"Then why are they doing this now?"

Tess shook her head. "His mother hired an attorney. She refuses to accept that her son committed this horrible crime," she said. "Mothers can be . . . stubborn that way."

"But he did do it, right?"

"Yes," said Tess firmly. "He did it. Now, come on, let's go get those pancakes."

"After breakfast I'm going out on Sean's bike," Erny announced. Half the reason Erny loved coming to Stone Hill, besides constant access to Leo the dog, was the freedom he had here to come and go on his own. In the city, he was more confined. "Dawn said I could."

Tess pressed her lips together. "It would be a big help to me if you would stay here with Dawn till I get back. I think it would be a big help to her, too."

"Why?" he asked.

Tess thought about her mother, having to relive her family's tragedy yet again. "She's . . . thinking about my sister a lot today. It makes her sad. You can help keep her mind off it."

Erny shrugged. "Okay."

Tess went over to him and kissed him on the top of the head. "Thanks. It's just till I get back."

* * *

When Tess entered the dining room, she saw Jake seated at a corner table with Dawn, shoveling down the last of his pancakes. He was dressed in work clothes, a buffalo-check shirt over a chamois shirt and jeans, but at least his clothes weren't spattered with paint. Tess sat down with them and Dawn asked Erny to go out to the kitchen to get Tess a plate.

"Did you sleep?" Dawn asked.

"Not bad. Considering," said Tess. She noted the dark circles under her mother's eyes and didn't need to ask her the same question.

Jake wiped his mouth with the napkin and drained his coffee cup. "I slept like a baby," he declared.

"The first thing this morning, when I woke up, I saw some guy out in the field," Tess said. "It gave me a start."

"Could have been a hunter," said Dawn. "Or just a guest. Out walking."

Tess shook her head. "No, he looked weird. I thought it might be a reporter."

"Those bastards," said Jake.

Dawn sighed. "It's public property back there."

"I know," said Tess. This place will always scare me, she thought.

Jake cleared his throat. "I brought Kelli's car," he said. "I thought you could use it while you're here. Julie'll come pick me up when she's done at the hospital."

"Oh Jake, that's really nice. Thanks," said Tess.

"No problem. Kelli doesn't need it where she's at."

"Have you heard from her lately?"

"She calls her mother like clockwork every Sunday," he said. "She's still at Fort Meade. No marching orders yet."

"I wish she could just stay there," said Tess.

Jake shook his head. "She had to go into the army. Nothing else would do. She says she can go to college for free when she gets out."

"Well, that's true," said Tess. "That's pretty responsible of her."

"She's a good kid," said Jake. "Anyway, you can drive her car around for a few days. It'll do the engine good. I took it out to Julie's dad at his garage. Had the oil changed and all. She's good to go."

Tess nodded as Erny returned and proudly placed a plate piled with pancakes in front of her. Dawn sat across from Tess, apprehension written on her face and in her sad, anxious eyes.

"Do you want me to call you from there when it's over?" Tess asked her mother.

"You don't need to," said Dawn, shaking her head. "We all know what the results will be. Just get back as soon as you can."

"I will," Tess promised.

"Ma, try 'em," Erny insisted.

"They look great," Tess assured him. Even though her stomach was in knots and she had no appetite, she picked up her fork and knife and began to slice through the stack.

* * *

Neither Tess nor Jake spoke a lot on the drive from the inn to the *Stone Hill Record*'s offices. Tess looked out the window at the quaint but severe-looking New Hampshire town with its well-kept Colonial-era houses and the brilliant foliage now past its peak and fading. They traveled past the shops on Main Street. The center of Stone Hill looked pretty much the same. The general store, which sold everything from paper lanterns and plastic glassware to pliers and bags of nails, still anchored the block. But a few trendy new shops had storefronts in the old, austere buildings. There was a gourmet deli and a video store and a shiastu massage studio called Stressless. Tess raised her eyebrows. "Shiatsu massage?" she said. "How New Age."

Jake chuckled snidely. "Yeah, a massage parlor. And guess who runs it? Charmaine Bosworth. The wife of the police chief. Former wife, I should say. I guess the chief wasn't man enough for her."

Tess was just about to insist that shiatsu was therapeutic, not licentious, when she was struck by what her brother had just said. "Bosworth? What about Chief Fuller?"

"He's not the chief anymore, Tess."

"He's not?"

Jake shook his head. "He had some health problems. He had to retire."

"Oh no," said Tess. "I was hoping he would be here. He was so . . . good to us."

Jake shrugged. "That was a long time ago."

Tess nodded and lapsed into silence as they rode along. The newspaper offices were in a relatively new building several blocks past Main Street. The building had its own parking lot, which was now overflowing with television news vans and people with sound and video equipment milling around, their cables crisscrossing the lot. A crowd of curious onlookers had gathered outside of the plate-glass facade of the *Record*'s offices.

"Don't talk to anybody," Jake said as he pulled into a parking space at the edge of the lot. "Just keep your head down and hang on to me."

Tess nodded. Together they picked their way through the milling crowd to the door. A few people called out questions to them, but Jake's jaw was set. "'Scuse us," he said, leading with his shoulder and pressing his way through the crowd. Tess did as he had told her and kept her head down. She wondered if they were going to be exiled at the back or even outside of the room, where the press conference was taking place, but as Jake managed to reach the door of the conference room, a murmur went through the crowd and immediately Tess heard a voice saying, "Let these people through. Stand aside. Let them through."

Tess kept her eyes down and clung to a corner of Jake's buffalo-check shirt as someone, whom she could not see, escorted them to a pair of seats toward the front. As they went past the rows of chairs filled with onlookers, she could see the head table where all the lights and microphones were set up. Seated at the table was Governor Putnam, looking official in a gray suit and a red tie. He was talking with the man she had met at the airport, the publisher, Channing Morris. Chan was wearing a white shirt and tie today and leaned against the table, his arms crossed over his chest.

At the other end of the table, on the governor's right, was Edith Abbott conferring with a man whom Tess assumed was her attorney. Edith was a tall, sinewy woman with frizzy, brown hair and glasses. She was wearing a purple polyester suit that swam on her bony frame and had an improbably large white corsage pinned to the lapel, as if today were Easter or Mother's Day. She appeared to be Lazarus Abbott's sole supporter. As promised, there was no sign of his stepfather, Nelson, in the room.

Edith's attorney, athletic-looking and dressed in pin-stripes, had a square jaw and a handsome, unlined face, but his perfectly groomed hair was prematurely silver. He was listening intently as Edith spoke rapidly, unceasingly into his ear. For a moment, he looked in their direction and his impassive, porcelain-blue eyes met Tess's cool stare. Their gazes locked for an instant and Tess felt an unexpected jolt of sexual electricity pass between them. Upset by her own response, Tess blushed. She felt as if she had, in that moment, consorted with the enemy. She quickly looked away.

She turned her gaze across the aisle to a ruddy-faced man with reddish hair cut into an old-fashioned crew cut and a brushy auburn mustache. He was wearing a navy-blue police officer's uniform with a tie that was too tight for his fleshy neck. He sat stiffly, drumming his fingers impatiently on the taut crown of his hat, which he held in one hand.

"That's the new chief," Jake said, indicating the police officer she was looking at across the aisle. "Rusty Bosworth."

"He looks kind of . . . impatient," Tess observed.

"He's a bully," said Jake. "I never liked him. He's Lazarus Abbott's cousin, you know."

"You're kidding," said Tess, staring at the chief with renewed interest.

"Welcome to a small town. His mother was Nelson Abbott's sister."

"Really," said Tess. "And does he agree with his uncle? Does he think Lazarus was guilty?"

"Everyone around here does," said Jake.

As if he could hear their conversation, Rusty Bosworth turned his basketball-size head and studied them. Tess immediately looked away and met Chan Morris's gaze. Channing excused himself from the governor. He loped over to where Tess and Jake were seated and bent down to talk to them.

"Would you two like to be seated up here at the table?" Chan asked. "It seems to me that you have as much right as these others—"

"No, really," said Tess before Jake could give some hostile answer. "Thanks anyway. We'll stay put."

"Okay," said Chan. "Thought I'd ask." Stepping over wires and cables, he made his way back to the table.

"That was nice of him," said Tess to Jake.

"Yeah, he's a peach," said Jake disgustedly.

"I thought it was nice," said Tess.

"He just wants to plaster our picture on the front page to sell newspapers," Jake scoffed.

"Does everybody have to have an ulterior motive?" Tess asked.

Jake slid down in the chair with his feet extended and crossed, his arms over his chest. "Yes," he said.

The governor turned to the audience, stood up, and tapped on the microphone in front of him, lifting it off of its stand. The noisy conversations in the room immediately ceased and the governor invited the assembled news people to come in closer. "Can everybody hear me?" he asked, speaking into the mike.

A murmur of assent passed through the crowd.

"Okay," said Governor Putnam. "Now, we all know why we are here today. Nearly twenty years ago in this very town, a young girl" — he stopped and clarified — "an innocent young girl named Phoebe DeGraff, who was visiting here on a vacation with her family, was raped and murdered. Lazarus Abbott was convicted of her murder and ultimately put to death for the crime. His mother, Edith . . ." The governor leaned over and indicated the woman in the purple suit. "Even long after her son's execution, hoped to prove his innocence. Her attorney, Mr Ramsey, knew of my feelings about the death penalty. He insisted we get together and discuss the case. He pointed out to me, very cogently during that meeting, that Lazarus Abbott was convicted mainly on the eyewitness testimony of a child. And it is now a well-established fact that eyewitness testimony is often unreliable."

Tess's face flamed. She thought she could feel Ben Ramsey's gaze on her, but she deliberately did not look at him. She kept her eyes focused to a point over the governor's head.

"Mr Ramsey convinced me that I should order a retesting of the evidence. Fortunately, the evidence in this case had been preserved by the Stone Hill Police Department . . ."

"Fortunately?" said Tess under her breath as the governor continued to explain the course of events. She felt a little frisson of anxiety.

"Don't worry about it," Jake whispered. "He's just a politician enjoying the spotlight. He's going to drag this out for all it's worth."

". . . and despite their obvious reluctance to reopen this case, the police were finally prevailed upon to produce this evidence for testing," the governor continued.

Tess glanced over at Chief Bosworth, who was staring at the people seated at the microphones with narrowed eyes.

His face appeared to be flushed with anger and he looked as if he were ready to explode.

Tess looked back at the governor, who was taking a deep breath.

"Now, as you know, there has never been a case to date in the United States where a person executed for a crime was later proved innocent of that crime by virtue of DNA evidence. But many people have walked free from death row. And those of us who oppose the death penalty have always feared that such a day would come. We are here to determine if this is, indeed, that dark day.

"The results of these tests, which were delivered to me yesterday in the strictest confidence from the Toronto lab that tested the DNA, can now be revealed to you. This was the report which was sent to me." He held up a few pieces of paper stapled together in the upper right-hand corner. "I'm going to read it to you now." He cleared his throat and began to read aloud. "'The evidence in this case which was presented by the prosecution at the trial, namely the semen and the traces of blood on Phoebe DeGraff's undergarments, and the skin collected from beneath her fingernails, has partially degraded over the years because of the conditions of storage . . .'"

A groan of frustration traveled around the room. "All this crap for nothing," Jake said to Tess in disgust. The governor held up his hand for silence and, when the noise in the room simmered down, he continued. "Because of this decomposition, it would be difficult, if not impossible, to definitively call this sample an exact match to a suspect's DNA. However, the DNA samples from the evidence are more than adequate to rule out a particular suspect. We have determined that all of these samples belonged to the same person. An unidentified male."

The governor lowered the report he was reading, cleared his throat, and looked slowly across the audience of people assembled there. His expression was grave. Then he lifted the paper again and resumed reading. "The DNA did not, in any particular, match the sample from the man who was convicted and executed for this crime — Lazarus Abbott."

CHAPTER 5

There was a wail from Edith Abbott as she rose from her seat and, with a feeble cry, collapsed. A cluster of people surrounded her, trying to revive her.

"NO," Tess whispered. The room had erupted into chaos with reporters shouting and shoving. While the people in the room surged around her like a wave, Tess sat immobile, frozen in shock, remembering the face of the man who had ripped the tent open those many years ago. Ripped their lives apart. Her heart was racing out of control.

Edith came around quickly, although the color of her skin remained pasty. Clutching her attorney's arm, Edith resumed her seat at the table. The police chief, Rusty Bosworth, was on his feet, demanding to be heard. The governor recognized him.

The chief lumbered up to the table and took the microphone from the governor. He glared out at the assemblage. "All right. As many of you already know, Lazarus Abbott was my cousin. But I never questioned the verdict in his case. Neither did anyone else in this town. Everyone figured he was guilty."

A murmur of disapproval went through the crowd.

"Now if these results are right, it seems maybe Lazarus was railroaded. I'm not making excuses for the police work involved because I wasn't chief at the time. I wasn't even on the force when this crime happened," Bosworth continued. "But I personally want to assure everyone here that this case will be reopened, and the police department will not rest until we get to the bottom of this."

"Thank you, Chief Bosworth," said the governor as the chief took a deep breath and appeared ready to elaborate on his promise. "That's very reassuring."

The florid-faced chief frowned and gave the microphone back to the governor, then resumed his seat.

Tess stared straight ahead. Her hands were clammy and her face felt stiff, as if it were not real, but a plaster cast set over her human face. The noise around her scarcely registered. She felt light-headed and her stomach was churning.

"The chief is quite right to remind us, and the officers of the police department of Stone Hill, that this case is now officially unsolved once again. I want to turn this over," said the governor, "to the woman who worked so hard to bring this day about, and I refer, of course, to the mother of Lazarus Abbott, Mrs Edith Abbott."

"This is bullshit," Jake muttered. "Pure bullshit."

The governor tried to hand the microphone to Edith, but she was holding a large, white handkerchief to her face and was shaking her head. The governor looked to the attorney in the navy pinstripe suit. "Mr Ramsey?"

The silver-haired attorney stood up and took the mike from the governor.

"Thank you, Governor," said Ben Ramsey. The mike amplified a deep voice that was perfectly modulated. "I want to thank the governor for having the courage to allow these tests to go forward, so that the truth, as terrible as it is, could finally come out. Our worst fears have been realized. The wrong man has been executed and there is no way to bring him back. With all due respect to the good intentions of the police department, this wrong can never be righted. There will be no justice for Lazarus Abbott."

"No justice, my ass," Jake swore.

"I think I'm gonna be sick," said Tess.

Jake looked at her. "Really? Like, puke?" he asked.

Tess nodded.

"You don't look good. All right, hang on. I'll get you out of here."

Jake stood up and helped his sister to her feet. Tess felt as if she couldn't breathe, as if the room were spinning around her. A number of reporters swung cameras and microphones in their direction.

"Move," said Jake. "Get out of my way. Give my sister some air."

A wall of reporters blocked their way. Chan Morris saw them getting up to go and leaned over to whisper in the ear of the governor. Governor Putnam rose to his feet again and indicated to Ben Ramsey that he wanted the mike.

"Excuse me, Mr Ramsey. For just a moment. Folks, before you go . . . I want to say to the family of Phoebe DeGraff that we haven't forgotten their sister. Her death was a tragic loss . . ."

Jake, who was attempting to lead Tess toward the door, elbowing reporters out of the way, stopped and turned. He looked daggers at the governor and the people assembled at the front. "You hack. Keep your fake sympathy and go to hell . . ."

"Jake, don't," Tess whispered, clinging to his arm. "Let's just go."

Reporters shoved their microphones at them, but Jake batted them away like greenhead flies. "Get away from me," he growled, "I swear to God . . ." Jake pulled his sister's arm through his own and lifted his shoulder, ready to batter his way through the crowd if necessary.

"Let those people alone," the governor insisted, his voice booming in the mike. "All of you. Just get out of their way."

Reluctantly, the news people began to part to make a pathway and let them pass. As Jake pushed open the plate-glass door of the newspaper office, Tess extricated her arm from his and rushed out, gulping in the fresh air.

"There," said Jake. "Now you'll feel better."

But Tess shook her head. Clutching her jacket closed, she ran toward the car. When she reached it, Tess was gasping. She steadied herself with one hand on the car's front fender and willed the spasms in her stomach to stop. It was no use. With a horrible gagging cry, she bent over and threw up her breakfast into the brown grass bordering the parking lot.

* * *

Dawn was watching at the front window of the inn's library when Jake pulled up and a white-faced Tess climbed out of the car on wobbly legs. Dawn rushed to the front door and held her arms out. Tess entered her embrace like a small child.

"Come inside. Come in," said Dawn.

Tess stiffened. "I can't sit out here. It's too . . . public."

"No, I know. We'll go to my rooms. Erny's back there right now."

The three of them hurried past the spacious common rooms of the inn and Dawn ushered them through the curtained French doors that led to the tidy little innkeeper's suite. Erny was lying on a braided rug, gaping at the television. Dawn walked up to the TV and lowered the volume.

"Hey!" Erny sat up in protest. Then he saw Tess. "Ma, we were looking for you on TV but we didn't see you."

Jake collapsed into a corner of the sofa, rubbing his face with one large, weathered hand. "Go on outside, Erny," Jake said.

Erny was peering at Tess. "What's the matter?" he said.

Tess sat down at the other end of the sofa. She shook her head. "Nothing," said Tess. "It's all right."

"They said on TV that guy didn't do it," said Erny. "I thought you said he did—"

"Not now, honey," said Dawn. "Your mom isn't feeling too well."

"Can we talk about it later?" Tess asked, her face haggard.

Erny hesitated, his own face reflecting her distress.

"Everything's okay, Erny. Really. I just need to . . . um . . . rest for a while."

Erny accepted her reassurance skeptically. Then he had an idea. "Can I ride Sean's bike now?" he asked.

"Yeah, go take a ride," said Jake.

"Far as I want?"

"Don't go to the mountain. Don't . . . talk to anyone you don't know," Tess warned him. "You hear me? If anyone tries to talk to you . . ."

"I'll ride away," Erny promised.

"Take your jacket," said Dawn.

The boy grabbed his heavy, hooded sweatshirt and disappeared. Dawn pulled up a cherrywood rocker to the end of the sofa where Tess was sitting and took Tess's hand, limp on the armrest, into her own, rubbing it solicitously. "It's just unbelievable," said Dawn. "I don't understand. How could it be?"

"Lazarus Abbott was a crazy bastard with a sex crime record and his own stepfather believed he was guilty," said Jake. "He did it."

Tess stared ahead, unseeing. "It was him," she said. "I saw him."

Dawn pressed Tess's unresponsive hand to her own cheek. "Oh Tess," Dawn crooned. "You were a little girl. Completely traumatized. If . . . this is true . . ."

Tess looked at her mother, her eyes wide. "Mom, I know it was him. I recognized him immediately that night when they brought him into the police station. I saw him in that courtroom. I've seen his picture millions of times. I know that Lazarus Abbott was the one who came into the tent that night."

"Honey," said Dawn gently, "I'm afraid we have to face the possibility that you . . . that there was some mistake. You said it yourself. The science would settle it — put the matter to rest. Now, as it turns out, it didn't put it to rest the way we expected . . ."

"You always believed me. Now you think that I was lying?" Tess angrily pulled her hand away from her mother's grasp.

Dawn raised her hands in a placating gesture. "Not lying. Of course not. But you were so little — and vulnerable. And the police were sure it was him. You had all these grown-ups pointing to Lazarus Abbott. They may have influenced you. You were just a child. And you had endured the worst experience . . ."

Tess stared at her mother. "No, I couldn't have been wrong. That would mean . . . I implicated an innocent man. I brought about his death."

Dawn shook her head. "Your father was right. He was always against the idea of Lazarus Abbott being executed. This is the problem with the death penalty . . ."

"Oh, for God's sake, Mother," said Jake, leaning forward. "Are you really going to get all teary-eyed about Lazarus Abbott? He was a psycho and I am not going to lose a minute's sleep over this. And neither should you, Tess. And don't be so quick to second-guess yourself. If you still think that he was the one who took Phoebe, I still believe you."

"Jake," Dawn chided him. "That's no help. No matter how we'd like to wish it away, we can't just pretend these tests didn't happen."

Jake shouted at his mother. "I'm not saying it didn't happen."

"Jake, don't yell at me," his mother bristled.

Jake lowered his voice. "I'm saying, Mother, that I believe Tess knew what she was talking about. She was a smart little kid. Nobody conned her into anything."

Dawn rolled her eyes. "Jake, we're all upset by this but your attitude isn't helpful. How could Tess be right when the evidence proves that it wasn't Lazarus Abbott who killed Phoebe?"

"Test results . . ." Jake scoffed. "Everybody acts like God himself ran the tests. Let me tell you something. I've got a guy on my crew — Sal Fuscaldo — you know Sal, Mom . . ."

Dawn nodded wearily.

"He wasn't feeling good, so the doctor sent him for blood tests at the hospital lab. The results came back positive for some kind of acute leukemia. Sal asked the doctor what that meant, worst case, and the doctor told him he might have only four to eight weeks to live. Can you imagine? Sal was making out his will and picking out his cemetery plot. His wife, Bea, nearly had a breakdown. But the doc thought Sal didn't seem sick enough for that diagnosis so he sent him for a spinal tap, just to make sure. Guess what? There was no cancer. The lab goofed. They sent Sal's results to somebody else. Some other poor slob thought he was off the hook and then found out different."

Tess shook her head. "This was important. I'm sure they checked those results several times," she said.

"Oh, and you don't think it was important to Sal whether he lived or died?"

"You know what I mean," said Tess.

"That's a true story, Tess. About Sal," Jake said. "You wait and see. They're going to find out they made a mistake at the lab."

"How I wish that were true," said Tess.

Dawn shook her head. "I'm almost glad your father didn't have to live to see this day. Lazarus Abbott declared innocent. After all that we went through . . ." The three sat in silence for a moment, numb, all lost in their own thoughts. Then the phone began to ring.

"Don't answer it," said Jake.

Dawn stared at the phone. "It could be a reservation."

"It's the press. Hounding us," said Jake. "Trust me."

Dawn hesitated and then took her son's advice and ignored the phone's ringing. The machine picked up. A reporter from CNN wanted to tape an interview with the family and left his number. Dawn shook her head "What do we say to them?" she asked.

"We don't have to say anything," said Jake. "It's not our problem. Lazarus Abbott had a trial. He went to prison for

Phoebe's murder. He lost about a million appeals. He was executed. End of story."

There was a tapping on the voile-curtained French doors that led to Dawn's quarters and they all jumped. Then Dawn sighed and stood up. "What now?" She walked over to the doors and pulled back the curtain, peeking out into the hallway. Then she let out a sigh of relief and opened the door. Julie came into the room, wearing a puffy mauve, quilted jacket over her hospital uniform.

"I came as soon as I could get away," she said to no one in particular. She pushed her glasses up on her nose and looked sympathetically at Tess. "The hospital was buzzing. Everybody's talking about it."

"That's not what my sister needs to hear right now," said Jake to his wife.

"Well, excuse me," said Julie. "I'm just telling you what I heard."

"It's all right," said Tess. She looked at her brother and his wife, still together but no longer in sync. Once, long ago, they were like bookends — Jake and Julie, youth and beauty. Now Julie waddled and wore glasses and kept her faded blonde hair styled in a sensible haircut. Jake, ungroomed but still good-looking, seemed to look at his wife with distaste. For a moment, Tess felt critical of her brother's superficiality. Julie might no longer be the eye candy he married, but she was still the same kind person who was loyal to Jake's family in their darkest hours. She had always been a practical girl and a source of strength.

"Is there anything I can do for you?" Julie asked Tess.

"You can tell her," said Jake, "how often those hospital lab tests get screwed up. You've told me stories like that. Remember when they gave Sal the wrong results? You were telling me some story about a woman who had a tumor and they told her she was pregnant . . ."

Julie, who was shrugging off her jacket, hesitated for a second and then she nodded. "Oh yes." She looked encouragingly at Tess. "It definitely does happen. I mean, they try to be accurate, but there are mistakes sometimes."

"Thanks," said Tess. She knew they were trying to help.

Julie hung her jacket up on a coatrack by the door and walked over to the sofa. "Scoot over," she said to her husband, wedging herself between Tess and Jake.

Tess suddenly felt as if she couldn't breathe. It wasn't so much the physical proximity of the other three in Dawn's tiny sitting room. It was more their sympathetic gazes and their well-meant reassurances that suddenly felt crushing. This affected all of them, but only Tess was truly . . . responsible. Only she had pointed to Lazarus Abbott in the courtroom and insisted that he was the guilty one.

Tess jumped up. "I'm going to go out and get some air," she said.

"See? You're squashing her," Jake complained to his wife.

"Nobody's squashing me," Tess snapped. "I just need to clear my head."

"Are you sure, honey?" Dawn asked. "Those reporters will see you. They're everywhere."

"I'll go out through the kitchen," said Tess. She could hear the note of panic in her own voice. Before they could think of any more reasons why she shouldn't go, Tess fled from her family.

CHAPTER 6

Tess made her way through the inn's kitchen to the mudroom door, which led to the back steps. In the mudroom, she lifted a knit cap off a hook and put it on, tucking her hair into it. She still had on her wool hacking jacket, but she was shivering all over. She pulled a parka off one of the hooks and slipped it on over her jacket. Then she opened the back door and stood for a moment on the step, inhaling the smell of autumn and wood smoke and looking out at the perimeter of the national park in the distance. Under gray skies, the brown fields behind the inn were ringed by evergreens and ancient trees still bejeweled with stubborn, unshed leaves of gold and garnet at the foot of the mountain. Her gaze, so accustomed to the camera's lens, automatically framed the beauty of the scene in front of her, even as her heart welled with the painful memories summoned by the sight. Her head was aching, but the damp air felt as soothing as a cool hand on her pounding forehead.

Tess looked warily down the deserted bridle path that wended through the field and to the mountain, and the campground. Even though she knew rationally that no danger awaited her there, she never ventured in the direction of the park when she took a walk. But today she felt it tugging her, insisting that she face up to the past.

For a minute she felt trapped, both compelled and afraid to go, and then she had an inspiration. She went back into the mudroom, picked up Leo's leash, and whistled. The yellow Lab, who was snoozing on his rug near the woodstove in the kitchen, looked up, tongue hanging out.

"Leo, come on," said Tess. "Want to go for a walk?"

Panting eagerly, the dog got up and padded out to where Tess was waiting. "Thata boy," she murmured as she hooked the leash on Leo and closed the door behind them. She let Leo pick his way across the back terrace and down to the bridle path where Dawn often took him for a walk.

Together they started down the path, crunching over ice-covered ruts of horses' hooves and brown, broken grass. Leo led Tess along, stopping to sniff every bush and tree trunk he passed. Normally, Tess would have been impatient with the erratic pace of Leo's explorations. But today the constant stopping and starting was good in that it kept her from following any train of thought too far.

As Leo stopped to mark yet another shrub, Tess pulled the hat off and stuffed it into her jacket pocket as she shook out her hair. No need for a disguise, she thought, on this lonely trail. She held the leash lightly and looked ahead at the jagged, granite-colored horizon. As they approached the entrance to the wooded campground, Tess felt her heart beating faster with anxiety. Sometimes she wondered how Dawn could even bear to live so close to the spot where all their lives had been upended forever.

Just before she entered the campground, she turned and looked back in the direction of the inn. The well-kept, clapboard-sided building looked charming and peaceful with smoke curling out of the chimney. Somehow, Tess thought, her mother had come to terms with living here, at the edge of their personal disaster area. It was almost as if it comforted her to be near the place where she lost Phoebe, as one might move to a place where a beloved child had disappeared, so as to be there if that child ever returned. But Phoebe had not disappeared and she would never return.

Drawing in a deep breath, Tess followed the dog into the dark woods. She was amazed to see that nothing seemed to have changed in those twenty years. She passed by the latrine, where she never dared to go without Phoebe, and wound through the trails and up to the campsite, where they had set up their two tents that long-ago summer's day. She had thought that perhaps she would not know the exact site if she saw it, but in fact, she recognized it instantly. It looked remarkably the same. She could picture their Volvo parked there, the doors and trunk open, their gear spilling out. She could almost hear their voices, calling to one another. Teasing. Her legs felt weak and she sat down at the pitted picnic table, Leo's leash held loosely in her hand. The dog sniffed eagerly at the campsite's unfamiliar smells, investigating a wide circle. Tess looked behind her and could see down the hill to the surface of the lake glinting through the empty branches of the trees. She gazed at the patch of dirt with its ring of rocks placed there to encircle a campfire. The ashes in the center of it were cold. Songs came to her mind, and ghost stories. Her heart was thudding madly, seeing it all again. Phoebe in the lantern light, and a ripping sound that woke her, and the man's face . . .

Leo's sharp bark startled Tess and she felt the dog straining at the leash. Tess looked up in the direction the dog was pulling and saw a man walking toward them from the direction of the trail. He was wearing a navy-blue sweatshirt, sweatpants, and watch cap. Tess scrambled to her feet, her heart hammering. She thought of the man watching her from the field this morning, and though she wanted to cry out, fear caught the words in her throat.

Leo barked again. The man slowed down slightly as he approached. "Take it easy, boy," he called out in a friendly voice.

Tess did not try to restrain the dog but let him bark. She glared at the man who raised his hands in surrender.

"Sorry," he said. "I was jogging on the bridle path. I rarely run into anybody up here since it started getting cold."

"Leo, sit," Tess commanded. The dog obeyed and became quiet. Tess glanced warily at the man who'd stopped at the edge of the campsite. "You startled us," she said accusingly.

"I can see that. I didn't mean to." He leaned over and reached out a hand for Leo to sniff. Leo approached him, pulling the leash taut, and examined the proffered hand warily. "You're a good boy," said the intruder in a gentle voice that thrummed through Tess, unnerving her. He looked up at Tess, smiling. "He means to protect you."

"Yes, he does," Tess agreed in a warning tone. She had a sudden, embarrassing realization that she recognized this stranger. Now that she was standing close to him, she felt his physical presence weaken her, and his eyes seemed to uncover her secrets as if he could see the pulse throbbing beneath her skin.

The man frowned as he straightened up. "It's Miss DeGraff, isn't it?" he said.

Tess's heart sank. There was no use denying it, although she didn't want to talk to him, or have to meet his eyes. She had a sudden impulse, which she resisted, to let go of the leash and command Leo to run him off down the trail. The jogger pulled off his watch cap, revealing shining silver hair.

The attorney for Edith Abbott had a grave look in his delft-blue eyes. "I thought I recognized you from this morning," he said. "I don't know if you remember me. I'm—"

"I know who you are," Tess said abruptly.

"I wouldn't think you'd want to be up here," he said. "Too many memories."

Tess did not reply.

"I'm sure those results came as a shock to you today," he said.

Tess lifted her chin. "And I'm surprised to see you out jogging. I would have thought you'd be busy doing interviews."

"I had to get away from that madness," he said. "I needed some air."

"No victory celebration?"

"This *is* how I celebrate," he said with a hint of a smile. "I run."

"I prefer champagne myself," said Tess.

Ben Ramsey shook his head. "This isn't a champagne occasion," he said. "An innocent man was executed."

"And you think it's my fault," she said.

"Your fault?"

"That *is* what you think."

Ben Ramsey shook his head. "No. Of course not. You were only a child."

"I told the court exactly what I saw," Tess said.

"What you thought you saw," he corrected her. He crossed his arms over his chest and assumed a comfortable stance. "You know, initially, when Edith Abbott approached me, I didn't want to get involved. I had my own problems and I knew it would be a drain on me. But when I read the transcript and saw that the conviction was largely based on the eyewitness testimony of a nine-year-old child . . . well, do you have any idea how unreliable eyewitness testimony can be? Even with adults? Psychologists have conducted tests that prove that over fifty percent of all eyewitness testimony is incorrect. That is a frightening statistic," he said. "Especially when you're building a death penalty case on it."

Tess stared at him without replying. He spoke as if he were discussing the case with a colleague, not with the very witness involved. She began to shiver again and her head hurt.

Mistaking her silence for interest, he said, "I'll tell you another sobering fact. Since 1989, a hundred and seventy-five prisoners on death row have been cleared on the basis of DNA evidence, and in seventy percent of those cases, they had originally been convicted primarily by eyewitness testimony. Seventy percent. That is mind-boggling."

Tess looked at him with narrowed eyes wondering how she could have found him attractive. He was obviously an insensitive jerk. "Why in the world are you telling me this? I was the eyewitness in this case."

Her indignation did not faze him. "I just thought you might want to know," he said, "that this kind of erroneous identification isn't some rare mistake. It's practically commonplace. Add to that the fact that you were a child under a great deal of pressure . . ."

"Nobody pressured me," said Tess. "I told the truth."

Ben looked at her, his gaze sympathetic. "I'm sure it seems that way. And after all these years . . . you know, the more we repeat a story or recount a memory a certain way, the more we become convinced that our memory is the truth. That's not just a courtroom fact. That's something we do in our own lives."

"You're wrong, Mr Ramsey," she told him coldly. "I saw Lazarus Abbott take my sister."

His gaze remained kindly. "You know, denial will give you ulcers."

"I wasn't wrong," Tess said. "And I'm not interested in your opinion anyway."

Hearing Tess's angry tone, Leo began to bark again. At the same instant, Tess heard a voice call out, "Ma!" She turned. Erny was riding his bike straight into the campsite, bumping up and down with every stone and rut.

"Erny," she cried. The boy pulled up beside her and stuck out his feet on either side of the bike to balance himself. "Hey, Leo," he said and the dog eagerly pressed up against Erny's leg and accepted a flurry of pets. Then Erny looked up at Ben Ramsey guilelessly. "Hi," he said.

"Hi," said the attorney in a friendly tone.

Tess had no intention of making any introductions. She turned her back on Ben Ramsey. Erny was used to his mother behaving politely to people. He looked quizzically at her and then at the stranger in the sweat suit. Tess pretended not to notice. "Why are you up here by yourself?" she demanded.

Erny looked back at her wide-eyed. "I was looking for you."

"I told you specifically not to come up here."

"I was just wondering where you were," he insisted.

Tess looked at him skeptically.

"It's neat up here," said Erny.

"Let's get back," said Tess. "Dawn will be worried." Erny shrugged and turned his bike around on the path. "Bye," he called out to Ramsey. Leo began straining at the leash to keep pace with Erny.

"Bye now," said the attorney, looking after the departing boy and raising a hand in farewell.

Tess glanced at Ramsey, who had turned to her with unguarded interest, as if he had a hundred questions he wanted to ask her. His face fell at the sight of her bitter gaze. With a curt nod but not a word, Tess turned away from him and followed her son and the dog out of the campground and onto the path back to the inn.

* * *

Dawn was at the stove, heating a teakettle, when the three of them came back through the mudroom door. "You found each other," she exclaimed. Tess nodded. Leo made straight for his customary spot on the rug, while Erny picked up a fistful of thumbprint cookies from a plate on the counter.

"Can I go watch TV?" he asked.

"Sure," said Dawn.

"Come on, Leo, come with me," Erny urged the dog. Leo did not have to be asked twice. He got up and followed Erny out of the kitchen and down the hall.

Dawn looked at Tess with relief. "That's better. That walk put a little color back in your cheeks," she said. "You were so pale. I thought you were going to faint before."

Tess didn't mention that it was anger from her upsetting encounter at the campground that had turned her cheeks pink. "Jake and Julie are gone?"

Dawn nodded. "He left Kelli's car for you and Erny to use while you're here."

"That's what he said," said Tess.

Dawn poured a mug of tea for Tess.

Tess took the tea and sat down on the bench in the breakfast nook. She looked out across the gloomy field and thought about Edith Abbott's attorney. There was no point denying that he was handsome or sexually appealing to her. Obviously, he knew it. It was probably a weapon he used freely to win over female jurors, she thought. But he was so smug with his analysis. Ben Ramsey had spoken to her as if she ought, obviously, to be agreeing with him. That was infuriating. Still, she could not deny that his words made her uneasy. For they had brought back to her an unwelcome memory that was unrelated to her sister's death.

Once, at college, during a painful estrangement from a boyfriend, she had come home from class one day to see him walking out of her dorm. Thinking that he wanted to make up, she had run after him, calling to him, but he didn't respond to her calls. Later, when she brought it up during a brief reconcilation, he told her that he had not been on the campus at the time she thought she had seen him. He had not even been in the state. No matter how she argued with him about it, he insisted that he had been home with his parents at the time. He said that he had no reason to lie about it, and she knew that it was true. She had not seen him. She had mistaken someone else for him. But she had been so sure at the time. So completely sure. She would have bet her life on it.

Dawn brought her own mug over to the nook where Tess was sitting. She sat down opposite her daughter. "I can see that you're torn up about these results. Look, whatever happened, Tess, it wasn't your fault," she said.

"No one believes me. It was Lazarus," Tess said. "You were there. Don't you remember?"

Dawn sighed and gazed into the past through the steam rising from her mug. "You and your father talked to Chief Fuller about the man you saw. My only concern that night was the search for Phoebe. That was all that mattered to me. To be truthful, I don't remember anything else."

Tess bowed her head. She was a mother now. She understood all too well.

"Those days are just a blur to me now," said Dawn softly.

"I wonder if Chief Fuller remembers," said Tess. She pictured Aldous Fuller as he'd looked the first time she met him. A burly man with light brown hair and glasses and a somber look in his eye. He had treated Tess, treated her whole family, with a respectful kindness at the time of Phoebe's kidnapping. Even when Tess's father, Rob, had shouted, pressed him for answers, and demanded results, Chief Fuller had maintained his sympathetic, unflappable demeanor.

Dawn shook her head. "I don't know. I understand he's been very sick."

"Do you think he would talk to me?" Tess asked.

Dawn frowned. "Well, he's retired now . . ."

"I could call him at home."

Dawn's attention seemed to drift away. "I guess you could," she said.

"You act as if it doesn't matter," Tess said ruefully.

Dawn opened her hands in a helpless gesture. "It's not that. It's just . . . it won't change anything."

Tess blinked back tears and looked out at the smoky twilight. "Maybe not. But I have to know," she said.

CHAPTER 7

The next morning Tess ducked out the side door of the inn, evading the assembled reporters, and drove out to the street address given to her by a woman who had answered the phone at the Fuller house. As she pulled up, she saw a thin, bespectacled man with a fringe of white hair sweeping the already immaculate front steps of the neat, barn-red Cape Cod house.

Tess frowned at the numbers on the paper, wondering if she was misreading her own handwriting. The man stopped and straightened up, leaning on the broom as she got out of the car and walked hesitantly toward the steps.

"I'm looking for Aldous Fuller's house?" she said.

The man peered at her. "Tess?" he said.

Tess stared at him, shocked at the drastic change in the former police chief. "I didn't . . . it's been so long," said Tess, shaking the cold hand he proffered.

"I know. I look terrible." He patted his chest. "Cancer," he said. "The treatment's worse than the disease."

Tess grimaced and shook her head.

Aldous shrugged. "Not much I can do about it."

"Thank you for seeing me," said Tess.

"Don't mention it. It does my old heart good to see you," said Aldous. "Didn't you grow up lovely. Here, come on. Come inside."

Tess followed him into the house. They went through a formal living room to a cheerful red-and-white kitchen in the back. Aldous indicated the chairs by the kitchen table. "Have a seat," he said.

Tess sat down and looked around the tidy room. "What a nice house," she said.

Aldous, who was filling a kettle at the sink, turned off the faucet and looked around at his home. "Well, my daughter-in-law and my grandchildren live with me now. That was my daughter-in-law you talked to on the phone. Mary Anne. She's a good girl. My wife died ten years ago, and then . . . two years ago I lost my son . . ." Aldous stared out the window above the sink.

"I'm so sorry," said Tess. She'd had enough loss in her life to know that it was best to be direct about it. "What happened to him?"

Aldous sighed. "He was playing touch ball with some of his old high school friends. Just a bunch of guys having a game. Their families were there having a picnic. A nice autumn day . . ."

Tess could picture the scene, smell the hot dogs, imagine the weather. And she felt the dread of what was coming.

Aldous took a deep breath. "His heart just stopped. Some . . . fibrillation something. Twenty-seven years old."

"Oh, Chief. That is terrible. I'm so sorry," said Tess.

Aldous Fuller shook his head. "We never know, Tess. We never know."

Tess nodded.

"Well, what am I telling you that for?" Aldous said with a trace of sheepishness in his voice. "So, anyway, it's been tough for Mary Anne to make ends meet." He did not mention his own illness, although Tess suspected that it must also have been a factor in their decision to share the house.

Aldous lifted the kettle. "I was just going to make myself a cup of coffee. Can I interest you in one?"

"Oh, no. No thanks," said Tess. "One cup a day is my limit."

Aldous sighed. "The doc says I should cut back on it. I've cut back on everything else but . . . I can't seem to give up my coffee." He shook his head and reached for a mug in the cabinet.

"I thought I might see you at the press conference yesterday," Tess said.

Aldous sighed. "I wanted to be there. But I wasn't feeling too well yesterday . . ."

Tess nodded and watched him as he poured his coffee and searched in the refrigerator for milk. Then he sat down at the opposite end of the table and set the coffee cup down on a paper napkin. She kept thinking of how he had been twenty years ago. A strapping man who spoke softly, but whose very bulk was a kind of reassurance to her. She felt sorry for him and, inexplicably, sorry for herself, as well.

"So, I hear *you* have a son," said Aldous, stirring the coffee in his cup.

Tess nodded and smiled. She reached into her bag for her wallet and pulled it out. She opened it up and showed Aldous Fuller a picture. "His name is Erny. I adopted him. He's ten now."

"Oh, he's a fine-looking boy," said Aldous, gazing at the photo.

Tess beamed and nodded, looking at the school picture. "Well, he's the best thing that ever happened to me."

"I'm glad to hear that, Tess. Mustn't be afraid to live your life."

Tess folded up her wallet and put it back in her bag. Then she placed her hands on the scarred wooden surface of the table. "I haven't been. I don't think," she said. "At least, not so far."

"So, enough fatherly advice. You wanted to see me. What can I do for you?"

"Well, I'm sure you heard about the announcement yesterday. The DNA results."

Aldous Fuller's eyes were weary behind his glasses. "I know this is tough on you, Tess. Hell, it's been tough on me. These reporters calling. It gets to you."

Tess nodded. "I couldn't sleep last night. All these years I've been so sure . . . then I ran into someone who told me something that shook me up. I have to admit it. This . . . person said that experiments had proved eyewitnesses were wrong about fifty percent of the time. Did you know that?"

Aldous Fuller nodded. "Yeah, I've been hearing a lot of those theories."

"I keep thinking, what if that's what happened. What if I was wrong?"

"Do you want me to tell you what I remember?" asked Aldous.

"Please," said Tess.

Fuller inhaled deeply. "Well, when we arrived at your campsite that night, I asked you to describe for me the man who took your sister. You remember that?"

Tess shook her head. "To be honest, not really. It's all a jumble."

"Well, *I* remember. You never hesitated. You gave me an absolutely dead-on description of the guy. Every detail. Here. I took my personal files home with me when I retired. After Mary Anne told me that you were coming by this morning, I pulled these out for you to see. These are the notes I made based on what you told me. Have a look."

Tess reached across the table and took the notebook. The entry read, "Tessa DeGraff, the victim's sister, 9yrs old: white man, filthy dirty. Bumps and scars on his skin. Glasses. Black rims. A greasy black ponytail. A broken front tooth." Beneath his notes, Chief Fuller had written "*LAZARUS ABBOTT!!!*"

Tess looked up from the notebook. "I didn't know his name at that time," she said.

"I wrote that," Aldous said. "While you were describing him, Lazarus came instantly to my mind. It was as if I had asked you to describe Lazarus Abbott for me. Plus he was a known pervert — a Peeping Tom and a flasher. His mother protected him. Always bailing him out. That's the only reason he wasn't in jail that night."

"So you were sure right away, too?" she asked hopefully.

"Damn right," said the chief.

And then Tess was struck by a sobering thought. "So you never really . . . considered anybody else?"

"Did I?" asked the chief. "No. Not really. We just went out and picked up Lazarus Abbott, and brought him into the station. Do you remember that? You started screaming when you saw him."

Tessa nodded slowly. "Yes. That I do remember." She remembered it vividly now — how terrifying it had been to see him walk in — the man she had seen in the tent.

The chief shrugged. "His only alibi was his mother, whom I gave no credence to. His stepfather didn't offer any corroboration. Lazarus had a record. A history of public indecency. We had no DNA testing at the time. Antigen testing was what we used. When we found Phoebe, the blood types were a match. The rapist was a secretor, type A, just like Lazarus. That wrapped the whole thing up with a bow. And you may have been only nine years old, but no DA ever had a better witness than you. The jury saw it the same way we all did. There was no one else it could be."

Tess sighed. "But the DNA says that I couldn't have been right. My brother thought maybe they made a mistake with these tests at the lab."

Aldous Fuller shook his head. "They were pretty thorough in their procedures. Rusty Bosworth told me he had to sign about a hundred documents when they came to get the old evidence. They checked and rechecked, just to be sure there was no possibility of error."

"So where does that leave us?"

"I don't know. But I do know this. They're going to try and make you recant, Tess. Rusty Bosworth and his bunch need someone to blame. They need you to say that I — or somebody else — put this idea in your head about Lazarus Abbott. That you were just a gullible child and I was willing to pin this crime on an innocent man, just to have a suspect." He wagged a bony finger at her. "But you know and I know, that's not the way it was."

Tess suddenly realized that Chief Fuller was worried about his own reputation. His recollections had been consoling to her, but now she felt a sort of defensive chill. "I'd never say that," she said stiffly. "Because it wasn't true."

Aldous Fuller looked relieved. "No, it wasn't."

For a moment there was an awkward silence between them. Tess couldn't help thinking he wanted to distance himself from this horrible mistake and make sure the blame fell on her shoulders.

"Well, okay," she said coolly, standing up. "I should go."

Aldous Fuller reached out and took her hand in his. His palms and fingers were cold and Tess shivered involuntarily. "Look here, Tess. It does seem as if there was some mistake. Perhaps the killer was someone who strongly resembled Lazarus Abbott."

"Resembled?" Tess echoed the word.

"But neither one of us has anything to be ashamed of. I mean, I did the best I could with what you told me. And you told the truth as best you could."

"I did tell the truth," she insisted.

Chief Fuller dropped her hand. "In any case, these perverts rarely stop with one," said the chief. "I spoke to Rusty this morning. Those DNA results have already been sent to the FBI's CODIS database."

"What's that?" Tess asked.

"It's a . . . a national DNA index system of people who have been arrested or convicted of a sex or other violent crime. They may find Phoebe's killer rotting away in some prison."

"And if they do," Tess said, "that means the death of Lazarus Abbott will be on my conscience forever."

She expected him to agree and understand, to say that it would be on his conscience, too. Instead, he shook his head. "That would be hard, Tess," he said.

CHAPTER 8

Reporters and cameramen shouted her name as Tess scurried, head down, back inside the inn and slammed the door behind her. She leaned against it, her eyes closed, and willed her frantically beating heart to slow down. The visit to Chief Fuller had not made her feel better. If anything, she felt worse.

"Ma, you're back," said Erny.

Tess opened her eyes and looked at her son smiling broadly at her, his teeth large and white in his thin, brown face. Healthy and happy. Rescued from a terrible life in the foster system. She reminded herself that she was a good person. No matter what anyone thought. "I'm back," she said.

"Can you take me down to Blockbuster?" he asked.

Tess's spirit seemed to shrivel at the thought of going out again, of being seen. "Can't you ride your bike?" she asked.

Erny frowned and looked out the door lights at the clamoring reporters camped outside. "I guess . . ." he said.

Tess saw the reluctance in his eyes. It was her fault that they were out there. Her fault that they had to run the gauntlet to get out of the house. "All right," she said. "I'll take you. Just give me a minute."

The phone in the foyer began to ring. "Go get your jacket," she said. "Don't forget that Blockbuster gift card you got from Aunt Julie and Uncle Jake."

"I won't," he said eagerly, rushing off to find his sweatshirt. Tess picked up the receiver. "Stone Hill Inn," she said. "How can I help you?"

"Liar," an insinuating male voice whispered. "Killer."

Tess stifled a cry and slammed the phone back down on the hook. She stared at the phone as if it had turned into a live snake in her hand. Who would do that? Bastard, she thought. I'm not the guilty one. She clutched her chest, waiting for her heart to resume a calmer beat.

No, she thought. This was wrong. She was not going to be bullied. And it was not too late to do something about it. She picked up the receiver again and pushed *69. A mechanical voice recited the last incoming number and Tess instantly dialed it back, but it was the number of a cell phone, which switched directly to voice mail. "Listen, you coward," Tess declared into the receiver. "Leave me and my family alone or the next time I will call the cops." She slammed the receiver down again and turned around.

Erny was standing there in his sweatshirt, looking worried. "Who was that?" he said. "What about the cops?"

Tess tried to sound calm. "Nothing, honey. Are you ready to go?"

Erny nodded.

"All right." She reached for the doorknob and then hesitated. "No matter what these people out here say to you, just ignore them and stick with me, okay?"

* * *

The Blockbuster was on Main Street, right beside the general store. Tess parked diagonally on the street. "Okay," she said. "Do you know what you're going to get?"

Erny shrugged. "Video game," he said. "Probably Madden."

Tess smiled. Dawn had purchased a PlayStation for her TV, just in honor of Erny's visits, but she had no games for it and didn't even know how to work it on her own. But Erny enjoyed having it at hand during his visits. Tess was glad he favored the sports games over the more grisly crime games that were available. "Okay. Well, you go on in and get it."

"Aren't you coming in?" he asked, surprised.

She didn't want to run into people asking questions. People who may have seen her face on the news. "I'll just wait in the car," she said.

Erny shrugged. "Okay," he said. He got out of the car and slammed the door behind him. Tess looked up the street. She thought about going to the gourmet shop and picking up something for their lunch, but her anxiety kept her trapped in the car. She peered at the Blockbuster window, and between the movie posters in the window she could see a red-shirted clerk gaping at an overhead TV monitor. She knew it would take Erny a while to look over the store's assortment of games. She could picture her son inside, resting, cranelike, on one leg, frowning intently as he read the game boxes. Tess sighed happily at the thought of him. Everyone told her that once he became a teenager, Erny would only ignore her or grunt at her. She dreaded that day. His smile always made her feel better, no matter what.

A movement in the doorway of the general store caught her eye and she turned to look. There, stepping out on the sidewalk only a few feet away from the hood of Kelli's car, was Edith Abbott. The tall, skinny woman was wearing white sneakers, faded plaid pants, and a blouse beneath a baggy blue denim car coat. The white corsage from yesterday, now brown around the edges, was pinned to the coat's lapel. Edith was going through her purse, looking for something.

Tess froze. She wished she could make herself invisible. To anyone else, Edith Abbott must look harmless, but to Tess, she might as well have been a dragon, able to shoot flames toward the windshield of the car. Tess sank down in the seat, hoping not to be seen.

Last night, when she could not sleep, Tess had thought a lot about Edith Abbott. People had called this woman stubborn and stupid for doggedly pursuing her son's case, even after his death. But yesterday her determination had paid off. In the lonely hours of the night, Tess had imagined herself in Edith's position. What if someone had accused Erny of such a crime? What if Erny were sentenced to death as a result? Wouldn't you be the last person on Earth to give up on him? she had asked herself. And what if he had actually died, and then it turned out to be a mistake?

Tess had thrashed in her covers, trying to imagine it, but it was too terrible to think about. Somewhere in the middle of the agonizing night, Tess had pictured herself going to Edith Abbott, speaking to her as one mother to another. Begging forgiveness. She had tried to imagine what she would say, but it was impossible. The right words wouldn't form in her mind. "I regret that Lazarus was executed because apparently he did not kill my sister, although I still do think he was the one . . ."

Horrible. There was no good way to say it. She just didn't want to face Edith Abbott. Not now. Not on Main Street with people watching, and her mind a blank.

In the few seconds it took for all those thoughts to race through Tess's mind, Edith Abbott located the item in her purse that she'd apparently been seeking. She pulled out a little round box and popped it open. She extracted something tiny with the tips of her fingers and put it in her mouth.

A mint, Tess thought. Or nitroglycerin for her heart.

"Ma," Erny demanded, rattling the door handle. "Open the door."

Edith Abbott looked up, blinking at the boy standing beside the car. Then her gaze traveled through the windshield and settled on Tess. Tess met Edith's gaze with trepidation, expecting a glare or an outburst. Edith blinked at her from behind her glasses, with absolutely no sign of recognition in her eyes. Then she hung her pocketbook over her forearm and gazed patiently at the general store, as if she were waiting for someone to emerge.

She doesn't even know me, Tess thought, with amazement and relief. She doesn't recognize me at all. How could she not know me? Tess wondered. And then, in the same moment, she realized that for Lazarus's mother, Tess was frozen in time. Forever a nine-year-old girl, pointing to her son in a courtroom and calling him a killer. And in all the commotion at the governor's press conference yesterday, Tess must have been just another face in the crowd to Edith. However she might feel about the child who had accused her son, Edith Abbott did not connect her with Tess, the woman she had gazed at through the windshield. That realization came as a welcome reprieve.

Feeling as if she had dodged a bullet, Tess took a deep breath and pressed the button on the driver's side to unlock the car door. Erny opened his door to get inside. Tess put the key in the ignition and waited for Erny to slide in. Suddenly a man's voice called out. "Hey. You there."

Erny, who had one foot in the car, looked up, surprised.

Nelson Abbott had come out of the general store, a roll of burlap under his arm and was walking toward his wife. His gaze had traveled from Erny to Tess, who was behind the wheel. "Tess DeGraff."

At the sound of the familiar name, Edith Abbott began to look around, confused. Nelson pointed at the car and Edith peered in at Tess with a dawning recognition in her eyes. Tess's heart sank. "Who is that?" Edith Abbott asked.

"This is her. The one who testified against Lazarus," said Nelson.

The older woman's eyes widened and she clutched Nelson's arm.

"What do they want?" Erny asked.

"Just get in the car," said Tess, opening her door and sliding out.

"No, Mom," said Erny anxiously. "Get back in."

"I need to talk to these people," she said.

"Why?" he pleaded.

"I'll tell you later."

"You should tell him," Nelson advised her. "Tell him what you did." Tess did not reply. She understood instantly that the bitterness in Nelson Abbott's eyes was now focused on her. He was no longer sympathetic, as he had been when he came to the inn the evening before the press conference to express support for her family.

Tess spoke quietly to Nelson. "Look, I don't think this is necessarily the time or place, but I really would like to sit down with you both—" she said.

Nelson sneered at her. "And say what? How sorry you are?" Nelson peered at her through cold, black eyes. "My stepson was executed because of you."

"All I did was . . . I tried to tell the truth," Tess protested.

"Did you hear what those results said yesterday? Lazarus didn't do it. You really don't want to own up to what you did, do ya?" Nelson said, shaking his head.

Tess was trembling. "Excuse me, but didn't you tell us that even you thought . . . ?"

Nelson's beady eyes flashed at her, warning her not to complete that sentence. He began to speak, drowning out her words. "The facts have changed everything."

Edith, still clinging to Nelson's arm, cocked her head and looked at Tess sadly. "Why did you say those things about my son?" Edith asked in a tremulous voice. "You didn't have to do that. I know someone took your sister, but why did you have to blame my Lazarus?"

Tess turned to Edith. She still didn't know what to say to this aggrieved mother. But there was no escaping her questions. "Mrs Abbott, I have wanted to speak to you about all this. I'm sure you blame me for what happened to your son . . ."

Edith nodded. "Well, you were only a child at the time. But child or not, that's no excuse. You're the one who lied," she said.

Tess felt her face burning. "Look, I told the police the truth about what I saw at the time. That was all I could do . . ."

The other pedestrians on the sidewalk were slowing their steps, aware of an argument and trying to catch the gist of it. Tess tried to ignore their curious faces.

Edith shook her head and began to sniff. She opened her purse and peered into it.

Nelson fumbled for a hanky in his pants pocket and handed it to his wife. "She's never going to own up to it, Edith. She thinks because she was a kid when she did it that nobody's going to hold her accountable. We'll just see about that."

"What do you mean?" Tess asked him in a quivering voice. "Is that a threat?"

"You'll just have to wait and see, won't you," Nelson sneered.

Tess thought of the voice on the phone, whispering "liar" into her ear. She wondered, for a brief second, if it had been Nelson Abbott, trying to intimidate her. She drew herself up. "I have to go," she said. "And take my son home."

"My son will never come home," said Edith indignantly.

Tess slid back behind the wheel and slammed the door. She did not look at Nelson or his wife as she pulled out.

Erny hunched his shoulders up around his ears. "What's the matter with that dude?" he asked, trying to sound nonchalant.

Tess shook her head, not trusting her voice to answer. She clamped her hands on the wheel and drove, although her arms were trembling and her insides were jumping. Erny was quiet beside her, looking at her warily out of the corner of his eye.

When they reached the inn, Tess pulled up to the front door. "Go inside."

"What about you?" he asked.

The lounging reporters were stirring, suddenly aware that the newcomers were prey. They began to surge forward. "It's okay. I'll park the car and come right in."

Erny jumped out of the car, ran to the front door of the inn, and started to open it. Tess tried to keep her face impassive and not look into the eyes of any of the news people who were surrounding her car. All of a sudden, just as Erny was slipping through the front door, out of the corner of her eye, Tess saw something fly through the air, hit the front door with a thud, and tumble to the welcome mat at Erny's feet.

Erny turned around, startled, and then looked down at the missile. He bent over and picked it up.

Tess opened the car door and jumped out. "Erny, what is that? Are you okay?" She shoved aside the people in her way and rushed up to her son.

Erny examined the granite chunk in his hand. "It's a rock," he said, bewildered.

Tess turned and looked around slowly at the faces in the crowd. Some of them showed consternation, others were impassive. Tess took the rock from her son's hands.

"Who did this?" she said, holding up the rock. "Who threw this stone? Are you crazy? You could have killed an innocent kid."

The crowd was quiet. Tess searched their eyes boldly, looking for a furtive glance, for someone who looked guilty in a sea of defiant or indifferent faces.

Hidden in the back of the crowd, a hollow-cheeked man in a gray parka quickly ducked his head so as not to allow her to catch his eye. Tess did not notice this as her blazing gaze swept over the assemblage. For a moment there was no reply and then a voice drawled, "Hey, Tess, how's the view from that glass house you're living in?"

"What does that mean?" Erny asked.

Tess reddened. "Nothing. He's a jerk," she said. "Ignore them. Let's go in."

CHAPTER 9

"Tess, pay attention, honey," said Dawn. "This is their driveway."

Startled, Tess made a sharp right turn into the long driveway that led to Jake and Julie's house. It was six o'clock and darkness had already descended on Stone Hill and its outskirts. Julie had called to invite them to their house for dinner and Tess had gratefully accepted. She wanted to get away from the inn and the reporters who were still camped there. Tess had been unprepared for the level of hostility she would encounter after the DNA results. For years everyone in Stone Hill outspokenly agreed that justice had been done. Now the DeGraffs' suffering seemed to be forgotten, as people hurried to disassociate themselves from the injustice to Lazarus Abbott. It was almost as if the whole town blamed Tess for this blot on its reputation.

Tess drove slowly, gravel crunching under her tires, up the winding drive between a bank of trees. The house, secluded from view by the trees, sat on a slight rise, surrounded by a lawn now brown from the early frosts. It was a small house with yellow clapboard siding, dark green shutters, and a metal chimney for their gas fireplace. Jake's white van, ladders fastened to the top, was parked next to Julie's neat little compact. On the lawn was a cement statue of a wood nymph holding a lantern, which illuminated the path to the front door.

Tess, Dawn, and Erny piled out of the car and Erny ran to the door, opened it without knocking, and charged inside. Tess and Dawn followed at a slower pace. They walked in and were greeted by rich aromas from the kitchen warring with the sweet, cloying fragrance of potpourri. Erny flopped down on the plump, flowered sofa, a pink knitted afghan draped behind him. One of Julie's four cats jumped up on his lap. The beige walls of the living room were covered with framed prayers bordered by pastel drawings of children and doilylike crosses embroidered with flowers and leaves. There were a number of framed photographs atop the television, including a wedding photo of Julie and Jake, Julie looking blonde and doll-like in her cinch-waisted wedding gown. There were several of Kelli at various milestones in her life — in mortarboard and gown, in a prom dress, and in an army uniform. Erny smiled broadly from an eight-by-twelve print of his school photo with its royal blue background, framed in silverplate. Over the mantel of the gas fireplace was a copy of a Thomas Kincade painting of a Cotswolds cottage amidst a bower of roses. Julie came out of the kitchen and greeted them, wiping her hands on a dish towel.

"Oh, I can hear Sassy purring from here," she said. "That cat likes you, Erny."

Erny smiled. "I know."

"How's your cat?" Julie asked him.

"Good," he said, nodding. "My friend Jonah is taking care of him."

Julie smiled at him. "Well, I'm sure he'll miss you while you're gone."

Erny shrugged. "Can I watch TV?"

"Go ahead if you want," Julie said.

Erny, still clutching the uncomplaining, seemingly boneless cat, leaned over eagerly to get the remote from the coffee table and turned on the set. Tess thought to protest, but then decided against it. At home, she limited his TV viewing, but during these visits to New Hampshire there were no children Erny's age around, and he ended up watching more television than normal. There's no harm in it, Tess reminded herself; he also did a lot more bike riding and exploring than he did at home.

"You two come in and talk to me while I cook," Julie said. "Jake's taking a shower."

Tess followed her mother through the tiny dining area and into the warm kitchen. "It smells great," she said.

"Chicken pot pie," said Julie.

"You make the best chicken pot pie," said Dawn.

Julie turned to Tess. "What kind of mother-in-law actually likes your cooking?" she asked incredulously.

Tess smiled.

"So, I hear you've had a rough day," Julie said as she pulled rolls from the oven to check them and then slid them back in.

Tess sighed. "Well, I feel like public enemy number one. We've had anonymous phone threats and somebody threw a rock at us when we came back to the inn this afternoon. It nearly hit Erny in the head."

Julie straightened up, hands on her ample hips. "You're joking. How could they?"

"It was no joke," Tess assured her.

Julie shook her head. "Everybody in town is so busy being outraged about the test results. They don't seem to remember what a creep Lazarus really was."

"He was, wasn't he?" Tess said, craving a little reassurance.

Julie nodded. "Oh, completely. The boys used to trail after him and try to provoke him but we girls just avoided him. I think the only job he ever had was working for Nelson. You know, his stepfather. Nobody else would have him. Nelson worked as the caretaker at the Whitman farm and Lazarus used to help him out. Although I don't think he was much good at it because Nelson was always mad at him."

Julie frowned, recalling events from long ago.

"He came to my father's garage sometimes. Nelson had a beat-up old truck he used for work and Lazarus used to bring it in for repairs and service. I remember that truck because Lazarus used to drive it up on Lookout Ridge where we kids all went parking. He'd drive up there by himself with the headlights turned off and stare and, you know . . . do other things." Julie shuddered, unwilling to name his onanistic acts. "He didn't have a friend in the world."

"Well, he seems to have some now," said Tess.

Julie sniffed. "It's just because his cousin's the new police chief . . ."

"That's what Jake told me," said Tess.

"But don't kid yourself. Rusty was ashamed to be related to him even back then. Rusty used to work for Nelson from time to time, but he was the first in line when it came to making fun of Lazarus."

"Hey, look who I found," said Jake, entering the kitchen with wet hair and clean clothes and Erny under his arm. He opened the refrigerator door and reached in for a beer. Then he looked at Erny. "You want one?"

"Jake, for heaven's sakes," said Julie.

"It's a joke," said Jake.

"I don't drink," Erny said gravely.

"Good for you," said Julie.

"Don't listen to her," said Jake. "What have you been up to?"

Erny shrugged. "Not too much. Hey, Uncle Jake, are you going to take me for a ride in your truck?"

"Honey, don't bother Uncle Jake," said Tess.

"No. It's no bother. I've been looking forward to riding around in the mountains with this guy. How about tomorrow? I'll come get you at your grandmother's. How's that?"

Erny's eyes lit up and he looked at Tess. "Is it okay?"

"Mmmm," said Tess absently.

"Okay. Cool," said Erny.

"Okay. You're on," said Jake.

"Can Leo come?"

"Sure. Why not?" said Jake.

"Thanks, Uncle Jake."

"Okay. Go on, now. Watch the tube till it's time for dinner. I want to talk to your mother."

Jake twisted off his bottlecap and tossed it in the trash as Erny ducked back into the living room. Then Jake turned to Tess. "What's the matter, Tess? You look kind of shaky."

"I am," said Tess.

"How come?" said Jake.

"They're being harassed," said Julie.

"By who?" Jake demanded.

"Malcontents," said Dawn. "That's all it is. People with nothing better to do."

Tess sighed. "I don't know. There are a lot of angry people around this town. I ran into Nelson and Edith Abbott today. I thought she would try to gouge my eyes out, but actually he was a lot nastier to me than she was. The very picture of righteous indignation."

"Nelson?" Jake asked. "Jesus, he's full of crap. Nelson resented every penny that his wife spent defending Lazarus. He'd tell anyone who'd listen how worthless his stepson was. Well, you heard him when he came to the inn the other day."

"He's changed his tune," said Dawn. "I guess he had to, or Edith would throw him out of the house."

"I don't like that man," Tess said. "I get a very creepy . . . feeling from him."

Jake drained the beer bottle he was holding, opened the refrigerator door, and reached in for another. "Nelson's one of those guys who feels like he got the short end of the stick. Thinks the world never really appreciated him. But don't worry about him. He's harmless."

"I suppose," said Tess.

"That's not what my dad said about Nelson Abbott," Julie corrected her husband. "He said that Nelson was a real bastard. He used to beat Lazarus within an inch of his life. There was testimony about that at the trial. Some people thought Lazarus shouldn't get the death penalty because Nelson abused him so bad . . ."

"Poor little Lazarus," said Jake in a singsong voice. "Whupped by his mean old stepfather. If you ask me, Nelson didn't hit him enough."

Suddenly there was a loud knock from the direction of the living room.

"Aunt Julie," Erny cried. "Somebody's at the door."

Julie frowned at Jake. "Who's that? Are you expecting anyone?"

"No," said Jake grimly. "I'll get rid of them." He disappeared into the living room.

"Could it be reporters?" Tess said wearily. "Sorry."

"Don't apologize," said Julie. "You've got nothing to apologize for."

"That's what Chief Fuller said. Just before he implied that it was all my fault," said Tess.

Jake reappeared in the doorway to the kitchen. "Tess. I'm sorry. You'd better come out here. It's the cops."

"The cops? What now?" said Tess. She looked helplessly at Dawn and Julie. Then she followed Jake out into the living room. Erny was huddled in the corner of the sofa, staring at the two burly police officers who were taking up a large amount of space in the small living room. Their buzz-cut hair, holstered weapons, and somber uniforms looked completely out of place in Julie's flowery, pastel decor.

"Tess DeGraff?" the younger officer asked.

Tess nodded.

"Chief Bosworth sent us. He wants to speak to you down at the police station."

"Now?" said Julie. "We're just about to sit down to dinner."

"Sorry, ma'am," said the older, taller officer. "He wants to see Miss DeGraff right away."

"What for?" asked Jake.

"About the Lazarus Abbott case."

"Wait a minute, wait a minute," said Jake. "I know this is big news, but let's remember — it happened twenty-odd years ago. What's the hurry? Why can't she come in tomorrow?"

"Chief wants to see her tonight," said the younger officer.

"Tasker," said Jake in a friendly voice to the older officer. "You know me. We've known each other for years. At least to say hello. My sister has been through a lot. What's the big rush here? You're treating my sister like a criminal."

The younger officer bristled, but Officer Tasker put a restraining hand on his arm and spoke to Jake in a confiding tone, gazing from Jake to Tess. "There's a lot of pressure coming from the public and the chief is short on answers. The chief was hoping they'd find the real perp when they ran the DNA results through the CODIS database. But they didn't get a match."

"What the hell's the CODIS database?" said Jake.

"The FBI has DNA records for every sexual pervert who was ever arrested. But we got the results and our perp wasn't in there. So the chief is picking up the pace a little bit. Miss DeGraff, would you mind?"

Tess did mind. She minded very much. But she did not want to start an argument in front of Erny. "Can I take my own car at least?"

"We'd prefer you come with us. Someone will bring you home afterwards."

Tess shook her head. "Fine," Tess said bitterly. "I'll get my coat."

Tasker tugged discreetly at the sleeve of the other officer. "We'll wait for you outside."

"We'll go with you, Tess," said Dawn as the officers went out the front door and closed it behind them.

"No, stay here and have dinner. I'll be all right," said Tess, picking up her jacket and putting it on.

"Ma, why are you going with the cops? Are you going to go to jail?" Erny cried.

"No, of course she's not," Julie said in a soothing tone.

"That Bosworth is a bastard," said Jake. "I never liked him. Even when he was a kid he was mean. Remember that, Julie?"

Erny looked up worriedly at his mother. "Why do you have to go, Ma?"

Dawn patted his hand absently. "It's nothing, dear. It's all right," she said.

Erny jerked his hand away from Dawn angrily. "No, it's not," he shouted. The cat, alarmed, leapt from Erny's lap. "They were cops. They're making my mother go with them. That is bad. Stop saying it isn't."

Erny's sharp words were like a slap in Tess's face, a stinging wake-up call. Tess looked at her son, who was glaring back at them all.

"Erny," she cried. She tried to reach for her son's shoulder, but he twisted himself away from her.

"If you go to jail, what happens to me?" he demanded. "Who's gonna take care of me?"

For a moment, Tess was silent, shaken by his angry cry. Then she said, "Erny, I'm not going to jail. Don't even say that."

Erny met her gaze defiantly. "Why not? My real mom did," he said.

He rarely mentioned his biological mother or the chaos of his life with her. He often said that he didn't remember her, but he knew the story of her demise all too well. His words pained her, but Tess did her best to conceal it. "It's not going to happen," she said. "Because I didn't do anything wrong."

Erny slumped down on the sofa, his arms crossed over his chest. He muttered something unintelligible.

"What was that?" said Tess sternly. "I didn't hear you."

Erny looked up at her defiantly, his chin trembling. "You did do something wrong. You told the cops that guy Lazarus was guilty. And that was a lie. Wasn't it?"

CHAPTER 10

Despite the fact that he had summoned her, Rusty Bosworth kept Tess waiting for about twenty minutes. She sat in the wooden office chair outside the frosted-glass-windowed wall of his office and waited. She could hear the murmur of a voice, rising and falling, inside his office. She presumed that he was talking on the phone, for there were long lapses in the conversation during which there was silence, but she could not make out the content of the conversation.

While she sat there, tapping her toe anxiously, Tess looked around the old station house. It looked very much as it had twenty years earlier when she had been brought here, wrapped in a blanket, and set down, shivering, on a green leather chair in front of the chief's desk. She could still picture Chief Fuller's worried eyes as he gently questioned her and feel the warmth of her father's hand, clutching hers, as she explained all that had happened, describing the man who had stolen her sister in the night.

God, I hope he doesn't still have that green leather chair, she thought. She was afraid she would pass out, or burst out crying, if she had to sit in that chair again. Just the thought of it brought every horrible memory rushing back to her.

Just as she was reassuring herself that she could face it, that she was tougher than that, the office door opened and Rusty Bosworth stepped out, clutching a wad of papers in his meaty fist. Tess stood up, expecting to be invited inside.

Bosworth's mustache twitched, and he looked at her with cold, assessing eyes. "Let's go down the hall," he said.

Without waiting for a reply, he began to lumber down the corridor. Tess picked up her bag and followed in his wake. His bulky frame took up most of the hallway and his large head seemed to graze the bottom of the light fixtures. When he reached a door that had "Interrogation Room" printed on the frosted glass, he opened it and gestured for her to go inside.

"Interrogation?" Tess said.

Bosworth's small eyes betrayed no expression. "Means questioning," he said.

Tess took a deep breath. "No kidding," she muttered as she went inside.

"Have a seat," said Rusty, pointing to a wooden ladder-back chair on the far side of a battered oak table. Tess walked around the table and sat down. The small room was bare. There was a white plastic carafe on the table and a stack of paper cups. In a nod to the new, a videocamera was mounted in the corner of the room. As Tess looked at it, a red light went on, indicating that it was running.

"Thirsty?" the chief asked.

Tess shook her head.

The police chief cleared his throat. His florid complexion and his rust-colored hair and mustache seemed to flame in the dun-colored room. "All right, Miss DeGraff, let me explain the situation to you."

I think I understand the situation, Tess wanted to say, but she restrained herself.

"I know you're probably wondering why you're here," said Chief Bosworth. "When those DNA results came back yesterday, it became obvious that a mistake had been made somewhere along the line. Now, it seems to me that there are two possibilities. Only you can tell us which one applies. Either you were mistaken in your identification of Lazarus Abbott . . ."

"I was not mistaken," Tess insisted.

Bosworth continued as if she had not spoken. "Or you were deliberately lying."

"Deliberately lying?" Tess cried. "I was nine years old. Why would I lie about such a thing?"

Rusty waited impassively. "I don't know. I'm asking you that."

Tess shook her head. "Lying? That's ridiculous."

The chief stared at her with steely eyes.

Tess looked at him impatiently. "Is that your theory? That I was lying?" Tess shook her head. "That makes no sense."

"Let me just give you a 'what if,'" said the chief, glancing down at the sheaf of notes that he had placed on the table. "What if, say, someone you knew entered the tent that night."

"Someone I knew!" Tess exclaimed. "The tent was slit down the side by an intruder with a knife."

"Well, if someone wanted to make it appear that it was an intruder . . ."

Tess looked at him and shook her head. "What?"

"You were just a child at the time. What if someone you loved . . . someone you were accustomed to obey, told you to say that the tent had been slit by an intruder . . ."

"What are you talking about?" Tess demanded.

Chief Bosworth cleared his throat. "I'm trying to consider every possibility."

"You've lost me," said Tess.

Chief Bosworth raised his voice and hardened his tone. "We need to clear this matter up, Miss DeGraff. And if you have been . . . protecting someone all these years, it's time to admit it."

"I have no idea what you're talking about," said Tess.

"The truth can't hurt him anymore, Miss DeGraff. He's beyond all that now."

"Hurt who?" said Tess.

Rusty Bosworth cleared his throat. "You may think that we are just small-town cops. But let me tell you, I've seen more than my share of the unsavory. The downright repellent . . . I know perfectly well that sometimes parents . . . fathers, in particular . . . have unnatural appetites . . ."

Tess's eyes widened and she jerked back in her chair as if his words had slapped her face. "My father? You are accusing my *father*?"

"I'm not accusing anyone," he said. "I'm asking you to tell the truth."

Tess shook her head. "No. I don't have to listen to this. That is the most disgusting—"

Rusty Bosworth leaned toward her. "More disgusting than putting an innocent man to death?"

"You keep your filthy accusations to yourself!" she said.

Rusty Bosworth stood up and slammed his hands, palms down, on the table. "Listen, Miss DeGraff, this police force is under attack. We are taking the blame for your mistake and I've had enough of it. Now, I intend to explore all the options this time around. Including the possibility that you lied to cover up your father's crime."

For a moment Tess was too outraged to even form a sentence. Finally she took a deep breath and said, "My father was a wonderful man whose life was destroyed by what your cousin, Lazarus Abbott, did . . ."

Rusty's eyes narrowed. "No need for you to remind me of my relationship to the victim," he said.

"The victim?" she cried.

"As you have pointed out, the victim of this miscarriage of justice was my cousin. But I think I can still be objective. You, on the other hand, were an impressionable child when all this happened. Now, I want to make this clear. You were a little girl. A good little girl. If someone told you not to tell . . . someone you cared for . . . like your father . . ."

Tess put her hands up. "All right, that's it. That's enough. You can say that until you're blue in the face. It won't make it true. It was not my father."

"Your brother, Jake, perhaps?"

"My brother Jake was at a dance in town that night," Tess snapped. "You know that. Every kid in Stone Hill was there."

"I'm aware of your brother's alibi," said Bosworth.

"Alibi!" Tess yelped.

"But your father had no such alibi. Perhaps he was lying awake while his exhausted wife slept. Lying there wondering if he could coerce one daughter into cooperation. And the other into silence."

Outraged, Tess glared at the chief. "Not in a million years. The only person who coerced me into being silent was Lazarus Abbott."

"That is not possible, Miss DeGraff," Rusty Bosworth said coolly. "Everybody knows that now. You have to stop saying that."

Tess felt her outrage ebbing, being replaced by confusion.

"Now, either you mistook someone else for Lazarus or you were lying," he said. "Which was it?"

Tess stared back at him. "I didn't lie. But . . . I . . . don't know . . . I can't explain it."

"Can't or won't?" he persisted.

Tess shook her head.

"If you lied about it, that's perjury, Miss DeGraff. That's a felony. It's called a delinquent act and you can still be arrested for it."

Tess stared at him in disbelief.

"It's time to tell the truth, Miss DeGraff."

"I told the truth," she said.

"I'll remind you again," he said in a menacing tone. "That is not possible. Let me give you the benefit of the doubt. Perhaps it was an honest mistake. Perhaps you were saying that you saw someone who looked a certain way . . . and the adults around you jumped to an incorrect conclusion."

Tess immediately remembered her conversation with Aldous Fuller. The former chief was afraid that blame would fall on him and now it seemed that Rusty Bosworth was suggesting exactly that. It was Lazarus, she wanted to say. Lazarus. But the words stuck in her throat. The chief was not going to listen to that. He was not going to listen until she at least acknowledged the possibility that she had been mistaken. Tess thought again of her college boyfriend. The one she thought she saw leaving the dorm, when he was actually several states away. What was the point of insisting on the impossible? She thought of Erny, and shame swept over her as she remembered his words: You told the cops that guy was guilty, and that was a lie.

Not a lie, she insisted silently.

"Miss DeGraff."

"I don't know for sure what happened," she said.

Rusty pounced, his eyes gleaming. "You were wrong. You admit it."

Tess stuck out her chin. "All I admit is that it doesn't make sense."

"That's not good enough," said the chief.

Tess summoned all her nerve. "That's all I can tell you. That's all I know. And that's all I'm going to say to you without an attorney present. I want to leave now. I'm not under arrest. I assume I can leave."

Rusty scowled at the mention of a lawyer and raised a hand, as if to detain her, but then seemed to think better of it. "All right. You can go. For now," said Rusty Bosworth. "But I warn you, Miss DeGraff. If I find out that you committed perjury, you will face criminal charges. Take my advice. If my hunch is correct, you'll be sacrificing yourself to protect a man who doesn't deserve your loyalty. Not if he killed your sister . . ."

Tess stood up, even though her legs trembled beneath her. "My father would have died to protect my sister," she said in a raspy voice. "To protect any one of us."

Rusty Bosworth peered at her. "But he didn't, did he?" he said.

Tess wanted to shout at him or slap his face. She wanted to shriek at him that no one had suffered more than Rob

DeGraff over what happened to Phoebe. She wanted to, but she didn't. Bosworth was an enemy who had made up his mind.

* * *

Erny was already in bed by the time Tess got back to the inn. Julie had sent a helping of chicken pot pie home with Dawn for Tess. Dawn heated it up for Tess and set it down in front of her, but Tess had little appetite. She picked at it and ate a few forkfuls.

"What did he want, honey?" Dawn asked.

Tess shook her head and avoided her mother's gaze. She was not about to tell Dawn about Rusty Bosworth's speculation that Dawn's husband was responsible for the murder of their daughter. Tess could not imagine even uttering the words, much less forcing her mother to hear them. "He was asking me about that night. What I remembered," she said blandly. "Just hoping I might be able to provide some new information for the case."

Dawn nodded. Tess excused herself after barely eating anything. "I'm exhausted," she said. "I'm going to turn in."

"Try and sleep," Dawn said, although, judging by the dark circles beneath her eyes, Dawn was unable to take her own advice.

Tess shook her head. "I'll try. Good night, Mom."

Dawn hugged her for a long time and Tess could feel her mother's frame shaking. "Are you okay, Mom?" Tess asked.

"Oh sure," said Dawn. "It's just . . . this never ends, does it?"

Tess left her mother in the kitchen and went down the hall to her room. The room was dark except for the moonlight that spilled in through the window. Tess got changed in the bathroom and slipped under the covers of her bed. Across the room, she could hear Erny's steady breathing. Tess lay on her back, staring up at the ceiling. She felt as if she were pinned there by a dead weight. In the last forty-eight hours, she had done nothing, it seemed, but react to the disorientation caused by unfolding events. The unexpected results of the DNA tests had upended the one certainty she had clung to about the death of her sister. The identity of the killer. She did not know why he had done it, or where, or why he had picked on them out of all the people in the world. But at least she had always known who was guilty. Lazarus Abbott. The man she described to the police. The killer.

Now even that was gone.

Who is wrong and who is right? And who is truly to blame? The room was quiet and Tess longed to sleep, but she couldn't turn her thoughts off, couldn't stop thinking about what she knew and didn't know. The DNA results were a fact. They exonerated Lazarus Abbott. That meant that he could not have raped Phoebe.

But no matter what preposterous theory Chief Bosworth floated about her father, she knew for a fact that it was not him. As for her mistaking Lazarus for someone else, Tess remembered the face of Lazarus Abbott. And even if, over time, she thought she might have altered the face she saw that night to fit the face of the man they arrested, Chief Fuller's words this morning came back to her. When she had described the man with the knife that long-ago night, Chief Fuller had recognized her description instantly. When Lazarus Abbott had been brought into the police station, she had screamed at the sight of him.

That reaction was not an accident. So where did that leave her? What if, she asked herself, your identification is right, and also the DNA is right? How, she wondered, can I reconcile two facts that seem to be mutually exclusive? It was Lazarus Abbott who took her. It was not Lazarus Abbott who killed her.

"Mom?"

Tess jumped and let out a soft cry.

"It's just me," said Erny, delighted with her alarmed response.

"You scared me. I thought you were asleep," she said.

"Nah. I was waiting until you got back."

"Well, I'm back," she said firmly. "Now you can sleep. Did you have a good time at your aunt and uncle's?"

"Pretty good. Ma, I'm sorry I said those things to you. I shouldn't have said you were lying. I didn't mean it."

"I know, honey. Don't worry about it. We're all a little stressed."

"What did the police chief say?"

Tess was not about to utter the accusation against Rob DeGraff, the grandfather Erny had never known. "We just went over the same stuff. He thinks I must have . . . remembered the wrong man.

"Did you?" he asked. "Did you remember the wrong guy?"

Tess sighed. "I don't think I did. I saw the man who took her. But it's a problem because the test results say someone else did the . . . crime."

Erny was silent for a minute. "Maybe it was his friend. Maybe his friend dared him to take her."

It seemed like an utter non sequitur. "His friend? What friend?"

"I don't know. Any friend. Your friends can get you into trouble sometimes," he said in a knowing tone.

Tess turned over in her bed and propped herself up on one elbow. She could see the other bed, the jumble of Erny's covers, and his shock of dark hair against the pillow in the moonlight.

"What do you mean?" said Tess.

"Oh, you know, Ma. Sometimes they say, 'Let's do something bad,' and you might not even want to do it. But you do it anyway."

Tess's heart skipped a beat. She knew he was speaking from experience. And any other night, she would have pursued his explanation, but tonight all she could think about was the possibility he raised. "That's true," said Tess slowly. Julie said that Lazarus had had no friends, but that wasn't necessarily true. Maybe if she knew more about his life . . .

Erny yawned while Tess turned the idea over and over in her mind. Then she said aloud, "But no. Wait. It couldn't be."

"What couldn't?" Erny murmured. Sleep was beginning to overtake him.

"If someone else did the . . . crime," said Tess, thinking aloud, "Lazarus would have told the police. Why would he take the blame?"

"He didn't want to be a snitch," said Erny, as if that were the most reasonable explanation in the world.

No, of course not. Tess was silent. A partner in crime. The thought opened up a realm of evil possibilities, like a deadly nightshade blooming in the dark. It would explain how she could have seen Lazarus and yet the rape, and possibly the murder, was committed by someone else. Maybe someone else had planned the whole thing. Goaded him into it. Lazarus never could have been the brains behind it. It had to be someone older or smarter. Someone he would be afraid to betray.

Tess looked over at her son in the dark, amazed by his simple suggestion. "You know, honey, you might be right."

But Erny had not heard her. He had flopped over on his side and was making a murmuring, sighing sound. Soughing like the wind. Dreaming.

CHAPTER 11

The next morning dawned sunny and warm, a moment of Indian summer. Dawn had opened the sitting room windows a few inches to air out the inn a little bit. Tess pulled back the curtain and felt the light, fresh air as she looked out at the inn's wide driveway. Tess noticed that the corps of reporters had thinned out a bit. The public's appetite for sensational news stories was insatiable, but their attention span seemed to be ever diminishing. Thank heaven, Tess thought. The fewer developments there were to report, the sooner the reporters would vanish. Those who remained were now assembling outside in a desultory fashion.

As she looked out the window, Tess saw Jake's white van, flanked on both sides and across the top with closed extension ladders, pull up at the end of the walkway to the front door.

"Erny," she called out. "Uncle Jake's here."

The front door opened and Jake came into the vestibule "Hey, Tess," he said. "Is the kid ready?"

"He's getting his stuff," she said.

"What happened with Bosworth?" he asked.

Looking at Jake, Tess thought of the chief's suggestion that their father might have been her sister's assailant.

It made her feel sick to her stomach. She did not want to imagine Jake's reaction if he heard about this theory that the chief had posited. "Nothing. Really. It was a complete waste of time. Where are you two headed today?"

"I'm gonna take him out to the Whitman farm. It's a great place for a kid to run around. He can go exploring while I finish the trim on those third-floor windows."

Erny appeared in the hallway wearing his sweatshirt and tugging Leo by his leash.

Jake frowned at the sight of the dog.

"You said I could bring him," Erny reminded him.

Jake shook his head. "I did? I must have been drinking. All right. Come on. See ya later, Tess."

"Have fun," she said to Erny.

As soon as they were out of sight, Tess picked up her bag and pulled her own jacket from the hook in the hallway. She drew in a deep breath to try to calm her jittery stomach. She told herself she was going to sail past those reporters as if they were invisible. She couldn't hide inside this morning. Erny's sleepy suggestion about a friend had given her an idea and she needed to pursue it. She kept her gaze straight ahead as the reporters, galvanized by the sight of her, began to shout out her name.

* * *

Ironically, unlike the Stone Hill Inn, the offices of the *Stone Hill Record* were subdued. A receptionist greeted Tess with a pleasant nonchalance when she asked to see Channing Morris. "Who shall I say is asking?" the receptionist asked politely. It was only when Tess said her name that the girl's eyes widened and she rang the publisher's office and spoke in a low, hurried voice.

She hung up the receiver and looked up at Tess. "He'll be out in just a minute. You can have a seat," she said, indicating the waiting area of the newspaper's modest office. Tess thanked her and walked over to the low-slung leather couch that sat beneath a wall of framed photos. They told a story in pictures of the newspaper's history. Most were photos of men dressed in banker's-style suits, shaking one another's hands and beaming avuncularly. The exception was a stern, square-jawed woman with snapping black eyes who was in the center of many of the pictures. Tess was studying the gallery when Chan Morris, handsome and casual-looking in an open-collared shirt, his hands stuffed into the pockets of his well-worn chinos, emerged into the waiting area.

"Miss DeGraff," he said. "You looking at my journalistic forebears there?"

Tess nodded. "You had a female publisher, I see."

"My grandmother," said Chan.

"Wow. Looks like she was kind of a feminist pioneer," said Tess.

"Oh yeah. No knitting and cookie baking for her. She was as tough as nails. But she taught me the newspaper business."

Tess smiled. "I guess you didn't have much choice."

Chan shrugged. "Luckily, I liked it. So, what brings you here? I thought you were avoiding the media entirely."

"I am. I was," Tess admitted. "But I need a favor."

"Come through," he said. "Tell me what I can do for you."

She followed him back into the paper's warren of offices. "I want to look at all the articles from the paper concerning my sister's abduction. I need the local viewpoint. I looked on the Internet, but you're only cataloged for the last five years."

"I know," said Chan sheepishly. "It's been a nightmare with all the news organizations covering this story."

"Are the back issues available?" Tess asked.

"Down these stairs," said Chan, indicating a basement staircase. "We have them in the archives. It's a nuisance to look through them, but yes, we do have them." Chan raked his fingers through his soft black hair. "Perhaps we can help each other out. How about just a few words of reaction from you about all this?"

"I'd rather not say too much," said Tess.

Ignoring her reluctance, Chan reached into his shirt pocket and pulled out a small spiral-topped pad and a pen. "Just tell me how you felt when you heard the governor's announcement?"

Tess took a deep breath. "Shocked," she said truthfully.

Chan scribbled on the pad. "You didn't have any doubts, all these years."

"I believed," she said carefully, "that the courts and the police had done their jobs. That the matter was settled."

"And now?"

"And now . . . it would seem that the case has to be reopened."

Chan wrote down her response and looked at her quizzically. "You sound very detached," he said. "Almost as if it wasn't personal."

"Oh, it's very personal," she said. "Are you finished?"

"One more question? If you don't mind my asking, what are you looking for in the archives?"

Tess was not about to tell him her "accomplice" theory. She did not want people to know that her search was motivated by the hunch of her ten-year-old son. She managed a vague excuse. "Well, naturally, I have questions and I am looking for answers. Not that I think I can find what the police couldn't, but I have to at least see if I can find something to jog my memory. Just for my own peace of mind."

"Jog your memory about that night," he said.

"Yes, exactly," she said. "Can I have a look now?"

"Sure." He seemed to accept her motive. He replaced his pad in his pocket and led the way toward the basement staircase. It crossed Tess's mind, as she accompanied him down the steps, that he wasn't a very aggressive reporter. They came out into a room that looked like a low-ceilinged library, lined with shelves, which were piled high with papers. Tess frowned, looking at the towers of papers around her. She had expected microfilm, at least.

Chan saw her expression of dismay. "Sorry . . . I just don't have the manpower to get these back issues cataloged."

"How do you find anything?" she asked.

Chan sighed. "It takes a while. Uh, the years you want would be over in that far corner," he said.

Tess sneezed.

"Dust," he said apologetically.

"It's okay," she said.

"There's a Xerox machine over there, if you want a copy of anything."

"Thanks, I'll be fine," said Tess. She followed the dates on the shelves and found the section where the papers she wanted to look at might be. She took the first sheaf over to a small table at the end of a stack and sat down.

"Mind if we get a photo of you looking through the archives?" Chan asked.

Tess felt frozen inside, but she nodded politely. It was the price she had to pay. "Go ahead," she said.

"I'll see if we've got a photographer in the house," he said and he sprinted back up the stairs, wanting to catch her before she got away.

Tess began to comb through the papers. It was an arduous task, both hard on her eyes and on her heart. She read the accounts of Lazarus's life closely, looking for any indication of a friend or an associate. In the process, she was forced to look past countless pictures of her own family, dressed in forgotten clothes, looking stunned and grief-stricken.

She was forced to stop for a moment to turn and look gravely at the camera of the photographer Chan had found for the job. Then she returned to leafing through the papers. She found a few items of interest among the many articles. There was an interview with one of Lazarus's old schoolteachers that talked about his life as a disliked and below-average student. No mention of friends or associates. On the contrary, the teacher was eager to label him, as so many killers were labeled in their youth, as a loner.

There was another interview with his aunt, Rusty Bosworth's mother, who insisted that their family was like a Norman Rockwell portrait of Americana, and there had to be some mistake. There was also one reporter's account of trying to interview Nelson Abbott, but being met with only his scorn and impatience.

It was fascinating to Tess and repulsive at the same time. She used the copier for a few articles she thought she might want to read again, but overall she was disappointed. No new names from Lazarus's life emerged or caught her attention. She was about to give up when she came across an interview with the Phalens, who had owned the Stone Hill Inn and had taken in the DeGraffs so kindly. Obviously the reporter was grasping at straws, trying to offer some new, human interest angle on a case that dominated the local headlines for weeks. The article was innocuous enough. Ken and Annette Phalen expressed sympathy for the DeGraffs and outrage at the crime. But it was the photo that accompanied the article that caught Tess's attention. Tess xeroxed the article and then sat back down at the table, staring at it. Ken stood awkwardly on the front step of the inn while Annette and their toddler, Lisa, sat on one of the benches that flanked the front door. Lisa was struggling to get free from her mother's grasp. Ken, unsmiling, was slouching, his hands in his pockets, his black hair pulled back in a messy ponytail. For a few minutes, Tess could not put a finger on why the photo seized her attention. And then, her eyes widened. She took out her black marker pen and began to draw on the xeroxed copy. She drew a pair of large, black-framed glasses on Ken Phalen's face and stared at the result, her heart racing.

* * *

Jake glanced over at his nephew, who had his forehead pressed against the window on the passenger side of the van. Leo was sitting straight up behind them, his furry head poking between them, panting.

"Hey, Erny, tell your friend here to stop drooling on me."

Jake was rewarded with a smile. Erny immediately began to pet Leo's furry ruff. "Good dog," he said mischievously.

They were approaching an all-too-familiar landmark — a humble gray farmhouse sitting on a neatly kept acre of property. Jake wondered for a minute if he would feel any different today seeing that house, knowing what he now knew about the DNA results.

Jake could easily have changed his route to avoid passing the Abbott place and thereby avoid being reminded of Lazarus Abbott and what had happened to Phoebe. Avoid remembering that it was his own fault that his sister had been unprotected when Lazarus Abbott tore open the tent and seized her. But there was no use in that. Fate, he thought, and no use crying about it.

A black truck was approaching from the direction in which they were headed. As the driver signaled to turn into the Abbott driveway, Jake recognized Nelson Abbott at the wheel, wearing his John Deere hat and his customary scowl.

Part of him wanted to point the truck out to Erny and say, "Your aunt Phoebe was killed by that man's son." It seemed as if the kid had a right to know that much about the family history. Jake could imagine the kid's silent wide-eyed stare. But he decided against it, and, he realized with a mild feeling of anxiety, the DNA results had something to do with his decision to remain silent.

Instead, he continued on the meandering back road until he came to the entrance to the Whitman farm. "This is it," he said. "This is where we're going." Erny looked around as they turned down the driveway, which had been cut through acres of trees. Jake drove up and down several hills, past forest and field, past rock gardens and apple trees and rosebushes that were in the process of being wrapped in burlap for the winter.

"Welcome to how the other half lives, my man," said Jake. "Quite a place, huh?"

"Yeah," said Erny. "Who lives here?"

"A guy named Chan Morris. He lived here with his grandmother."

"Is he a kid?" Erny asked.

"No, he's not a kid now. He was a kid when he moved here. When his parents died. But that was a long time ago."

"Did they die from drugs?" Erny asked thoughtfully.

"Drugs? No," said Jake, frowning. "I don't know what they died of. I don't really remember."

Erny turned his head and looked out the window silently.

Jake glanced at him and suddenly realized that Erny was identifying with Chan, another child orphaned at an early age. That's why he'd asked about the drugs — because that was what happened to his birth mother. Jake grimaced, remembering the awkward silence last night when Erny mentioned his birth mother and how she'd gone to jail. He flailed around in his mind for a change of subject. Looking out on his left, he noticed the large, algae-covered pond rippling in the breeze under the branches of some overhanging trees.

"Damn," said Jake in an overly loud voice. "I wish I'd remembered to bring fishing poles. We could've tried fishing over there."

"That's okay," said Erny, but there was disappointment in his tone.

"No, you know what? I know a better place. Remember the lake near the mountain where we fished the last time? Well, maybe tomorrow I'll take you over there and we'll fish for a little while."

Erny looked at him. "Really?"

"Yeah really," said Jake.

Erny smiled. "Okay."

Coming up over a final rise, they spotted the Morris house nestled in a natural valley. It was a huge Colonial-style house surrounded by trees and gardens.

"Wow," said Erny.

"I painted that whole place," Jake boasted.

"Awesome," said Erny respectfully.

Jake pulled the van up in the driveway beside the house. He got out and opened the side door so that Leo could get out. Erny had clambered down on his side and come around the truck. "All right now, listen to me, you two," said Jake. "You can run around here. There are fields and stuff. Rock out. Just . . . no going in the pond. I've heard it's pretty deep. Have a good time. It's gonna take me an hour or so to finish this." Jake pulled a boom box from inside the van.

"We can go anywhere?" Erny asked.

"Don't go so far that you can't hear me when I call you. And when I holler for you I want you to come back. You got it? All right, scram."

Erny took off at a flat-out run with Leo chasing him, barking.

Jake smiled, watching them disappear over a hill, and then he set his boom box down and snapped it on to his favorite oldies station. Jake retrieved his brush and can of white semigloss from inside the van. Then he unhooked the ladder he would need. He knew it was dangerous to do a job like this without another guy to spot him on the ladder, but all his guys were working at a new job. And he had to get this finished. The season for outdoor painting was just about done for. This was likely the last nice week they would have. Besides, Jake was not afraid of heights.

He carried the ladder over to the side of the house where he needed to paint the third-floor trim and squinted up. It was so high up that it was hard to tell if the window trim had been scraped or not. He stuck a paint scraper and sanding block into his tool belt with the paintbrush. All right, he thought, let's get this show on the road.

Humming absently to the eighties tunes on the boom box, Jake scraped and painted, working without stopping, other than to occasionally climb down to move the ladder. When, after an hour, he finished painting the last windowsill and stuck the lid back on the can of semigloss, he felt relieved to have the job finished. While he had been working, the mild day had vanished. The sky was turning dark and the wind had risen.

Jake descended the ladder slowly this time, holding on tightly because of the stiff breeze. As he carefully backed his way down and came eye level with the first-floor windows, he glanced inside. And then he stopped and looked again.

A slight blonde woman he recognized as Chan's wife, Sally, was sitting on the living room floor, propped against the sofa like a rag doll, her arms limp, her legs akimbo, her eyes glazed with pain. Jake hesitated. He didn't want to be taken for a Peeping Tom, but the woman looked dazed, as if she needed help. He tapped on the pane and her vacant gaze traveled to the window.

"Mrs Morris," he shouted over the noise of the boom box. "Are you okay? Do you need a hand?"

She looked at him balefully, and for a moment Jake wished he had minded his own business. Then, slowly, she nodded.

"Okay. I'm coming right around." Realizing she probably couldn't hear him, he nodded and gestured toward the front of the house, to let her know his intentions. Jake quickly descended the ladder, went around the side of the house, and rushed up the porch steps. Just as he was opening the front door, he heard the sound of barking. He turned and saw Leo, barreling toward the house alone, barking a warning, like a canine Paul Revere.

CHAPTER 12

Tess thanked Chan for his help and left before he could suggest another, longer interview. Clutching the articles she had copied, and keeping her gaze lowered, she hurried toward the door of the newspaper office and nearly collided with a man who had reached it at the same time. "Sorry," she murmured without looking up.

"We've got to stop meeting like this."

Tess looked up at the silver-haired man who had spoken and blushed furiously.

Ben Ramsey raised his hands in surrender. "I'm not tailing you. I swear."

"I didn't think you were," Tess said, feigning coolness as she opened the door to the vestibule and slipping outside. Ramsey caught the door and followed her through. She did not look at him, but started quickly down the sidewalk to the parking lot. Unfazed, he fell into step beside her. "I met a reporter here to do an interview about the case, actually," he said.

"Love that press coverage," she said grimly. "Good for business."

He ignored the implied criticism. "I thought you would be avoiding the press."

"I was looking something up in the archives," she said.

"What were you looking for?" he asked.

Tess sighed. Why should his persistence surprise her? He was a lawyer, after all. Persistence came with the territory. "It wouldn't interest you," she said.

"Actually, if it's about this case and Lazarus Abbott, it would interest me very much," he said seriously. "I thought a lot about what you said when I met you at the campsite the other day. The fact that you still believe you were right in your identification. I mean, you seem to be a very intelligent, observant person. Maybe it's not as simple as a case of mistaken identity."

Tess did not want him to know how much she had thought about what he'd said during that conversation. She thought about the photo in her pocket of Ken Phalen, transformed by a pair of drawn-on glasses. "Or maybe it is," she murmured.

Ben Ramsey squinted at her. "What are you thinking about?" he asked.

Standing there on the sidewalk, Tess could feel the warmth of the springlike day seeping into her. Ramsey's concerned expression, and his broad chest and shoulders were magnetic. She was tempted to lean against him. Tess shook her head. "Look, I can't talk to you about this. You're the Abbotts' attorney. You just won the victory of a lifetime for them."

"For Mrs Abbott," he said. "Only for Mrs Abbott. Mr Abbott was not equally fond of me. In fact, he told me, on one memorable occasion, that I could 'stuff my bill where the sun don't shine.'"

Tess smiled in spite of herself. "Well, it seems now that Mr Abbott is one of Lazarus's biggest supporters. And among the late-comers rallying to the cause is his nephew, the police chief, who thinks I lied to protect my deviant father," Tess said in disgust.

Ben Ramsey shook his head. "Well, that's just insulting."

Tess felt grateful to him for saying that. "Yes, it is."

"So what was it that brought you here today?"

"I shouldn't be talking to you," she said. "We're adversaries."

"No, we're not," he said seriously. "We both want to know the truth."

Tess met his gaze and thought that if he was lying to her, he was the best liar she'd ever seen. She felt as if his eyes were drawing her to him, speaking silently to her in a secret language known only to the eyes. "I don't know," she demurred.

"I know how much fun it is to search through that pile of old papers," he said wryly. "I spent some time doing that myself, trying to get a clue as to what happened. I had a sneezing fit. Several of them, in fact. What about you? Did you find anything?"

Tess hesitated. "I'm very mixed up at this point," she admitted. "When I came here this morning, I had a theory. Something my son said to me got me thinking."

Ramsey did not even smile. "What? What did he say?"

His open, interested gaze made her feel safe, as if he were an ally. And part of her really wanted to tell him, but she knew better. It was time to terminate this conversation, she thought. Don't start romanticizing this guy, she thought. That is dangerous. He is not your friend. "Nothing important," she said dismissively.

Ben noticed her change of attitude. "You know, I understand why you wouldn't trust me, but I probably know this case better than anyone in this town right now," he said. "And I can tell you that it became more than just a job to me. I've studied that trial transcript a thousand times looking for that missing piece of information that would explain what really happened. I'd be very interested to hear your theory."

Just as she was about to shake her head and hurry away, Tess suddenly realized that this might be an opportunity, and that Ramsey might be just the person to talk to after all. She looked at him with narrowed eyes. "Do you still have a transcript of Lazarus Abbott's trial?"

"Sure," he said.

"Do you think I could take a look at it?"

"Well, if it would be of use to you, sure."

"Great. Could I get it now?" she asked.

"If you don't mind coming with me," he said.

"To your office?" she said.

Ramsey grimaced. "Tess. Can I call you Tess?"

Tess nodded.

"I'm Ben," he said. "Call me Ben. Look, I know this doesn't sound too professional, but . . . I have to be honest with you. I just . . . um . . . got a pup, and I have to go home and deal with him."

"A pup?" she said, surprised.

"A puppy. He's only ten weeks and he's at that stage where he's kind of . . . high maintenance. Well, you know. You have a dog."

Tess realized after a moment's confusion that he was referring to Leo. "It's not my dog," she said.

"Oh. I thought . . ."

"Leo belongs to my mother."

"Well, in any case, I have to run home for a few minutes. It's only about ten minutes from here. And I'm coming right back . . ."

"I can't wait," said Tess stiffly. "I have to get back."

"No," said Ramsey. "You don't understand. The trial transcript is at my house. I meant, do you want to ride out there with me?"

"To your house?"

Ben raised his black eyebrows apologetically. "I'm sorry. I have to go. It won't take long.

Tess hesitated, knowing she wanted to agree to it.

"Come on," he said.

* * *

The road to Ben Ramsey's house wound through the woods and around Lake Innisquam. Tess caught an intermittent glimpse of the sun gleaming on the waters of the lake. In the car, they hardly spoke at all. His house, when it appeared, turned out to be a good-size fishing cottage built in view of the lake. "This is it," he said.

He got out and walked up to a screened porch that wrapped all the way around the house. He opened the door and called out to her. "Come on in."

Tess stopped to take in the view. The mild, clear day and the dark water of the lake, its surface silvery from the sun, made her want to kick her boots off and wade in. Instead, she followed Ben up the walk to his house. She opened the screen door and heard him inside, murmuring endearments while a dog yipped delightedly. The house had four long windows and a door that opened out onto the screened-in porch. She could see him in the living room, sitting on a hooked wool rug in his good suit, while the pup, newly released from its crate, leaped happily at him, licking his face. Tess walked into the house.

"Yes, yes," he was saying. "I'm glad to see you, too. And we have a guest. Scout, meet Miss Tess DeGraff."

Tess reached down and stroked the puppy's silken fur. "Hello there, Scout," she said. "Call me Tess."

"All right. I've got to take you out," said Ben, rising to his feet. He lifted a leash from a hook beside the fireplace and bent down to put it on the dog's collar. Then he handed it to Tess. "Here, hold this a minute."

Tess took the leash but was about to protest when she saw that he was rummaging through the papers on a desk in the corner. "Here it is," he said. He brought the thick bound sheaf of paper with a plastic cover over to Tess and handed it to her. "I'll trade you," he said, gesturing to the leash. Tess handed the pup's lead to him.

"Sit down and have a look through it, if you like," Ramsey said, indicating the sofa. "We'll be right back."

"Can't I take it with me?" Tess asked.

"You can," he said. "I just thought you might be impatient to have a look."

"It's true. I am," said Tess. She sat down on the sofa and opened the document, wondering if she'd find any clues that the best legal minds might have missed. She heard Scout yipping cheerfully and rustling in the leaves outside as she read over parts of the sentencing phase of the trial. After a few minutes, she looked up from the transcript, ruminating about what she had read, and her gaze scanned the comfortable living room. She noted that the well-maintained house had a rustic look, but it was a city person's idea of rustic. It was tastefully decorated — everything was coordinated in shades of forest green and wine, plaids and muted prints perfectly matched. She recognized furniture, cushions, lamps, and even the rug from catalogs that she received herself at home in Washington. It was as if everything in the house had arrived, at great expense, by UPS.

Tess remembered Jake's saying that Ben was a widower and that this had been his and his wife's vacation home. There were definite signs that a man now inhabited the place alone. For one thing, she thought, a woman probably would have set that dog cage somewhere other than the living room rug. On the oak dining table in front of the long windows was an empty mug, still stained with coffee, a crumb-covered plate, piles of mail, and a heap of newspapers with the *Stone Hill Record* on top. The fireplace was filled with cinders, as if no one ever thought to clean it. A canvas jacket hung over the back of one of the dining room chairs. On the mantel, beneath a framed map of New Hampshire, was propped a small oil painting of a woman with her face partially turned away from the artist. Tess peered at it curiously.

"Brrr . . . the weather's changing," Ben said, coming back into the house with the puppy. "You finding what you wanted?"

The transcript was open on her lap, but Tess's attention was distracted. "I was just looking at that painting," she said truthfully. "It's really nice." It looked as if it had been painted in a forest and the shadows on the woman's averted face had a tinge of green in the gray.

"Oh, thank you," he said. "I painted that."

Tess saw no reason to pretend not to know he was a widower. "Is it a painting of your wife?" she asked.

Ben looked away from the painting. "Yeah," he said brusquely.

Tess reddened. "I'm sorry. I didn't mean to offend . . ."

"It's all right," he said. "Sometimes I forget it's there."

Tess nodded. "I understand that," she said. "I've had a lot of that lately."

He frowned at her. "A lot of what?"

"Well, you think you've adjusted to a loss and then something reminds you. It jumps up and grabs you by the throat when you least expect it."

Ben's gaze returned to the painting. He shook his head. "I'm over it," he said.

Liar, she thought. But instead she said, "It's a beautiful painting. You have some talent."

Ben shrugged dismissively. "It won't pay the rent." Ben gave his dog a treat and then pulled out a chair from the dining table and sat down, facing Tess. "So, are you going to tell me what you're looking for in there?" he asked, nodding toward the transcript.

Tess hesitated. He had asked for nothing in return for showing her the transcript. A little part of her wanted to see what he thought of her theory. Clearly he was intelligent. His opinion would be interesting. She decided to share her thoughts and hoped it wasn't a mistake. "I've been wondering if Lazarus might have had an accomplice," said Tess.

Ben frowned. "You think Lazarus Abbott had an accomplice?" he asked.

For a moment she thought of the photo of Ken Phalen and she hesitated. No, she thought. She had to stop second-guessing herself. "Lazarus was the man I saw that night, no matter what you — or anybody — might think."

"You could be right," said Ben. He turned his head and looked out through the screen porch windows to the lake. Dark clouds were beginning to blow up and the temperature was falling. A sudden breeze whipped dry leaves against the mesh of the screens.

"What?" Tess finally asked as he sat silently.

"Nothing. It's an interesting idea," he said. "It's possible. And, if you're right, there might be some clue in those proceedings as to who it might be."

"Well, I know it's not what you want to hear after the great DNA revelation," she said. "You don't want to think that he might have been involved after all."

Ben Ramsey sighed and leaned over, absently stroking the pup's head as it nestled at his feet. Tess was shocked to feel a moment of envy for the puppy as she wondered how it would feel to have those fingers touch her skin with that languid stroke. She forced herself to look away, to concentrate on his words.

"No. You're wrong. I don't have anything invested in the innocence of Lazarus Abbott. He seemed to have been a man with a troubled life and very few redeeming qualities. He may well have acted with an accomplice."

"But . . ."

Ben hesitated and seemed to struggle in choosing his words. "Is it possible that you've hated Lazarus Abbott for so long that this might be a way to keep him somehow . . . tied to the crime?"

Tess froze, and stared at him without replying.

Ben took a deep breath. "Look, don't take this the wrong way, Tess. But even if he did have an accomplice, that doesn't change the fact that Lazarus Abbott's execution was a mistake that can never be rectified. He was executed for a crime he didn't commit," Ben said calmly. "Even if he had ten accomplices, that wouldn't justify his execution."

Tess struggled to control her temper. She should never have confided in him. She replied to him in a clipped tone of voice. "I get that. Believe it or not, I do get it."

Ben nodded. "I'm sure you do."

Tess gazed at him. "The death penalty. That's what this is all about for you. Your opposition to the death penalty."

Ben looked at her grimly. "Obviously, it's something I feel strongly about. I mean, I don't blame crime victims for wanting vengeance. But to give the state the authority to take vengeance is completely irrational. Particularly because it is meted out arbitrarily. If you're rich, you escape it. If you're poor, maybe not."

"Don't forget the fact that it's not proven to be a deterrent," said Tess coldly. "You left that out."

Ben looked a little sheepish. "You've heard all this before."

Tess shook her head. "You have no idea," she said. "None."

Ben Ramsey grimaced. "I'm sorry, Tess. I know it's personal for you in a way that I could never understand."

"You're right about that," she said.

He did not flinch from the anger in her eyes. "I know my view is very . . . different from the victim's perspective."

"Just for your information, my parents were always opposed to the death penalty. My father was a very intelligent man — a professor at MIT. He considered capital punishment barbaric. Until his own daughter was raped and murdered. Then it ceased to be a philosophical question for him."

"He changed his mind?" Ben asked.

Tess thought about her reply. "No. It wasn't that simple. He was torn apart. He had no peace of mind either way. I can remember hearing him and my brother having screaming battles about it. Jake would accuse him of betraying Phoebe's memory."

"But that's a puerile argument," Ben insisted. "I mean, either you believe in a principle or you don't. If it applies to the killer of your own daughter, why not to the killers of other men's daughters? I can't imagine an intelligent man not seeing the contradiction."

Tess rose abruptly to her feet, trembling, and shoved the transcript under her arm. "Well, you're lucky, you know. There's nothing like consistency. It's so . . . reassuring. And easy. You never had to hear your own father locked in his study weeping. I have to go now."

Ben looked at her sadly. "I'm sorry, Tess. I've had so many arguments about this over the years. I forget sometimes that we're talking about people's real lives. I didn't mean any offense. Truly."

Tess gazed at him coldly. "None taken," she lied.

CHAPTER 13

Leo stood at the foot of the steps barking frantically.

"Take it easy, buddy," said Jake. "Take it easy. Stay there. I'll be right back." Jesus, he thought. What the hell happened? The mild day had vanished. The sky had turned dark and the wind was up.

Jake ran into the house and over to Sally, who was still in the same spot on the floor, leaning against the sofa.

"Whose dog is that barking?" Sally asked.

"It's my mom's dog. He was out running around with my nephew. I hope the kid's okay. The dog just came back by himself," said Jake as he reached under her arms and lifted Sally up. She was virtually weightless, but she let out a cry of pain as he pulled her to her feet.

"Where do you want to be?" he asked, hoping she wouldn't say upstairs or something. He could hear Leo barking and his anxiety about Erny was mounting.

"Over there," said Sally, pointing to a love seat that was centered under a painting of a beautiful blonde girl in a debutante gown. Sally's cane was leaning against the settee. Jake guided her over to the love seat, practically lifting her off her feet to speed the process. "There you go," he said, setting her down.

She slowly unwound her arm from around his shoulders.

"Thank you," she whispered. "I'm lucky you saw me."

"You should have one of those medic alerts," he said. "So you could call someone."

"I probably should," Sally said grimly.

"Are you okay now?" he asked. "I've got to go."

"Go ahead," she said. "Go. I hope everything's okay."

No kidding, Jake thought. Erny, what the hell happened? He was working up an angry head of steam, not allowing himself to think that some harm might have come to the boy. He could not picture himself telling that to Tess. Not possible. Not after . . . all that had happened. Hooking a leash onto Leo's collar, he began to lope up the steep driveway while being tugged along by the dog. When he'd come down the driveway in the truck, he'd scarcely noticed how long and hilly it was. Running up it was a different story. It was uphill to the first rise and then he started down the slope on the other side, pausing to holler out, "Erny! Answer me. Time to go." His voice seemed to vanish in the rising wind. Where is that damn kid, he thought? I told him not to go too far.

Leo was whining, straining at the leash. "Where is he, Leo?" Jake demanded aloud. He hesitated for a moment, wondering if he should let Leo loose and try to follow him. The dog could move much faster than he could, but at least Leo would lead him in the right direction. Finally, Jake unhooked the leash. "Go get Erny," he said.

Leo bounded off, disappearing into the orchard, a honey-colored blur. Jake hurried after him, trying to trace the dog's path through the trees. In the distance he could hear Leo barking.

"Erny, goddammit! Where are you?" Jake shouted. He didn't know if Erny was the type of kid who lost track of time or routinely disobeyed. Tess had never said anything negative about him that he could remember, although Jake didn't always pay that much attention when the talk turned to children. "Erny!" he cried.

Jake came out of the orchard and loped past the gardener's shed and toward the pond. He veered away from the orderly rows of plants and began to climb past a rock garden that led to the water's edge. Jake's heart was racing, both from anxiety and the exertion.

Leo's barking sounded closer as Jake entered another copse of trees whose bare branches extended out over the pond. Jake gazed around the gloomy little glen. All of a sudden, halfway around the pond's perimeter, he saw the dog's golden-brown coat. Leo was at the edge of the water, barking. Jake looked closer. Lying face down near Leo's feet he saw the shape of a dark-haired child, dressed in black Nike hip-hop sneaks and a sweatshirt.

Jake felt a thud in the pit of his stomach. "Erny," he whispered. He ran around the pond, toward his nephew. "Shit. Erny," he cried.

But there was no reply.

Jake stumbled to where Erny lay, his heart pounding. The boy was lying still on the mossy bank. Beside him on the bank was a fishing pole the boy had fashioned from a tomato plant stake and a piece of twine, with a little metal lure tied to the end. "Goddammit," Jake cried. "You couldn't wait. Oh my God. What happened? Erny, wake up."

> Mr Hall: *Now, Dr Belknap, you have examined Lazarus Abbott. We have heard testimony from teachers and family friends about the abuse that he endured at the hands of his stepfather. Can you tell the court what effect that abuse may have had on his psychological development?*
>
> Dr Belknap: *Well, it had a deleterious effect on him, obviously. He was very frightened of his stepfather. Terrified, actually. It seemed to Lazarus that he could not escape the wrath of Nelson Abbott, no matter what he did, and his stepfather's temper would erupt with no warning. As a result, Lazarus lived a secretive life, knowing instinctively that he had to conceal all the normal, developmental impulses that*

a teenage boy has in an effort to avoid his stepfather's punishments. In his mind, sexual thoughts and feelings became connected to the idea of violent punishment. In this way, his disorder was formed.

Tess lowered the transcript and reached for the mug of tea on the night table beside her bed with a trembling hand. When she'd returned from Ben Ramsey's, she'd looked for her mother but Dawn had not been around. Tess had brewed herself a cup of tea and took it and the trial transcript to the bed in her room, and huddled under a quilt there, exactly as a sick child might curl up after having been sent home from school. The wind, which had risen when she returned from Ramsey's house, was blowing fiercely now and the sky had darkened. She looked anxiously from the gloom outside the window to Erny's hastily made bed, worrying about him being caught outside in the rain. Would Jake think to keep him dry? she wondered. She didn't want Erny to get sick.

Trying not to fret, Tess returned to the transcript. When she had first opened it, she had turned immediately to the record of her own testimony at the trial as if it were a code that, once broken, would unlock a doorway back to the child she had been. Although she still remembered sitting in that witness box, her own words proved unfamiliar. She had no memory of the questions she was asked, nor the way she responded. Still, reading those words so long after the fact, she had felt her heart aching for the child that she had been, answering bravely and clearly, telling the story of her sister's abduction without faltering.

After she had read her own testimony, she had reread the sentencing phase of the trial. A number of witnesses had come forward during that part to attest to the cruelty Lazarus Abbott had suffered, both at home and from the bullying of other children. One of his teachers from grade school, the pastor of the Abbotts' church, and a friend of Edith's named Josephine Kiley had come forward to tell the same story. The psychologist tried to put all the testimony into perspective for the jury. Of course Tess knew how it ended. The jury had remained unmoved. They had voted unanimously for the death penalty.

Tess sipped her tea. For the first time that she could remember, Tess began to feel pity for Lazarus Abbott. It was clear to her from reading the testimony that while Lazarus may have been a warped young man, he was not entirely his own creation. He had been the butt of jokes at school. And at home, it was obvious that Nelson Abbott had shaped his nature with his cruelty.

She sighed, set down her mug, and returned to the grim testimony.

All of a sudden, the door to the bedroom opened and Dawn stood on the threshold, her eyes anxious, her lips pressed together.

Tess looked up at her. "Mom, you're back. Where were you?" Before Dawn could reply, Tess noticed the look on her mother's face. "What's wrong?" she said.

"Honey, that was Jake on the phone."

"What's the matter? What happened?"

Dawn's expression was pained. "He's over at the emergency room . . ."

Tess jumped from the bed, the transcript falling to the floor. Her heart was thudding. "Erny?"

Before Dawn could answer, Tess knew by the expression on her face. "Oh my God," she said.

"Come on," said her mother. "I'll drive."

* * *

When they arrived at the emergency room, Jake was pacing the waiting area, talking on a cell phone. He snapped it shut when he saw them come in and strode toward them.

"Where is he?" Tess demanded.

"I'll show you," said Jake. "Follow me."

Tess raced after her brother down the hospital corridor and through a set of double doors. They met a doctor who was emerging from a curtained cubicle. "He's in there," said Jake. "This is his doctor."

"I'm Erny's mother," Tess said.

The bald-headed physician smiled and patted her hand reassuringly. "Take it easy," he said. "He's gonna be all right. He was knocked out by the fall. He's conscious now, although he's going to have a little headache. He's bruised up but otherwise he seems to be okay. We're still waiting for some of the X-rays."

"Oh thank God. Is he awake? Can I see him?" Tess asked.

"Sure, go on in," said the doctor.

Tess pushed back the curtain and walked into the cubicle. Erny was lying on the bed under a white sheet. His face, normally a nutty brown, looked unnaturally pale.

She leaned over the bed and carefully enfolded him in her arms. "Honey, what happened? Are you okay?" she asked.

"Ouch, that hurts, Ma," he complained.

Tess released him gently. "I'm sorry. Are you in a lot of pain?"

Erny shrugged. "Not too much," he said.

"The doctor said you're kind of bruised up but you're going to be fine. How did this happen, Erny?" Tess asked.

"Well, I wanted to try and go fishing. So I found this long stick and some string and I made a fishing pole. I even found a lure for it. And then I climbed up this tree and shinnied out on the branch. I figured that would be a good place to fish from." Erny shrugged as if the result was self-explanatory.

"Did it break off? The branch?"

Erny shook his head. "The wind started blowing all of a sudden and the branch was creaking and . . . I don't know. I tried to climb back down from it and I fell."

"It must have been scary," said Tess.

"It didn't scare me," Erny said.

"Well, it scared me," said Tess. "When I heard you were knocked out it scared me half to death."

Erny looked at her with wide eyes. "I didn't get hurt that bad," he said.

Tess brushed a curly lock of black hair off his skinned forehead. "Thank God."

"Did Uncle Jake get my fishing pole? I made it myself."

"I think he was a little bit too busy getting you to the emergency room."

"Maybe he got it," said Erny.

"Maybe," said Tess.

"Can I go home now?" he asked.

"Soon," said Tess. "They need to get a few more X-rays and then we'll take you home. You just rest. Can I get you anything?"

"A Sprite?" he said.

Tess smiled at him, feeling absurdly relieved by his simple request. "I'll see what I can do. I'll be back."

The boy nodded. "Thanks, Ma."

"You rest." She backed out of the curtained cubicle and then walked down the hall and through the double doors to the waiting room.

Jake, who was sitting beside Dawn, looked up when she walked in. He and Dawn both rose to their feet and approached her.

"How's he doing?" Dawn asked.

"He's going to be all right."

"Thank God," said Dawn with a sigh.

"Yeah, he's asking for a Sprite. And his fishing pole."

"I saw a soda machine down the hall," said Dawn. "Let me get him one."

"Would you, Mom?" Tess asked. "Thank you."

"Sure." Dawn hurried off.

Jake chuckled. "He couldn't wait. He had to go fishing. Made his own pole. That's what I would've done at his age."

Tess turned on her brother. "Where were you when this happened?"

Jake raised his hands helplessly. "I was just finishing my work. He and the dog were out playing. I told them not to go too far. The dog came back by himself. So I went looking for him."

Tess looked at him balefully.

Jake scratched his head. "It was one of those things, Tess. The kid just wanted to try something . . ."

"He could have been seriously hurt!" she said, her voice louder. "Or killed."

"Well, he could have been, but he wasn't," Jake said.

"No big deal, right?" said Tess.

"Hey, he's gonna be fine. And I'm sorry, okay? But it wasn't my fault. I didn't know he was gonna do something crazy. Fishing from a tree branch," Jake said, shaking his head but with a slight smile. "I better go back and get that pole or I'm going to lose my most-favored-uncle status."

Tess was in no mood to be distracted by jokes. "So the fact that he fell is his own fault," she said sarcastically.

"Ahhh . . . boys are like that. It's . . . the way they are. They do crazy things."

"Yes, but you're the adult. You were supposed to be watching him!"

"What? He never hurt himself before? You gotta let the kid take his lumps. You'll turn him into a sissy. He's all right. That's what matters."

"No matter what happens, you've got an excuse," Tess said disgustedly.

"I'm not making excuses, Tess. It was an accident. The kid will live."

"I should have known better than to trust you," she fumed.

Jake looked at her through narrowed eyes. "Oh. So now I can't be trusted?"

"Could you ever?" Tess snapped.

Jake's gaze was venomous. "What do you mean by that?"

Tess opened her arms indicating the hospital waiting room. "Look where we end up!" Tess's heart was hammering in her chest, knowing she would regret reopening old wounds but she couldn't help herself. "Why am I the only one who feels guilty, Jake? It's never your fault. How do you skate away with no guilt at all? It must be nice."

Jake's expression was cold and closed. "If it makes you feel any better, Tess, I was scared half to death. All right?"

"Well, I should hope so," she snapped.

"Tell Erny I'll see him later." Jake turned and stalked out of the waiting room, slamming through the double doors that led out to the parking lot. Tess watched him go, her eyes blazing. It was the first time she could remember, since they were kids, that she had ever gotten angry at her brother. But it felt as if that anger had been coiled within her for a long time — back to the time when he had deserted her and Phoebe, with disastrous consequences. Her parents had always told her it was wrong to blame Jake, wrong to blame herself. But was it wrong? she wondered. She already blamed herself. She always had. Wasn't Jake even more to blame than she was?

Dawn came back holding a can of Sprite. She glanced around the waiting room and then asked, in a soft voice, "Where's your brother?"

"Gone," said Tess. "Where else would he be? Gone."

CHAPTER 14

Three hours later, Erny was released and Tess was able to get him back to the inn, where she tucked him into his bed and then went into the kitchen to heat up some soup for him. By the time she returned to their room, he was sprawled out on his stomach fast asleep. Tess closed the door to the room gently, leaving her son to sleep, and carried the soup bowl and spoon back to the kitchen.

Dawn was preparing a tea tray with cookies to set out in the sitting room for the guests. The afternoon was completely gray now and cold rain spattered the kitchen windows. Dawn looked up when Tess entered the room. "How's our boy doing?" she asked.

"Sound asleep," said Tess.

"He's had quite a day," said Dawn. "Your brother felt terrible about what happened. These things do happen with kids."

Tess evaded a conversation about Jake. "I'll never get used to the worry. How did you ever manage with four of us?" Tess asked.

Dawn's gaze was far away. "Oh, you do get used to it. All your father and I ever wanted was a big family," she said. Then she sighed.

Tess averted her eyes from the pain in her mother's face. It had been a simple enough wish, Tess thought. Not a greedy plan. Just a desire to love and be loved. And it had been very successful, too. Until a maniac had destroyed their peaceful life.

Dawn put the last of the cookies on a plate along with a steaming flowered teapot, a sugar bowl, and a matching pitcher. Tess was constantly amazed by her mother, who never shirked her duties to her family, to her job at the inn, even when she had the weight of the world on her shoulders. Who could ever have imagined, Tess thought, on that sunny, holiday afternoon when they first met the Phalens, the owners of the Stone Hill Inn, that they would all end up so enmeshed in this place.

"Mom, you know, I wanted to ask you something," said Tess.

"Hmmm . . . ?" said Dawn.

"Do you remember the people who used to own this place? The Phalens."

Dawn nodded. "Yes. Of course. What about them?"

"How well did you know them?" Tess asked.

"Not . . . too well. They were . . . they seemed like good people," said Dawn. "They were very kind to us."

"Didn't their daughter commit suicide?" Tess asked.

Dawn's expression was wary. "Yes, she did. Why?"

"No real reason," said Tess. "But . . . suicide at fourteen. It makes you wonder . . ."

"Wonder what?" said Dawn.

"It's just . . . unusual," said Tess.

"You mean you wonder if it was their fault? Her parents'?"

"I'm just thinking about everything and every . . . one in a new light," she said. "Now that we know the DNA results."

Dawn frowned at her. "I don't follow you."

"Well, I mean, we didn't really know Kenneth Phalen. He lived right near the campground. And his daughter killed herself when she was fourteen. Just a year older than Phoebe was. Is it possible he might have . . . had a side we didn't see?"

"Tess, for heaven's sake," said Dawn. "How can you even think of slandering innocent people with speculation like that?"

"I'm not slandering anyone," said Tess. "The Phalens aren't even around here anymore. I was just . . . thinking out loud."

"Well, don't," Dawn insisted. "Just stop it."

Tess winced at her mother's angry response. She thought about the photo of Ken Phalen that she had altered with her black pen. It didn't really look that much like Lazarus. Besides, it was just a photo. In real life, she doubted if they looked anything alike. "You're right. I'm grasping at straws."

Dawn was still simmering. "Why do people always blame the parents? The ones who suffered the most?"

Tess thought of Rusty Bosworth, suggesting that Rob DeGraff might have killed Phoebe. "I don't know why people do that," Tess said. "You're right. It's cruel."

Dawn picked up the heavy tray. "I have to take this out," she said.

"I'll take it out for you," said Tess.

Dawn's shoulders seemed to slump. She set the tray back down. "Thank you. I'm tired," said Dawn. "I think I'll sit down."

"Why don't you?" said Tess. "Sit down and rest." Dawn turned her back on Tess and sat down in the breakfast nook. Tess carried the heavy tray carefully out through the dining room and into the comfortable sitting room where the afternoon tea was always served. A couple was seated in front of the fire and both of them looked up as Tess walked in.

"Oh good," said the woman, setting down her magazine and getting up. "I could use a pick-me-up."

Her husband, who was wearing well-worn corduroys and an expensive golf sweater, said to Tess, "Do you spike that stuff?"

Tess forced herself to smile as she set down the tray. "We don't, but you may."

The man turned to his wife. "Did you hear that? I told you I should bring my flask on this trip."

His wife shook her head, smiling. Tess excused herself and left the room. She started back toward the kitchen when the front door opened behind her and a man came in wearing an Irish tweed hat and a beige raincoat.

"It's gotten nasty out there, hasn't it?" Tess asked.

"Sure has," said the man pleasantly. "I don't want to mess up your rug."

"It's all right. These rugs can take it. Can I help you?"

The man opened his coat, reached into his pants pocket, and pulled out a handkerchief. He removed his glasses, gave them a quick swipe, and then put them back on. Then he began to fumble in the inner pocket of the raincoat.

"I'm looking for Tessa DeGraff," the man said.

"That's me," said Tess.

The man drew a manilla envelope out of the inside pocket of the coat and handed it to her.

Tess reached out and took it, frowning.

"You've been served," the man said. Before Tess could reply, he turned, opened the front door again, and went out. "Have a nice day," he said.

"What . . . ?" Tess tore open the envelope and pulled out the papers inside. She scanned the first few pages. It did not take her long to realize what the legal documents meant. The papers informed her that she was being sued for damages in civil court by Nelson and Edith Abbott for the wrongful death of their son, Lazarus.

Wrongful death . . . Tess felt as if she had been punched in the gut. She thought about her encounter with Nelson on the street and the way he had maundered on about getting justice for Lazarus. Justice for Lazarus, indeed, Tess thought. What he really meant was that he saw an opportunity for a great big financial settlement for himself. What had begun as a vague feeling of dislike for Nelson Abbott was now cementing itself into emnity in her mind.

Tess crushed the legal papers in her fist. "You bastard," she muttered. But she wasn't referring to Nelson Abbott. She was thinking of Ben Ramsey. It was pointless to deny to herself that she found him attractive. And despite their clash over the execution of Lazarus Abbott, she had felt a certain respect for his principles. But this . . . this was something else again. How could he have acted so sympathetically when all the while he was getting ready to file this lawsuit against her? It pained her to think that she had considered trusting him while he was planning to betray her. Tess looked at her watch and jammed the stapled sheaf of papers into her pocketbook, pulled an umbrella from the porcelain stand by the door, and checked to be sure she had the car keys. She walked back and poked her head into the kitchen. Dawn was still seated there, staring into the gloom.

"Mom, I'm going out. Will you keep an eye on Erny for me?"

Dawn looked around. "Where are you going?"

Part of Tess wanted to pull the legal papers out and show her mother, but she could see the weariness, the sadness in Dawn's eyes. It would be one more thing for her mother to worry about. One more thing she didn't deserve to have on her mind.

"I just have to take care of something," said Tess.

CHAPTER 15

Even in the rain, it was easy to find the law offices of Cottrell and Wayne. Ben had pointed his office out to her only hours earlier when he drove her back to town, explaining that he was not yet a partner because he had only worked with the firm for a year. But he had the office pretty much to himself, for Cottrell now had emeritus status and Wayne divided his time between New Hampshire and his vacation home in Florida. The office was off the town square and the building must, at one time, have been a private home. Tess walked into the neatly tended building, through a carpeted vestibule and waiting area, and up to the desk of the middle-aged receptionist seated behind a bank of family photos and a dusty bowl of fake flowers. She was eating a snack cake and drinking a mug of coffee. "I'm here to see Mr Ramsey," Tess announced.

"Do you have an appointment?" the woman asked pleasantly.

"No, but please tell him that Miss DeGraff needs to see him right now."

The woman hesitated, as if taken aback by the irregularity of the request, but then, possibly in a desire to get back to her snack cake, she buzzed Ben Ramsey's office and then told Tess to go in. "Third door down the hall on the left, dear," she said.

Tess marched down the hall and burst into Ben's decorless, book-lined office. Ben, still in his tie but with his jacket off and his sleeves rolled up, was seated at his desk. He looked up at her, his eyes alight, and then his smile faded at the sight of her face.

"You know," she began without preamble, "you have a lot of nerve doing this to me. I guess it's all about the money with you."

"What?" he cried. "Doing what?"

"Don't play dumb. This morning you were all about the ethics."

Ben stood up behind his desk and faced her squarely. "Hold it. What the hell are you talking about?"

Tess was surprised by his reaction. She had to admit to herself that he looked clueless. "The lawsuit," she said.

Ben shook his head, as if to say that he still didn't understand.

"The lawsuit you filed against me for the Abbotts. The papers just arrived."

Ben picked up a pencil and tapped it on the desktop. "I didn't file any lawsuit against you," he said.

"You didn't," she said skeptically.

"No. I didn't. Did you check the letterhead? Because it certainly wasn't mine." Tess hadn't actually looked at the letterhead. She had simply assumed that the Abbotts would bring all their legal business to Ben.

Tess's indignation faltered. "No," she admitted. "Just a minute. The papers are in my bag." She put her purse down on his desktop and rummaged around in it. She pulled the papers from her bag and looked at the letterhead. Her cheeks flamed. She shook her head.

"Can I see?" he asked.

Mutely, Tess handed him the document. Ben looked at the letterhead and then scanned the document. She expected him to reproach her for jumping to a hasty conclusion.

Instead, he shook his head. "Wrongful death? That's a stretch."

"Why do you say that?" Tess asked.

"For one thing, the statute of limitations has run out on a wrongful death claim." Then he frowned. "They're probably going to argue that the statute of limitations needs to be adjusted because of the DNA results. It's . . . creative. I'll give them that."

"How come they didn't come to you for this?"

Ben frowned. "I suspect this attorney approached *them*. This firm is from North Conway. They specialize in civil suits. The attorney probably followed the case on the news and called them to suggest the suit. These civil suit guys . . . there's no end to their . . . creativity when it comes to blame."

"Sorry," she murmured, humiliated.

Ben handed the papers back to her, unsmiling. "Natural enough mistake, I guess."

"Do they have a case?" she asked.

Ben shook his head. "Against you? Well, civil suits are not my specialty. But no jury is going to see this as your fault."

"I hope you're right," she said.

"Of course, a crafty attorney can keep one of these suits dragging on for years. And Nelson Abbott is just the kind of client they love. Self-righteous and mean-spirited."

Tess nodded, feeling both embarrassed and chastened. She wanted to retreat as hastily, if not gracefully, as possible. "I'm very sorry . . . Ben. I . . . I know you're busy. I really am sorry . . . let me just get out of your hair."

Ben resumed his seat behind the desk. "You're not in my hair. I'm glad you came. Especially since that has nothing to do with me," he said, pointing his pencil at her pocketbook.

Tess nodded.

"You will need to get yourself an attorney, though," he said. "To fight this."

Tess shrugged. "Interested?" she asked.

Ben shook his head. "Not my area of expertise. And it could be a conflict of interest. But I can recommend my senior partner . . ."

"I have an attorney at home. He handled my adoption of Erny. I'll call him and send him the papers."

"You might want to have somebody here in town," he said.

"I'll be fine," she insisted stiffly. "I don't want to take up any more of your time." She pulled tight the belt on her coat. "Thanks," she said, turning to leave.

"Wait. Don't go," he said.

Tess frowned at him. "Why not?"

Tess thought she noticed his face color slightly. "The fact is," he said, "I wanted to talk to you. I was thinking about what you said earlier."

"What I said?" Tess asked.

"Yes. Do you have a minute?"

Tess nodded.

"Sit," he said, pointing to the client's chair. Tess hesitated and then sat down.

"After I got back to the office, I was thinking about what you said about Lazarus having an accomplice."

"This morning you accused me of clinging to that idea so that I could still blame Lazarus."

"I asked you if that was a possibility," Ben said. "I didn't say it was a bad idea."

"Wait a minute," she said, holding her forehead. "It's a conflict of interest for you to represent me, but you want to talk about whether or not Lazarus had an accomplice?"

"Lazarus wasn't my client," he said.

"That's splitting hairs," she said.

"Not to my mind," he said. "We're just . . . friends, having a conversation."

Tess tilted her head and studied him. She had noted his hesitation on the word "friends" but she wasn't about to mention it. "Does this mean that you think there might be something to the accomplice idea?" she asked.

"Well, if we assume that you were right in your identification of Lazarus . . ."

"You're assuming I was right?" she cried.

"Just for argument's sake," he said.

"Ah," said Tess calmly. But she felt almost giddy with surprise and . . . gratitude.

"It would explain the DNA discrepancy," said Ben. "I was doing some research this afternoon. The experts seem to agree that in a pair of killers there is usually a dominant personality and a subservient one. The subservient one is in some kind of thrall to the dominant one. The dominant one can be cruel and controlling. It's very often a relationship based on fear. Now, if there was such a pair at work here, it's unlikely that Lazarus was the dominant one. He would have been the passive one, the follower. Doing the bidding of the other."

Instantly, as he spoke, a face appeared in Tess's mind's eye and she blanched.

"What?" he asked.

"I was just thinking. According to the sentencing phase of the trial transcript, and what I've heard from everyone else, Lazarus was a loner who had no friends. He didn't have dealings with anyone outside the family."

"That doesn't mean that he didn't have any relationships—"

"Wait, hear me out," said Tess.

Ben nodded.

"Now, apparently, his only occupation was working for his stepfather, Nelson Abbott. And Nelson Abbott was always angry at him. He abused him for years."

"That's true. Nobody ever said that Lazarus . . . wait a minute." Ben peered at her. "Are you suggesting . . . ?"

Tess stared back at him.

"Not Nelson," Ben scoffed.

"Why not?" she asked.

"Well, for one thing, Nelson has no record as a sexual predator."

"Yes, but he's got a history of violent behavior in his own family."

Ben shook his head. "I don't see it."

Tess leaned forward in the chair. "Ben, they know that Phoebe's body was transported to the ditch in Lazarus's truck. A witness recognized the truck leaving the scene. There was no time to clean up the truck. Phoebe's blood was in that truckbed. Shreds of her clothing. But that truck actually belonged to Nelson. He just let Lazarus drive it."

"Tess, the police searched the Abbott house after they found the body. And the garage and the basement. They couldn't find any proof that he kept her there."

"But he may have," said Tess. "He might have cleaned it up."

"Well, it's true that if we'd had the forensic techniques we have nowadays, they might have found evidence," said Ben. "By now, of course, it's too late."

"Ben," said Tess carefully, "if Lazarus kept her in that house, or on that property, who else would have had . . . access to Phoebe there?"

Ben tilted back in his own chair, gripping the armrests. Then he shook his head. "No. If that were the case, why wouldn't Lazarus have implicated his stepfather? His life was at stake."

"Well, that's a good question. But he didn't implicate anyone. He just said he was innocent." Tess shrugged. "He was afraid of his stepfather. Terrified of him."

"He was facing execution . . ." Ben protested.

"I know," said Tess. "A normal person would have named his accomplice. But of course a normal person wouldn't have committed the crime in the first place. And it's hard to imagine what went on inside the snake pit that was Lazarus Abbott's mind — I'm just speculating — but I know that abuse victims rarely accuse their abusers."

"That's certainly true," said Ben. "It's a crime that's so difficult to prosecute."

Tess leaned forward in her chair. "In fact, nowhere in the sentencing phase of the trial did Lazarus ever even acknowledge that his stepfather beat him and humiliated him. That all came from people outside the family."

Ben frowned.

"And who really cared? Nelson was a solid citizen. His stepson had a record as a pervert," Tess continued.

They sat in silence for a moment.

"I'm not accusing anyone," Tess protested. "I just wonder if it would be possible to make a discreet comparison of Nelson's DNA to the test results."

Ben shook his head. "There's no way Nelson would voluntarily give a sample."

"Could the police . . . demand a sample? Legally?" Tess asked.

Ben frowned, tapping the pencil absently on his desk. "They could. But Rusty Bosworth is Nelson's nephew so I think you can forget about that happening," said Ben. "And Nelson can't be forced to give a DNA sample. That would violate his fourth amendment rights . . ."

Tess reached a hand out and put it lightly on his, to still the tapping. She felt his warmth radiate up through her fingertips. She pulled her fingers back. "Isn't it possible to obtain a person's DNA without their knowledge?" she asked. "People leave DNA on drinking cups or clothing or hairbrushes, don't they?"

"Sure, it's possible. But the police aren't going to try and obtain a sample at all, never mind illegally." Ben looked at her meditative profile with a kind of possessive admiration. His blue eyes were at once bemused, and chiding. She was pressing her steepled fingers against her lips. "And neither should anyone else. Tess?"

Tess looked up at him, her gaze opaque. "No," she said absently. "No. Of course not."

CHAPTER 16

A redheaded woman with freckles wearing a baggy, oxford cloth shirt opened the front door of the neat, barn-red Cape Cod house and frowned. "I know who you are," she said bluntly as Tess attempted to introduce herself.

"I wondered if I could see the chief for a minute," Tess asked.

"He's in very bad shape," said the woman. "It would be too exhausting for him."

"Mary Anne," came a feeble cry from inside the house. "Who is it?"

Nothing wrong with his hearing, Tess thought.

"Tess DeGraff," said Mary Anne.

"I promise I won't stay long," said Tess.

"Tell her to come in," said the weak voice.

Mary Anne hesitated and then stood aside, a long-suffering look on her face. She inclined her head toward the room behind her. "He's in the family room. Go on through there."

"Thanks," said Tess.

Tess walked through the pristine, rarely used living room to the arched doorway of the family room. The paneled room had obviously been added on to the house. A beige chenille-covered sofa faced a large gas hearth and an enormous television set. Beside the sofa was a gray, black, and beige plaid recliner with the footrest extended. Huddled on the recliner, under an afghan, was Aldous Fuller.

"Chief," she said.

He turned to look at her. The huge gray circles under his eyes made his bald head look like a skull. His skin was waxy. He managed a smile.

"Tess," he said.

Tess went over to the chair and squeezed his hand, which lay limp on the armrest. His bony fingers were icy. "I'm sorry to bother you," she said. "But I need your help."

"Sit down," said the chief. "Not there. Sit where I can see you."

Tess, who had been about to sit on the edge of the sofa, got up and pulled a wooden chair from beside the fireplace over to a spot in front of the recliner. "Is this better?" she asked.

Chief Fuller, whose breathing was labored, nodded.

"I need a favor," Tess said.

"I'm not good for much right now," said the chief. "But I'll help you if I can."

"That's all I ask," said Tess. She took a deep breath and explained her proposal.

* * *

Because of the rain, Tess passed the Abbott place several times before she finally located the entrance to the driveway. She turned in and slowly drove up to the house. She parked in the drive and sat in her car, staring at Lazarus Abbott's boyhood home, her heart thumping.

In answer to her questions, Chief Fuller had explained what he knew about DNA collection. One could, he had said, find saliva on a discarded paper cup, a bottle, or a piece of gum, or perspiration from a T-shirt, or hairs trapped on a hat or a comb. And yes, once that object was obtained and placed in a plastic bag, Chief Fuller did have contacts at the state crime lab who could compare it with the DNA of Phoebe's killer. But Aldous Fuller had been very clear — it was dangerous and a bad idea for Tess to get involved in this.

Tess pretended to take his warning to heart. But, as she got up to leave, she was already putting her plan into motion. Tess went out through the kitchen where Mary Anne was stirring a pot on the stove. She had thanked Mary Anne for letting her speak to the chief and then said that the chief was asking for a glass of water. With a sigh, Mary Anne ran some water into a glass and started back toward the family room.

Alone in the kitchen, Tess quietly opened three cupboard drawers before she found what she was seeking — Ziploc plastic bags. What kitchen would be without them? Tess mused. She had tucked a handful of them into her coat pocket and let herself out the back door. Then she drove directly to the Abbotts' place.

Tess had hoped that Nelson's black truck might be in the driveway. People often drank take-out coffee in their cars, she reasoned. She thought she could open the door of the cab, snatch his paper cup, toss it into a plastic bag, and be gone before he even came out of the house to see why someone was idling in his driveway.

But Nelson's truck was not there. And there were no lights on in the house. No one seemed to be at home. Tess got out of the car, opening her umbrella. She walked up to the foot of the porch steps and looked around at the neatly kept property while the rain made a persistent clatter on the gutters of the stark-looking gray farmhouse.

Tess climbed the steps and tried turning the front doorknob, but it was locked. She felt both disappointed and relieved. She didn't know if she would have had the nerve to open the door and just walk inside. Now the decision had been taken away from her. She shielded her brow with one hand and peered through the wavy glass of the old windowpanes into the front room of the house. It was a drab, sparsely furnished room with a few stiff-looking chairs, a dun-colored sofa, and faded wallpaper. The rug that sat in the center of the floor was flowered and far too small for the space. A grandfather clock stood near the door, ticking off the minutes. She tried to picture the Abbott family living in this house: Lazarus sitting in one of those straight-backed chairs as Nelson cuffed him and yelled in his ear.

Now that she was here, gazing into the Abbott parlor, she was distracted from her purpose, overwhelmed by thoughts of her sister. Phoebe, she thought. Did he bring you to this house when he took you away from us? Was he tired of being the only one who suffered here? Or did he bring you here to satisfy the perverted appetites of another, more powerful person? Tess shuddered at the idea of it.

She straightened up and walked to the edge of the porch. The garage was not attached to the house, but sat back at the end of the driveway, a small gray building with the same multipaned windows as the house. The doors of the garage were closed. The windows of the garage were covered from within by what appeared to be yellowed paper shades. It was impossible to see inside. Tess felt thwarted, as if the eyes of the garage were looking back at her blindly. She wanted to see inside. She felt . . . entitled to look in there. To see the interior for herself. To try to determine if she could feel the presence of her sister. She was sure that somehow she would be able to do what the police had not been able to do — tell whether this building was the place where Phoebe had been held captive and killed.

Tess climbed down the porch steps and walked toward the shuttered garage through the blowing rain, holding her opened umbrella over her head. Every so often a gust of wind would shake the umbrella frame and Tess had to grip it tighter. At the garage door, she reached out and grabbed the wrought-iron handle and shook it. The door did not budge. She tried the other handle, jiggling it back and forth. It was no use. The doors were locked tight. "Dammit," she said.

She turned away from the garage and walked back toward the house. Don't forget why you're here — the DNA, she reminded herself. The DNA. Get busy. They could come home at any minute. Crossing the immaculately kept backyard she passed an old-fashioned pole clothesline that had some laundry flapping on it, drenched by the sudden rain. Tess stopped and thought about taking one of the men's T-shirts, but that would be of no use. She was sure, judging by the tidiness of the house and yard, that Edith did a thorough job with her laundry. Every last identifying cell was probably washed and bleached away.

There were a set of slanted wooden doors beneath a kitchen window that obviously led down to the basement. Tess walked toward them. Was it there that he took you, Phoebe? she wondered. When she was found, Phoebe's body was bound and gagged and bruised all over. After all these years, Phoebe's face was almost a blank in Tess's mind. She remembered pictures of Phoebe rather than Phoebe herself. Gazing at those cellar doors, she felt as if she could suddenly see her sister again, in her T-shirt and sweatpants, her long blonde hair swinging like a curtain around that face that Tess could no longer visualize, as Lazarus lifted those creaking cellar doors and hoisted her up over his shoulder, carrying her down those steps like a rolled-up rug.

Tess turned away from the cellar doors, her stomach in knots. There's no time for ruminating about the past, she thought. You have to get that DNA sample now, while you have the chance. She glanced at the plastic trash cans. Surely there would be items in the trash with Nelson's saliva on them, but they would be useless, according to Chief Fuller, if they were bundled in proximity to the rest of the trash. She lifted a lid, hoping that one bin would be recycling and that she might find a beer bottle inside it. But both barrels contained trash tied up in plastic bags. Everything neat and tidy and cross-contaminated, she thought.

Tess looked around and then lifted one of the wooden cellar doors. She looked down at a storm door and the darkness of the basement beyond it. Was there anything useful down there, even if, by some fluke, that inside door was not locked? Somehow she doubted that these people ever left anything out of place. Tess hesitated, feeling sick at the thought of entering that basement, knowing that Phoebe may have taken her last breath in that gloom. Knowing that the Abbotts could return at any moment.

Do it, she thought. For Phoebe. She looked around, lowered her umbrella, and hurried down the cement block steps. She tried the handle on the door at the bottom of the stairs, rattling it vigorously, but it did not budge. The musty smell from inside seeped out, assailing her nostrils. She peered through the storm window. By the light that filtered down the stairs, it was too dark to see more than a few feet into the basement. Directly in front of her Tess saw a tool bench, with all the tools neatly hung on hooks and all the nails and screws in jars divided by size. There did not appear to be so much as a dirty rag on the surface of the workbench.

If I could only get in there, she thought, I could go through the basement and up into the house. Into the house where there would be a bathroom, with everything she might need. A toothbrush, a comb, nail parings. For a moment she toyed with the thought of breaking in, but she dismissed the idea almost as soon as it came to her mind. What if Nelson Abbott came home and found her in his house? He might have a gun, and if he did, he could shoot her and be justified. Even if there was no gun, he could call the police on her and be within his rights to have her arrested. Tess sighed, pressing her face against the pane, trying to peer inside. And then, suddenly, she froze. Above the whistle of the wind, she heard a car door slamming.

Oh my God, they're back. They've seen my car. I have to get out of here, she thought. She turned away from the storm door window and quickly ran up the cinder-block steps. Looking all around, she emerged from the stairwell and turned to lower the wooden cellar door as carefully as possible, so as not to make a sound.

Then, clutching her bag and her closed umbrella, she straightened up and hurried toward the driveway side of the house. She turned the corner and came face-to-face with

Nelson Abbott, peering at her from beneath the brim of his John Deere cap.

Tess let out a cry.

"What the hell . . . ? What do you think you're doing?" Nelson demanded.

He advanced on her. Tess stumbled back. She had a sickening feeling that he knew what she was doing. That he could read her intentions in her eyes. "I came here to see you," she stammered. She brushed her wind-whipped hair off her face.

"To see me? In the backyard? Behind my house? What are you playing at?"

"Nothing," said Tess. "I . . . just was . . . I thought you might be . . ."

"You thought I might be what? Huh? Speak up. Why are you trespassing on my property?"

Tess's heart was thudding. They were alone. There was no sign of Edith Abbott anywhere around. And Tess was at a loss to explain her presence here. She felt as if the letters "DNA" were flashing on her forehead.

"I've got a good mind to call my nephew, the police chief. He's none too fond of you as it is," said Nelson in a steely tone, pointing a finger at her. "Your lies have given him more headaches than he knows what to do with. Well, you've lied once too often, missy. You lied about Lazarus and you are going to pay dearly for that. As a matter of fact, you're soon gonna find out there's a lawsuit against you . . ."

The legal papers, Tess thought with relief. The lawsuit. She almost sagged against this man, her enemy, in gratitude. Her reason for being here was obvious. He had pointed it out himself. Now, she thought, tread carefully. Hide your indignation. Be . . . conciliatory. "Yes," she said in a deliberately even tone of voice. "Yes. I received those papers from your attorney. That's why I'm here. I wondered if we could talk about that."

Nelson peered at her suspiciously. "We got nothing to say. We'll say all that we need to say in court."

It made her flesh crawl to appeal to him — this man whom she suspected of being Phoebe's actual killer. The thought of trapping him through the DNA helped her to overcome her revulsion. "I was just hoping that you and your wife and I could maybe . . . discuss this whole thing. I mean, I probably shouldn't admit this to you, but I do feel . . . very responsible for what happened to Lazarus."

"My wife's not here," he said flatly. "She's at the church."

Tess raised her hands in supplication. "You and I then. Could we sit down and talk about this . . . ?" The thought of entering the house made Tess feel weak with dread, but she couldn't give up. If he would only invite her in, she knew she could get to the bathroom, to get what she needed. "Could we just go inside and talk . . . ?"

"I don't know what it is you want to talk about," said Nelson suspiciously.

"Just . . . to, um . . . clear the air," said Tess.

He peered at her and seemed to be calculating something. "Clear the air how?" he said.

"I don't think we . . . necessarily need an intermediary. I mean, lawyers can get in the way. And they're expensive. Would you mind if I came in?" she said. "It's awfully wet out here."

Nelson turned his back on her and walked up the front porch steps, rummaging in his pocket for the keys. He inserted a key into the front door and turned the knob.

"Mr Abbott," Tess said politely.

He turned to gaze at her, still standing beside the steps, and there was a chilling little flash of cunning in his eyes. "Well, come in if you're comin'," he said abruptly.

Tess felt victorious and utterly wary at the same time. Where was that sudden, sly satisfaction coming from? She climbed the steps and followed him into the parlor she had viewed through the window earlier. Nelson Abbott took off his hat and his jacket and hung them on a clothes tree by the front door. Tess started to take off her wet slicker to hang it and her furled umbrella on the clothes tree, as well, but Abbott interrupted her. "I didn't say to make yourself at home," he said.

"It's just . . . I'm dripping," she said.

Nelson Abbott made a face and then sighed, indicating his unwilling approval. Tess hung up the umbrella and the slicker over it. Nelson pointed to one of the wooden chairs and Tess sat down on it in the center of the dank room. Nelson remained standing, his arms crossed over his chest.

Instantly, Tess realized that they weren't going to be sharing a friendly drink. So much for any hope of secreting away his drinking glass. He was staring at her, tapping the palm of his hand impatiently on his upper arm. "Say what you come to say," he barked.

Make this good, Tess thought. Be appeasing. "Well," she said, "I know that you and Mrs Abbott feel as if your son was the victim in this . . . whole thing. And of course he was," she said, nearly choking on the words. "But my sister was a victim, as well. So I thought, maybe, instead of blaming each other, we should be placing the blame where it really belongs . . . on the state and the . . . death penalty."

Nelson looked at her in disbelief. "That's what you wanted to say? That's it?"

Tess felt flustered. "Well, I, yeah . . ."

Nelson rolled his eyes in disgust.

"I mean . . . I just thought we could talk," Tess said.

Nelson snorted. "And here I figured you wanted to settle this thing. I thought you come to make us an offer."

"An offer?"

"A financial offer," he said. Then he shook his head. "Avoid the court business. I should have known. Just a lot of talk," he said. "If that's all you're good for, get out."

Too late, Tess realized that she had missed her chance. Nelson would have been happy to sit and bargain. He might even have made them both a cup of coffee. Now it was too late to backtrack. He would not believe she was actually here to negotiate. In fact, he looked as if he was going to lift her from the chair and toss her out. Tess stood up, mindful that her last hope to obtain the sample was at hand. She knew that what she was about to say might seem strange, but she had to do it. "Excuse me," she said, "but would you mind if I used your bathroom?"

Nelson stared at her in amazement. "The bathroom?"

Surely you have one, Tess thought. But she didn't say it. "Yes," she said.

"No need for that," he said. "You're leaving."

"You won't let me use the bathroom?" Tess said incredulously.

Nelson was unrepentant. "No. You've wasted enough of my time. Get out of my house."

"All right," said Tess, her scalp prickling. "Never mind." She looked around the tidy room, hoping that something, somehow would strike her. Some source of a sample.

"Let me tell you something," said Nelson. "You *ought* to think about offering a settlement. Because if you don't, a jury is going to make you pay dearly. You're not going to get out of this. You hear me? It is going to cost you."

She walked over to the clothes tree while Nelson planted himself behind her so that there was no way for her to reenter the room. He grabbed the doorknob, pulling the front door open. Tess reached out for her slicker, still shiny and wet, and then she realized that all hope was not lost after all.

"Is it still raining?" she asked.

Nelson glanced out the front door. "Still coming down," he said.

Tess nodded as she put on her coat and clutched her umbrella and her pocketbook to her chest. "Well," she said, "I'm sorry to have disappointed you. I guess we'll have to leave this to lawyers after all."

"Don't come back," said Nelson. He barely waited until she was out the door to slam it behind her and lock it. Tess pulled up her hood while she was standing on the porch. Then she went down the front steps and hurried to her car.

Once she got inside the car, she turned on the ignition, set the windshield wipers in motion, and locked the doors.

Then she reached into her purse and pulled out one of the plastic bags she had taken from the Fuller house. Wrapping the bag around her hand like a mitten, she reached inside her slicker, under her arm and down the sleeve. She extracted a worn, stained hat with "John Deere" written above the brim. It had been hanging on the clothes tree beside her slicker and umbrella. When Nelson Abbott had looked out the front door at the rain, Tess had stuffed the hat into her sleeve as she pulled the slicker off its hook.

Now Tess folded the hat with the use of her plastic "glove," pulled it into the plastic bag, sealed the top, then placed it into the inner pocket of her slicker.

The hat in its protective plastic seemed to glow warm against her own thudding heart. Hair, perspiration, a veritable treasure trove of Nelson Abbott's DNA. Later, when he went to get his hat, Nelson would frown and try to remember if he had worn it in from the car. Perhaps he would assume that he'd left it somewhere. He'd probably check his truck, to see if it was on the seat. Or look around at the places where he worked. Tess backed out of the driveway, smiling at the thought. By the time he figured out that she had taken it, the results would be in.

CHAPTER 17

Chief Fuller scolded Tess soundly when she returned to his house with her treasure, but he also called in a favor from an old friend — a technician at the police lab in North Conway — who dispatched the lab's courier for rush jobs to come and pick it. Aldous Fuller assured Tess that he would let her know as soon as he received the results.

By the time Tess returned to the inn it was dark. Tess expected to find her mother comfortably settled in for the night, but Dawn went to the closet to get her coat as soon as Tess returned. "I have to go out," she said.

"Where are you going?" Tess asked.

Dawn pressed her lips together. "I'm going to a CF meeting."

Tess understood what meeting she meant. Compassionate Friends was a national organization composed of parents who had lost a child. Members shared their grief and tried to help other members come to terms with their devastating loss. Dawn had begun going to the chapter in Boston after Phoebe's death and occasionally attended meetings at the local chapter when she moved to New Hampshire. "I didn't know if you were still attending meetings," said Tess.

Dawn sighed. "This week brought it all back to me. I feel like . . . I need to . . . go tonight."

"I understand," said Tess. "Thanks for watching Erny. I'm sorry I was gone so long. I hope I didn't make you late."

"Where were you all this time?" Dawn asked as she buttoned her coat.

Tess wanted to tell her mother about her hunch, about procuring Nelson Abbott's DNA, and about the fact that she was now waiting to hear the results. But's Dawn's eyes were distant and distracted. Tess knew better than to detain her. Over the years, talking with those people who truly understood her loss had helped her mother to survive. "I'll tell you later," Tess said. "Go on. Don't be late."

"Erny's watching TV. There's some spaghetti sauce in there for you two," said Dawn. "Just cook up some pasta."

"I will," said Tess. "Thanks." She kissed her mother on the cheek, saw her out the door, and then went into Dawn's cozy parlor to see her son. Erny was curled up on Dawn's couch under a blanket. Tess sat down beside him and he rested comfortably against her as she absently stroked his curly black hair. "How do you feel now?" she asked him.

"Pretty good," he said, yawning.

"How about if I get you some supper after this?" she asked.

Erny's eyes widened appreciatively. "Yeah," he said. "I'm hungry."

"Good," said Tess.

Once the TV program was over he shuffled along with Tess to the kitchen where she made them both spaghetti, using Dawn's sauce, and they ate in the kitchen under the glow of the stained-glass lamp that hung over the table.

Erny dug into his food eagerly.

"My mother makes the best spaghetti sauce," said Tess as she handed him the cheese shaker for the third time.

"Yours is better," said Erny, polishing off his second helping. "But this is almost as good as yours."

"You are a born diplomat," said Tess. She gazed at him, smiling.

"What?" said Erny, looking up at her.

"I'm just so glad you're okay," she said.

Erny yawned again. "Can I have ice cream?"

Tess gave him some ice cream and cleared the plates. By the time she was done, Erny was resting his head in his arms on the table.

"You look like you're ready for bed again," she said.

Ernie yawned. "I'm tired," he admitted.

"You've had quite a day," said Tess.

"Will you read me more of *Unfortunate Events*?"

"Sure," said Tess. Her son, like so many kids, relished the bestselling ghoulish tales of orphans visited by every imaginable disaster. She sometimes wondered if Erny didn't relate to those orphans in a way that other kids might not.

She hung up the dish towel and together they went back to their room. Erny climbed up under the covers and handed Tess the book from the bedside table. Tess nestled down beside him on top of the covers and turned to the bookmarked page. She was no more than three pages into the new chapter when she noticed that Erny had dropped off to sleep again.

She closed the book and set it down, carefully got up off the bed, and kissed him on the forehead. Leaving the night-light on, she closed the door to their room and wandered down the hall.

Tess went into the library to look for something to read. She needed something to get her mind off the results she was waiting for. One of the guests had his laptop set up on the table by the front windows. He looked up at Tess and said hello politely when she came in and then returned to his computer. As Tess perused the shelves, taking out first one title and then another, she came across a framed plaque, propped up between the books. It had been awarded, years ago, to the Phalens, by the Chamber of Commerce for the improvements they had made to their property. As Tess pulled it from its spot to look at it, a newspaper clipping that had been tucked behind it fluttered to the floor. Tess bent down and picked it up. It was a picture of a beautiful young girl with long, straight hair and sad, kohl-rimmed eyes beneath the headline "Middle School Student, Lisa Phalen, 14, Dead from Drug Overdose." Tess stared at the picture. It was hard to believe this was the same little toddler who had careened through this inn so many years ago. She had grown into a pretty but hard-looking teenager. The article referred to several stints in rehab. What troubled you? Tess wondered, staring at the photo. Once again, despite her conviction that she would be proved right about Nelson Abbott, she found herself wondering if there was some connection between Lisa's death and Phoebe's. And then she was chastened by the memory of her mother's lament. Why do we blame the people who've suffered the most?

Tess replaced the plaque, putting the article behind it, and found an old Ruth Rendell hardback whose title she didn't recognize. She took the book back to the main sitting room. There were no guests in the comfortable room. Tess went over to the hearth and put a match to the fire that Dawn had laid, flopped down in the corner of the sofa, opened the book, and tried to read. But even her favorite author could not keep her attention tonight. She glanced up at the rain-spattered windows, the phone on the table by the door and wondered when Chief Fuller would have the results. "Rush job" did not mean that the lab would be working 'round the clock. Tomorrow, perhaps. But still, her gaze kept traveling to the phone. She got up and went around to the tray of sherry and tiny glasses that her mother always put out in the evening on the table behind the sofa. Several of the glasses on the tray were right-side up, having already been used by guests. Tess turned a fresh glass over, poured herself some sherry, and took a sip.

The phone rang and Tess jumped, nearly spilling the sherry. She set down her glass, picked up the phone, and answered cautiously. "Hello."

"Tess. It's Becca."

Tess was at once pleased and disappointed to hear her friend's voice. "Hey."

Becca knew her too well. "You sound disappointed. Who were you hoping to hear from?"

Becca's question made Tess realize that there was someone else she was hoping would call besides Chief Fuller. She had not even thought of Ben Ramsey since she left his office, but now, as she waited by the phone, the image of his face had crossed her mind more than a few times. "It's a long story," said Tess.

"We've been following the news," said Becca. "It's been all I can do to keep Wade from hopping the next flight up there. He keeps talking about what a missed opportunity it is."

"NO," said Tess. "I hope you keep reminding him that I expressly forbid him to try and make a movie out of it. This is not a game."

"I know. I'm keeping him under control," said Becca. "How are you holding up? How's Erny?"

Tess sighed. "Well, let's see. Erny fell out of a tree today."

"You're kidding," said Becca. "Is he all right?"

"He got the wind knocked out of him. A slight concussion. My brother was in charge, so naturally . . . there was an accident. But he's okay. He'll be fine. He was trying to fish from a tree limb."

"Well, at least he was having some fun. The papers make it sound so grim. Have you two been able to do anything to escape it all?"

Tess frowned. "No. Not really. A couple of Sudoku puzzles. I was just reading to him for a while. But I've hardly had a minute to spend with him."

"Sudoku puzzles? You can do that here. You should go on a picnic or something. Get away from all the madness."

"We should," said Tess.

"Or better yet, you should come home," said Becca. "What's keeping you there now? Why stay there any longer?"

Tess shook her head. "Unfinished business. After all, I'm the one responsible for Lazarus Abbott's death."

"I knew you were going to say that," said Becca. "Tess, that is so not true. You've got to stop thinking that way."

"Thanks, Becca. I know you're sincere when you say that."

"No one blames you. All your friends feel the same way about it."

"Well, I wish I could feel that way, but I have to try to . . . get a few answers while I'm here."

"Never mind answers. That's the job of the cops. Hurry back. We need you here. Tell Erny that Sosa is fine and Jonah is taking good care of him."

"I'll tell him," said Tess.

Tess said good-bye to her friend and they hung up. She took another warming sip of sherry, but felt even more warmed by the call, which reminded her of the good life she had made for herself and her son. Almost immediately the phone rang again. Tess picked it up, smiling. "What'd you forget?" she asked.

"Tess, you're there," a man's voice said.

The sound of his voice coursed through her like a current. For a moment Tess felt too surprised to reply. "Ben?" she said at last.

"I was thinking about you," he said.

Tess felt happy but flustered at the same time. She didn't know whether he meant it in a business or personal way. "I'm glad you called," she said.

"I ran into a friend of mine who works at the hospital. She said they treated your son in the emergency room today."

This is a small town, Tess thought. Word got around. "That's right," said Tess.

"What happened? You never mentioned it when you were in my office today. Is he okay?"

"He's going to be fine," said Tess. "Thanks for asking."

"How did he get injured?"

Tess sighed. "My brother was supposed to be keeping an eye on him, but he was busy working. Erny decided to fish from the branch of a tree and he fell off when the wind blew up. He got a bit shaken up, but he's okay."

"Kids," he said. "They can be a handful."

His words surprised her. It was as if he were offering her a little opening into his private world. "You say that like you know," Tess observed carefully.

"Not from personal experience. I . . . just remember my own reckless youth."

She was reluctant to pursue the topic of children since it would surely remind him of his late wife and marriage — a subject that, he had made clear earlier in the day, was off limits. She was casting about in her mind for another less personal conversational topic when he said, "I always wanted them, though. Kids."

Tess felt herself blushing, despite the fact that his statement had nothing to do with her. "Really," she said.

"My wife and I used to talk about it but we never got around to it."

All right, Tess thought. You brought it up. "Do you wish you had?" she asked.

"No," he said abruptly. Then he softened his tone. "No. I don't think I could have managed it on my own. I mean, I admire you for going it alone but . . . for me, it's probably better this way."

"Well, it's not like you couldn't still have kids. You're still young."

"Ah, the silver fox look didn't fool you?" he said.

Tess smiled. "The gray is obviously . . . premature."

There was a hesitation at the other end of the line. "Well, I was one of those people you hear about who go gray . . . almost overnight."

"They say it can be caused by a shock," Tess said.

"It's true," he said. "Mine was."

"Your wife's death?" Tess ventured.

"Yes," he said. There was a steely note in his voice that forestalled another question. But she was left wondering about his marriage. She felt suddenly, absurdly jealous of a wife whose death was so traumatic that it turned a young man's hair to gray. Clearly it was a subject he couldn't bear to think about. A subject that was now, definitely, closed.

"So," he said, "did you, um, give any more thought to what we talked about this afternoon? About Nelson Abbott."

The mention of Nelson Abbott reminded Tess of the call she was waiting for. Would her suspicion be borne out by the facts, she wondered? She considered telling Ben about it, but then decided against it. Even though he seemed sympathetic, she still wasn't quite ready to tell him what she'd done. He had made it clear this afternoon that he would not approve.

"I have been thinking about it," she said.

"And . . . ?"

"And . . . I am certainly . . . on the trail of something," she said. "We'll see where it leads."

"Do you have time to . . . follow a trail? What about your job?"

Tess smiled ruefully. "I'm trying to keep my job from coming to me."

"What does that mean?" Ben asked.

"I work for a documentary film team in Washington. I'm a cinematographer. My partners think this whole . . . situation would make a great film."

"Isn't it a little late? The main event already occurred when the DNA results were announced," Ben observed.

"Oh, that's no problem. There is footage galore of that event. What they want is the personal perspective on the whole thing. You know, interviews with the people involved, as well as footage from both past and present."

"You don't sound enthused," said Ben.

"This isn't something I can be objective about," said Tess. "That kind of intrusive attention could drive any reluctant witnesses even further underground. Besides, I need to be objective when I work on a film. I mean, it's good to be passionate about your subject, but I'm just too close to this. For me, this is not about making a movie. This is about finding out what really happened."

"It seems like you have your priorities straight," he said.

"I hope so," she said.

A silence fell between them. "Well, I'd better let you go," he said. "Get some sleep."

"Right," said Tess. "Thanks for asking about Erny."

"I'm glad he's all right," Ben said. "Good night."

"'Night." Tess put the receiver carefully back in the cradle, but her heart was feeling anything but careful. She hadn't felt that excited about a man in a long while. She gazed into the fire, but she did not see the flames. She was picturing him, wondering about him.

The front door of the inn opened and Dawn called out, "I'm back."

Tess looked up as her mother came to the doorway. "Hey, Mom. Come and sit."

"Honey, I'm beat," said Dawn. "Can we talk tomorrow?"

"Sure," said Tess. "How was the meeting?"

"Grueling," said Dawn. "They always are. But somehow, afterwards, you feel better. Tired. But better. How's our boy?"

"Asleep," said Tess.

"Good. I'm going to do the same," said Dawn. "I'll see you in the morning."

Tess looked at the phone. The results were not going to be coming in tonight. "Me, too," said Tess. She set her unread book on the table and picked up her sherry glass, which she set on the tray.

"That goes . . ." said Dawn.

"I know, into the kitchen," said Tess, kissing her mother's cheek. "Go to bed. I'll close the place up."

Tess carried the tray back into the kitchen and rinsed out the used glasses. Then she turned down the kitchen lights, leaving the light on over the sink. She walked back out and down the hallway, checking the library to be sure that she was not turning out the lights on a guest. The library was empty now. Tess left one lamp burning on the library table. She made sure the fire in the sitting room was banked and then she went to the front door to turn out the outside lanterns and the gaslights that illuminated the parking area. As she glanced out, she heard an engine idling and saw a plume of smoke rising in the air. She thought it must be a car's exhaust. Then she looked again. The smoke was drifting from the half-open window of a fawn-colored sedan, which was facing the inn. All of a sudden, Tess realized that it was smoke, not from the exhaust, but from the driver's cigarette. Tess strained to see the driver's face, but all she could make out was his head, which looked skull-like in the dark, his eyes sunken. He flicked his cigarette out the window onto the gravel of the driveway and Tess saw his extended arm. He was wearing a gray parka.

Tess backed up into the vestibule, slammed the front door, and flipped the switch. All the lights in the parking area went out at once. Then she looked through the door light. Now the car was bleached colorless in the moonlight. The car idled for a moment more and then slowly turned and pulled away.

Tess's heart was beating hard. It's nothing, she told herself. A gray parka. A million people could own a gray parka. It doesn't mean anything. It could be anyone, she thought. An inn is a public place. And then she remembered the front door. She turned the lock and the bolt snapped into place. She looked through the door light again, but the car was gone.

CHAPTER 18

While Tess's mother dusted the sitting room the next day, Tess was cleaning out the ashes in the sitting-room fireplace just to have something to do other than wait for the DNA results on Nelson Abbott. Shortly after noon, both turned and looked toward the front door where Julie came squeaking in on her rubber-soled shoes, dressed in her nurse's scrubs and her coat, and carrying an X-Men action figure, still in its plastic packaging.

"Hey," said Tess.

"It's my lunch hour. I figured I'd come see how my nephew is doing. Jake told me about his fall."

"He's doing okay," said Tess. "I let him take Leo out for a short walk."

Julie handed Tess the packaged action figure. "Well, I picked this up for him. I guess I'll leave it with you."

Tess smiled at the gift and then gave her sister-in-law a hug. "Thanks. That was sweet of you."

"Least I could do," said Julie, raising an eyebrow. "Maybe if my husband had been watching him like he was supposed to . . . he told me you were plenty mad at him."

Tess shrugged and avoided Julie's gaze. "I'm sure he also told you I was being an overbearing worrywart."

"He didn't use those exact words," said Julie.

All of a sudden the phone on the table by the door rang. Tess jumped. "I'm sorry. I have to get that," she said.

"Go ahead," said Julie.

Tess rushed over to the table and picked up the phone with a trembling hand. "Hello."

"Tess?"

Instantly she recognized Aldous Fuller's thready voice. Tess's heart thudded and she felt light-headed. Calm down. He's probably just calling to say he won't know anything until tomorrow, she told herself. "Chief Fuller," she said.

"I have the results," he said.

Tess felt as if someone was grabbing her throat. Squeezing it. "And?" she managed to squeak.

"Looks like a match," he said.

Tess's knees buckled and, for a moment, she actually saw spots in front of her eyes. She took a deep breath. "A match?"

"It's not perfect, Tess," said the chief. "The sample from the original crime is so deteriorated. But they do these things by points. Apparently . . ."

Tess was hearing his voice, but not actually listening as he detailed the test results. She kept picturing Nelson Abbott's face, his cruel little eyes, as he confronted her at his house. Demanding to know what she was doing there. Menacing her. Gloating over his lawsuit and piously proclaiming his desire to have justice for Lazarus. And all the while, he was the one who had killed Phoebe. Defiled her. Tess's stomach twisted and she stifled the urge to gag.

"So . . . a pretty good hunch on your part," said the chief.

Tess tried to speak calmly. "What happens now?"

"I called Rusty and explained the results to him. He was steamed. Said it wouldn't stand up in court, but I threatened to take the results to Chan Morris and the rest of the news vultures if he didn't do something about it. So he did agree to send two of his men to pick up Nelson and bring him in for questioning down at the station."

"Why do they have to question him? Doesn't this prove it?" Tess demanded.

"Well, it certainly implicates him."

"What else do they need?" Tess cried.

"That depends," said Aldous vaguely.

"Never mind," said Tess. "Thank you, Chief. Thank you so much."

"You just sit tight, Tess. If there's any news you'll hear about it."

Tess set the receiver back down in the cradle and turned around.

Julie, who was chatting amiably with Dawn, frowned at her. "Tess, what's the matter? You're red as a beet."

"That was Chief Fuller," she said.

"What did he want?" Julie asked.

"They know who did it."

"Who did what?" Julie asked.

Dawn was peering at her. "What are you talking about, honey?"

"The police. They know who killed Phoebe," said Tess. "It was Nelson Abbott."

Julie let out a cry. "What? No. Why would they think that?"

Tess nodded. "It was him. His DNA matched the old evidence."

"Oh my God," Julie cried. "Oh Tess. Oh my God. Wait until Jake hears this. Nelson Abbott. That lying hypocrite. I just . . . I can't believe it. Oh my God. I have to catch Jake at lunch. I want to be the one to tell him. I don't want him to hear it on the TV or something. He will be wild when he hears this. Just out of his mind. I'd better go. I'll see you both later." Julie hurried toward the front door.

Tess picked up the phone again. "I have to call Ben," she said. She called information for the number of Ben Ramsey's office and had it dialed automatically. As the phone rang, Tess looked at her mother. Dawn was dead white except for the gray smudges under her eyes. Even her lips looked livid. "Mom, are you okay?"

Dawn shook her head and walked into the sitting room.

"Cottrell and Wayne," said the receptionist.

"Mr Ramsey," said Tess. "I need to speak to him. It's very important."

"Mr Ramsey is unavailable," the receptionist said firmly. "Can I take a message?"

Tess looked worriedly at the door through which her mother had disappeared. "Tell him to call Tess please. As soon as he's free. Thank you," she said. She hung up the phone and went into the sitting room.

Dawn sat on the sofa, blinking, as if she had been struck in the face and was still stunned by the blow. She was shivering from head to toe. Tess came and sat beside her mother, draping an arm protectively around her shoulders.

Dawn looked into Tess's eyes with a bewildered expression on her face. "I don't understand any of this, Tess." Dawn shook her head. "Nelson Abbott? How could it be?" Then she looked at Tess. "You don't seem . . . surprised."

"I was the one who . . . first suspected him. I got a sample of Nelson's DNA and Chief Fuller sent it to the lab . . ." Tess admitted.

"*You* got it?" said Dawn. "How? What made you think of Nelson?"

Tess started to explain her thinking that had led to the unmasking of Nelson Abbott but as she talked she could see the distracted suffering in her mother's eyes. All Dawn could think about was her daughter Phoebe, set upon by two depraved men, father and son. Tess cut short her explanation.

Dawn shook her head and looked away from her daughter. "He always seemed . . . normal. A regular man. Not a monster. I mean, I should have known better. I remember the stories of how he used to treat Lazarus. I thought they were exaggerating how bad it was, to save Lazarus. But I never dreamed . . . to think that Nelson stood here, right in this very room, just days ago, and told us that he thought Lazarus was guilty . . ."

"I know . . ." said Tess. "Mom, I want to be there when they arrest him. I have to go down to the police station. Will you be all right if I leave you alone here?"

"I'm all right, Tess," Dawn said vaguely.

"If Mr Ramsey calls, tell him . . . tell him I'm heading to the police station. Give him my cell phone number."

"I will. You go on. Be my brave girl."

Tess kissed her mother's dry cheek and hurried to get her jacket.

* * *

The word was already out. The assemblage of reporters had vacated the parking area outside the inn and reassembled at the police station. There were officers coming and going through the front doors of the station house, refusing requests for comments from the reporters who waited in the cold, their clouds of breath visible against the blue sky.

Tess saw a pretty young woman being videotaped as she spoke to the camera with the station house as a backdrop. The nearby van had the call letters of a local TV station. Although she strained to listen, Tess could not hear what the reporter was saying. Tess jammed her hands in her pockets and hunched her shoulders, hoping no one would recognize her. She wasn't ready to make any public comment on Nelson's arrest. Even though it was her own purloining of the John Deere hat, her own suspicion of Nelson's guilt that had brought this moment about, Tess still felt too shaky to talk publicly about her feelings.

Tess jumped as someone tapped her on the shoulder from behind. She turned around. Channing Morris, wearing an olive green field coat, was standing beside her. "Fancy meeting you here," he said.

Tess shrank from his curious gaze.

"I heard they've arrested someone for your sister's murder," said Chan, absently pushing back his shiny black hair.

Tess hesitated. "Arrested?" she asked.

"Well, they have a suspect they're questioning." Chan shook his head and his black locks fell into his eyes again. "It's just hard to believe that after all these years, all that's happened, they could find the real killer so quickly."

Tess avoided looking at him. "It is amazing."

"We could be waiting here for quite a while. Can I buy you a cup of coffee while we wait?" he asked.

"I suppose so," said Tess.

Chan pointed to the Dunkin' Donuts across the street, which was doing a brisk business thanks to the assembled news people. People were streaming out of the store carrying paper trays of steaming coffee cups and bags of food. "Let's go over there. At least we can sit down."

"All right," said Tess. He must have been a beautiful child, she thought, glancing at his square jaw and his long black eyelashes, and then, inevitably, her thoughts returned to her own child. "I guess my son created a little excitement over at your house yesterday," Tess said as they hurried along the sidewalk to the store.

Chan looked puzzled. "I'm sorry. What do you mean?"

"Oh, I figured you knew."

"Knew what?" Chan asked.

"My son, Erny, was . . . fooling around and he fell out of a tree on your property. Jake had to take him to the emergency room."

"Really? You're kidding."

"Fortunately, he wasn't hurt. Just bruised and shook up," said Tess, although Chan hadn't asked.

"Well, that's good. No, I didn't know anything about it," Chan said. He reached out to open the door and ushered Tess into the bubble gum pink-and-white interior of the donut shop. Most of the TV people were collecting their orders and leaving, unwilling to miss a moment of recordable action or a sound bite, so the tables and booths in the store were mostly empty. Chan chose a beige Formica-topped booth in the rear and brought back two steaming cups.

Tess thanked him. She did not want to be recognized, so she sat with her back to the counter activity. Chan, on the other hand, wanted to keep an eye on the station house, just in case someone emerged to give a statement, so he sat facing the door. He shrugged off his field coat. Beneath it, he was wearing a striped broadcloth shirt with rolled-up sleeves. "I hope we'll find out what's going on soon. I have to put the paper to bed this afternoon and if there is an arrest I'd like to get it on the front page." Chan blew on his coffee. "Do you have any idea who the suspect is?" he asked.

Tess continued to stir her coffee, her gaze riveted to the plastic stirrer. The steam from the hot beverages rose up around them, enveloping them in a private haze. "No," she said.

Chan frowned. His pale gray eyes narrowed. "I've heard rumors that it might be . . . Nelson Abbott."

"Nelson Abbott?" Tess exclaimed, trying to feign surprise.

Chan nodded. "I know. It's freaking me out."

"Doesn't he work for your family?" Tess asked.

Chan raked back his hair. "Yeah. For years. My grandfather hired him when they first moved to the farm. And then, after he died, even during that business with Lazarus, my grandmother kept Nelson on. She couldn't have managed without him. She was too busy running the newspaper. My mom always said the newspaper was Nana's real child." Chan leaned across the table and spoke to her in a confidential tone. "You know, you didn't seem all that surprised when I mentioned Nelson Abbott as the possible suspect."

"I didn't?" said Tess, flustered.

"You knew, didn't you?" he said.

"No, really. I didn't," she insisted.

Chan looked at her skeptically. "I have to wonder, what kind of evidence would have led them to Nelson Abbott after all these years?"

Tess looked at the publisher incredulously. "Oh, come on," she said. "Are you serious? Do you really have to wonder?

I mean, when you think about how this case was reopened in the first place?"

Chan frowned. "Ramsey got it reopened," he said.

Tess frowned. She wondered if Chan was being deliberately obtuse. DNA results were the heart and soul of this case. She remembered Jake scoffing that Chan was no journalist, that he was a lightweight who had simply inherited the paper. She wondered if her brother might be right. "Well," she said, "I'm sure it will all be common knowledge very soon."

"You know what the evidence is, don't you?" Chan asked.

Tess gave him a half smile. "I'm afraid I can't be much help to you."

Suddenly there was a burst of activity at the front of the store. Chan sat up straight and looked out at the street. "Uh-oh," he said. "Something's happening." Tess turned around in her seat. She could see several people gathering in the vestibule of the police station.

Chan jumped up and pulled on his jacket. "Let's go," he said.

Tess followed him at a run. All the reporters and news people were converging on a podium that had been set up in front of the station. Chan managed to snake his way through to the middle of the crowd and he let Tess sneak into an empty pocket that had formed in front of him. Rusty Bosworth stepped up to the podium. Though she craned her neck, Tess could not see who else was behind him.

The redheaded police chief tapped on the microphone, sending a whoosh of noise through the clear, cold mountain air.

"All right, can I have your attention," he said. "Now I know," Chief Bosworth said, "that the rumors have been flying. So I want to just straighten out a few things. It's true that we do have a person of interest in the murder of Phoebe DeGraff and we have been questioning him. But his attorney has raised a number of issues and, as of this moment, our suspect is not under arrest. Until we make an arrest, we'll be releasing no other names or details at this time . . ."

A general murmur of disappointment and frustration traveled through the press corps as reporters realized that their lead story was still as lacking in substance as a soap bubble.

"As soon as we have more information, we will let you know . . ." Rusty Bosworth said grimly.

The crowd of technicians began to pack up their gear when suddenly a loud voice began to shout from the back of the crowd, "Bullshit! This is bullshit!"

Tess turned around, along with everyone else, and saw her brother, Jake, his golden-brown hair disheveled, his collar turned up against the cold, his rugged face distorted by anger. The chief, who was surrounded by officers and making his way back into the station, pretended not to hear him, but Jake would not be denied.

"This is pure bullshit, Bosworth. Nelson Abbott's DNA matches the killer's and you know it," Jake shouted. "How come you haven't arrested him?"

"What?" Chan Morris cried. "What is your brother talking about?"

How does he know that? Tess wondered. And then she remembered. Julie had been there when Chief Fuller's call came. She had rushed off to tell Jake.

"He did it," Jake was screaming. "You've got the DNA results to prove it and you're still asking questions? What is there to ask? He's gotten away with my sister's murder all these years and now you're lettin' him go? Doesn't this bastard have to pay for what he did?"

People around Jake were trying to calm him down, but Jake was in no mood to be placated. He shoved away their well-meaning reassurances. "What about it, Bosworth?" Jake cried. "Is this how you treat a pedophile and a killer? I guess it's okay to let him go if he's your uncle."

Rusty Bosworth glared into the crowd. "I'll let the suspect's attorney answer that." Rusty turned around and looked behind him. "Mr Ramsey?"

Tess felt as if she had been punched in the sternum. "Ben Ramsey?"

Ben Ramsey stepped up to the podium. The sun gleamed on his silver hair. He leaned down to the microphone. "As of right now, my client is not charged with anything, and I want to advise the members of the press not to broadcast or print any statements that can be construed as slander or libel. You're forewarned." Ben Ramsey stepped back and Rusty Bosworth took the microphone.

"Okay, show's over," snapped the police chief. He whispered to a couple of officers who waded out into the crowd and surrounded Jake, urging him to move along. "Just for the record, I didn't say we were letting our suspect go. We are still questioning him. When we have something to tell you, we'll tell you," Bosworth said. Beside him, Ben Ramsey's face was impassive as his eyes scanned the crowd. When Tess met his gaze, her eyes blazing with hurt and anger, she thought she saw him flinch.

You traitor, Tess thought. How could you?

Protesting loudly, Jake was hustled by a wave of blue uniforms out past the edge of the crowd. Tess turned and started to follow them.

Chan caught Tess by the sleeve. "Wait a minute. What is your brother talking about? What does he know about those DNA results?"

Tess raised her hands as if to ward off his questions. "I can't tell you anything," she said. "Really. I don't know anything about it. I have to go."

Chan brushed aside her protests of ignorance. "So the cops are saying that Nelson Abbott's DNA matched the results from . . . the old evidence."

Tess shook her head. "I told you, I don't know."

Chan shook his head. "I don't get it."

"What don't you get?" Tess demanded impatiently. "If he's the one who raped and killed my sister, then naturally his results would match the DNA on the evidence."

Chan put a hand to his forehead, as if the effort of thinking were painful. "But he always said that Lazarus was guilty. He told anybody who would listen . . ."

"Apparently, it was a lot easier for Nelson to let Lazarus be put to death than to face his own execution."

Chan peered at her. "It was you who said that Lazarus took your sister. How could you have made a mistake like that? Those two don't look at all alike."

"I didn't make a mistake," she said angrily. "Don't you see? They did it together."

Chan looked startled. "Together?"

Instantly Tess realized that she had said too much. The publisher was staring at her as if she had suddenly started speaking Mandarin. "I don't know. I don't know any more than you do," she insisted as she turned away from him. But she could see from the triumphant look dawning on his face that her protestations were too feeble, and too late.

CHAPTER 19

From all her mother's years in residence at the Stone Hill Inn, Tess knew that there was a path that could be entered on foot half a mile down the road and led in a meandering route to the back door of the inn. She also knew that the reporters, frustrated by their lack of a story and titillated by Jake's outburst, would soon be congregating again in front of the inn. She decided to take the path.

She came out of the field at the back door, went in through the mudroom, and walked into the kitchen. A shrieking whistle filled the room and a gaunt-faced man in a gray parka was standing by the sink. He turned on her as she entered the room.

Tess cried out. It was the man whom she had seen in the field, looking in at her that first morning. The cigarette smoker, from the car, last night.

He raised his pale fingers. "Whoa, Tess," he said. "Take it easy."

"Who the hell are you?" she demanded. "What are you doing here?"

Dawn came into the kitchen from the laundry room carrying a pile of dish towels. "Tess, what's wrong? Didn't you hear the kettle?"

Tess could see instantly that her mother was not surprised to find the man in the kitchen. "Who is this, Mother?" she demanded. "What's he doing here?"

Dawn looked embarrassed by her daughter's reaction. "Don't you remember Mr Phalen? Kenneth Phalen?"

Tess stared at the man's sunken eyes, his short, salt-and-pepper hair, and gray face that matched the color of his parka. She thought of the picture in the paper, the one on which she had drawn the glasses. Kenneth Phalen.

"Mr Phalen?"

"Call me Ken," he said with half a smile. "We're all grown-ups now."

Tess looked at him warily. "I've seen you. Hanging around here," she said.

Dawn set the towels down and turned off the flame under the kettle. "We're just about to have a cup of tea. Do you want to join us?" Dawn was pouring the boiling water into a pair of mugs on the counter.

Tess shook her head.

Ken took off his coat and draped it carefully on the back of a counter stool. Dawn pointed to the breakfast nook. "Sit down, Ken," she said.

Kenneth edged past Tess and onto one of the benches in the nook. "'Scuse me," he said. Dawn came over and set down the mugs. She slid into the bench on the other side of the table, sliding toward the window so that there was room on her bench. "Sit down, Tess," said Dawn. "Tell me what happened."

Tess looked at her blankly.

"With Nelson," her mother reminded her.

"Nothing happened," said Tess. She did not sit. "There's nothing new. The police are questioning . . . their suspect. Jake came and . . . got a little out of control."

Dawn shook her head. "Oh no."

"You can't blame the boy," said Ken Phalen.

Tess looked at Ken in surprise. "Boy?" she said.

"I guess that's how I remember your brother," said Ken.

Tess peered at Phalen. "You never answered my question. Why are you here?"

"Tess," Dawn reproved her.

Ken stirred the coffee in his mug and then set down the spoon on a napkin. "Well, I ran into your mother last night at the Friends meeting . . ."

"Although I have to admit I didn't recognize him," said Dawn.

"I haven't weathered too well," said Ken.

The Compassionate Friends. Of course, Tess thought. She felt a moment of guilt as she realized that Ken and her mother did have that unbearable loss in common. But the guilt quickly passed. "I meant, why are you here in town?" she demanded. "It seems kind of a coincidence . . ." she said. "Now, when all this is coming out about Phoebe's murder."

Ken shook his head. "It's no coincidence. I was having lunch with one of the editors I work for. He tries to throw as much work my way as he can. We were tossing around ideas and he mentioned this case — the DNA and death penalty thing. I told him about my personal involvement and he got very excited. He thought I should come up and try to get an article out of it."

"Mr Phalen's a writer," said Dawn.

"I never did finish that novel I was working on when I met you," Ken demurred. "But I do a lot of magazine work. My editor thought I might have an interesting angle on the whole thing. After all, we were here when Phoebe . . . when the crime happened. Your family stayed here during the trial."

"How fortunate for you to have the inside track," said Tess coldly.

Ken sighed. "I don't know how fortunate it is. I didn't want to come at first. I haven't been back here in years. Since my daughter, Lisa, died. I wasn't sure I was . . . ready to make the trip. You know."

"But, now that you're here, why not exploit your advantage, right?" said Tess.

Dawn glared at her daughter. "Ken did not come here to exploit anyone."

"How come you were in our parking area last night?" Tess demanded.

"Tess, your tone," said Dawn sharply.

"I recognized your mother, of course, and I wanted to talk to her, but I . . . didn't want to intrude."

But somehow, you brought yourself to do just that, Tess thought.

"You should have come in last night," said Dawn. "You did look familiar to me. I just couldn't place you. I'm really so glad to see you again."

"I've been trying to work up my nerve. The idea of walking through that door again . . ." he said.

Dawn reached out her hand and placed it over his on the table. "I'm glad you finally did. This was your home through good times, too, Ken. It wasn't all bad. You have to remember that."

Ken shuddered and then he nodded.

"How's Mrs Phalen?" said Tess.

Dawn gave her a warning look.

Ken looked up at Tess. "We're divorced now. She . . . had a very rough time after Lisa died. She became an alcoholic. Refused to get any treatment."

"That's too bad," said Tess.

Ken nodded. "I could understand it. I just couldn't live with it anymore." He took a sip of his tea, then set the cup down carefully in front of him. "So your mother says that at long last," he said, "it looks as if they've got the real killer?"

Dawn looked proudly at her daughter. "It was Tess who figured it out," she said.

"Really?" said Ken. "How did that happen, Tess?"

"I'm not really in the mood for an interview," said Tess. She turned to Dawn. "Is Erny back?"

"In your room," said Dawn.

Tess turned and left the kitchen. She went out into the main hallway and then around to her room. She was still fuming at Ken Phalen's question. Forget it, she thought. Another opportunist. Tess took a deep breath, tapped on the door, and walked in.

Erny was sprawled on the bed, working on the puzzle book.

Tess came and sat down on the edge of the bed. "Hey," she said. "How was the walk with Leo?"

Erny shrugged. "Good."

"How's the head feel?"

Erny nodded. "Good. Can I go fishing tomorrow with Uncle Jake?"

"No," said Tess, too sharply. Then she reached out and rubbed his messy hair. "But maybe tomorrow you and I can do something fun."

"Maybe," he said, frowning, and pulled away from her touch. "I'm hungry," he said, sliding off the bed. "I'm going to the kitchen."

"Don't eat too many snacks," said Tess. "It's almost dinnertime."

Tess followed him out into the hallway and closed the door behind her. Dawn ruffled Erny's hair as she passed him in the hallway.

Tess looked up at her mother. "Erny wants a snack."

"He knows where everything is," said Dawn.

"Where's Kenneth?" Tess asked.

"He left. I'm sure he didn't feel very welcome here. What was the meaning of that behavior anyway?" Dawn demanded. "Kenneth was my guest."

Tess frowned. "Your so-called guest is a journalist, Mother. You're offering him the kind of access every one of those vultures waiting around outside the inn wants."

Dawn shook her head. "We were talking, Tess. Kenneth and Annette helped us in a very difficult time. I'll always be grateful to them."

"Don't worry. You're paying him back now," said Tess.

"I don't understand you. You were rude to him the minute you saw him."

"I've seen him lurking around this house for days," Tess exclaimed.

"He was trying to get up the courage to face the past," said Dawn. "Is that so hard for you to understand?"

Tess folded her arms over her chest. "I don't like it. Now suddenly he finds the courage to come back? Now, when there's a story in it, that will probably earn him a bundle of money?"

"Oh Tess," said Dawn, shaking her head. "It's not that simple. He's suffered a great deal. He knows that I, of all people, can understand it."

"In other words, you're an easy mark, Mother."

Dawn shook her head. "Tess, you've got to have a little faith in people."

Tess thought of Ben Ramsey, acting concerned and brainstorming with her about Phoebe's killer. Calling her about Erny. Seeking her out. Flirting with her, in his own careful way. And now the handsome attorney, who had begun to invade her daydreams, was busy searching for a loophole. An excuse to get Nelson Abbott exonerated. The thought of his betrayal caused tears to spring to her eyes. But she willed them away. She couldn't call it a betrayal when he had not promised her any loyalty. Hell, he hadn't even asked her out. She had blamed his reticence on his bereavement, not his lack of interest. Now, she berated herself for imagining that he felt the same attraction which she felt. It had all been a fantasy. As painful as it was to admit, she had not really seen him for the man he was. "Everybody suffers, Mother," said Tess. "That doesn't mean they deserve your trust."

CHAPTER 20

The next morning, the sky was a clear blue-gray and the air was cold. When Tess woke up, Erny was already gone from the room. The first thing Tess saw when she reached the hallway outside the dining room was a neat pile of newspapers sitting on the sideboard, topped by the *Stone Hill Record*. The headline read, "Nelson and Lazarus Abbott — Victim's Sister Alleges: They Did It Together." Tess's cheeks flamed as she realized that Chan Morris, no lightweight after all, had taken advantage of her unguarded remarks. She scanned the story beneath the headline, quoting the accusation she had made so irresponsibly to the publisher. Then she set the newspaper back down, hesitating, considering the possibility of hiding the entire pile of papers. She sighed and realized it was no use. She had said it and now she had to live with the result. Tess found her mother sitting with Erny, finishing breakfast. Dawn looked up at her wearily.

"Hello, darling," Dawn said.

"Did you see the paper?" Tess asked.

Dawn nodded.

Tess poured herself a cup of coffee. "I should have kept my mouth shut."

"There have been a lot of calls. I put them all off."

"Reporters?"

"That. And one from that fellow on your documentary team. Wade something. Hoping it wasn't too late to come up here and start filming."

"Maitland," Erny piped up.

"Becca must have had her back turned. Well, the answer is stilll no. Not in a million years," said Tess firmly.

"That's what I told him," said Dawn.

"Thanks, Mom." Neither one of them mentioned their disagreement over Ken Phalen. Tessa sat down next to her son. "How you doing?"

Erny shrugged. "Good."

Dawn got up with her empty plate to take it to the dishwasher in the kitchen and Erny began to follow suit. Tess asked him to sit down a minute. Erny replaced the plate on the table and reluctantly pulled his chair back out.

"What?" he asked.

She gazed at him a minute. In the wee hours of another sleepless night, Tess had thought about her friend Becca's urging her to do something fun with her son while they were in New Hampshire. She thought about Erny wishing he could go fishing with his uncle, even though Jake had abandoned him to fall out of a tree. And this morning, Tess did want to make herself scarce and let justice take its course with Nelson Abbott. Despite Ben Ramsey's best efforts to thwart justice, it was just a matter of waiting now. It was a perfect opportunity to concentrate on her son for a change. She felt as if she had dragged Erny along like an extra suitcase on this trip for all the time she had spent with him since they'd arrived here.

"Erny," said Tess, "I know this trip has been no fun for you. I've been preoccupied over this DNA business and you had that fall from the tree when you were supposed to be having fun with Uncle Jake."

Erny shrugged. "Doesn't matter."

Tess tapped on his forearm. "Yes. Yes, it does. I meant it when I said that I want us to do something fun today. Just you and me."

Erny frowned at her suspiciously. "What?"

"Well, what would you like to do? We could drive to North Conway and go to a movie. They probably have all the latest releases." Tess waved to her mother, who walked back into the dining room carrying a basket of breads toward the breakfast buffet table.

"What are you two plotting?" asked Dawn, stopping beside their table.

"We're going to do something just for fun today," said Tess.

"What about a canoe ride? Like we did with Uncle Jake that time!" Erny exclaimed.

Jake had taken them out on a short river canoe trip several summers ago. They had run into several fast-moving sections of the river and nearly capsized twice. Once their canoe had gotten wedged under a fallen tree branch and it had taken Jake twenty minutes to free them. Erny had loved every minute of it.

"Oh, I don't know, Erny," Tess demurred. "I haven't had that much experience with canoes. I wouldn't be comfortable taking us out there alone."

"We could ask Uncle Jake to come with us," Erny said.

Tess suddenly felt trapped by her own suggestion. She was not about to ask her brother to take them, not after their argument at the hospital. "Honey, there was a big storm the other day. That river will be much too fast."

"You said we could do what I wanted today," Erny protested.

"What about the lake?" Dawn suggested. "They have a canoe rental place down at Mayer's Landing. It's a nice calm day. The lake will be very smooth. You could paddle over to the beach and have a picnic."

One of the inn's guests, a man wearing a jacket with elbow patches who was standing at the buffet, turned and looked at their table. "Excuse me," he said to Dawn. "I'm sorry to interrupt, but do you have any more granola?"

"Sure do. Just a minute," said Dawn. She walked over to the buffet table, set down the basket of muffins, and picked up the empty granola container.

Tess watched her mother, realizing that her suggestion was the best solution, but knowing that she was stalling all the same. She, who had once looked forward all year to the family camping trip, now avoided that lake beach and the surrounding woods. The very thought of going there made her feel exposed and vulnerable. That fear was a legacy from Phoebe's death and she had accepted that she would never be free of it. It was like a handicap that she had learned to live with. "You'll turn him into a sissy," Jake had said. Well, she wasn't about to take her parenting cues from Jake. Still, she knew that it was unfair to infect her son with her fears. "Okay," she said at last. "How about that? We could go out on the lake. Just you and me this time."

"Cool. Can we take our lunch?"

"Sure," said Tess, relieved to see his enthusiasm return.

"Awesome," he said.

"Go get your stuff," said Tess. Erny bolted from the chair and raced out of the dining room. Tess watched him go, trying to calm the apprehension in her own heart. You can do this, she said. For Erny, you can do it.

* * *

Tess followed the sign for Mayer's Landing, which led her down a bumpy dirt road to the lake. However, when they finally reached the lakeside clearing, they found the place deserted. A stack of canoes piled on a metal frame was covered with a tarp and the shack where one signed up for rentals had a closed sign over the boarded window.

"Oh no," said Erny.

"I guess the season is over," said Tess. "Why didn't I think of that?"

"We can't go?" Erny said.

Tess looked helplessly around the clearing. Part of her was secretly glad that the place was closed. For her, the woods would be, forevermore, a place where a maniac could easily hide. She already felt uncomfortable being here among the dark, forbidding pines. You tried, she thought. You did your best. But the disappointment in Erny's eyes chastened her, told her she had to try harder. "Hang on a minute," she said.

Set back in the trees was a small house that looked inhabited. There was smoke drifting up from the chimney and an old pickup parked next to it. Tess walked up on the rickety porch and knocked on the door.

A stooped old man in a flannel shirt opened the door, frowning. "Yeah," he said.

"Are these your canoes?" Tess asked.

"We're closed," he said.

"I know. And I'm sorry to bother you. But my son and I are visiting my mother who lives here and we were just hoping . . ." Tess noted the flicker in his eye when she mentioned that her mother was a local. In a tourist town, that always carried a little bit of weight.

"I don't get too many customers this time of year," he explained gruffly.

"I know. I should have thought of that. I just . . . is there any chance that you could rent us one for just a couple of hours?" Tess asked.

The man hesitated, frowning. He looked back ruefully at the flickering TV in his living room. Then he snorted, but he put on a battered fishing hat and stepped out onto the porch. Hampered by a slight limp, he climbed down the steps and trudged over to the tarp-covered frame that was stacked with canoes. He lifted the tarp and began to ease one of the boats off of its berth.

"Yeah!" Erny cried, leaping around the clearing.

"Do you need help with that?" Tess asked.

"Nope," said the man. "Wait down there."

“Good work, Ma,” Erny whispered as they walked down to the water’s edge.

“Thanks,” said Tess. She looked across the lake at the sheltered beach of the campground and the mountain looming behind it. It didn’t look too far away and the surface of the lake was indeed calm. But Tess was filled with apprehension.

The old man set the canoe down and went back for paddles and life jackets, at Tess’s request.

“Is it all right to row over to that little beach?” Tess asked when he returned.

“Yeah,” said the man. “It’s safe enough. Just avoid the rocks on this side.”

Tess gazed anxiously at the boulders along the water’s edge, from which once, long ago, she had seen her brother swing out on a vine, like Tarzan, yodeling his invincibility for the sake of the female onlookers.

“You two know how to paddle this thing, right?”

“Yeah, we know,” Erny assured the old man.

Tess was not so sanguine. “You use the J stroke, right?” She remembered the term from their trip with Jake.

“Or you can take a stroke and just pry your paddle against the hull.”

“Come on, let’s go,” Erny cried impatiently, picking up their plastic bag of lunch and jumping into the back of the boat.

“You go on up in the bow. Let your mother sit in the stern, sonny.”

Erny did as he was told.

“All right then,” the old man said to Tess. “Get in. I’ll hand you the paddles.”

Erny settled himself on the bow seat. The man tried to hand him a small paddle, but Erny insisted he could manage the big one. The man shrugged and handed him the larger paddle. Tess did not want to discourage him, even though the paddle looked like a bit much for him to handle. Tess took the other paddle and sat in the stern. Despite Erny’s protestations, Tess insisted that they both put on their life jackets. The old man handed them each a stained, frayed orange vest, which looked as if it would sink immediately on contact with water.

"What's in the bag?" the old man asked.

"Our lunch," said Erny proudly.

"It's gonna get all wet."

Too late, Tess realized he was right. Dawn had tried to talk her into taking a cooler, but she had been in a hurry and wanted to travel light.

"We don't care," Erny assured the man. "Let's go, Mom."

Tess gripped her paddle firmly as the man gave the canoe a push and the boat glided out onto the surface of the lake. The perimeter of the lake was lined with evergreens and gray-barked trees with branches almost completely denuded of leaves. The mountains loomed up on the other side of the lake, outlined against the sky by ragged pines. The lake was silvery gray and quiet but for the sound of bird calls and the occasional splash of a fish leaping and then falling back into the water. Erny looked all around him with an expression of innocent delight on his face and for one moment Tess was very happy that she had not been deterred from this by her fears. She let them glide for a little bit, until they were away from the shore and then she dipped her paddle into the placid water.

Even though she stroked and lifted her paddle as best she could in the prescribed J motion, the canoe began to veer a little bit. "Erny," she said. "You'd better help me paddle."

"Oh yeah," the boy said, turning around and rocking the canoe beneath them. He reached for his paddle, which was under the seat behind him. He pulled it loose, stuck it in the water, and promptly lost his grip. The paddle sailed out into the lake. "Ma, oh no. Look." He started to lean over the side to try to reach it.

"Erny, sit down," Tess cried. "You're going to capsize the boat."

"My paddle!" he yelled.

"Just sit still. I'll try to catch up with it." Tess's heart was pounding. This was exactly the sort of mishap she had feared would occur. Every time she lifted the paddle from the water and moved it across her body, their lunch was splashed with water. The boat responded to her frantic paddling with jerky, uneven movements. Erny gazed anxiously at his escaping paddle, which seemed to be setting out on its own journey. "Come on, Ma," he insisted. "We have to catch it."

"I know," she said, her forearms already aching. "I'm trying to."

"Come on, you've almost got it," he cried.

Tess managed, with one final push, to get them close to the paddle. Using her own paddle as a hook, she extended it out and managed to snag the wide end and guide it toward the canoe. As the paddle came near, Erny leaned out again.

"Erny, don't . . ."

But before she could tell him to stop, he managed to grab the handle and jerk it toward him, over the side of the canoe. The dripping paddle teetered and then fell into the boat.

"All right," Ernie crowed.

Tess lifted her paddle back into the boat and exhaled. She let them slowly drift for a moment. The beach, which had seemed so close, now looked to be a daunting distance away. And there were the rocks to think of. What if they were hiding below the surface and she accidentally rammed the boat into them?

"I don't know, Erny," she said. "I'm not sure we should go all the way over to the beach."

"It's not far," Erny said.

"It is when you don't know what you're doing," said Tess.

"But you promised we could . . ."

Tess felt as if all her shaky confidence had slipped away with the paddle. "Stop, Erny, please. I know what I said, but—"

"Ma, look," Erny cried, wide-eyed and pointing to the shore. Tess peered at the trees and was about to ask him what she was supposed to be looking for, when suddenly she saw and understood. Standing still at the edge of the water, gazing out at them, was a large, shaggy moose with mild eyes and rounded antlers.

"Do you see it, Ma?" he cried.

"I do," said Tess. "It's amazing."

"Hey, Mr Moose," Erny called out.

"Quiet, you'll scare him," said Tess. But she was smiling, both at the unexpected sight of the moose and her son's joy at having picked him out from the camouflaging surroundings.

"Man. Wait till I tell Jonah," said Erny and Tess realized that, even at this exciting moment, he was thinking of home. He was not the only one.

"Can we get closer?" Erny asked.

"I don't want all the splashing to scare him away," said Tess.

Erny heeded her caution and sat like a statue in the prow, gazing on the magnificent animal with delight. The moose returned their gazes impassively for a few moments and then lowered his head and turned away, ducking back into the trees and shambling off in the opposite direction from the beach.

"He left," Erny lamented.

"Well, he's a wild animal," said Tess. "He doesn't want us getting too close to him." But something about the sighting of the moose seemed to have shored up her shaky confidence. It was as if his appearance in their view had been a sign. This was a good idea for an excursion today. It would be an adventure her son would remember. And she would banish, once and for all, the anxieties that had paralyzed her for so long. After all, Nelson Abbott must be under arrest by now and it had been her determination that had made it happen. There was nothing to be afraid of now.

"All right, you," Tess instructed her son gently. "Pick up that paddle. Next stop, the beach."

CHAPTER 21

"Look, it's got a picnic table," Erny cried out as their canoe neared the shore.

Tess gazed at the hill thick with evergreens that ran down to the narrow strand of sand. The lake water lapped docilely, gently over the pebbly bed. "I know," she said.

Erny twisted around to look at her wide-eyed. "Did you ever go swimming here?" he asked.

"Yes," she said. "Long ago."

He leaned eagerly forward in the prow and scanned the fast-approaching shoreline.

"Mind your paddle there, Erny. Stick the wide part down into that pebble bed. It'll act as a kind of brake."

Erny jammed the paddle down and the canoe lurched to a halt and then the stern began turning crazily toward the shore.

"Easy, honey. Lift it up and extend the paddle out," said Tess. "That's it. Just like that. We're going to pull ourselves up onto the sand. Watch me. Do what I'm doing."

Erny obediently watched and then imitated her motions. The boat came about and surged forward, crunching across the bumpy lake bed and up into the sand.

"All right," Erny crowed. "We did it. We're here."

"We're here," Tess agreed as her son clambered out of the canoe and onto the sand. Tess followed him out of the front of the narrow boat and together they dragged it up onto the brown grass, far enough so that Tess was certain the boat would not be picked up on a swell caused by a passing motorboat and sucked back into the lake and away from them. It was not as if they would be completely stranded. There were roads that led to the park campgrounds and the trails through these woods led back to Stone Hill. One of them even came out at the rear of the inn. But Tess did not feature either a swim through the icy water to try to catch a runaway canoe or a walk back to town. Not through these woods.

Erny ran up and down the beach, crouching to examine some glinting treasure magnified by the water or tossing a stick onto the lake's shimmering surface, as Tess retrieved their bag of lunch from the boat.

"I wish I brought my fishing pole," Erny said. "I made a pole. Did I tell you that?"

"You told me," said Tess.

"I hope Uncle Jake remembered to get it for me."

"Don't count on your uncle," Tess muttered.

"What?" Erny asked.

Tess stifled a sigh. "Here. I thought we could use that picnic table to eat our lunch."

"Do you think we should make a fire?" Erny asked.

"I didn't bring anything to cook," said Tess.

"We could just make one to keep warm," he suggested.

"Well, maybe a little one," said Tess, wondering if there was some park regulation against fires on this beach. "Maybe after we eat."

"Oh cool," Erny cried and he spun in a circle, his arms outstretched.

Tess, who had been feeling vaguely guilty about the missed fishing opportunity, brightened. Erny liked it here. It had not been a mistake to come. On the contrary, she felt as if she were releasing her anxieties into the pure air like so many balloons. The time had come, she thought, to seize this beautiful place and own it, for her son's sake. Time to leave behind the terrible memories.

"Maybe we'll bring your pole next time we come," she said. "Or we could come swimming here in the summer."

He had seated himself on the bench across the table from her and was already chewing on his sandwich.

"Have a drink," she said, tossing him a juice box across the table.

Erny ate and drank in silence for a few minutes, contentedly surveying his surroundings. "I like it here," he said. "It's like a secret hiding place."

Tess nodded and looked around as she ate her sandwich. "It is, isn't it?"

"Wait," said Erny dramatically, holding up a finger.

"What?" she said.

"I hear something. Listen . . ." he whispered.

Tess listened. She could hear the sound of a car's engine in the woods. "Someone else is here," she said.

"Aliens," Erny whispered, wide-eyed.

Tess smiled at his imagination. "Campers, more likely. There are campsites back there. Or maybe fishermen. It's a national park, honey. We aren't the only people who can come here."

Erny shook his head. "Aliens," he said gravely.

Tess shrugged. "You never know. Want an orange?"

Erny shook his head. "Cookies."

Tess rummaged in the bag. "You're in luck." She pulled out a plastic bag of thumbprint cookies and fished a few out for Erny. Erny ate them in a flash.

"Can I go exploring?' he said, looking curiously at the forest that edged the hill and the narrow beach.

"I guess we could take a little walk. We need to collect some twigs and branches for our fire."

"That's right," he said. "What can we put them in?" He looked around, frowning. Then his face lit up. "I know." He unzipped his sweatshirt and pulled it off. Underneath he was wearing a T-shirt. "We can put them in this."

"Honey, you'll be cold," said Tess.

"It feels better without it on," he insisted.

Tess shook her head. Erny, like all of his schoolmates, went off to school each day, even in the winter, with only a sweatshirt for warmth. Erny always insisted he was warm enough and, she had to admit, he didn't seem to suffer from poor health as a result. She always reminded herself of how her own grandmother, Dawn's mother, used to say that it did a child good to be out in the cold air. Maybe it was true.

"If you're already hot, why do we need a fire?" Tess teased him.

"Ma . . ." Erny wailed at her lack of imagination.

"Okay, okay. That's a good idea you had. We'll put them in the sweatshirt. Turn it inside out so you won't be full of splinters when you put it back on."

As Erny was obediently reversing the sweatshirt, inverting the sleeves, Tess's cell phone began to ring. She pulled it from her jacket pocket and looked at the ID. The Stone Hill Inn. She felt a little anxious throb in her throat. Her mother wasn't one to call without a good reason.

Tess frowned. "I'd better take this." She pushed the button and held it to her ear. "Mom?" she said. "What's up?"

"Tess, you won't believe it," said Dawn.

Erny had gotten up from the table and started filling his hoodie, now a wood carrier, with twigs he was scavenging among the leaves. "Stay where I can see you," said Tess.

Erny nodded and continued his search. Tess watched him for a minute and then returned to her call. "Won't believe what?" she asked.

"Nelson Abbott," Dawn said.

Tess frowned. "What about him?"

Dawn hesitated. "They let him go."

Tess went rigid. "Let him go? When?"

"Last night, apparently. I just heard it from a reporter who called here. The lawyer, that Ramsey fellow whom Edith hired, said there was something wrong with the evidence and he got the judge to go along with it. The judge said Nelson was free to go. They're not going to arrest him."

"I don't understand. They have the DNA," she protested. "What more do they need?"

"That's all I know, honey. Nelson's attorney convinced them."

Goddamn him, Tess thought, picturing Ben Ramsey's ice blue eyes. He had found his loophole. "I guess I must have violated Nelson's civil rights somehow. I mean, what's more important? The way the DNA was obtained or the fact that he killed my sister?"

"I don't know, Tess," Dawn said wearily. "I'm not a lawyer."

Tess's mind was roiling. She understood that there were legal procedures that had to be respected, but now that they knew he was guilty, couldn't the police have held Nelson Abbott until they obtained evidence through other, more . . . traditional means? Besides, Tess was pretty sure that private citizens were allowed to do things that the police couldn't do. Private citizens could tape phone calls and it wasn't called wiretapping or entrapment. Surely this was the same kind of thing?

"Tess?" Dawn asked.

"I'm here," said Tess. "Yes. All right, look. We're coming back. Erny's not going to like it, but . . ."

Her gaze swept the beach but he was not there. Not enough twigs, she told herself. Not enough twigs on the beach. He must have gone up to the edge of the woods. All of a sudden, from the direction of the woods, she heard an inchoate shout. To her ears, in her gut, it sounded like Erny calling for her. Tess glanced around, telling herself it was her imagination. Then, clearly, she heard a wailing sound and the thud of a car door or a trunk slamming.

"Erny?" she cried.

"What is it?" Dawn was asking on the phone, hearing the panic in her daughter's voice.

"I'll call you back," said Tess. She snapped the phone shut and began to run. "Erny," she screamed. "Erny, where are you? Answer me this minute!"

There was a sound of an engine revving and tires screeching.

"Erny?"

No, she thought. No. Be here. Call out to me. Jump out from behind a tree. Scare me. "Erny!" she screamed. She ran up the hill, stumbling, crying out for him, looking around. She plunged into the woods and toward the trail that led to the campsites. There was no sign of a car, but there was dust in the air and pines and bits of leaves drifting back to earth where a car had pulled away.

"Erny, where are you?" she screamed. But he did not answer. She looked all around her, but it all looked the same. Pine needles and dead leaves among certain bushes and trees still strangely green though winter was nearly here.

"Erny." She kicked through the leaves, rushing first one way and then another, looking up the trail helplessly for some sign of him.

"Oh my God," Tess wailed, but it came out as a squeak. No, no. It can't be. He's hiding. He's here. She started back toward the beach, trying another path. Her heart was pounding hard and she stumbled, landing against a boulder as the toe of her boot kicked into something soft and heavy. Something that gave way, moved.

She looked down and saw what she had kicked. A hand lay open, fingers curled. Tess clapped her hand over her mouth to stifle the scream and steadied herself against the boulder. She jumped back from the boulder and then forced herself to go around it to look. It was a man, lying on the ground among the dead leaves. His eyes were open, but he was not alive. She could see that instantly. Under his head was blood, sticking to the leaves, running down into his neck matting his short, graying haircut. Nelson Abbott, his mouth hanging open, as if in surprise at the suddenness of his own death.

Beside him was the beginning of a hole. A trough someone had started to dig. A grave, left half-finished, as if the digger had been interrupted in mid-task.

"Oh my God," she breathed. "Oh my God." She looked up from the murdered man's face, looked around at the trees that rustled in the gentle breeze. "Erny?"

And then, before she could even formulate the next question in her mind, her gaze landed on a hapless bundle just beyond the boulder. And the sight of it was more horrible to her than the sight of any bloody dead man. Of any ten men with their heads smashed in. For there, tossed aside on the ground by someone who didn't know or care what they were discarding, lay a hooded sweatshirt, tied in a bundle, half-filled with twigs.

CHAPTER 22

The uniformed officer held a wadded sweatshirt in his gloved hands and pressed it to the nose of the leashed hound. The black dog jerked his head back and then forward again into the cloth, then nervously stepped away from the proffered sweatshirt, straining at his lead. "Okay, Diablo," said the handler. "Find it." The dog took off, sniffing the ground and the tree trunks, pulling his handler toward the deep woods.

Tess shook her head. "We're wasting time," she insisted. "He's not in the woods. He would hear me calling for him. He'd come back. Don't you see that?"

Rusty Bosworth crossed his arms over his broad chest and squinted into the trees. "Boys get lost in these woods all the time. If he's out there, we'll find him." The dirt roads that ran through the campground were clogged with police vehicles and the ATVs of volunteers who had fanned out to search for Erny. Members of the press were being kept back behind a police line, but there was a constant hum of chatter from their direction.

"I told you what happened. Erny must have witnessed . . . something," Tess cried, unable to keep her tone rational. "Whoever killed Nelson Abbott took Erny. My son's life is in danger."

Chief Bosworth assessed Tess coolly. "Well, now, that's your idea of what happened, but it could be completely wrong. I mean, you know from past experience that your version of events can be . . . inaccurate."

"How dare you?" Tess exploded. "My son is missing and you—"

Rusty raised a hand. "Calm down. I'm agreeing with you. To a point. Your boy may have seen something, panicked, and took off running into these woods. Dropped his sweatshirt as he ran."

"I heard him scream," Tess cried. She was almost screaming herself and her face was white with the strain. "I heard the car tearing away. The tires screeching."

"Well, we only have your word for that, Miss DeGraff. You claim that when you found Nelson Abbott, he was already dead. But I have to consider all the possibilities. Now, you say there was a car, but what if there wasn't? What if you asked Nelson Abbott to meet you here and things got ugly. After all, you were so sure he was involved in the death of your sister."

My sister, Tess thought, looking helplessly around the woods, the campsite, the path to the beach. The same nightmare, in the same place. But this time it was her son who was taken. This time it was Erny.

"Excuse me, Chief, can I have a word?" asked a gray-haired man with glasses dressed in coveralls.

Rusty turned away to speak to the crime scene expert. Just as he did so, his phone rang and, after looking at the caller ID, Rusty took the call, turning his back on Tess. When he finished his call, he spoke again to the gray-haired man in coveralls. The expression on Bosworth's face darkened with every word he heard. Finally, clearing his throat, Rusty nodded and turned back to Tess. "All right. I'm gonna be upfront with you. The head of my forensic team here tells me that Nelson Abbott did not die on this spot. He was already dead when he was placed here."

"Of course, he was already dead," Tess cried. "Someone was trying to dig him a grave. Can't you see that?"

Rusty ignored her angry tone. "That would tend to corroborate your story about the car. The fact that he was brought here and dumped. Also we've determined that the estimated time of death seems to coincide with the time when you were renting the canoe over on the other side of the lake. I had a man check out your version of events. That was him on the phone. Apparently the old man with the canoes said your story was true. So this pretty much lets you off as a suspect."

"A suspect?" Tess cried in disbelief.

"Don't act so surprised, Miss DeGraff. You were very angry at Nelson Abbott . . ."

Tess stared at him, but did not respond.

"But you were not the only one. Your brother, Jake, also publicly accused the deceased of being your sister's killer. He had to be dragged away from the press conference, he was making such a fuss."

"Jake was upset," Tess insisted.

"He was more than upset. He looked mad enough to kill," said Rusty. "Now, I've sent a couple of officers to pick up Jake for questioning. Once we catch up with him, we'll know more."

"You're accusing Jake of snatching his own nephew? That's absurd," Tess cried.

"Is it really?" said the chief, his eyes flashing angrily.

A squad car roared into the clearing and stopped. The driver got out and came around to the passenger side. He opened the door and Edith Abbott struggled to climb out. The young officer took Edith's arm and helped her over to where the body of Nelson Abbott lay under a gray tarp. Rusty walked over to her.

"Aunt Edith," he said. "You might want to wait to see him until they've cleaned him up a little bit. Uncle Nelson doesn't look too good right now."

"I want to see him," said Edith stubbornly.

Rusty nodded to the bespectacled man in the coveralls, who crouched down and pulled back a corner of the tarp.

Edith Abbott stared down impassively at her husband's battered head. Then she looked up at Rusty, blinking behind her glasses. "Who killed him?" she said.

Rusty shook his head. "I don't know yet, Aunt Edith. We'll find out."

Edith looked over at Tess. "Her?" she asked.

Rusty frowned. "Like I said, we don't know yet. After his lawyer got him out, what did he say to you? Did he say anything to you today about where he was going?"

Edith stared down at the covered body, appearing slightly dazed. She shook her head for a moment. Then she looked around the clearing, now filled with police vehicles and the cluster of reporters gathered in the area, which the police had roped off for the press. "He was going to the newspaper," she said, her voice trembling. "To talk to him," she said, looking directly at Chan Morris, who, thanks to his local connections, was standing in the front row of the crowd of journalists.

Rusty Bosworth collared one of his officers. "Get Channing Morris," he said. "Bring him over here."

The officer went over and indicated to Chan Morris that he should climb under the rope. Chan pointed to himself, puzzled, and the officer nodded. Chan bent down and ducked under the rope. Then he walked over to where the chief was standing with Edith Abbott.

"Chief," said Chan.

Rusty Bosworth did not acknowledge the greeting. "Mrs Abbott here tells us that Nelson Abbott was on his way to the paper to see you when she saw him last."

Chan's gray eyes looked pained. "Well, yes, he did come to see me."

"What about?" Rusty asked.

Chan grimaced. "He wanted me to know that he was cleared of all charges. He threatened to sue me for the article in the morning paper. The article that said that Miss DeGraff implicated him in the murder of her sister."

Edith Abbott let out a low moan. "How could you? How could you, Channing Morris, after all those years Nelson worked for your family? You should be ashamed of yourself."

"I'm sorry, Mrs Abbott. It was a big story. I had to do my job," said Chan. "Obviously, I made a mistake."

Rusty glanced at Tess, who looked back at him defiantly.

"Anyway, he wanted me to print him an apology," said Chan. "Especially since the lawyer had proved it wasn't him who did it."

"He proved no such thing," Tess cried. "Nelson was freed on some kind of technicality."

Rusty turned on her. "You're talking about something you don't know anything about." He turned back to Chan. "What did you say?" Rusty asked.

Chan shrugged. "I said I would do it. Print an apology."

"And that was it?" Rusty said.

Chan shook his head. "He implied that he knew who really killed Phoebe DeGraff."

The muscles in Rusty's jaw twitched. "Who?"

Chan shook his head. "He didn't say."

"You didn't ask him?"

"I asked him," said Chan.

"Did he tell you?" Rusty asked. And then he shook his head, answering his own question. "He wouldn't tell you," said Rusty in steely disbelief.

Chan stuck out his chin defiantly.

"Don't play games with me, Morris. If you know who did this," said Rusty, glowering, "you'd better speak up. And don't give me any of that journalistic integrity bullshit or I'll throw your ass in jail."

"Do you know who has my son?" Tess screamed, lunging at Chan. "Do you? If you do . . ."

Rusty and another officer reached out and held her back.

Chan looked from the chief to Tess gravely. Then he shook his head. "Believe me, if I could help you, Tess, I would."

Rusty looked at Chan in disgust. "He doesn't know anything. He wants to look important." He poked a finger in Chan's chest. "Get back behind that rope," he said. "Stop pretending you're a journalist."

As Chan was unceremoniously escorted back behind the police line, Rusty turned to his aunt, who was sneaking furtive glances at the body of her husband, as if she felt as if it were wrong to look at him.

"Aunt Edith, do you know anything about this?" he asked. "Did Uncle Nelson tell you who he believed was the guilty party?"

Edith Abbott's shoulders slumped and she shook her head. "He always believed that Lazarus was guilty. Now I hear that he had another idea. I don't know. He didn't say so to me. But then again, he never did tell me much," she explained. "He had a secretive nature."

Rusty beckoned to another officer. "Find out where my uncle went after he left the newspaper offices. There has to be somebody who'd seen him. And let me know as soon as you get a line on Jake DeGraff."

Tess felt as if a vise were tightening around her head. Her son had been kidnapped and these people were standing around talking. "What are you doing?" she shrieked. "Why won't you listen to me? My son is not with my brother. He was taken by whoever was driving this car. We have to find the car. Look," she strode past the people who were gathering evidence and pointed to the dirt path. "There are tire tracks here. Someone should be following them. Someone has to have seen the car." She began to head down the road that led to the clearing. "If we follow these tracks . . ."

"Tess," a familiar voice cried. Tess looked up and saw Dawn, who had just arrived, waving frantically to her from behind the police lines.

At the same moment, Rusty Bosworth grabbed Tess roughly by the upper arm. "You could be destroying evidence. Get out of the way and let us do our jobs."

Tess jerked her arm free from his grasp and rubbed it with her other hand. "Your job is to find my son." She pointed behind her. "You've sent half your people out into the woods and my son is not out there. He did not run away. You're wasting precious time asking questions about Nelson Abbott's death. I know he was your uncle, but since when is a dead body more urgent than a missing child? You should let someone else take over. Someone whose priorities aren't all messed up."

Rusty Bosworth glared at her, his face red. "When I want your advice about how to handle things, I'll ask for it," he said. "There's your mother. Go home with her. When we have something to tell you, I'll let you know."

CHAPTER 23

"Stop the car, Mother," Tess cried, glimpsing a hiker on a neighboring trail. "Maybe this guy knows something."

Dawn glanced in her rearview mirror as her car bounced along the rutted, dirt road. Her face was chalk white and impassive. "All right," she said.

Tess leaped from the car and began to stumble through the brambles, calling out to the young man on a nearby trail who was wearing a backpack and a knitted hat with earflaps.

The young man stopped and looked up at the frantic woman who was crashing through the woods in his direction.

"Help me!" Tess cried. "I need your help. Did you see a car with a young boy in it coming along this trail maybe — I don't know — an hour ago? Probably going very fast?"

The hiker, who had a tufted beard and mild eyes, shook his head and his earflaps rose and fell. "The cops already stopped me and asked me. I told them I wasn't on this trail. I was on the other side of the lake forty minutes ago. I didn't see anybody over there."

Tess's small flicker of hope was doused by his words. "Are you sure?"

"Yeah. What's going on anyway?"

Tess shook her head. "Never mind."

"Wish I could help," the young man said.

"Thanks." Tess trudged back to her mother's idling car and slid into the front seat.

"Nothing?" Dawn asked.

Tess shook her head and pressed her face against the car window, trying to peer through it into the curtain of bare branches and evergreens, dense and twisted, that stretched as far as the eye could see. "How will I ever find him?" she asked. "Nelson Abbott is dead."

"I know," said Dawn.

"I thought it was Nelson, but it wasn't. There's another killer."

"I guess so," said Dawn.

Tess turned and looked at her mother. "Where is Kenneth Phalen today, Mother?"

Dawn yelped in dismay. "Ken!"

"Yes, Ken," Tess cried. "Why should he be above suspicion? He was around when Phoebe was killed. His own daughter was a suicide at that same age. All of a sudden, after all these years, he shows up here out of the blue—"

"Tess," Dawn cried. "Stop. Just stop it."

Tess fell silent.

"Sweetheart, I know you're desperate. I know exactly how you feel. But it's not going to help to make a scapegoat out of that poor man."

Tess glanced over at her mother's sagging profile as she drove through the woods. Dawn had been through this same ordeal once before in her life. "How can you go through this, Mother?" Tess asked. "Again?"

"Don't think like that. It's not the same. It's different these days. When a child disappears, the FBI gets involved right away . . . it's not going to end that same way. It can't," Dawn said, keeping her eyes fixed on the narrow road.

Tess looked back out the window as the car crept along the road leading out of the woods. Erny. She wanted to call out his name, but she knew that he would not answer. He was with Nelson Abbott's killer. Whoever it was who had come to the forest to bury Nelson had snatched Erny, not as part of a plan, but impulsively. She could only pray that Nelson's killer was not someone who would hurt a child.

"The DNA proved that Nelson was guilty," said Tess. "But somebody killed Nelson. Somebody who was desperate."

Dawn nodded with a distant look in her eyes.

Tess sighed, rolled down the window, and leaned her head out. She knew it was futile but she had to do something to relieve the pain in her heart. She began to scream Erny's name.

* * *

When they got back to the inn, another car had already pulled into the parking area and two men who were clearly not guests were getting out of it. One man pulled a transmitter from inside his wind-breaker and began to speak into it. "The police are here," said Tess. Dawn nodded agreement. "I'm going to ask them to keep the reporters away," she said.

Tess didn't even wait for Dawn to pull into her parking spot. She asked her mother to stop near the front door. She jumped out of the car and went inside, not looking up when reporters called her name. She hung up her jacket and went through the inn, to the phone in the kitchen. She had to speak to someone who could explain to her how it was possible that Nelson Abbott had been set free. Obviously, she was not going to call Ben Ramsey. She called Chief Fuller, whose number was written on a pad by the phone. His daughter-in-law answered on the second ring. Tess identified herself and asked to speak to the former chief.

"He's can't come to the phone," said Mary Anne.

"Can you have him call me?" Tess asked hopefully.

"No, he won't be calling anyone. He can't talk. He had a terrible night. He's, um . . . we had to put him on hospice care this morning."

"Hospice!" Tess exclaimed.

"You knew he was sick," Mary Anne said accusingly.

"I know. But I didn't realize he was that bad."

"Well, he is," said Mary Anne in an angry tone.

"Is he there? Is he at home?"

"Yes, he's at home," Mary Anne said indignantly. "But he's extremely weak. He can't talk on the phone. Now leave the man in peace." Without waiting for Tess to reply, she hung up the phone.

For one moment, shaken by this news about Chief Fuller, Tess forgot about why she had called. And then, instantly, it returned to her, like a stabbing pain in her own heart. Erny.

She came out of the kitchen and into the hallway. Her mother was standing between the two casually dressed men she had seen in the parking lot. One was short with dark hair and a mustache and the other was a large overweight man with small porcine eyes.

"Miss DeGraff?" said the dark-haired man. "I'm Chuck Virgilio. This is my partner, Mac Swain. Chief Bosworth sent us over. We sent the press jackals packing like your mother asked us to. I don't know how long they'll stay away, but . . . for the moment . . ."

Tess nodded. "Thanks."

"We'll be monitoring your phones in case anyone calls about . . . ransom."

Tess's knees felt like jelly. "Ransom."

"Don't get me wrong. We're still betting your son got lost in the woods. The search party is going to keep on looking for him. But meanwhile, we're covering this end. Believe me, I understand how stressed out you are. I'm a parent myself. Anything we can do to help, we will."

"Thank you," said Tess.

"I'm here to help, too, if I can."

Tess turned around and saw Ben Ramsey emerging from the library. Tess stared at him, too shocked to speak.

"Listen, I heard about Erny's disappearance," said Ben. "I had to come."

"You've got a lot of nerve," she said.

"Why don't we step outside," Ben said. "You look like you could use the fresh air." He pulled her jacket from a hook in the foyer and offered it to her.

Tess snatched it from his hand. "Please leave," she said.

"Tess, come outside for a minute," said Ben in a low voice. "I really need to talk to you."

"You heard the lady. You'd better clear out of here, Counselor," said Officer Virgilio. "Get going."

"Okay, I'm leaving," said Ben to the police officers. "Tess. Two minutes. Please. I may be able to help you."

"If you know anything pertinent to this case, Mr Ramsey," said the larger officer, Officer Swain, in a menacing tone, "you'd better tell us about it right now."

"That's right," said Tess. "If you have any idea where Erny is . . ."

Ben shook his head. "Of course I would tell you. Immediately. Please, Tess. I just want a word with you. Come outside with me."

"I don't want to go outside," Tess complained. "It's cold. And I need to be here if Erny calls or—"

"I'll come get you right away," said Dawn. "Go ahead and talk to him. Just stay close by."

Tess saw the intense expression in her mother's eyes and realized that Dawn was not making a suggestion. It was more like a command. Tess sighed and then threw on the jacket Ben had handed her. "Two minutes," she said. She opened the door, walked out, and stood on the granite stone of the entryway. She heard Ben step out and close the door carefully behind him. Tess gazed past the circular gravel driveway to the wooded lane bounded by a stone wall. With the reporters gone, it was the image of peace and tranquility. It was the kind of picturesque view that drew people to New England. Historic and unchanging. A fairy-tale place. A mirage. "All right, what is it?" she said without looking at Ben.

"Come and sit down," he said.

He indicated the pair of wooden, church-pewlike benches, painted the same green as the shutters, that flanked the front door. Behind each one was a white wooden lattice screen that extended up to the low overhanging roof. In summer, roses grew on the lattice. Now, in late October, there were only brown vines. Tess hesitated, but she could not resist. She did feel wobbly on her legs. She sat. He sat beside her. She still did not look at him. It was chilly sitting on the wooden bench. She shivered and jammed her hands into her pockets.

"Look, I know you're angry with me . . ." he began.

Tess turned and looked at him. His silver hair glinted, even in the gloom of the afternoon. And his frowning eyes seemed to refract light like a prism. "Do you think so?" she said.

"I'd like to explain to you what happened," he said.

"No, I'll tell you what happened," said Tess. "You got Nelson Abbott sprung on some technicality and somebody killed him and tried to dump his body. And in the process, that person kidnapped my son. My son is with a murderer. For all I know . . ." She tried to continue, but her voice broke. She wiped her eyes angrily and looked away.

Ben ignored her tears. His voice remained calm and matter-of-fact. "Look, I know you want to blame someone, but I had no way of predicting this. And I'm as sorry about it as I can be. Both for you and for Nelson."

"Nelson Abbott?" she cried. "You feel sorry for him?"

"Tess, it was not some technicality, as you'd like to think, that exonerated him."

"Sorry. I meant to say 'constitutional protection,'" Tess said sarcastically. "The rights of the accused. I know all about it. You found out that I obtained that hat with Nelson's DNA without telling him. Went into his house and walked out with his filthy hat. I can just imagine your righteous indignation. I'm surprised you didn't have the cops arrest me."

Ben shook his head, but did not respond.

Tess pointed a shaking finger at him. "The police were doing nothing. Somebody had to trap Nelson Abbott in his lies. When I brought the hat to Chief Fuller, he said it would be okay. And it was, until Nelson hired you — the crackerjack lawyer. It's your job to find loopholes. And you seem to be very good at it. Anybody that tries to hurt my family, you find them an out." She could feel her cheeks flaming, and she knew very well that it was unreasonable to impugn him for doing his job, but she felt helplessly furious with him.

Ben's expression did not change. "Stop it, Tess," he said firmly. "I'll explain to you what really happened, if you will listen. I think you might want to hear this. It's important."

Tess stuck out her chin defiantly, but remained quiet.

Ben spoke in a low urgent voice. "While Nelson was being questioned, I asked for, and was given access to, the DNA results that supposedly implicated him. I'm sure Bosworth thought that it would just look like a jumble of numbers to me, but I've had a lot of experience with DNA evidence. And what I saw in those results set off alarm bells in me. I had another lab — a highly reputable lab — check them for me. The lab I sent it to said that the results did not match Nelson's DNA."

Tess shook her head. "That's crap. Chief Fuller's guy said that they did match. Why would he lie about it?"

Ben sighed. "Chief Fuller was trying to help you, but he went too far. His friend at the lab gave him a shabby report that said what Aldous Fuller wanted to believe."

"It's science. He said the sample matched Nelson's!" Tess cried.

"When in fact," Ben corrected her, "the sample only had some markers in it that matched Nelson's. The sample did not match perfectly."

Tess shook her head. "You're splitting hairs. Goddammit! Everybody knows that the sample from Phoebe's case was deteriorated. After all these years of being stored under less-than-ideal conditions . . . it never was going to be perfect. But it was enough. It was enough to get Lazarus 'exonerated,' as you say. I notice you had no problem with that."

Ben shook his head. "That's different. In that case, there were *no* markers that matched Lazarus. He was ruled out completely by the DNA."

"Ruled out. Exonerated. What's the difference? The guy from Chief Fuller's lab was able to match it to Nelson."

Ben explained in a patient tone. "Listen to me. Nelson was Lazarus's stepfather. They weren't actually related. There was no match to Lazarus. But the sample *did* have markers that matched Nelson's. It also had markers that didn't."

Tess peered at him. "What does that mean?"

"I'm saying that a person's DNA sample is always going to be a perfect match of itself. No extra markers. No differences. A perfect match. My lab guy found other markers."

"Then they were Phoebe's cells," she said.

Ben shook his head. "No. My guy checked for that. It was not Nelson who was in league with Lazarus. It was not Nelson who killed Phoebe," Ben said. "It wasn't. That's not speculation. It's fact."

"NO," Tess wailed in protest. "How could the sample be mistaken for Nelson's? What are the chances of that happening? Are you saying that the guy at the state lab lied deliberately? Why would he do that? It makes no sense."

"No. I'm not saying that he lied. There *were* markers that matched."

Tess shook her head. "I'm utterly confused. What the hell are you saying? Some markers matched by coincidence?"

"Not at all," said Ben. "Not coincidence. It wasn't Nelson who killed Phoebe. But it *was* someone related to him."

Tess stared at his grave face and felt her heart flip over like an acrobat on a trapeze. She was not exactly sure of the implications, but she understood the central point. "Related to him?"

Ben nodded. "I was with Nelson when the report came in. It wasn't until I explained the science to him that the light dawned. I could see it in his eyes. Something suddenly made sense to him that had never made sense to him before. I tried to get him to tell me, but he absolutely refused. But he'd realized the truth. And I think it got him killed," said Ben.

Tess was shivering as she considered what he had just told her. Then she had another thought. "Nelson had no children," Tess said, looking into Ben's intelligent crystalline eyes.

Ben glanced at the front door of the inn, which was still tightly shut. Then he looked back into Tess's eyes. "He has a nephew," Ben said.

CHAPTER 24

Tess's heart lurched in her chest. "Chief Bosworth?" she whispered.

"Rusty Bosworth is the son of Nelson's sister."

"He's the chief of police," said Tess.

Ben gazed at her somberly. "That's why I wanted to talk to you out here, where we wouldn't be overheard," he said.

Tess clutched the sleeve of his jacket as if to steady herself. "Are you saying you think he could have done these things . . . ?" she whispered.

"I don't know, Tess. What I do know is that we can't go to the local police with our suspicions."

"Who can we go to?"

Ben frowned. "Well, the state police or the FBI. I have to tread carefully, though. We need proof. Not conjecture."

Tess shook her head as if she could not take it in. "Are there any other siblings. Cousins?"

"Well, we need to find out before we start accusing the police chief," said Ben.

Tess looked at him with keen, troubled eyes. "I don't get it. Why are you helping me now? Why did you come here and tell me this?" she asked.

Tess saw the blush which moved up his neck to his cheeks.

"Because it's you," he said. "It's your son." He turned and looked her directly in the eyes. "Because it seems like you are all I think about these days."

Tess looked at him in amazement. Before she could form a reply, a white truck came rumbling down the gravel driveway and pulled up in front of the inn. Jake jumped out of the driver's seat. He opened the van doors, pulled out a long stick, and came walking toward Tess and Ben.

"Hey, Tess," Jake said with a forced heartiness. "Are you speaking to me yet? Tell Erny I'm here. I brought back his fishing pole." Jake looked fondly, and with a certain pride, at the pole he was holding. "He did a good job. Clever little guy. Look how he made it. He used a garden stake, a piece of twine. He even put a lure on it," said Jake, plinking his thumb and forefinger against the piece of metal tied to the end of the line.

Tess stood up and stared at her brother. All her anger at him melted away at the sight of his familiar face. "Jake, where have you been? You don't know what happened?" she asked.

Jake stood the pole up carefully against the lattice behind the bench and looked at Tess warily. "No. After I picked up the fishing pole I had to drive to North Conway for supplies. Why? What happened?"

Ben stood up also and put a protective hand on Tess's shoulder. "Erny has . . . disappeared," he said. "We think he was abducted by Nelson Abbott's killer."

"What?" Jake yelped. "Killer . . . ? Wait a minute. Nelson was killed? Who did it? How did they get ahold of Erny?"

Tess saw the genuine bewilderment in her brother's eyes. She needed to back up and explain. "This morning, we took a canoe ride to the beach at the campground. Erny and me. Someone had dumped Nelson's body there. He was getting ready to bury it, we think. Anyway, Erny went into the woods, looking for twigs . . . and he must have seen . . ." Tess dissolved into tears. She shook her head, unable to continue.

"Jesus, Tess . . ." Jake rushed to his sister, wrapping his arms around her. Tess huddled against her brother's broad familiar shoulder. She felt his empathy, his support, as he enfolded her. He only wanted to comfort her. Not, she thought ruefully, to berate her for letting Erny out of her sight, the way she had berated him for the same sin only a day earlier. It would never have occurred to him to do that, she realized, as a sob escaped from her throat.

Before Tess could regain her composure and tell him she was sorry, there was the sound of a siren's wail and the roar of a car engine. A black-and-white police car, its roof light flashing, rounded the curve of the driveway and sped into the circle in front of the inn. It squealed to a stop behind Jake's truck, spraying gravel to the sides of its wheels. Another siren could already be heard coming toward them down the driveway. The front door of the inn opened and the plainclothes officers who had been in the hallway came outside, with Dawn following hard on their heels.

Two officers jumped from the first car, guns drawn and approaching cautiously.

"Jake DeGraff?" said the first uniformed officer who had emerged from the car.

Jake let go of Tess and looked at the police, perplexed. "Yeah," he said. "I'm Jake DeGraff."

A second police car roared up beside the first and stopped short. Two more policemen got out and waited by their car.

"What the hell?" said Jake.

"Your truck was spotted on the road into town heading in this direction. Do you have the boy?" the second cop from the squad car asked.

"What boy?" Jake asked, incredulous.

"Your nephew. Erny."

"Of course I don't have him. I just found out he's been kidnapped!"

"We have orders to bring you in for questioning, sir, in the murder of Nelson Abbott," said the first uniformed officer.

"I didn't kill that son of a bitch," Jake protested.

Chuck Virgilio, the plainclothes cop with the mustache, said, "You'll have to go with them, Mr DeGraff."

Jake looked at Tess. "Tess, tell them. I didn't even know Abbott was dead . . ."

Tess appealed to Officer Virgilio. "My brother couldn't have done this. He wouldn't have taken Erny. It's Erny you should be looking for. Every minute that goes by, my son's life is in danger."

"Sorry, ma'am," said the uniformed cop from the patrol car. "We have orders to pick your brother up. He threatened the murder victim within earshot of a lot of people. So we are going to bring him in. Are you going to come with us voluntarily, Mr DeGraff, or do I have to arrest you?"

Dawn, who had been standing quietly by, watching with huge haunted eyes, suddenly approached the officer with raised fists and began to shout. "Stop this! Now! Leave my son alone. Why are you people persecuting us?"

The officer turned on her. "You'd better calm down or you'll find yourself down at the station, too."

"Watch how you talk to my mother," Jake warned him.

"No, Jake. Don't. I'm all right," said Dawn.

Ben took a step toward Jake and spoke in a low quick voice. "Jake, go with the police," said Ben. "Don't make trouble. I'll come with you."

"Who are you?" Jake demanded.

"Ben Ramsey. I'm an attorney."

The light of recognition dawned in Jake's eyes. "Ramsey. You're the one who was working for . . . who got Lazarus . . ." Jake sputtered. "You were the one who was defending Nelson."

Tess grabbed her brother's arm and spoke quickly into his angry suspicious face. "Let him help you, Jake."

"What are you talking about, Tess? This is the enemy."

"No, Jake, listen. He knows . . . what we're up against." Tess exchanged a serious glance with Ben. "Someone . . . could be looking for a scapegoat. Don't let them use my brother, okay?"

Ben nodded, unsmiling, understanding exactly what she meant. "Nothing will get by me," he said. "I promise you."

"Mr DeGraff," said one of the uniformed cops. "You can go peacefully or we'll put these cuffs on you. Your call."

"Jake, we'll go down there with them and I'm sure in no time we can straighten this out," said Ben. "There has to be someone who remembers seeing you in North Conway. Or a surveillance camera tape. Don't worry. We'll corroborate your alibi."

"Alibi? Why do I need an alibi?"

"Mr DeGraff," the cop snapped.

"Jake," said Tess. "Let Ben help you. He's the best at what he does. Who knows that better than us?"

"All right. All right," said Jake irritably. "But this is just crap."

"I'd come, too, but . . . Erny," said Tess. "Someone might call."

"I'm going with him," Dawn insisted. "I'm going with my son."

"No. Mom, stay with Tess," said Jake. "I'll be okay. I didn't do anything wrong. Call Julie. She's at work. Tell her about this. Go on, Mom. You call her. I'll be fine."

As the uniformed officers led Jake to the squad car, Officer Virgilio opened the door of the inn for Dawn. Dawn marched past him without acknowledging his gesture.

"Tess," said Ben. "I'll be back with your brother as soon as I can. You sit tight. Don't worry. We're going to get Erny back."

Tess nodded numbly and watched as the uniformed officers accompanied Jake and nudged him into the backseat of the patrol car. Ben quickly ducked into his car and fired up the engine.

Tess watched them leave the driveway in a caravan, headed for the police station. Standing alone in the driveway, she began to shiver uncontrollably. She felt as if she were coming apart inside, fracturing into a thousand pieces. No, she told herself. NO. Keep it together. If Ben's theory was right, the police could be working against her, covering up for their chief. One thing was for sure. She could not wait around here, hoping the police would rescue her son. Even if they weren't in collusion with the chief, the last person they would ever treat as a suspect was Chief Bosworth. You have to do it, she thought. You have to do something.

Tess's heart was thudding and her insides were ajitter. Get a grip, she thought. This isn't helping. She wanted to just collapse in a heap on the gravel driveway and hide her head in her arms. Stop it, she thought. Concentrate. She forced herself to think about the DNA results and Rusty Bosworth. Could the police chief have hidden her son somewhere? If he did, she thought, trying to find a shred of hope, maybe that gave her a little time. At least Erny might be safe for the moment. The chief would be in the public eye all day because of this high-profile murder of Nelson Abbott. If she could find his house, maybe she would find her son there. Tess fumbled in her jacket pocket and found her cell phone. She dialed information and asked for Chief Bosworth's number. "It's on . . . Maple Road," she said, fabricating an address, hoping the operator would supply the correct address.

While Tess waited for the operator to respond, her thoughts raced. Could Rusty Bosworth have been the long-ago accomplice of Lazarus Abbott? They were cousins, close in age. Summers, they worked together, helping Nelson. In a way, it made sense.

The operator came back on the line. "I'm sorry, that number is unlisted."

"Unlisted? No. It's very important . . ."

The operator clicked off, leaving Tess staring at her phone. Don't panic, she told herself. Someone will know. Julie, she thought. Quickly she punched Jake's number on her directory. In a moment, she heard Julie's voice sounding frantic.

"What is going on, Tess? I'm talking to your mother on the other line. Dawn said that Jake has been arrested! For taking Erny? That's insane. How could they possibly think that Jake would do that? To his own nephew?"

Tess couldn't take the time to speculate. "Jake will be all right. He has an attorney with him. Listen, I need your help."

"I've got to get to the police station, Tess."

"Julie, listen to me. I need you to help me. Where does Chief Bosworth live?"

"Rusty Bosworth? What's that got to do with anything?"

"Julie, you know everybody in this town. Where does he live?"

"I don't know. He and Charmaine had a house but they separated and he moved out. I don't know where he lives now. Look in the phone book."

"I tried information. He's unlisted."

"Tess, what is this all about?"

"Julie, can you help me or not?" Tess demanded.

"I don't know," said Julie. "Ask Charmaine. She has a place on Main Street. A massage place. She'll know."

Immediately Tess realized why the unusual name sounded familiar. She remembered Jake pointing out the massage parlor to her and making a joke about Rusty Bosworth's wife. "Right," said Tess. "They're divorced. Right?"

"Separated," said Julie. "I have to go, Tess."

"Okay. Thanks, Julie." Charmaine would know where her estranged husband lived, Tess thought. She would also know if Rusty had any other blood relations who might fit the DNA profile. "What's her place called?"

"Stressless," said Julie. "It's called Stressless."

CHAPTER 25

A flutelike bell tinkled as Tess opened the door to Stressless. Water burbled and circulated over shiny stones in a round fountain in the window and the walls of the small space, painted a soothing celadon green, were decorated with framed Zen koans, photos of dew-laden blossoms on a branch against an out-of-focus background, and Japanese drawings of cranes, snowcapped mountains, and high-rising ocean waves with red Japanese characters running down the sides of each picture. A CD of tuneless music plunked on a stringed instrument played softly in the background. A square woven basket full of pamphlets about yoga classes, AIDS, and women's health issues sat on the blond wood counter, which was obviously the reception desk, though it was unmanned at the moment. A light fixture and a fan hung from a stained, dropped ceiling, marring the otherwise clean and soothing effect of the space.

There were no customers seated in the ergonomically correct chairs arrayed around a tatami mat in the waiting area, but Tess could see shadows moving behind a wood-framed standing paper screen at the back of the room. "Hello?" Tess called out.

A trim woman with finely lined skin, Western features, and a skinned-back, dyed blonde bun anchored by a chopstick came out from behind the screen and bowed. Then she smiled benignly at Tess. She was barefoot and wearing a kimono-style jacket and cropped black pants. "Take a seat, why don't you, and just breathe for a while. I'll be with you shortly."

Before Tess could reply, she slipped back behind the screen. "Excuse me," Tess called out. "Are you Charmaine Bosworth?"

"Yes," the woman's voice trilled, at once pleasant and reproving.

Tess could tell that she was clearly disturbing the vibe. "I'm sorry, but I need to talk to you right now."

The woman folded back one panel of the screen. Tess could see that there was someone lying face down on the table, wrapped in a bathsheet-size towel. At first glance, Tess thought it was an adolescent boy whose bruised limbs were flaccid, lacking in muscle tone. Then Tess realized that it had to be a female. A boy would only be wrapped to the waist.

"I am unable to help you right now," said Charmaine firmly.

"It's very important," said Tess. "I wouldn't interrupt otherwise."

"This is a treatment session," said Charmaine, raising her eyebrows and indicating, with an inclination of her head, the wheelchair that was folded against the wall. "Surely it can wait."

"It's all right, Charmaine," said a small raspy voice from the direction of the massage table. "I'm fine for a few minutes." The client turned her head to face Charmaine and Tess recognized the tiny woman on the table. It was Sally Morris, the publisher's wife. For one minute Tess felt fearful that maybe Sally would recognize her or her voice, but she reassured herself that it was unlikely. They had only met briefly at the airport and even though Sally had turned her head on the table, Tess was completely out of her line of sight.

Tess winced at the sight of the woman's wasted body with its assortment of bruises, some fresh and some faded to yellow. Probably from the kind of fall she had taken at the airport. Tess felt a pang of sympathy for the woman's pitiable condition. A desire to speak a kind word to the woman on the table crossed her mind, but Tess instantly dismissed the impulse. It was critical to her plan that she not be recognized. She was relieved when Charmaine Bosworth sighed and adjusted the screen so that Sally was no longer in view. "What is the problem?" she asked.

On the way over, Tess had imagined the possible scenarios of this visit. Already she realized with relief that she was over the most daunting hurdle. Charmaine's cool gaze betrayed no sign that she recognized this intruder. Tess's avoidance of interviews and photographers had proved valuable. Charmaine had no idea that it was Tess DeGraff she was talking to, despite all the media coverage. Besides, Tess thought, Charmaine probably avoided the news to maintain her calm aura. This made Tess's mission that much easier. She knew that asking this woman for the home address of her estranged husband would arouse suspicion. And certainly, there was no normal way to inquire about Rusty Bosworth's blood relations. Tess had thought it over carefully and figured out a way to proceed. Now she put her plan into action. She began with an effusive apology.

Charmaine seemed somewhat appeased. "That's all right. How can I help you?"

"You are Mrs Russell Bosworth?"

"Well. Technically," said Charmaine.

"My name is . . . Terkel. June Terkel. I work for a brokerage house in Boston. We are trying to locate Russell Bosworth."

"What for?" Charmaine asked.

"He, and any siblings or cousins he may have had, have been bequeathed a brokerage account at my firm from a distant relation who never actually knew the family."

"A brokerage account? You mean like stocks and bonds?" Charmaine asked.

"Exactly. We tried to reach him but found that he was no longer at your address."

"We're separated," said Charmaine. "But Rusty's the chief of police. You can find him at the police station most likely."

"Yes, I know that he is. I've left several messages with his sergeant, but your husband has failed to return my calls."

"He's been really busy," said Charmaine.

"I'm afraid he might be ignoring my calls because he thinks I'm trying to contact him about investing money or some such thing. That's why I decided to seek you out. I would prefer to speak to him away from his place of employment. This is really a matter I need to discuss with him privately. Also, I need his address for purposes of correspondence."

Charmaine hesitated. "He doesn't like people knowing where he lives."

"Well, I can understand that," said Tess evenly, though her heart was thudding. This was the critical hurdle. "If you prefer, maybe you could contact him for me and tell him about our conversation."

Charmaine seemed to give the matter some thought. "No. I'd rather he thought I didn't know about it. Is it a lot of money?"

Tess suppressed a sigh of relief. It was going to work. She could see the calculations going on behind Charmaine's eyes. She and Rusty Bosworth were not yet divorced. Community property had not yet been legally divided. Charmaine wanted to give her estranged husband enough rope to hang himself. When, in listing his assets, he failed to mention having this account, she would be able to catch him in a deception in front of the lawyers or the court. Obviously Charmaine was trying to achieve a higher spiritual plane, but when it came to Rusty, she could be as ruthless as any injured spouse.

"It's a considerable sum," said Tess. "Of course, it may have to be divided among a number of people."

"Oh no," said Charmaine. "Rusty has no other family. He had one cousin but he's . . . deceased."

"I see. So Mr Bosworth would be the sole heir."

"Yes," Charmaine said eagerly.

Tess fumbled for a notepad and pen in her purse, trying to conceal both the hope and the distress that this news caused her. No siblings. No cousins. It had to be Rusty Bosworth who had colluded with Lazarus. And it also had to be the police chief who had abducted her son. Tess tried to calm herself, so that her hands wouldn't shake as she wrote in the notepad. "All right," said Tess, "if you could just give me that address."

"He's renting a condo out by the Stone Hill Mountain ski area. Two-fifty-three B Millwood."

"And his home phone?" Tess asked, trying to keep her voice calm as she wrote.

"He doesn't want me to have it," said Charmaine.

"Really," Tess murmured.

"I know. Do you wonder why we're separated?"

"Charmaine," Sally called out softly from behind the screen.

"I'm coming, sweetheart. Are you okay?"

"I'm okay," said Sally. "I just need to turn over."

"I'll help you. Just a sec."

"I won't keep you any longer," said Tess. "Thanks so much for your help."

"Don't bother going over to his place right now," Charmaine advised. "He's got a big case going on. He won't be home till all hours."

"That's fine," Tess said. "Thanks again." She forced herself to smile and make a serene exit, despite the fact that she wanted to take off at a run. The tinkling sounded behind her as Tess closed the door and Charmaine returned to Sally Morris. Now, Tess thought, she had all the information she needed. As she started up Main Street, a shiny black Mercedes pulled into the handicapped parking space in front of Charmaine's storefront. Chan Morris got out, arriving to pick up his wife from her therapy. His soft, black hair was instantly disheveled by the wind and he pushed it back off his face.

Tess averted her gaze and pulled up the collar on her jacket, hurrying up the street toward Kelli's car before Chan saw her. She knew that if he saw her, he would greet her and probably want to start asking questions. She couldn't afford to have her identity revealed to Charmaine, who might glance out the front window and see them talking together. She didn't want Charmaine asking Chan how he knew June Terkel. No, Tess thought. That was not going to happen. She had the information and now she needed to get to her son. Hang on, Erny, she thought. I'm on my way.

CHAPTER 26

The trees along Millwood Road were still ablaze with the last of the autumn leaves. The road had once been a scenic pathway to the summit of Stone Hill Mountain. Now interspersed among the trees, on both sides of the road, were vacation condos built by developers from New York and Boston. From Thanksgiving to March, when snow was on the ground, the Millwood area was abuzz with luxury cars topped by ski racks and colorfully arrayed, well-to-do weekend athletes from out of state. Today, a weekday in late October, showed signs that the area was beginning to awaken. A few of the ski shops had opened and there was some light traffic up and down the mountain, but it was still very quiet.

Tess drove slowly along the winding road. Some of the condos, mainly the newer ones, were designed with a perfunctory nod to the surroundings, with crisscrossed wooden timbers on the facade to suggest ski chalets in the Alps. The most recently built were designed as more businesslike structures with false stucco facades, garages underneath, and even a convenience store incorporated into the complex. 253B Millwood was clearly one of the oldest buildings, functional but not luxurious. It was neither cleanly modern, nor charmingly quaint. It was built in a quad style and had begun to look a little bit shabby. Tess pulled into one of the visitor's parking spaces provided beside the complex and sat, shivering in the warm idling car. Now that she was here, she knew she had to be careful about how she proceeded. It seemed unlikely to her that there would be security cameras or the kind of patrolling that one might find in a newer kind of complex in the Washington, D.C., area, for example. Most people only used these units seasonally and rarely kept anything of value in them except for their ski equipment. Even so, Tess wondered how Rusty was able to procure one of the units for rental, but then she reminded herself that he was the chief of police. He undoubtedly had some influence among the developers of these condo warrens. Influence enough to have a spare unit at his disposal.

Tess looked up at the bland beige building with its cedar shingle roof and windows that overlooked the mountainside. Erny, are you in there? she thought. How did he get you inside without anyone noticing? Or did he take you somewhere else? Somewhere more private, where it would be easier to stash an abducted child.

Tess shook her head. She couldn't think about that. She had to find out about this place first. If she couldn't find her son here, then she would face the worry of where else in this vast area he might be hidden. Right now she had to get inside 253B. She turned off the engine and, feeling the rapid cadence of her own heartbeat, stepped out of the car.

Looking all around to be sure she wasn't seen, she slipped inside the outer door of number 253 to the tiny vestibule where the four mailboxes for the quad of condos were located. She wondered, with a sinking feeling, if anyone was home in any of them, someone who might buzz her in if she pressed their bell. She tried all four buttons, but with no luck. No answering buzz released the catch on the door. Erny, she thought. Are you in there? Can you hear the buzz and know that someone is here and close to finding you? She thought about going around to the back. Maybe if she could figure out which window belonged to the B unit, she could peer in and see something — some sign of her son. She was just about to leave the vestibule when a dirty dented compact car pulled into the parking area and a skinny woman of about forty, dressed in jeans and a sweatshirt, got out. She reached into the backseat of the car for a paper shopping bag and then came toward the vestibule. Tess immediately began to rummage in her bag, as if she were searching for her key. The woman pulled the door open, came in, and smiled at Tess. Her entire face crinkled into folds. "Couldn't be much gloomier out there, could it?" she asked pleasantly.

Tess smiled back. "No, it really couldn't."

The woman inserted her key in the lock and turned it. "Can't find your key?" she said sympathetically.

"I'll find it," said Tess.

The woman shrugged, but did not hold the outer door open for her. She went through and down the hall, carrying her bag. Tess just managed to catch it by shoving her toe in before the door locked shut again. Tess held it open just an inch while she waited for the woman to get into her own apartment. Tess felt her heart hammering as she heard the sound of a door opening and then slamming shut down the hall. Luckily there was no one passing by to see Tess lingering in the vestibule of the quad. After a couple of minutes had passed, Tess thought it was probably safe. She pushed the door open and looked down the hall. There were two doors on each side. The near doors were marked A and D. That meant the far doors were B and C. She walked down the hallway to B and tried the knob. Of course it did not open. From the place next door she could hear a loud humming, as if from an air conditioner or a fan. It created enough white noise to mask her voice. She put her mouth to the door and said, in as loud a voice as she dared, "Erny. Erny, are you in there? Erny, it's Mom. Can you hear me? Can you make a sound?"

There was no reply from inside. Thankfully, though, none of the other doors opened. Tess looked in frustration at the doorknob. How did you unlock a lock? She'd seen people do it in the movies with a bobby pin or a credit card. She had to try. She reached into her purse and pulled out a credit card from her wallet. With trembling hands she inserted it between the door and frame and pulled up. Nothing happened. She tried it again and pulled the credit card out. Then she reached for the doorknob and twisted it in frustration. Still nothing. "Erny," she cried in a low urgent voice, bending toward the crack between door and frame.

The white noise stopped abruptly and Tess straightened up. Then, to her shock, the door of Rusty Bosworth's apartment opened in front of her face. The skinny wrinkled woman from the vestibule was standing there and she started at the sight of Tess.

She put a scrawny hand against her chest. "Oh, you scared me. I thought I heard something, but I had the vacuum going."

Tess was too taken aback to speak for a moment. "I'm sorry. I thought . . . I mean, I thought that . . . Rusty Bosworth . . ."

"Oh, sorry. I'm Vivian. I clean for Chief Bosworth," the woman explained. Then she frowned. "Didn't I just see you in the foyer?"

"Yes," said Tess. "I . . . I was looking for . . . him."

"Chief Bosworth's not here," Vivian said. Then she stared out at Tess suspiciously. "How'd you get in the building anyway? I thought you said you lived here."

Tess's mind was reeling. If Erny were in there, surely this woman would know it. She would have noticed something, even though she had not been in the condo for long. And Vivian obviously came and went as she pleased. She must have her own key. Surely Rusty Bosworth wouldn't have dared to try to hide Erny in a place where his cleaning lady could come and go at will.

"Hello?" said Vivian, waving her fingers in front of Tess's eyes. "How did you get in?"

"Oh," said Tess, recovering as best she could. "I'm sorry. I do . . . I live here . . . across the hall."

The woman folded her arms over her chest and raised her eyebrows. "Borrowing a cup of sugar?"

"I was here . . . with . . . Rusty last night," said Tess. "I think I may have left my . . . glasses here."

The cleaning woman pressed her lips together and a spot of color appeared in her weathered cheeks. "Oh."

"Would you mind if I came in and looked for them?"

"I can look for you. Where were you sitting?"

Tess edged her way through the door. "Well, here . . . on the sofa. And . . . in the bedroom."

Vivian cleared her throat. "I'll have a look in there," she said brusquely, indicating the hallway to the bedroom. "You can check the sofa."

"Thanks," said Tess. She waited for Vivian to disappear down the hall and then she looked around frantically, opening every door and cupboard in the combination living room/kitchen and dining area.

"Were they in a case?" Vivian called out.

"No," said Tess. "They have blue frames. They might be in the bathroom."

"I'm looking," Vivian called back.

Tess closed the doors on the home entertainment console and stood up with an oppressive heaviness in her heart. Erny wasn't here. There was no way that the chief would have left him for the cleaning woman to find. Not if he knew she was coming. And most cleaning people worked on a schedule.

Tess looked helplessly around the room. There were few personal effects to warm up the chilly, cookie-cutter look of the condo. There were exactly two framed school photos of children, set up on the coffee table, and a fish that looked fake, mounted on a large, wooden plaque. The plaque was propped up against the side of the entertainment center, as if waiting to be hung up. Tess picked it up. Beneath the fish and behind a glass window was a faded photo of a redheaded kid holding up an enormous fish. Tess realized, to her surprise, that it was the selfsame fish on the plaque. Not fake, after all, but stuffed. For a moment, Tess marveled at the skill of the taxidermist and couldn't help thinking how Erny would covet such a trophy.

Tess looked more closely at the photo and realized that the redheaded boy in the photo, standing on the dock proudly displaying his catch, was a young Rusty Bosworth. Crouched beside him in the photo was another older boy who was homely and wore glasses. The older boy had a hangdog look, as if he was disappointed, or maybe a little ashamed, not to be the lucky angler. With a start of revulsion, Tess suddenly recognized him. She was looking at Rusty and Lazarus Abbott as youngsters. Nothing about Lazarus Abbott betrayed the monster he would become. He looked like any other awkward adolescent. She squinted at the photo trying to see past Lazarus's expression. But there was nothing to see. Just a boy at a lake on a summer's day.

A round-faced, red-haired man, probably Rusty's father, stood behind Rusty, proudly resting his hand on the boy's shoulder. Perhaps, even at that moment, he was planning to have the fish stuffed and mounted for his son. Behind Lazarus, a lanky, black-haired man in a T-shirt looked on enviously, almost angrily, as Rusty displayed his catch. In an instant, Tess recognized those angry eyes. It was Nelson Abbott. A thinner younger version, his face unlined, but Nelson Abbott without a doubt. Tess set the plaque back down beside the entertainment center. It was a memento of a fishing trip that had ended in glory for one cousin and ignominy for the other. Still, it gave Tess a disorienting feeling of having forgotten something.

"Nope," said Vivian, coming back into the room. "I didn't find 'em. Did you? I looked high and low."

Tess looked up. "No. I don't know. I'll ask Rusty to look for them."

"Okay," said Vivian. "Sorry I couldn't help you."

"I'll let you get back to work," said Tess. "Thanks."

"No trouble," said Vivian.

Vivian closed the door behind her and Tess felt as if her last hope had been closed off with that door. Tess closed her eyes. Where is my son, you bastard? she shouted at Rusty Bosworth in her mind. Where are you keeping him? Tess heard the whine of the vacuum again, now realizing that the sound was actually emanating from inside the chief's apartment. Vivian would clean every inch of that condo, Tess thought. Wherever Erny might be, Tess knew that she would not find him here.

CHAPTER 27

Tess ran the gauntlet of a bunch of reporters who, despite the police warnings, had reassembled outside the Stone Hill Inn. She avoided making eye contact with any of them.

"Do you know who took your son?" one of them shouted.

"Any news yet, Tess?" another called out.

"Do you feel you're being punished because of Lazarus Abbott?" cried a third.

Tess jerked open the door to the inn. She was shaking as she entered the foyer. Officer Virgilio was leaning against the sitting room door frame, talking on his cell phone, while the other larger man, Officer Swain, stood in the library, jiggling one foot as he leafed through the newspaper. He looked up as Tess appeared in the hallway.

"Is there any news, Officer Swain?" Tess asked.

"Sorry, ma'am," he said putting down the paper. He sounded sincerely sorry.

Tess nodded and sighed. "Those reporters are back. My nerves are really on edge. I can't stand much more of this harassment."

Mac Swain set the paper down on the table. "I'll get rid of them for you, ma'am," he said with quiet determination.

He walked outside and Tess could hear him ordering the reporters to vacate the premises. Tess shook her head. It was like trying to chase away a swarm of gnats. They might disperse for a moment, but she knew they would be back. Still, the sound of their grumbling retreat made her feel slightly better. Mac Swain opened the door and came back into the house.

"Thank you, Officer," she said.

"Happy to do it," he said.

"Have you seen my mother?" Tess asked.

Swain shook his head. "Sorry."

"Never mind," said Tess. She walked back to the kitchen and then over to her mother's quarters, tapping on the voile-curtained French doors. "Mom?"

Julie opened the French doors, clutching a wadded tissue in her hand. She was wearing a shirt-style jacket of colorful squares of fabric. Her eyes were red-rimmed and angry. "Oh, it's you," she said in an accusing tone.

"I'm looking for Mom," said Tess.

"She went out. With Mr Phalen," said Julie.

"With Phalen?" Tess cried. "What is she thinking? Didn't you try to stop her?"

"She's a grown woman, for God's sake. Besides, I have my own problems," Julie said petulantly.

"What happened at the police station?" Tess asked. "Is Jake still there?"

"Yes, he's still there," said Julie, shutting the door behind Tess. "Of course he's still there. Why in the world did you send that attorney down there with him?"

"Because I thought they were going to arrest him. You know Jake publicly threatened Nelson Abbott. He needed an attorney."

"Maybe so. But not that Ramsey guy," Julie insisted. "The police absolutely loathe him. It's doing more harm than good to have him there." Julie collapsed in a patchwork heap on Dawn's couch. "Jake would have been better off on his own. He's known most of those cops for years.

They probably would have been nice to him if he hadn't come in with that shyster lawyer. They blame that lawyer for everything that's happened."

Tess dug her nails into her palms and counted to ten. "Look, I'm sorry you feel that way. I was just trying to help Jake."

"Some help." Julie sniffed.

Tess raised her hands, palms out. "I can't . . . I don't know what to say. I'm a little preoccupied right now. My son is missing. He's out there all alone with a killer . . ."

Julie's eyes watered again and she immediately looked sheepish. She dabbed at her red nose with the mangled tissue. "I know. I didn't forget Erny. I never would."

Tess realized that this was true, but still, she felt a little bruised. She glanced at the door to be sure it was shut and then spoke in a low, angry voice. "I'll tell you something else. I know who is responsible for all of this. The chief of police is responsible, so if you want to blame someone, blame him."

Julie blinked away her tears and stared at Tess. "What are you talking about? Are you crazy?"

"No, I'm not crazy."

"Then where did you get an idea like that?" Then she frowned in disapproval. "Is this why you wanted Rusty Bosworth's address?"

Tess sighed. "Yes. And I got it from Charmaine. I went to his condo but Erny wasn't there. That would be too easy. He's put him somewhere else."

"Put him . . . ? What are you talking about? Now you think that Rusty Bosworth killed Nelson? And took Erny? Did you tell that to the police?" Julie asked.

Tess looked at her balefully. "Sure," she said. "Tell them I suspect the chief."

Julie shook her head. "I don't know, Tess. I can't picture Rusty Bosworth doing something like that."

"Yeah, well, I'm sure you can't . . ." Tess said dismissively.

"I mean, the last I knew, you were blaming it all on Nelson Abbott," said Julie.

Tess turned on her sister-in-law. "I wasn't *blaming* him. I had information."

"Well, it couldn't have been very good information."

"It was incomplete," Tess snapped.

"Wrong, you mean," said Julie. "Just like with Lazarus."

Tess gasped, as if she had been slapped. "Thanks, Julie. Thanks a lot. You're a big help." She turned on her heel and left the apartment, slamming the French doors behind her. She felt cornered, with nowhere to turn. The police were still camped out down the hall. And outside the reporters were, no doubt, still lurking. Tess went to her room, opened the door, and looked at the two beds. Hers was neatly made while Erny's was thrown together, the bedspread lumpy, the pillow askew. Tess went over to his bed and sat down on the edge, taking his pillow up and holding it to her heart, burying her face in it, rocking back and forth as the tears she had tried to hold in all day began to fall. Tess felt as if she couldn't breathe, as if she couldn't catch her breath any longer. In her heart she kept saying his name: Erny. Where are you? Are you still alive?

As a child, she had only told the truth as she knew it. The adults around her had done the rest. But perhaps the perverse order of the universe had ruled that she had not yet suffered enough for her unwitting part in the injustice done to Lazarus Abbott. How much, she wondered, do I have to lose before my debt is paid? Where is my boy? she thought.

She felt as if Julie had attacked her when she was at her weakest. Attacked her when she didn't need reminding of her failings. She never forgot, not for one moment, that it was her word that sealed the fate of Lazarus Abbott. She may have ignored those reporters, but she had heard their insinuations.

They had no idea what was in her heart. None of them. They did not know what it was like to grow up in the aftermath of such a crime. Tess remembered the day of the execution with utter clarity. The family had been told they could attend the actual execution at the prison, but they all declined. Even Jake. When Lazarus was executed, Tess was at college, hiding in a library carel pretending to study, waiting for the news to come that would "end" her family's suffering.

But after it was over, long before she learned that Lazarus might not be guilty, Tess learned the sorry truth about vengeance and closure. After the execution was done, Tess realized that she felt no better for it. No less guilty for having stayed quiet as her sister was stolen in the night. No less secretly angry at Jake for having left them alone in the tent that night to go to a dance. Vengeance would not bring back her innocent, lovely sister or spare her father from the anguish that had led to his fatal heart attack. Or heal her family. She understood, too late, that the execution of Lazarus Abbott, even when she believed him to be guilty, had done no good. No good at all.

The bedroom door opened and Dawn came in wearing her car coat with the collar turned up. "Tess, are you all right?"

Tess furtively wiped her tears away. She got up from the bed, sniffling, and walked to the door where her mother stood. "Where were you?"

"Ken and I have been out driving around, looking for Erny. I've just come home to change into some rubber boots. We want to walk up the bridle path to the campground. At least as far as they'll let us go. Maybe I'll see something they missed. It's worth a try. I can't sit here and do nothing. Did you have any luck?"

Tess shook her head and followed her mother out of the bedroom.

"All right, let me see if I can find those boots," said Dawn as she turned down the hall to head for the mudroom. "Tess, go put a sweater on. You're shaking."

Tess didn't feel like arguing. Obediently, she pulled on a warm sweater and then walked down the hall. She looked into the sitting room. Kenneth Phalen was sitting in the Windsor chair by the fireplace. He seemed to feel Tess's gaze and looked up.

"Tess. I'm so sorry about your boy," said Ken. "I thought I'd help your mother look for him. You have to help in the search at a time like this. Just to keep your sanity."

"Yes," said Tess.

"I know how it feels when your child is missing. I'll never forget that sense of helplessness when we couldn't find Lisa." He shook his head. "She ran away about a dozen times before . . . the final time."

"Erny did not run away," said Tess. "That's what the police want us to believe, but it's not true. Somebody took him."

"Oh, I know. I know. But the feeling is the same. Just the sheer terror that something awful is going to happen to them. I can't tell you how many nights I went out looking for Lisa, making bargains with God that if I found her and she was all right . . . Well, when they get into drugs, it's a nightmare."

Tess crossed her arms over her chest. "Kids don't just . . . get into drugs, do they? I mean, aren't there warning signs that they're very troubled to begin with?"

There was a flicker of resentment in Ken's eyes. And then it subsided. "How old is your son?"

"Ten," said Tess.

Ken shook his head. "Well, that's what you tell yourself now. You think that you'll make sure your kid has a happy life and then it won't ever happen to them."

"Isn't there some truth to that?" said Tess.

Ken shrugged. "If you're lucky," he said.

Dawn came down the hall wearing her rubber "Wellies." "Ken, are you ready?"

Ken rose immediately to his feet. "Sure," he said. He put on the gray parka that was hanging from a hook by the door. Then he pulled a walking stick from the umbrella stand. "Might need this," he said.

"Well," said Tess stiffly, "I appreciate your . . . helping out."

He grasped her shoulder briefly. "Courage," he said.

Tess felt tears spring to her eyes and she avoided his gaze.

"Let's go out the front," said Dawn. "We'll walk around the inn."

"Okay," said Ken. He led the way out the front door.

"Tess, walk us out. Get a breath of air," said Dawn.

Tess did as she was told, walking arm in arm with her mother out the front. Tess pulled her sweater tight around her and scanned the parking lot.

"I guess the vultures have scattered for the moment."

"They'll be back," said Dawn grimly. "Ken has his cell phone with him. We'll check in with you soon."

Tess nodded and breathed in the damp, gray air. "Thanks."

"Don't be afraid," said Dawn.

Tess released her mother reluctantly. Dawn stepped off the front step and started down the path where Ken had led. He was using the walking stick to part the grasses as he went along. Dawn turned back to look at Tess. "I won't be gone long." Then she frowned. "Now, what's that doing there?" Dawn asked as she spotted something out of place in the inn's carefully maintained front yard. She walked back across the gravel and picked up the pole that was propped against the latticework behind the bench.

Tess looked at the object Dawn was holding. "Oh," she said, "that's the fishing pole Erny made. Jake brought it over."

Dawn's expression softened as she looked at the makeshift fishing rod. "Oh," she said. "That's wonderful. What a kid."

"Oh, Mom," Tess cried.

Dawn shook her head and handed the pole to Tess. "Don't, Tess. Don't give up. You go put it in the mudroom. He'll be using it again before you know it," she said firmly.

"I will," said Tess.

"We'll be back soon," Dawn promised and then she disappeared around the side of the house.

Tess nodded and clutched the pole to her chest with both hands. She waved at her mother, though Dawn was already out of sight. Then Tess sank down on the bench, planting the fishing rod on the stone step in front of her and gazed at it. She could picture her son making it. Busily hunting up the elements he needed for the job. The long tomato plant stake. The twine, which had probably been used to secure the vine to the stake. Where did he find this stuff? she thought, smiling through her tears. Jake's house? Neither Jake nor Julie was much of a gardener. Then she remembered Jake saying that they were out at the Whitman farm. He probably found this stuff in one of their many fields that Nelson Abbott had tended so dutifully over the years. Luckily Nelson would never know that Erny had lifted this pole and twine from his garden to fashion a fishing rod.

Tess clutched the childish contraption to her, to her heart. He was hoping to catch a big fish and instead . . .

Tess pulled the twine through her fingers until she came to the small, rectangular metal lure that he had clumsily secured to the end of the twine through an eye at one end of the rectangle. She took the piece of metal in her fingers and turned it over. Then her heart leaped to her throat.

Erny's lure was a silver medallion, worn and scratched by time and dirt. Engraved on it was one word: "Believe." Tess felt confused and . . . suddenly frightened, as if she had stepped out of an open door and found herself on a high ledge. Mine? she thought, examining the medal. It had to be. The blood was pounding in her ears as Tess fumbled inside the top of her turtleneck and pulled out her own chain. Her medallion was still there, as it always was. Her hands shook as she put the two medallions together and saw that they were the same, although the one attached to the twine was scratched and battered. She turned the fishing lure/medallion over again and peered at it more closely. Etched faintly into the back, barely visible, were three numbers. Tess's heart was thudding and there seemed to be a rushing sound in the air around her. The three numbers formed a date. It took her a moment to comprehend it. Her brain felt woolly and it was difficult to make those numbers correspond to a day, a month, a year. To the date they represented. To Phoebe's date of birth.

CHAPTER 28

"Phoebe?" she whispered, squeezing the battered medallion as if it were an amulet and she could summon her long-lost sister by breathing her name over it. "Phoebe . . ."

For one moment, she felt suspended in time. Felt as if, somehow, because she was holding this long-missing talisman, she might turn around and everything would be different. Her blonde-haired sister, still thirteen, in sweatpants and braces, would be hovering behind her, close enough to touch. Smiling at her . . . Phoebe's face, so long lost, now nearly forgotten, was suddenly vivid in Tess's mind's eye. Tess tried to hold on to it, to keep it with her somehow, but the edges began to blur and the image faded. Tess's heart sank and she felt as if a magic spell had been broken.

She looked down at the twine laced through her fingers. She had to free the medallion from the knot Erny had made to fasten it to his fishing line. There was no sensation in her fingers. They were white and numb. Somehow she managed to rapidly sort through the childish system of knots until she worked the end free and the twine fell away, coiled like a slinky, and she was able to pull the medallion loose. She pressed it, for a moment, to her lips. Phoebe. Your necklace. You were wearing it that last day . . .

The unpleasant tang of metal against her tongue jolted her back to the reality of the present. Her thoughts of Phoebe were replaced by thoughts of her son, who had recovered Phoebe's necklace. Found it, obviously, in the place where he found the tomato stake and the twine. Found it in the place where Phoebe's killer had hidden her, so long ago. At the Whitman farm. Where Nelson Abbott, his son, Lazarus, and his nephew had all worked.

Tess stood up on unsteady legs and ran toward the corner of the house where Ken and her mother had recently disappeared. She looked down the path, but there was no sign of them. "Mother!" she cried out. Tess felt almost dizzy with longing to show this relic of Phoebe's life and death to Dawn. Oh my God. Mom. Wait until you see what I have found. What Erny found . . .

But her shouts dispersed in the air. Dawn and Ken were nowhere in sight nor within shouting distance, apparently. Tess tried to gather her thoughts. Maybe she could call Dawn on her cell phone. But as soon as she thought of it, she knew it was futile. Dawn was from another generation. She never took her cell phone along on a walk. Dawn said that Ken had his, but Tess didn't know his number.

Clutching the medallion in her palm, her heart racing, Tess took a deep breath. Maybe I can run after them, she thought. But then she shook her head. It would be possible to find them, of course, but it would take time. And there was no time to lose. She felt certain that wherever Phoebe's killer had hidden her, that was where he had hidden Erny also. The Whitman farm. Chan Morris's place. It made perfect sense, now that she thought about it. She had never visited the Whitman farm, but she had passed by it. She assumed it had outbuildings, a barn. Hiding places for a stolen child. Hiding places that Lazarus Abbott would have known about from working there. Hiding places that his cousin, Rusty, who worked there in the summer, would have known about, as well.

It couldn't be hard to find, she thought. Her mind was racing in six directions, but she forced herself to concentrate.

The Whitman farm. It was off a back road in Stone Hill. She remembered seeing the sign for it when she had driven Erny on other trips, to admire the changing leaves, the mountains. Her eyes narrowed. Harrison Road? she thought. That wasn't right. Tess squeezed her eyes shut, tried to visualize it. Harriman Road, she thought. That's it. Harriman Road. Now she had to get there.

She went back into the inn. She needed her coat, her cell phone, her car keys. She tried to move deliberately, without haste. Officer Virgilio studied her movements and Officer Swain greeted her pleasantly, but to Tess they suddenly resembled occupying soldiers from a foreign army. She forced herself to move slowly and appear calm and circumspect.

She pulled on her jacket, wrapped a wool scarf around her neck, and picked up her bag. "I have to go out for a few minutes," she said.

"Did you get a call or something?" Officer Virgilio asked suspiciously. "Don't go being a hero, Miss DeGraff. If somebody contacted you with information, you'd better tell us right away."

"Nobody contacted me," said Tess truthfully.

"I need to be able to reach you if there is a ransom call," said Officer Virgilio. "I may need your authorization where your son is concerned. In fact, maybe you'd better stay put," said the officer. "Just in case."

Tess hesitated, torn. "I have my cell phone with me," she murmured.

"And I'll be here," said Julie, closing the door to Dawn's quarters and coming down the hall, looking like a walking quilt in her colorful patchwork shirt. She glanced at Tess briefly.

Tess gazed at her sister-in-law's honest, bespectacled face, her no-nonsense haircut, her pudgy form pulled up to its most erect carriage. Julie did not ask where Tess was going or why. Their recent angry words forgotten, Julie was simply loyal. Ready and willing to do whatever Tess needed her to do. The same comforting, reliable presence she had always been. "Erny's aunt can speak for me while I'm gone," said Tess. "I trust her with my son's life." She turned to Julie. "You know my cell phone number, right?"

Julie's little dumpling of a face took on the sternness of a warrior's. "By heart," she said.

* * *

Tess got out of the car and looked up at the large old Colonial house ringed by evergreens, with its pitched roof and rows of shuttered windows. The mountains loomed behind it like a theatrical backdrop. She had tried to call Chan Morris at the paper while she drove to the Whitman farm, but his secretary said he was in a meeting and couldn't be interrupted. As Tess climbed the front steps to the house, she noted that there was no wheelchair ramp up to the porch. How does Chan's wife get out of here when he's not home? Tess wondered as she waited for someone to answer her knock.

Maybe they have servants, Tess thought. A housekeeper or something. Obviously a woman as fragile and handicapped as Sally could not take care of a house this size. Tess rang again. All right, she thought, if nobody answers, I'm going to start searching the grounds and, if they complain about finding me on their property, I'll just explain it to them. She started to turn away from the door when she heard a voice from inside, faint but distinct, calling out softly, "Come in."

Tess realized, when she heard that voice, that she had almost hoped no one would answer so that she could begin her search without explanation, but now that the voice had summoned her, she had to go in and state her purpose. She turned the knob on the front door and found that it opened readily. She stepped into the musty-smelling, dimly lit foyer. The foyer faced a long hallway and staircase with a curving walnut banister. "Hello," Tess called out. "Mrs Morris?"

"Who is it?" a voice said weakly.

"It's Tess DeGraff. Can I talk to you for a moment? Where are you?"

"Here. Off the hall . . ." The voice seemed to fade away.

Tess walked along the central hallway, looking into the rooms on either side. She passed a wheelchair, which was folded up and leaning against the staircase. The sound of her footsteps echoed on the wooden floors. The decor was surprisingly austere for such a large house. Despite its elegant wide moldings and high ceilings, the house's furnishings were a monument to New England reserve and the house had an air of having seen better days. Tess looked into a living room that had gray-striped wallpaper and a grouping of chairs, a sofa, and a matching love seat with threadbare upholstery. On the wall above the mantel was an imposing oil painting of Chan's grandmother. Tess recognized the severe features and the snapping black eyes from the photos at the newspaper office. On another wall, above the love seat, was a much less impressive portrait of a pretty, young woman in a white gown. Chan's mother? Tess wondered. She took a step closer to look at the portrait and jumped when she heard a voice say, "Here."

Tess turned and saw that there was a cane propped against one of the wide-backed wing chairs. Sally Morris's tiny frame was huddled in the wing chair, her clogs lying by one of the chair's claw feet. "Sorry, I didn't see you," said Tess. "I was just looking at . . ." She gestured to the painting.

"Chan's mother," said Sally with a sigh. Then she turned her head and stared blankly into a tiny fire in the hearth that Tess had not noticed from the door of the room.

Tess nodded. "She was very pretty," she said.

Sally nodded and pushed her hair back off her face. Tess saw that there was a healing gash along her hairline on the right side of her face. Tess had not noticed it earlier, at Charmaine's, although when she looked at Sally — now swathed in baggy pants, socks, and a bulky sweater — she couldn't help remembering all the bruises she had seen on her wasted body when she'd been lying on the massage table. Sally looked up at her. Her eyes were shadowy in the gloomy room.

"I'm sorry you made the trip for nothing," said Sally. "I realized as soon as I hung up that it was a mistake. I tried to call you back but I got no answer."

Tess looked at her blankly.

"Aren't you the woman from SHARE?"

"Share?" said Tess.

Sally's eyes widened in alarm and she drew back against the chair back. "Who are you? What are you doing here?"

"I'm Tess DeGraff. Don't you remember? We met at the airport."

Sally looked at once puzzled and then disappointed. "Oh. What do you want?"

"I'm, um . . . I'm looking for something. Uh . . ." Tess realized that she had not prepared an adequate explanation. "My son . . . was here the other day and I think he left something."

"His fishing pole," Sally said in a dull voice. "Your brother already came for it."

Tess pressed her lips together. "He left a jacket, too. My brother was supposed to be taking care of him, but, you know men . . ."

Sally looked back into the tiny, dwindling fire in the hearth and did not reply.

"Anyway, would you mind terribly if I looked around for it? He was down by your pond and in the fields."

"I don't care," said Sally, her voice a dull monotone.

"Thank you," said Tess, starting to back out of the room. "I really appreciate it."

Sally lifted her hand a few inches and waved it, as if to wave her away. Suddenly Tess heard the front door slam. It must be Chan, she thought. He would immediately realize that this had something to do with Erny's disappearance, and while she could use his help, she had to be careful what she said because she was not ready for it to be all over the news. But before she could think of how she might explain things to Chan, a large woman with thick brunette hair and high color, wearing a voluminous gray tweed coat, appeared in the door.

"There you are, Mrs Morris," she said cheerfully. "I'm Gwen. I'm here from SHARE."

Sally looked at Gwen in alarm. "No. I don't need you. You have to leave."

Gwen ignored the panic in the woman's voice. She turned to Tess and extended a hand. "Are you a friend of Sally's?"

Tess shook her hand but also shook her head. "No. No. I just came to ask Mrs Morris if I could look for something . . . on her property."

Gwen's smile faded. She went over to the chair where Sally was sitting and pulled up a chair beside her. She looked pointedly at Tess. "Could you excuse us?" she asked. "I need to talk to Mrs Morris privately."

Sally began to cry and put a limp hand on the forearm of Gwen's tweed coat. "Really . . ." she said. "I am grateful to you for coming, but I shouldn't have bothered you. I was just feeling . . . a little weak. If I can just get some rest, I know I'll feel better."

"You were right to call," Gwen insisted.

Tess backed quietly out of the room and then hurried toward the front door. She realized that this must be another medical crisis for Sally. Maybe SHARE was an organization for people with muscular diseases.

Tess walked out on the porch. A maroon van with the SHARE logo on its side was parked directly at the foot of the front steps. Otherwise, the vast farm seemed deserted.

Where? she thought. Where, on this property, had Rusty Bosworth hidden her son? She got into her car and began to drive slowly. She passed a barn and horse pasture. Several horses grazed in the shadow of the white-capped mountains. The barn? she thought. She got out of the car and walked toward it.

Unlike the house, the faded red structure looked as if it had not been painted in years. There was an air of neglect about the place. She went inside and looked around, but apart from a barn cat who stared at her indignantly, the barn was filled with dingy tackle, hay, and little else. Besides, the barn doors were opened on both sides. No one would try to hide someone and leave the doors open, she thought.

On one side of the barn was a closed door and the sign on the door read "Office." Tess tried the doorknob and jiggled it. It did not open. "Erny," she cried, twisting the doorknob. She leaned all her weight against it and the door, not locked but swollen shut with moisture, opened. Tess stumbled into the room. The walls were papered with feeding schedules written in a careful hand, a calendar of pin-up girls on tractors, and other farm machinery and lists of chores and equipment maintenance. The desk was piled high with receipts and reminders. This has nothing to do with Erny, she thought. She was about to turn away when it occurred to her to open the desk drawer and see if there were keys inside there. She did not want to have to break down every locked door of every outbuilding on the property. She tugged at the drawer and it opened. But there were no keys inside. Dammit, Tess thought. Just as she was about to close it again, something pink and lacy caught her eye. Tess reached into the drawer. Tucked away in a corner, under a couple of equipment operating manuals, was a pink envelope. Tess pulled it out and looked at it. The envelope was torn open and the lacy edge of a valentine was visible. Tess pulled out the card, which was worn and creased from having been handled many times. In that same neat hand that had made the feeding charts, someone had written "Valentine's Day, 1961." Inside the card, beneath the lovelorn message, it read: "To N. Always and forever, M."

A noise behind her made Tess jump. She whirled around and saw a barn cat staring at her. Tess stuffed the card back into the envelope and replaced it beneath the pile of manuals. Then, she left the barn and went back to her car. As she turned out onto the winding road that led through the farm, she saw the maroon van sailing toward the entrance gates with the tweed-coated Gwen at the wheel.

Tess turned Kelli's car up one of the network of dirt maintenance roads that crisscrossed the property. Slowly, like a fishing boat trolling the water, she drove slowly past an orchard, the ground around it littered with rotting apples the color of dried blood, past fields knee-deep in brown grass, past gardens with bushes now wrapped for the winter in burlap, past the pond where Erny had fallen from an overhanging tree branch.

She peered around her as she drove, searching for a building, but not knowing what it was exactly that she was looking for.

And then, when she was beginning to wonder if she had drawn another erroneous conclusion, Tess came over a rise and saw before her, half-hidden by trees, a long, low, one-story wood building. Beside it was a worn, dirt patch that had obviously long served as a place to park a truck or a car. Tess's heart started to race. She pulled her car onto the worn spot and got out. She walked slowly down the length of the building. The near end of it had two open bays where a riding mower and a small tractor were sheltered from the weather. At the far end was a shed with a large windowless door, padlocked at the hasp. A shed where someone might keep supplies and equipment, like tomato stakes and twine. A gardener's shed. The structure on this farm that was the most familiar to Lazarus Abbott. The place where he and Rusty and Nelson always began their day's work

Tess licked her dry lips and began to walk toward the padlocked door. Her legs felt wobbly beneath her. There was no light emanating from inside the shed. She approached it quietly, holding her breath. Please God, she thought, let him be in there. Please. Let him be alive.

She walked up to the shed, made a fist, and rapped on the door. "Erny," she said urgently. "It's Mom. Are you in there? Erny?"

There was no reply. Tess's heart sank. She had been so sure that she was right about this. So sure again. So wrong again. She wondered disgustedly when she would stop turning every hunch she had into a belief. Her son was not here. He was gone. Gone and she would probably never see him again.

Tess felt an agony in her heart of regret and self-hatred. Why did I take you to that godforsaken spot in the woods? Hadn't I lost enough there already? Why didn't I watch over you? How could I have let it happen? She felt herself sinking into darkness, as if water were closing over her head, and she struggled to breathe against the blackness weighing her down. The end of her hope. And then, all at once, she froze. She heard a soft, small voice whisper from behind the door.

"Mom?" Erny said.

CHAPTER 29

Tess's heart leaped. She flattened herself against the door of the shed. "Erny?" she cried. "Is that you? Are you all right?"

"Ma!" he said. "Open the door. Hurry up!"

Tears sprang to Tess's eyes and she offered a silent, fervent prayer of thanks. "Just a second," she said. "It's locked. I'm going to get it open."

Tess jerked the padlock up and down, rattling it with all her might, but it did not budge. It's all right, she thought. It's all right. You can do this. "Just a second, honey," she called to him. "I'm going to get something to break the lock. Just . . . sit tight."

She glanced into the shed where the tractor was, but there was nothing in there that she might use to break the padlock. Her gaze swept the desolate surroundings and fell on Kelli's car. The jack. She could use the jack to smash the hasp. She ran to the car and opened the trunk, praying there was a jack in the wheel well. She fumbled through the jumble of golf clubs, ski boots, and rock-climbing gear in Kelli's trunk, opened the wheel well holding her breath, and then let out an exultant cry. The jack was right there where it was supposed to be. Of course it was. Kelli was a soldier.

Of course she would have the right equipment. Tess wrested it from the trunk and ran back to the padlock.

"Okay, Erny," she called to her son. "Listen to me. Stand back. Get away from the door. I'm gonna smash this thing."

"Ma, you rock!" Erny yelled back at her.

Tess laughed, in spite of herself. "Thanks."

As she lifted the jack, her heart felt as if it would fly out of her chest with joy. Erny was all right. Must be all right. His voice was strong. He could never sound that chipper if Rusty Bosworth had hurt him. History was not going to repeat itself. She knew she should probably go up to the house and ask Sally, or call Chan Morris and ask him if there was an extra key to the padlock, or call someone for help, but she was not about to wait. She was not going to leave this spot without Erny's hand in hers. She was going to free her son, even if it meant breaking the door down.

Tess swung the jack down on the padlock with a mighty force. The padlock leaped and spun, but was unscathed. The dry, wooden door of the shed, however, splintered around the hasp. She lifted the jack and brought it crashing down again on the spot where the screw fastened the hasp to the door. Paint and wood splinters flew. She raised the jack again and again, smashing at the door until there were deep gouges in the wood around the hasp. She threw the jack to the ground and tried to pull the hasp, its screws, now slightly exposed, free from the door. She still could get no purchase on the hasp to break it free.

"Hurry, Mom!" Erny cried from inside the shed.

"I am, honey," she insisted. She needed something to lever it out. A crowbar or even the claw of a hammer, to wedge behind the hasp and pull the screws from the wood where they were embedded. She ran from the tractor bay to the bay for the riding mower, but there was nothing there that she could use. She looked at the car, thinking about the contents. Then she had an idea. She rushed over to the trunk and pawed through the jumble of Kelli's sports equipment until she dislodged the small, lightweight golf bag. She rummaged through the few clubs that Kelli kept on hand. A putter. A driver. And then she found it. Two irons. A five iron. That'll do, she thought. She tugged it free, rushed back to the door, held the iron upright, and wedged the angled metal head of the club between the hasp and the door. Now, she thought, as she reached up and settled her grip on the shaft of the club. Pull that sucker off. She jerked the shaft of the club down toward her shoulder. After two tries, there was a loud splintering sound. The screws were pulled from the wood and the hasp hung off the door, the padlock hanging uselessly there.

Tess tossed the club down and put her fingers around the edge of the door, pulling with all her might. The door started to open and Erny let out a cry and began to push from inside the shed. In a moment he was free, and he barreled into her arms, knocking her off balance. Together they crumpled to the ground, Erny holding on for dear life.

"Are you all right?" she said. "Are you hurt?"

He was filthy from head to toe, his dirty face streaked with tears. He shook his head and clung to her, shivering, his skinny chest heaving.

"Thank you, God," Tess breathed as she squeezed him in her arms. "Oh baby, I am so glad you're all right."

They rocked there for a moment, awash in relief and mercy. Finally, Tess caught her breath and spoke into his grimy ear. "Erny, listen to me. Listen to me," she said. "Look at me." She managed to persuade him to loosen his grip just enough to look at her. Her heart ached to see the haunted look in his eyes.

"Erny, we have to go before the man who put you in there comes back. Okay?"

He nodded, his eyes widening. His skinny little frame was still trembling. "How did you know where to find me?" he asked.

Tess smiled at him, her eyes welling up. She pressed her lips together. She didn't want to cry. Not now. There would be time for that when they were safe. "You left me a clue. On your fishing pole."

Erny frowned at her. "My fishing pole? No way."

Tess nodded. "The medal you used as a lure? It was actually a medallion from a necklace that belonged to my sister. A long time ago, she was hidden in this same shed apparently."

"Your dead sister?" he asked.

Tess avoided the question. The implications were obvious, and sickening. "I figured if you made the fishing pole here, you must have found the medal here. So I came here to look for you."

"Leo found it," Erny exclaimed. "I was using a long stick and some string I found in that shed to make the pole," he said eagerly, gesturing behind him toward the open door of his erstwhile prison. "Leo was digging around in the dirt and he found it."

Tess pushed his dusty hair back off his forehead. "Wow," said Tess. "I owe that dog a bone."

"A really big bone," said Erny, nodding.

"Come on," said Tess. "Are you okay? Can you walk?"

"I'm shivering. It was freezing in there."

"I'll put the heat on in the car. Here, take my jacket." She took off her wool jacket and put it over his narrow shoulders as she hustled him toward the car. He climbed into the front seat, pushing her leather sack to the floor, and pulling the jacket around him. "Hurry up with the heat, Ma," he said.

Tess did not need to be urged. She rushed around to the driver's side, slamming the trunk as she passed by it. She got in, leaned over and locked the doors, turned the engine over with the ignition key, and pushed the heat up to its maximum. She started to untie the wool scarf from around her neck. "Here, take this, too," she said.

Erny recoiled. "I don't want that. It's pink. You wear it."

Tess smiled in spite of herself. "It's not pink. It's cranberry. But okay. Okay," she said, half to Erny, half to herself. "We're going to be okay now." She began to back out onto the maintenance road. "We're going to go and call someone we can trust."

"You should call the cops, Ma," he said. "Tell them."

"I can't call the cops," she said grimly as the car began to bump down the dirt road. "The guy who took you is a cop. He's actually the police chief."

Erny stared at her. "No way," he breathed.

"I'm afraid so," she said.

"How do you know?"

"It's a long story," said Tess.

"He killed that guy?" said Erny. "The guy at the campground?"

"Apparently, he did."

Erny was silent for a moment. "Why?" he asked.

"That's a good question. I don't really know."

"Wow," said Erny.

Tess looked over at him, huddled under her jacket, wedged up against the car door. His eyes were huge, like black checkers. "Erny, did you see him kill the guy?"

Erny shook his head gravely. "No. He was digging in the ground when I saw him. I was looking for firewood and I saw him digging a hole."

"Where was the . . . body?" Tess asked.

"In the back of the car," Erny explained eagerly. "I didn't know it, but it was in the backseat. When I looked in the car, I yelled. That's when the guy who was digging came after me with the shovel."

"Did he hit you with the shovel?" Tess asked.

Erny shrugged. "I pretended it hurt more than it did."

"Where?" she demanded.

"Right there in the woods," Erny said.

"I meant where on your body did he hit you?"

Erny feigned nonchalance and gestured vaguely toward his side. "Along here somewhere."

Tess made a mental note to have a doctor check him over thoroughly when they got back to the inn. "I'm so sorry, Erny. I'm sorry for everything. I'm sorry you had to see that body. I'm sorry he hit you. I'm sorry he locked you up like that."

Erny grimaced. "Well, I shouldn't have been looking in there. In the car. I guess if I wasn't looking in his car, I wouldn't have seen the dead guy. And I wouldn't have screamed and he wouldn't have come after me."

"Believe me, Erny, it wasn't your fault."

"I couldn't help it, Mom. It was so cool. I just wanted to see it. I never saw one of them before. Not up close."

Tess frowned at him. "What, a dead body?" she asked.

Erny rolled his eyes. "Not a dead body. A Mercedes, Mom. A Merc."

CHAPTER 30

Tess jammed on the brake and they both lurched forward. She put the gear in park, turned, and looked at Erny. "A Mercedes?" she said.

Erny nodded. "A black one."

Tess's palms were damp as she gripped the wheel. "Erny, what did the man look like who took you? Was he a great big man with red hair and a mustache?"

Erny made a face, as if he could hardly believe she would make such an obvious mistake. "No. He had black hair. His eyes looked like one of those eskimo dogs."

Tess sat staring out the windshield. Black hair and the pale gray eyes of a malmute. It was Chan Morris. He drove a Merc — one of the few people in this area who could afford such a car. And the shed where Erny was locked up was on his property. It all fit. It was obvious. It just didn't make sense. Why Chan Morris? Her mind felt like it was spinning. She had to stop speculating. Once again she had accused the wrong man. It wasn't Rusty Bosworth. And right now, she had no time to puzzle it out. Just moments earlier, when she got Erny into the car she had felt safe. She felt safe no longer. This was Chan Morris's property. He could drive in at any minute. He could be here already, heading for the gardener's shed. Coming to dispose of the witness who could put him in jail for murdering Nelson Abbott.

"Erny," she said. "Listen to me. You get into the backseat and crouch down behind here. Put my jacket over you so you can't be seen and just stay there while I drive us out of here, all right?"

"Why do I have to?" Erny said.

"Because I said to. Hurry. That man could be back at any minute. Hurry."

Erny unbuckled his seat belt and got out of the car. He opened the back door and climbed into the space behind the passenger seat in front. "I can't close the door," he said.

"I know. I know. I'll help you. Just . . . stay down." Tess got out and went around the car. She leaned into the backseat, arranging her jacket over her son. "Now, stay there," she said. "Stay very still." She stood up, looking all around, and slammed the back door shut. She went around the car and got back into the driver's seat.

"That guy said he was going to kill me," Erny's voice came, small and frightened, from the well behind the passenger seat.

"Well, he's not," said Tess. "Now, don't talk till we're out of here."

She shifted into drive and began to move very slowly down the maintenance road toward the long drive that bisected the farm. I can't protect him by myself, she thought. If I could only get some help. Jake was in custody. She couldn't call the police. And then, suddenly, she remembered. A feeling of complete relief washed over her. She *could* call the police. It wasn't Rusty Bosworth she needed to fear, after all. Once she called the police and explained where and how she found Erny, they would come to the rescue. She glanced over at the passenger seat where she had put her bag with her cell phone. Erny had pushed it onto the floor when he got in. She leaned over and tried to catch the strap in her hand as she continued toward the driveway. She couldn't manage to grab the strap and keep her eye on the road at the same time.

"Ma, what are you doing?" Erny asked, seeing the movement on the passenger side through the space between the seats.

"Trying to get my cell phone," said Tess.

"I'll get it for you," he offered.

"You stay put," she said.

But she knew she wasn't going to be able to reach the bag and drive at the same time. Once we get through the gates at the top of the driveway, she thought, I can pull over and call . . . But it seemed foolish, even dangerous to wait. I need help now. I need to tell someone what happened. I need those police to swoop down here in their squad cars and escort us safely home. The image in her mind was so tantalizing that it was irresistible. Safety. The nightmare over. I'll pull over. It won't take but a second to make the call, to let them know where we are. And then we'll be safe.

The maintenance road curved toward the driveway around the pond. She assumed it was the same place where Erny went fishing and fell from the tree, but she didn't mention it or ask him. She didn't want him throwing off the jacket draped over him and popping up from the backseat to look. The road followed the shoreline of the pond and turned out onto the driveway in the direction of the farm entrance. Once she made the turn, she pulled the car to the side of the drive, put it in park, and bent over the passenger seat. Tess grabbed her bag by the strap and pulled it onto her lap. She rummaged in the bag and felt both delight and relief when her groping fingers identified the cell phone and grasped it. She drew it out of the bag with a sigh. As she straightened up, and flipped the phone open, there was a rap on the driver's-side window.

Tess screamed and jumped. She turned her head and saw the black-ringed gray eyes of Chan Morris staring in at her. Tess glanced in the rearview mirror. The black Mercedes, pulled to the side of the road, purred silently, a car length behind her. Drive away, she thought. He can't stop you. Or act normal? Which was better? Before she could choose, he reached for the door handle on the driver's side and opened the door. Too late, Tess realized that unlike her own car, the car she was used to, Kelli's car did not have doors that she could lock automatically. Chan held the door open and glanced around inside the car. Her options had dwindled. Her only option now was to lie and hope he didn't realize it. Stay quiet, Erny, she thought. Oh please, don't move or make a sound.

"Hello, Tess," said Chan. "What are you doing here?"

Tess exhaled and gave him the brightest smile that she could muster. "Oh, hi, Chan. You startled me."

"You should have told me you were coming," he said.

Tess heard the chilly note in his voice. "I asked your wife if it would be all right," she said. "You can ask her."

"I'm asking you," Chan insisted. "What are you doing here?"

"Brrr . . . it's kind of cold," said Tess. "Would you mind if I shut the door?" She reached for the inside handle and tried to pull it toward her. The door did not budge.

Chan did not explain nor did he let the door go. "It's not that cold," he said. "Now, why are you here?"

"Well, when Erny was here the other day he lost his sweatshirt and I thought it might still be here."

Chan cocked his head. "A lost sweatshirt? That's why you're here?"

Even as she nodded, Tess realized her mistake.

"Your son was kidnapped this morning," Chan said. "And all you've got to do is come over here looking for his sweatshirt?"

Too late, Tess knew how ridiculous her excuse sounded. She stared through the windshield ahead of her, her cheeks flaming.

Chan reached into a bulging pocket of his olive green field coat and pulled out an object that he swung in front of her eyes. "What do you know about this?" he said.

Tess stared at the metal padlock that hung from the broken hasp. Chan shoved the padlock back into his pocket, reached into the coat's inner pocket, and pulled out a gun. He pointed it at Tess.

"Nothing," she whispered.

"Get out of the car," he said.

Tess stared at him, frozen to the seat.

Chan roughly grabbed her by the upper arm. He jerked her from the front seat, smashing her head against the door frame, and then, still grasping her arm, the gun pointed at her head, told her to open the back door. "Where's the boy?" he demanded, although he avoided her gaze. "Open the back door."

"No, Chan," she said. "No, please don't."

"Open it," he cried, his voice cracking. "Do you want me to start shooting?"

Tess shook her head. She was shivering, both from fear and the cold. Numbly, she reached for the door handle and opened it. Chan leaned over and looked inside. He pointed to Tess's jacket, covering Erny on the floor of the backseat. "You know, Tess, if you're cold, you should wear your jacket. Pick that up for me, why don't you?"

"No, it's all right . . ."

"Do it!" he cried.

Feeling helplessly trapped, Tess leaned into the car and pulled her jacket off her shivering child hidden in the well. Erny looked up at her with wide eyes. Their faces were inches apart.

For a moment, Tess felt as if they were frozen in time and space. She had almost saved her son. Almost gotten him away. And now, because she had stopped to call for help, instead of stepping on the gas, they were both in mortal danger. Erny was shaking all over, staring at her, looking to her for an answer. Tess looked directly into his eyes. "Listen. If I say 'run,'" she whispered, "open that door and go. And don't stop. Hear me?"

"What are you saying to him? Come out here," said Chan. He reached in and jerked Tess toward him by the scarf around her neck. She gagged as it tightened against her throat. She grabbed at the scarf, trying to pry it from her throat, to relieve the pressure as she tottered clumsily backward.

Chan leaned over and looked into the car at Erny as Tess crumpled against the door, gulping in the air. "I told you not to leave that shed. But here you are. Doesn't your mother teach you to mind?" he cried, pointing the gun at the frightened child in the backseat.

The sight of Chan pointing a gun at Erny was horrifying. Tess wanted to yell out in protest and then she realized how dangerous that would be. He was clearly nervous and agitated. She didn't want to startle him. Try to be calm, she thought. Pretend you don't know anything. Try to reason with him. "Chan," she said. "I don't understand what's going on. Why was Erny in that shed?"

Chan shook his head wearily. "Don't pretend, Tess."

"I don't know what you mean," she said.

Chan ignored her protest. "How did you know he was there?" he asked. "Does anyone else know? Who were you calling when I came up on you?"

Tess took a chance. She tried to look apologetic. "You may as well know. I just got off the phone with the police. They're on their way. There's no use in hurting us. They already know."

Chan peered at her. "I saw your car stop. You didn't have time to call the cops."

"It doesn't take long," she said.

"Even if you did, they wouldn't believe you," said Chan, shaking his head. "You're the girl who cried wolf."

Tess realized that there was some truth to what he said. Still, she persisted. "Look, Chan, I told several people I was coming over here. You can't get away with this," she said, wishing that were true.

"No. You were just playing a hunch or you would have brought the cops along. But what was it? What made you think of me?"

Tess wanted to tell him about the mistake he had made, so long ago. About the "Believe" pendant found in his shed and the fact that she had proof. And then, before she blurted it out, she realized that the pendant was still in her pocket and that she had told no one that she had found it. All he had to do was get rid of it, and them, and there would be no one to suspect him. "I . . . I had a very good reason," she said.

"What reason?" he demanded and Tess jumped.

She and Erny were alone on this vast farm with Phoebe's killer holding a gun on them. And wherever she had gone, Sally, who was the only one who knew they were here, would not be concerned about Tess. Clearly, she had her own problems. "I don't have to tell you. And people do know I'm here . . ." Tess insisted, but she could hear the note of desperation in her own voice.

Chan peered at her, still pointing the gun at her chest. "There's nothing, is there?" he said. "It's not too late."

Tess seized on the hint of doubt in his tone. "It is," she said. "It's way too late."

He frowned a moment, thinking, and then he shook his head again. "No. If you'd called the cops, they'd be here by now. No. If I get rid of the two of you, I'm safe."

"Sally knows I'm here. Your wife. I spoke to her. She'll tell the police."

Chan shook his head. "Sally's gone," said Chan.

Tess thought of Gwen, the woman from SHARE. Sally must have left with her after all. She must have been in the passenger seat when she drove away. "Yeah, but when she gets back . . ."

Chan stared back at her and suddenly Tess was struck with a terrible realization. "You mean, gone, as in . . . ?"

"She had another fall," he said. "We quarreled a bit and she fell down the stairs."

Tess pressed her lips together to stifle a sob. "Let us go, Chan. Please."

"Look, you brought this on yourselves," he said, almost apologetically. "I never wanted to hurt anybody." He was thinking aloud. "Now, I need to get rid of any trace of you. Any way they can link you to this place. Here, get back in the car. In your car. Get behind the wheel. We'll drive far away from here." He gestured with the barrel of the gun for her to reassume the driver's seat.

"And then what?" said Tess, although she was afraid that she knew.

"I'm not sure," he said.

"You're not going to let us go," said Tess.

Chan shook his head. "Perhaps a fall for you, too. Now, get in the front. My gun and I will get in the backseat with Erny. That way, I don't have to worry about you doing something stupid at the wheel."

He was going to kill them. There was no reason in the world to think he wouldn't. For a second she thought that maybe the best thing would be to do as he said. Maybe when they were out on the road, she could signal someone with her lights. And then her heart sank. He would watch her every move. And a signal like that would be all he needed to kill Erny. Erny, who had seen the dead body of Nelson Abbott in Chan's car. No. She was not going to get into the driver's seat and let him hold a gun to her child's head. No, she couldn't do that.

In the next second, Tess formulated a crude plan and made up her mind. In one swift motion, Tess stepped close to him, reached into the pocket of Chan's field coat, and jerked out the broken padlock. "Hey," Chan protested, startled. Tess smashed the padlock down against his hand that held the gun. Chan let out a cry and the gun dropped from his hand to the blacktop. Tess prayed for good aim and kicked it beneath the car.

Chan dropped to his knees and began to grope for the gun beneath the car. Tess pulled back her foot and kicked him as hard as she could with the toe of her boot. This blow also caught him solidly, but it was cushioned by the thick coat, and he began to rise to his feet, his eyes wild, growling like a wounded bear. She knew she would not be able to fight him. He would overpower her easily. And if he wanted his gun, he could simply drive the car a few feet forward and uncover it. She had to prevent that. Tess only had a moment to think as he turned and came toward her. She reached inside over the driver's seat, grabbed the keys from the ignition, and pulled them free. She straightened up, raised her arm, and threw them, as far as she could, into the pond that bordered the road.

"Erny, run!" Tess cried.

Erny reached up, opened the car door on his side, tumbled out, and took off.

With a roar, Chan grabbed for Tess. Tess avoided his grasp, but fell to the ground on her knees. Chan lunged at her but Tess scrambled to her feet. And then, as much as every instinct told her to follow her child, her poor shivering child who was racing up the driveway toward the road, her brain reminded her that Chan could not chase two of them at once. And she was the greater threat. Tess turned and sprinted as fast as she could in the opposite direction, back toward the Mercedes that was idling in the drive. If she could only get inside the running car and lock him out . . . The gleaming, black car stood ready to save her. The prize that would go to the swiftest. She rushed toward it, but he was right behind her.

She heard his oaths in her ear and felt his hands clamp down on her from behind, jerking her backward. She saw his fist out of the corner of her eye. She tried and failed to avoid the blow that fell on the side of her head. Dimly, as Tess crumpled to the ground, she raised her hands against a rain of blows.

CHAPTER 31

Chan secured her hands with duct tape he had in the trunk of the Mercedes. Then he pushed her into the front seat of his car and slammed the door.

He came around to the driver's side and got in. "I'll find him. He won't get far," he muttered.

Tess did not reply. She was regaining her senses, although she ached all over from being struck. He pulled up beside Kelli's car and reached beneath the driver's seat of the Mercedes. He pulled out a long-handled ice scraper and turned off the engine before he got out of the Mercedes. Locking her inside the car, Chan went over to Kelli's Honda and flattened himself out on the ground. He stuck the ice scraper beneath the car and managed to fish out the gun that she had kicked under the chassis. When he had retrieved it, Chan stood up and held the gun high where Tess could see it.

Tess turned her face away. She lowered her eyes so that he would not have the pleasure of waving it in front of her. He was going to track down Erny and then . . . She felt overwhelmed by the hopelessness of her situation. Think, she thought. Don't give up. Think. As she looked frantically around her, her gaze fell on a pamphlet, obviously wadded up and tossed into the console between the passenger seat and the driver. She could see the word "SHARE" in big red letters. Beneath the acronym logo, the group's name was spelled out: Stone Hill Abuse and Rape Emergency. Suddenly, Tess understood. She thought of the bruised woman huddled in the chair by the dying fire. Afraid to stay, incapable of leaving on her own. Sally's bruises had not all been the result of accidents or her medical condition. She had been the victim of her husband's anger. Sally had finally called for help, and then, at the last moment, she had panicked and sent that help away. And now she lay dead in that house. Tess felt tears prick her eyelids, for Sally, for herself, for Erny. And then she reminded herself — it was not too late for Erny.

Chan popped the locks, opened the driver's-side door, and got back into the car. He jammed the gun into his inside jacket pocket and turned on the engine. "All right. Now, I'll find that kid."

"My car is right there in the middle of your driveway," said Tess, feeling some satisfaction that she had left such a huge, immovable clue.

"I can hot-wire it," he said. "Once I get rid of the two of you. First I have to find your . . . stupid kid."

"He's a good boy," said Tess, trying to keep her voice from wobbling. "None of this is his fault. How can you even think about hurting a child?" And then, she realized what a foolish question she was asking. This was the person who had killed her sister. It had to be. And even though her heart was thudding with fear, she needed to make him confirm it. "What am I saying? You killed Phoebe, didn't you?"

Chan did not reply.

Tess felt the old fury bubble up in her chest. "Why, Chan, why? What possessed you?" she said.

Chan was driving at a snail's pace, peering into the trees like a hunter. Watching for any sign of movement that would betray Erny's whereabouts.

Tess was frantic to distract him, engage him. "What I can't imagine," she said, "is how you and Lazarus Abbott ever became partners in crime. You, the golden boy, the heir to the Whitman farm, getting involved with a disgusting pervert whom everyone made fun of . . . what were you thinking?"

"Oh right," said Chan, scanning both sides of the road with narrowed eyes. "Your theory. That Lazarus had a partner."

Tess stared at him. "Don't try to pretend you weren't involved," she said.

"We were never partners."

"But you killed my sister," Tess said.

Chan put his foot on the brake and yanked the gearshift into park. "I can't see anything from here. I'm going to look for him on foot. You stay here."

"No," Tess protested. "Please, Chan. Answer me. Can't you tell me that much? I have to know."

Chan studied her for a moment and he seemed to be weighing his response.

"Please. Tell me what happened. For twenty years it has tortured me."

"I'm sure you two will be together soon," he said with a soulless smile. "You can ask her yourself."

Tess knew what he was threatening. She didn't care. She wanted Erny to get away. And she wanted an answer. "Please," she whispered.

He frowned and then he sighed. "Lazarus did abduct her. You were right about that. He took her, and he stashed her in that shed where you found Erny. As I was coming home from the dance that night, I saw him putting her in there."

Picturing Phoebe, terrified and helpless, Tess felt the horror of it afresh. "I don't understand. You saw him do that. And you didn't try to save her . . ."

"Who said I didn't try to save her?" Chan countered.

Taken aback, Tess stared at him.

"At first, I didn't know what was going on," Chan said. "So after he left, I went in. The minute I walked into the shed she started begging. Begging and crying. Pleading with me not to hurt her. To let her go."

"So you killed her . . . ?" Tess cried. "That doesn't make any sense," she said. "You went in to help her and ended up killing her?"

"I had my reasons," he said.

"What reasons? Because a terrified girl pleaded with you to help her? Or was it the fact that she was at your mercy and you could rape her? Was that it? Was it the sex? A bondage fantasy that just got out of hand?"

Chan raised his hand and smacked her face with his open palm. Tess felt her teeth rattle in her head.

"That's not it. I'm not a pervert like Lazarus," said Chan.

"How did Nelson know it was you?" she said. "The DNA proved that it was a relative of Nelson's and you're not . . ."

Tess gazed at Chan's cruel, handsome face and felt the same nagging sense of something forgotten that she had felt earlier in the day. And then she remembered when she had felt it. It was when she had invaded Rusty Bosworth's rented condo and saw the plaque of the fish — and the accompanying photo. And then, suddenly, she began to see. She understood, at least, why Nelson Abbott was killed. She understood what he had really told Chan when he learned the DNA results. When he visited Chan at the newspaper.

"What are you looking at?" said Chan. "Stop staring at me."

Tess nodded. She had to be right. The nagging sense of something forgotten, of some connection hidden in her mind, fell away when she thought of it. "You look just like him," Tess said. "When he was young."

Chan glared at her. "What are you talking about?"

"Your father."

"Richard Morris and I did not look anything alike," said Chan through gritted teeth. "Now shut up. We're wasting time. You're going to be sorry."

Tess felt oddly fearless despite his threats. She knew his secret. She could see it in his eyes, which avoided meeting hers. "How long have you known that Nelson Abbott was your father?" Tess asked. Tess could see that her question had broken his concentration, was preventing him from resuming his search. She knew he would make her pay, but she didn't care. Every second that passed, Erny had a better chance of getting away. At least one of them would escape.

"Shut your mouth. Who told you that?" Chan cried.

"Nobody told me. Earlier today I saw a picture of Nelson as a young man."

Chan clenched the muscles in his jaw. "Oh, you're suggesting that my mother slept with the gardener?" he asked in a voice dripping with sarcasm. "I don't think so."

But it was all coming together in Tess's mind. The resemblance in the photo. The treasured valentine from M. to N. She needed to know for sure. "What was your mother's name?" she asked.

"My mother's name? What business is that of yours?"

"What was her name?" Tess demanded.

"Meredith. Her name was Meredith. Are you happy now?"

"In the barn, I found a valentine. An old one, that your mother gave to Nelson long ago." Tess's heart was thumping, but she could not afford to let him terrify her into silence. For Erny's sake, she had to keep him talking. She was bound up in tape and otherwise helpless. It was all she could do. Besides, this man was Phoebe's killer. And she had to know the rest. "That was what Nelson came to tell you at the newspaper, wasn't it?" she persisted. "That he realized you had to be Phoebe's killer because of the DNA. It had to be you because he knew you were his son."

"Shut up!" Chan shouted. He glared at her as if he could kill her with his bare hands. "Just shut up. You don't know what you're talking about."

Tess summoned all her courage and continued. "Nelson always believed that Lazarus killed my sister. It never crossed his mind that it might be you. Until he learned about the DNA results. He must have known all these years that you were his son."

Chan snorted. "No. He says he always suspected. But he didn't know it for sure." Chan fell silent but she could see him mentally reliving his last conversation with Nelson. Finally, he sighed. "My nana threw her out when she found out my mother was pregnant. Nana never knew that Nelson was the father." Chan's laugh was scornful. "She would have fired him. Hell, she would have castrated him. Nana didn't put up with much."

"She never told you any of this?" Tess asked.

"My mother?" Chan snorted derisively and then stared, unseeing, through the windshield. "No. She never told me about Nelson. She never told Nelson, either, but he always suspected. But not me. Hell, I thought Richard Morris was my father until the day of his funeral."

"When was that?" Tess asked gingerly.

Chan shook his head. "When I was fourteen years old. My mother was furious at me that day because I refused to wear a tie. She started screaming about how I had to pay my respects to Richard for all he'd done for me. How he'd treated me like his own."

Chan shook his head in amazement at the memory, even after all these years. "I was stunned. I said to her, 'What do you mean, *like* his own?'

"'Oh, you were two years old when I married him,' she told me. 'I was all alone in the world,' she said. 'Your grandmother put me out of the house and cut off all funds 'cause I was pregnant and planned to quit college and have the baby. I had to take work as a clerk in a department store. Not many men with a house and a good job like Richard's would have taken on a woman with a two-year-old,' she said."

Chan sighed and shook his head, as if he had fallen into a funk. Then he turned and looked at Tess in amazement. "When I thought about what my life had been . . . I couldn't speak for a while. Finally, I said to her, 'What about my real father?'

"She said he was married. That he didn't even know about me. Besides, she said, 'You didn't need him. You had Richard.'

"That's when I . . . lost it. My whole life I had gone along with it . . . suffered. And then to find out . . ."

To her amazement, Tess saw something glistening in Chan's eyes. He sighed several times and then he shook his head, as if to shake off the memory. "So I said to her, 'Did you know that Richard was a pervert? That Richard made me do sex acts with him ever since I was little?'"

Tess grimaced at the sight of the outrage in his eyes. She felt a genuine pity for him. "Is that true?"

"Of course it's true!" he cried. "And you know what my mother said? She looked at me and said, 'Don't talk like that about Rich. He always took good care of us and now I don't know what I'm going to do.' That's exactly what she said. 'He took good care of us.'" Chan's eyes were furious. "Luckily, she got cancer and died about six months later."

"God," said Tess. "That is a terrible story."

"It's not a story," said Chan. "It's my life."

"I didn't mean—"

Chan drew himself up. "All right. That's enough. Where's that fucking roll of duct tape?" He got out of the car and began to rummage through the backseat. "I'll shut you up once and for all."

Tess turned her head and looked out the car window at the trees and the smoky autumn sky. She thought about all the misery that had brought them to this point. Chan, once a victim, had created victims of his own. All that stifled anger, erupting into violence. It was as sad as it was horrifying. Gazing through the open car window, knowing that Chan was about to come back and muzzle her, Tess suddenly saw a movement in the woods, beyond the lake. Her heart stopped for a moment as she tried to make it out and then, when it moved again, she recognized what she was seeing. Erny. He was crouched by the dark trunk of a flame-colored tree and he was looking at her. Their eyes met and his frightened gaze locked onto hers. Tess stifled a gasp and then she assumed an expression so stern it was almost a glare. She jerked her chin up as if to indicate the direction of the road and mouthed the words "run — go." Erny, crouched in the grass, read her lips with wide eyes.

He didn't understand, Tess thought with a sinking heart. He's hovering there, waiting for me to get free. At this rate we'll both be killed. And then, in the midst of her despair, she saw him lift his hand and point in the direction of the road. He jabbed his finger twice toward the front gates and then pointed to his own chest.

A wave of relief passed through her. Tess closed her eyes for a moment and gave thanks. Then she opened her eyes wide, held his gaze, and nodded her head sharply. Erny hesitated a moment, and then he disappeared behind the tree.

In the next moment, Tess heard a ripping sound. The passenger door opened, obstructing her view, and Chan Morris leaned in and plastered a large rectangle of silver duct tape over her mouth. Tess tried to gasp, but couldn't. She closed her eyes and prayed for Erny to keep running.

CHAPTER 32

Jake and Julie embraced and Dawn beamed. "It's all right now, it's okay," Jake said, although it was questionable whether he was talking to himself or to his wife. Julie struggled to hold back tears as she clutched his back, her small diamond ring winking in the light of the inn's foyer. Kenneth and Ben stood by awkwardly, witnessing the family reunion.

"How did you manage it?" Kenneth asked the young attorney. "Dawn was really worried."

"Well, it took a while to track down the guy who was mixing Jake's paints at the paint store in North Conway. But we found him."

Kenneth nodded. "Lucky he had you to help him. I'm Kenneth Phalen, by the way. I . . . I'm a friend of Dawn's. I used to live here. A lifetime ago."

"Ben Ramsey." The two men shook hands.

"Let me get one of those," said Dawn to her daughter-in-law.

Julie reluctantly let go of her husband. Jake gave his mother a brief, fierce hug. Then he released her and turned to Ben. "I owe you, man," he said.

"Glad I could help," Ben demurred, smiling. "We should tell Tess you're back."

"Tess isn't here," said Julie.

Ben's disappointment was visible in his face. "She's not? Was there some news about Erny?"

"No, there wasn't and I'm worried sick," said Dawn. "We've been trying to call her for the last hour and there's no answer on her cell phone."

Ben frowned. "That doesn't make any sense. She's got to have that phone in her hand, just in case there's news about Erny."

"I know," said Dawn. "Believe me, I know."

"And you have no idea where she went?" Ben said.

Dawn shook her head. "I wasn't here when she left. Kenneth and I walked up toward the campground looking for some sign of Erny. In vain, it turns out."

"I was here," said Julie.

Ben turned to her. "What did she say exactly?"

Julie was clutching her husband's hand. "Well, the cops . . ." Julie turned and looked down the hall, but the officers had not yet returned from the kitchen where they had gone to get a cup of coffee. Julie lowered her voice. "One of them challenged her. Said she shouldn't be leaving with Erny missing, in case some kind of decision had to be made, you know?"

Ben nodded gravely.

"Tess insisted she had to go and said that if any decisions needed to be made that they could ask me. That she would trust me with . . ." Julie's voice choked for a moment. "Trust me with Erny's life."

Jake shook his head. "What is she up to?"

Julie frowned. "I had the feeling . . . it was just a feeling, mind you . . ."

"What?" Jake demanded.

Julie shook her head. "I don't know. Like she didn't trust the police. For some reason, she didn't want them to know where she was going."

Ben's eyes widened. "Oh damn."

"What?" said Jake.

"Nothing. Never mind," said Ben.

"Well, I'm going to look for her," said Jake. "I don't know where the hell to look. But I know Kelli's car. I'll look for that."

"Oh don't," Julie pleaded. "It's too dangerous."

Jake turned to her with a surprisingly gentle demeanor. "Don't worry," he said. "I'll be okay. What about you, Mr Ramsey? Ben?"

"I think . . . I might talk to Edith Abbott. Maybe she's remembered something useful. It's worth a try."

Dawn and Julie looked at him anxiously, clearly doubting that he would be getting anything helpful from Edith. "Jake," he said, "let's keep in contact while we're out there. Call me if you hear anything. About Erny or Tess."

"You, too," said Jake.

The two men shook hands.

"I can take another turn around, as well," offered Kenneth.

Jake eyed him suspiciously, but Ben nodded. "We can use all the help we can get."

"Call us. And be careful," Dawn pleaded as the men went out to the driveway, and got into their vehicles.

Jake roared off first in his truck and Kenneth followed. But Ben sat in the driveway idling for a moment before he set out. He looked over at the bench where he and Tess had sat earlier in the day, recalling their conversation. He had as much as suggested to her that Rusty Bosworth might be the one responsible for Nelson's death and Erny's abduction. But Ben had spent the entire afternoon with Rusty Bosworth either sitting in the same room or coming and going with a phalanx of officers. Rusty literally hadn't had a moment in which he could have waylaid Tess. Wherever she was, it wasn't with the police chief, who had been preparing for a press conference as Jake and Ben were leaving the station.

No, he was forced to admit to himself, if someone was holding Tess, Rusty Bosworth was not the guilty party. Ben was going to the Abbotts' to ask Edith if she might know of another relative of Nelson's who would share his DNA markers. There had to be someone. And something he could do. He had to find Tess.

Ben drove up the driveway and out onto the road in the dim purple twilight, putting on his headlights as he headed toward the Abbott place. As he drove, he thought about Tess. She had aroused a feeling of possibility that seemed dead in him after Melanie's death. He had first noticed Tess during the tumult of the press conference about Lazarus. With that creamy skin and dark hair, she was too beautiful to overlook. But he told himself that he was immune to beautiful women. After all, Melanie had had the face of an angel.

But that same afternoon, at the campground, when he encountered Tess walking Leo, he had felt an unmistakable spark. There was an intelligence, and a sort of gallant loneliness about her that touched him. And he was intrigued by the fact that she had a son who seemed too old to be hers by birth. Since that day, each time he saw Tess or spoke to her, he was more and more drawn to her.

It had seemed that he would never get over Melanie. His hair had turned gray. He had left everything behind that had been familiar. Three years later he was still bitter and stunned by Melanie's betrayal. She had told him she was going on a weekend trip to Florida with a college girlfriend. He had learned the truth when he was contacted by the Miami police and found out that she was staying in a luxury hotel suite in Coral Gables with a junior associate in his own law firm. It was there that Melanie had died of a burst aneurysm while her lover lay passed out in bed beside her.

Even now, when he thought about it, his face flamed and his heart felt like a heap of ash, incinerated by shame and fury. He had quit his firm, abandoned the city, and tried to forget, but you could never forget. He'd thought he'd known his wife. And he had never known her at all. It seemed impossible that he would ever trust someone again. And then, something in Tess's beautiful sad eyes, when she looked at him, made him think he might want to try. He could see that she was cautious, that he would have to go slow with her. And he wanted to, more than he cared to admit. If only he had the chance.

"Where are you, Tess?" he whispered aloud as he drove. "What's happened to you?" He reached the Abbotts' driveway and drove slowly up toward the house. There were several cars parked beside the house and it was alight in a way it had never been on previous visits. Ben always had the impression that Nelson was penurious and probably insisted they turn off each light as they left a room. But tonight, light spilled from every window. Ben parked behind an old Chevy station wagon, walked up the steps, and knocked on the door.

A small, round woman with gray hair and flushed cheeks pulled the door open and smiled at him. "Hello," she said, glancing admiringly at his suit and tie. There was the sound of voices and tinkling glasses coming from the kitchen.

"I'm looking for Edith," he said. "I'm her attorney. Ben Ramsey."

"Oh, of course," said the woman. "I'll call her. Come on in."

"I hope this isn't a bad time," he said. "I know she's been through so much."

The woman shook her head. "Not a bad time. She's doing all right. We're just having a little bottle of wine and relaxing a bit. I'm her friend, Jo, by the way."

"Nice to meet you, Jo," he said.

Ben walked into the spartan living room and waited as the woman at the door yodeled for Edith. After a moment, Edith came into the living room. Her normally colorless skin was an unfamiliar shade of pink, everywhere but around her eyes, which were decidedly not red-rimmed behind her glasses. "Oh Mr Ramsey," she said. "Aren't you nice to come." She walked unsteadily to Ben, raised herself up on her tiptoes, and kissed him on the cheek.

Ben tried not to betray his surprise at the gesture, which was completely out of character with the severe, taciturn woman he knew. "How are you doing, Edith?"

Edith gave an abrupt nod of her head. "I'm doing well. A few people are here with me. You met Jo."

Ben nodded.

"Come on in. Have a glass of wine with us. My friend Sara brought a cake that's delicious."

The expression on her face was placid, almost . . . relieved. The loss of her husband did not seem to be weighing on her heart this evening. Ben noted, from the sounds of laughter in the other room, that the atmosphere was closer to that of a party than a wake. "I can't stay, Edith. I do have an important question for you, though. Could you spare a minute?"

"For you. Of course," said Edith. She indicated one of the straight-back chairs in the living room and she sat down on the other and looked at him expectantly.

"This is about Nelson. His death."

"What about it?" Edith asked.

"It appears that Nelson may have been killed by someone related to him."

Edith seemed unfazed by this information. "I know. Rusty told me that. I told him it wasn't me." She smiled at her own pleasantry.

"I mean a blood relation," said Ben. "Because of the DNA evidence. As far as blood relations went, he had only one sister and his nephew, right? No other children, or siblings . . . ? No skeletons in the family closet, if you know what I mean?"

Edith rocked back in the chair, pursing her lips and raising her eyebrows.

"Edith?" he said.

"The police have already asked me all this stuff," she said bluntly. "Earlier today. I told them all I knew."

Ben looked at her keenly. The wine had loosened her normally rigid manner. He had the impression that she was suppressing something that she wanted to say. "You and I have always been able to speak very frankly, Edith. It's important to me that we speak frankly now. In fact, it's a matter of life and death. For someone I care deeply about. And I promise, I would keep any confidence. This would fall under attorney-client privilege. You know you can trust me. Is there something else? Something you didn't tell the police?"

To Ben's amazement, tears came to the old woman's eyes. He had never seen tears in those steely eyes, even when she'd learned that Lazarus was vindicated. Perhaps he had misjudged the depth of her feeling for Nelson. "I'm sorry," Ben said. "I didn't mean to imply that Nelson . . . well, that there was any . . . wrongdoing on his part."

Edith shook her head. "No." She gazed at Ben with an almost tender expression on her face. Then she said, "You were the only one. The only one who helped me. The only one who believed me about Lazarus. If it weren't for you . . ."

Ben raised his hands as if to ward off her praise. "It's okay. Really," he said.

Edith frowned and seemed to be considering what to do. Finally, she said, "I don't know of anything, for a fact. Not for a fact."

Ben stared at her. "Idle speculation will do. Anything."

Edith raised her eyebrows. "This is just a . . . suspicion I once had."

Ben held his breath.

Edith twisted her worn, scratched wedding band on her ring finger. "When we were married a few years, I'm pretty sure Nelson cheated on me. She was young and pretty and . . . bored, I guess. I don't know for the life of me why else she would have lowered herself. He thought I didn't know about it, but I did. Wives have a way of knowing. I just didn't say anything. I hoped it would blow over and it did. She left town, and it seemed like that was that. But then, when he was a teenager, her son came back. The minute I saw that kid, I knew. He's the image of Nelson as a young man. I don't think Nelson even realized it. We never do see ourselves as we really are, do we? Anyway, I'm not saying he's the one who killed Nelson. I mean, why would he? But if you want to know . . ."

Ben stared at her. "Nelson had a son?" he said. "Who?"

CHAPTER 33

Chan rummaged around, first in the trunk of the Mercedes and then under the hood of Kelli's car. Then he returned to the driver's seat. Using a screwdriver and a pair of pliers, he fiddled with wires under the steering wheel until the engine suddenly roared to life. He sat back with a look of satisfaction on his face. "There we go," he said. "Hey, I'm pretty good." He turned the car in a K-turn so that it bumped off the road and came to rest, idling on the edge of the pond's bank.

Tess looked over at him. Chan was gazing across the water. Tess followed his gaze, which scanned the pond, quiet but for the call of the marsh birds that wheeled out over its surface. "You know, I should have thrown Nelson in there," he said. "None of this would have happened. I mean, this business with you and your kid. But I panicked. He came to the paper and confronted me. I said I couldn't talk there and that I would meet him here, where it was more private. But after I killed him, I didn't want to bury him here on my property. I was afraid someone would find him." Chan shook his head. "So I tried to bury him at the campground. That was stupid. I wasn't thinking clearly.

"There's no excuse for it except that he took me by surprise, telling me how I was his son, and how he knew it was me, not Lazarus, who had killed your sister. He said that Lazarus had always tried to blame me, but he never believed him. He threatened Lazarus for even daring to breathe such an outrage, but, what do you know, it turned out to be true." Chan chuckled, but without pleasure. "Nelson offered to protect me. Hah," Chan barked. "Another father to protect me. That's rich. I wonder what this one's protection would have cost me. He'd probably want to get paid in money rather than blow jobs. But you never know. I wasn't about to find out."

Chan sighed. He turned to Tess and spoke earnestly, with something resembling regret in his cold, gray eyes. "I want you to know that I have nothing against you personally," he explained. "I just don't have a lot of options. If your son hadn't looked in my car and seen Nelson . . . if I hadn't panicked . . . I don't know. The day I found your sister in that gardener's shed . . . I should have walked away from her. I should have." Chan shook his head. "But when I saw that it was her, the desire for revenge just got the better of me."

Even in the midst of her revulsion, her fear, Tess noted the strangeness of the word he chose. Not lust. Or frenzy. Revenge. On Phoebe? Chan didn't even know Phoebe. Why would he take revenge on her?

"I figured Lazarus would be blamed," Chan went on. "The pervert. He did take her in the first place. Probably meant to kill her. Anyway, I should never have come back to this town," he said. "And now . . ." His voice trailed off. Then he looked at her. "I need to get rid of you and this car. Even if your kid gets away, they'll think he's lying. That pond just seems like the best solution."

Tess followed his gaze back to the placid surface of the pond.

"It's called a pond, but it's pretty deep," he observed.

The terror in Tess's eyes was more eloquent than words. Her heart shriveled in her chest. She started trying to plead, to protest, but all that came out from behind the tape were muffled noises.

"No use dragging this out," said Chan. "I'm sorry. You probably don't believe that, but I am. I'm really sorry." He did not look at her when he said it.

He released the parking brake and put the car into park. Then he reached his hands toward Tess's neck. She thought he was about to strangle her and she pressed herself up into the space where the seat met the car door. Chan smiled and shook his head at the misunderstanding. He untied the woolen scarf at her neck and tugged it free. Then he rolled the scarf up from the narrow end, until he had a roll about the size of a coffee can. He leaned over and shoved the rolled scarf under the brake pedal. "There," he said. "We don't want you to halt the march of progress," he said. He rolled the windows up tight and opened the driver's-side door. "It won't take too long to sink," he said, throwing the gearshift into neutral. "Just let it take you," he advised.

Then he slid from the driver's seat and slammed the car door behind him. Slowly, Kelli's Honda began to roll forward, down the bank. Tess tried to scream, but the only sound she could make was a gargled moan. She rubbed her wrists together frantically behind her back, trying to get free. Her chest was heaving and even though the car was still aboveground, she felt as if all the air around her had been sucked away. She pressed herself back against the seat, planting her feet under the dash, as if she could somehow halt the forward motion, but the front of the car was angled down and it was rolling. Rolling down into the water as Chan applied his shoulder to the task, pushing the car from behind. She saw the top of the hood start to descend toward the water. NO, she tried to scream. Oh please God, NO. But the car was tilting now, and there was no sound inside the car except for the sucking of the water as Kelli's Honda floated out onto the water's surface and hung there. And then slowly began to sink.

* * *

Erny crouched in a huge, black knothole that formed a hollow in a tree trunk, made himself as small as he possibly could, and wished with all his might that Leo was here. If Leo was here he would jump on that Chan guy and bite him with his big sharp teeth until the guy was begging Erny to call Leo off. But he could beg all he wanted. Erny would not call him off. He'd make that guy let his mother go and then he'd tell Leo to keep on biting him and biting him until the cops came. With Leo by his side, everything would be all right, and his mother would be safe and they would all go home. But Leo wasn't by his side. Erny was alone.

Although he hadn't been able to hear her voice, he understood the words his mother had said when she'd spotted him hiding in the trees. Run. Get away. And he'd recognized the look she was giving him. It was that look she always gave him when she was really serious about something. That look that said she really meant it. He knew enough to obey.

But he didn't know where to run to, and he didn't want to leave her behind. What if that guy hurt her or . . . he couldn't think about the rest. You have to run, he thought. Ma said to get away. Erny's stomach churned as he thought about plunging into the woods, not having any idea where he was going. It was getting dark and there might be wild animals or vampires or . . .

He took a deep breath and reminded himself of something important. If he could find his way back to the road, maybe he could get help. There might be somebody there who could help him and his mother. The thought of that possibility made him feel a little less shaky. He knew he had to do it. He peeked around the tree's huge trunk but he could no longer see them.

Erny did not know why the man was doing all these things, but he did know that this was the same bad man who had locked him away in that dark, stinky shed. And now, after his mother found him and got him out, the guy had his mother as a prisoner. You have to run now, Erny thought. Do it now. You have to go!

Erny screwed his courage up and inched away from the shelter of the gaping knothole. Then, with a burst of crazy, fear-driven energy, he took off at a run. He didn't know where he was heading. He heard strange noises as he ran in a zigzag path around the trees, scuffling through a carpet of dead leaves as he plunged on into the woods. Several times he tripped over ropy roots and nearly went down, but then he caught himself and kept running. He didn't know where he was running to, or when he was supposed to stop, but he kept going anyway. It seemed as if he went up one rocky slope and down another, over and over, the trees a chainlike blur of stinging branches and gray bark. Erny ran until he was out of breath and his heart felt ready to burst and he felt like he was completely lost.

And then, just when he was sure that he would die right here in these woods, he saw a light up on the embankment ahead of him. He thought it might be the moon, but it was brighter than the moon, and besides, he thought he recognized the sound of a car engine passing by. He clambered up the embankment and through a row of trees he saw that the light, which he had spotted and followed like a star, hung from a pole over the front gate of the farm. The road! He had managed to make it all the way to the road. Yes! He pumped his fist in the air. He had found his way out.

But now what? He leaned out over the shoulder of the macadam and looked up and down. There were no lights, no houses as far as he could see. Now, which way to run? From somewhere deep in the Whitman farm, he heard the sound of a car's engine roar. It's him. He's coming after me! Erny's head swiveled as he looked both ways, trying to pick which way to run. Then, randomly, he decided, and tore off along the edge of the road to the right, away from the gate, his elbows pumping as he gasped for breath.

Suddenly, up ahead, coming down the road in his direction, he saw a car. A car with a driver. Someone who could help him. Erny could see nothing but headlights, but headlights were enough. He darted out into the street, waving his arms over his head. "Help," he cried. "Help me! Please help me!" Too late he realized that he had startled the driver. That he shouldn't have jumped out into the car's path.

There was a horrible screeching of brakes. Erny was frozen in the headlights, too paralyzed by his own fear to jump out of the way. The car swerved toward the shoulder of the road and then bumped and jounced to a stop, narrowly missing a tree.

Erny approached the tan-colored car cautiously, afraid the driver was going to scold him for sending him off the road. Part of him wanted to run away, but then he remembered his mother, still with that man. He knew he had to be brave. The driver, a thin man in a gray coat, opened the car door, got out of the car, and stood up. He put one bony hand on the roof of his sedan and looked around. Then he spotted Erny, crouched by the side of the road, shivering.

"Mister, I need help," Erny said to the driver. "It's an emergency."

"Come over here where I can see you," said the stranger.

CHAPTER 34

Chan Morris, Ben thought, as he pulled out of the Abbotts' driveway and headed in the direction of the Whitman farm. It didn't seem possible. He had spoken with the publisher many times in the last two years. Chan was nice-looking in a kind of cold, preppy way and he seemed . . . shallow, but personable. He struck Ben as an intellectual lightweight but, all in all, he seemed to be a decent person. He had that pretty wife with the muscle disease. He was always so solicitous of her. Chan Morris?

Ben didn't doubt that Edith was right about Nelson's having had an affair with Chan's mother. Women seemed better at detecting that kind of thing than men, Ben thought ruefully. But had Edith meant that Chan was Nelson's son? Did that connection make Chan Morris a killer? Did it mean that Chan was Erny's captor?

Ben was suddenly struck by the possibility that if he were, Ben might be the one to deliver Erny back to his mother's arms. He could picture Tess's dimpled smile, the joy that would light up her sad eyes. She would never be able to stop thanking him.

Ben forced himself to stop fantasizing and think rationally. He could call in the police, but what real evidence did he have to blame these horrible crimes on Chan Morris? Besides, he knew he was in particular disfavor with the Stone Hill Police Department right now, thanks to his role in the exoneration of Lazarus Abbott. What chance was there that the police would even listen to him, much less believe him? And why should they? Ben thought. It wasn't as if this was anything more than speculation.

No, he thought. It was unlikely that the police would lift a finger to help him. But he trusted Edith's hunch. She was a woman of determination, not imagination. And he was going to have to take her guess on faith. He was going to go to the Whitman farm and confront Chan Morris head-on. Ben wished he had a gun to take with him, but he had never really liked guns. He would just have to move cautiously, keep his head, and hide his purpose from Chan.

* * *

Tess struggled against the tape that bound her like an animal caught in a trap. The more she pulled and jerked her wrists apart, the tighter the tape seemed to become. She could feel the car rocking, adrift in the water. Tess felt light-headed and almost hoped she could faint, so that she would be unaware of her own drowning. But the part of her that was Erny's mother would not allow her the luxury of unconsciousness for her last moments.

Tess thought her heart might burst from the horror of it. Drowned. Suffocated. No escape. The car began to tip and Tess inched her way up onto the console between the seats, straddling it, trying to balance the weight. She knew instinctively that if the car turned over, all hope was gone.

What hope? she thought miserably. There was no hope. And then she gave herself a mental slap. As long as she was still alive, there might still be a way. But she had to calm down. Stop, she told herself. Breathe through your nose. Think. She looked through the windshield and saw the front of the hood begin to tilt down. Don't look, she told herself.

Don't look. Then, in the midst of a full-blown panic attack, a thought occurred to her: Be James Bond.

It was a desperation strategy she had devised for herself once when she was in junior high school and had to unlock her gym locker in a hurry, while a cluster of tough, older girls were taunting her. The more she rushed to work the lock, the more it refused to open. For some reason, at that moment, the movies about the suave, fictional British spy had entered her mind. Even faced with a ticking bomb, James Bond always concentrated, moved calmly, and without a wasted motion. She had tried it. It had worked for her then. Her lock had clicked and opened. Now, this minute, she needed to channel James Bond again, this time for much higher stakes.

Tess sat very still and forced herself to concentrate. She looked around the inside of the car. On the dashboard of the driver's side was the pair of pliers Chan had used to hot-wire the car. Tess turned her back on the windshield and lifted her bound hands behind her, ducking her head and shoulders to avoid the ceiling of the car's cabin. She groped around the top of the dash until she felt the cold metal beneath her fingers. Yes, she thought. Carefully, she wrapped one hand around the pliers and pulled them to her. She turned herself back around, still balancing on the console, and, after shifting the pliers to her left hand, used the fingers of her right hand to try to explore the twisted tape on her wrist. Don't think about the fact that the car is going under. Pay attention, she told herself. Her fingertips sought the loose corner that marked the end of the tape. She forced herself not to fumble for it, and after a moment or two, she felt it. All right, she thought. Good.

Tess did not look out at the hood, now lower and lower in the water. All that mattered was that loose corner of tape. She kept her little finger on that triangle of hope as she maneuvered the pliers until their teeth caught the end of the tape. She felt a moment of exaltation, but she reminded herself that there was nothing to celebrate. She was trapped in a sinking car. The thought instantly made her heart hammer. No, she told herself. Stop. Stay calm. Think James Bond. Carefully, painstakingly, she pressed the plier handles together and began to tug. After a couple of false tries, the pliers held the corner and she was able to pull. The sound of the tape tearing away from itself was like a symphony to her ears. Once she had pulled a few inches of the tape free, she was able to grip it with her fingers, to pull and unwind it with the fingers of first one hand and then the other. The hood was fully underwater now and the water had risen halfway up the windshield. Don't panic, she told herself. Keep calm.

The adhesive gave way and, with a mighty rip, Tess pulled her hands apart and they were free. She flexed her fingers joyously and then reached up and ripped the tape from her mouth. It felt as if she had pulled all the skin from around her lips, but she didn't care. It felt wonderful to breathe, even to smile. Now she could get out. She tumbled into the passenger seat and the sinking car listed dangerously to that side. But she couldn't worry about the car tipping over. She had to get the door open. She leaned all her weight against the door, turned the handle, and tried to force it free. It was no use. The door did not budge. It was completely underwater. Frantically she grabbed the crank and tried to roll down a window. The only thing she managed to do was to break off the crank. The windows remained closed tight. The water was at the top of the windows now and the car was drifting downward. In a moment, she would be completely submerged.

"No," Tess screamed. She had gotten herself free and now she wasn't going to be able to get herself out. She picked up the pliers and began to smash at the windows with all her might, but it was no use. A few chips appeared, but she was no match for the water pressure outside the car and the shatterproof glass. The water was beginning to enter into the car. Tess felt something cold around her feet and realized that the water was seeping in past the rubber gaskets, sloshing over the floor mats. She scrambled back up onto the console and the car rocked again, and then, after a thud, became eerily still. It took Tess a moment to realize that the car had come to rest on the bottom of the pond. Around her, everything was black. Water was seeping through the rubber gaskets everywhere in the car now, splashing her from every side. She huddled, shivering, in the darkness.

"Oh my God. Help me. Get me out of here," she pleaded. But no one answered.

* * *

Ben turned in at the lighted sign for the Whitman farm and drove slowly down the driveway, trying to look all around him in the dark. There was no sign of Tess or the car she had been driving. No sign of Erny. Ben pulled up in front of the huge house and parked beside the black Mercedes. The farm seemed peaceful and bucolic in the moonlight. Not the sort of place where a small boy would be held a prisoner. For a moment Ben doubted himself, wondering how he could even suspect such a thing.

Don't, he thought. Don't give in to the self-doubt. Just go in there and see what you can find out. Feeling a little foolish, but determined all the same, Ben got out of the car, mounted the steps, and knocked on the door.

Chan Morris opened the door, wild-eyed.

"My God, I'm glad you're here," Chan said to Ben. "Come inside. Hurry. I need your help."

Ben stared at him.

"My wife's had an accident," Chan said, turning away from the door and pointing inside the house. Ben looked in the direction in which he was pointing and saw a tiny woman crumpled at the foot of the stairs. "It's Sally. She fell down the stairs."

Ben rushed past Chan and went swiftly to the spot where Sally lay, at the foot of the staircase. He knelt down beside her, picked up her tiny wrist, and felt for a pulse. Then he put his ear to her mouth.

"She doesn't seem to be breathing," said Chan. "I couldn't feel her pulse."

Ben gazed grimly at Sally's waxy face. He suspected that she was already dead but he wasn't about to be the one who declared that. "We need to get her to the hospital."

"I heard the crash and this is how I found her." Chan raised his hands helplessly. "She was trying to come downstairs by herself, I guess. She has a . . . condition. She . . . she can't get around very well."

"Did you call an ambulance?" Ben asked.

"I was going to," said Chan.

"Well, do it," said Ben.

Chan ran his fingers through his hair. "I can't believe this." He knelt down beside Sally's body and brushed her spiky hair tenderly back from her face. "I should have been with her. God, I think it's too late. Here, help me pick her up. I want to put her on the sofa."

Ben stared at Chan in disbelief. "What are you waiting for? Get your phone. Every second could be critical."

Chan looked down sadly at his wife's face. "I don't think there's any point."

Ben shook his head in disgust and reached into his own pocket, pulling out his phone.

"What are you doing?" said Chan.

"Calling for help, of course," said Ben.

"Put that away," Chan insisted. "They can't help her now."

"Suddenly you're sure of that?" said Ben.

"She's dead," said Chan. He reached down and moved a hair off her forehead with his index finger. "Anyone can see that."

Ben stared at him. If this were Tess, he thought, I'd be screaming for help, trying to flag down the rescue vehicle. "I thought you were desperate for help. Now you don't even want to try to save her?" Ben said.

Chan stood up. "You can't save someone who's dead," said Chan. "I just don't want to leave her there on the floor. Now if you're not going to help me move her, why don't you get out of here and let me grieve for my wife in my own way."

Ben stared at Chan, who was behaving as if his wife's body was a piece of broken china that needed picking up. This didn't have a thing to do with grieving, Ben thought. Chan just didn't want any intruders in his house, asking questions, even if it meant forfeiting Sally's last chance for survival. "You don't want the police here," said Ben.

"Excuse me?" said Chan.

Ben got to his feet. "You heard me. You're more worried about the police being here than you care about saving your own wife."

"She can't be saved," said Chan. "She's dead. They're policemen, not magicians."

"Why is that, Chan?" Ben insisted. "What do you have to hide?"

"All right, that's it. Is this how you treat a man who has just lost his wife? Get out of my house."

"You have Erny here, don't you?" said Ben. "Is Tess here, too?"

"What are you talking about? Have you lost your mind?" Chan demanded.

In a way, Ben thought, yes, he had lost his mind. He knew with every fiber of his being that Chan's reaction was completely abnormal. Did that mean that Chan had Erny hidden somewhere in this faded mansion or on the grounds? Ben wasn't going to give Chan the benefit of the doubt. Ben was, indeed, out of his mind with worry.

"I know they're here somewhere. Just tell me where," Ben insisted.

"I don't know what you're talking about," said Chan.

Ben lunged forward, grabbed Chan's neck in his hand, and began to squeeze. "Don't fuck with me, Chan. Where is Erny. Where is Tess?"

Chan's gray eyes seemed to turn a shade darker while his skin reddened. He grasped Ben's hands on his throat, trying to loosen Ben's grip. "Let me go. I don't know anything about Tess. Or her little spic kid. Let go of me," he squeaked.

Chan tried to struggle, but it was no use. Ben's grip was a vise.

"You've got one second to tell me where they are or I swear . . ."

"All right, all right," Chan pleaded. "Stop."

Ben loosened his grip on his throat and Chan gasped for breath. He did not meet Ben's penetrating gaze. He rubbed his throat. "Goddammit, Ramsey. You're crazy."

Ben took a menacing step toward Chan. "Are they in this house?"

Chan shook his head. "No. But you're free to look. Why would you think that anyway? I have nothing against Tess."

"You're Nelson Abbott's son. She found out, didn't she?"

Chan went completely still for a moment. And then his eyes narrowed. "Where did you hear that?"

"I know all about it," said Ben. "Nelson's wife told me."

Chan's eyes widened. "I'm not."

"Don't play games. I know everything. Now where is Tess?" Ben demanded. "Where is Tess's son? If you've hurt them . . ."

Chan raised his hands in surrender. "All right. All right. Stop. They're all right."

"Take me to them. Now!" Ben cried.

"All right. I'll show you," said Chan irritably. "It's outside."

"What is?"

"Where I put them," said Chan.

"Hurry up," said Ben, shoving him in the direction of the front door.

Chan stumbled forward and then righted himself. "Just let me get my coat," he said. He reached toward the coatrack beside the front door, but instead of pulling the jacket off the hook, he stuck his hand in the pocket and pulled out his gun, which he pointed at Ben. The whites were showing around Chan's eyes. "She's at the bottom of the pond, actually. Now you can join her."

“The bottom of the pond?” Ben said. “She’s dead?”

Chan glanced at his watch and nodded. “Unless she’s got gills.”

In that split second Ben understood that this . . . creature had killed her. He let out a groan. Was it possible? Tess was gone before he had ever even held her in his arms. Before he could even tell her what was in his heart. They were just about to start, and now Chan had killed the last hope Ben had in the world to be whole again. Ben’s brain reeled and his heart wailed for vengeance. He lunged at Chan, who hesitated a second and then fired. Ben felt a searing pain in his chest. He staggered and grabbed at a nearby table for support. Instead, he pulled the table over as he fell.

CHAPTER 35

Ben was splayed out on the floor, his hands covering his bleeding chest. The wounded man gave a feeble groan. Chan lifted the gun in his shaking hand and pointed it down at the attorney. At that instant, Chan heard the door open behind him. He turned and was immediately tackled by someone hurtling through the open door. The gun flew from his hand as Chan collapsed with two policemen on top of him.

The cops held Chan as Rusty Bosworth burst into the foyer behind his officers. Rusty saw Ben Ramsey lying on the floor, blood across his shirt and tie. "What happened?" he cried. "You shot him?"

"I found him here with my wife. She's dead. Look by the stairs. She's dead," Chan cried. "It's not me. It's him. He killed her!"

Rusty peered down the hallway and made out the crumpled body of Sally Morris at the foot of the stairs. Then he strode over to the door and hollered out, "Get those EMTs in here, stat."

Outside of the house, a fawn-colored sedan pulled up behind the ambulance. Kenneth Phalen, Dawn, and Erny jumped out.

"Where's my mom?" the boy cried.

"Stay back," said Dawn. "The police will handle this." Kenneth had picked up Erny on the road and had driven the frantic boy back to the inn. Officer Virgilio and Officer Swain tried to calm the boy as he told them about Tess being held captive by Chan. They were on the radio, calling for help, before he could even blurt out all he knew.

"Thanks to you, Erny, I'm sure they got here in time and they'll find your mother," said Dawn, although in her heart she was crying out, God, you can't do this to me again.

Erny looked up at Dawn. "Swear," he said. "Swear they'll find her."

Dawn could feel Kenneth's sympathetic gaze on her but she did not meet it. Dawn felt sick to her stomach. She looked around the property, now swarming with police cars, emergency vehicles, and arriving television vans. "I swear," she said.

"I want to go up there," said Erny.

"You can't. There are people with guns."

"I'm going. She needs my help."

Dawn crouched down and grasped him by the upper arms. She looked at him steadily, but Erny saw that there were tears standing in her eyes. "Erny, I want her back just as much as you do," Dawn said. "And I'm as worried as you are. But right now all I can do for your mother is to keep you safe. And that's what I'm going to do."

Erny sighed and pushed out his lower lip.

"Try and be patient," said Dawn.

* * *

As the freezing water reached her knees and splattered her from every side, Tess tugged frantically at the door handle, but it refused to budge. Waves of horror rolled over her. What a way to die, watching the water rise, feeling the air sucked out of your lungs. She started to hyperventilate again in the submerged vehicle, but then she stopped herself with a mighty effort of will. Say your prayers, she thought. Try and make your mind peaceful.

She thought, first, of her son. Maybe he got away, she thought. Maybe he was able to get help and he will tell people what happened. If Erny got away, then I won't have died in vain. The water was pouring into the car now, reaching her chest. She felt more alone than she ever had in her whole life and it made her think of Phoebe and her sister's last moments. Maybe I'll see Phoebe in the next life, she thought. If there is a next life, she will be there. And Rob. Her father. He would be there, too. If . . .

Tess wasn't able to think anymore of people or prayers to say. The fear was filling her whole body just as the water was filling the car. It was up to her shoulders, her neck. She had never been so cold in all her life. Her teeth were chattering and she was shivering from head to toe. She began to hum the tune of "Amazing Grace" to keep herself from screaming. How could she die like this? Who died this way? In a car at the bottom of a pond?

Pond, she corrected herself. And then she thought about a car in a river. It was a memory from her childhood. Tess must have been twelve or thirteen. Two college boys, who had been her father's students, accidentally drove off the bridge into the Charles River while under the influence of some combination of drugs and alcohol. She remembered hearing her parents discuss it in hushed tones, the awfulness of it, the distress of the boys' families. Why think about this now? she thought. Is this how people will talk about me? They'll shake their heads and agree that it was, indeed, a horrible way to die. And then, suddenly, like a ray of light in the freezing blackness around her, Tess remembered her father's words as he recounted the terrible incident to Dawn.

"If they hadn't been so stoned, they might have remembered their physics. They might have realized that once the car had totally filled up with water, they could have opened the car door."

For a moment, Tess's heart seemed to stop. Had she really heard her father say that so long ago? Was she hallucinating? Why would the door open once the car filled up?

Her father had taught physics. Maybe it was some law of science. Some principle that Tess had never bothered to learn. Or maybe it was her own brain, trying to protect her from what was about to happen to her. Her mind was letting her think that she would be able to open the door. That there was hope.

The water was up to her neck now and splattering her face from every angle. Part of her just wanted to sink down into it and accept what was going to happen. But she had always listened to her father. And now, even if this memory was only the figment of her terrified imagination, she had to cling to it. Let the car fill up. Hold your breath. Either it will work or it won't. One way or the other, you will find out. Tess kept her head back, her nose and mouth above the water, for as long as she could. Her body was so numb, it felt as if it had become detached from her head and yet she felt as if she were being pierced with thousands of icy knives. The panic was almost uncontrollable, but she kept her mind fastened on her father's voice, be it a memory, or a hallucination, or his way of welcoming her from beyond. At the last minute, when there was only an inch or two above her face, Tess gasped, inhaled as much air as she could, and let herself drift down, immersing herself in the cold blackness, still holding her breath and groping for the door handle. The car was completely filled. Now or never, she thought. For a moment, the faces of the people she loved passed through her mind and swelled in her heart, and then her fingers found the door handle and pressed.

As if she had found a magic password, the door that had refused to budge for the hours or moments it had taken for the car to fill suddenly swung out.

Tess almost let go of her breath in her shock, but stopped herself in time. She forced her body into the open space between the door and the door frame and pushed herself out of the car, swimming awkwardly, her limbs numb, her lungs bursting. At first she could not see where she was going and she felt a moment of panic that she would not find the surface. And then, above her, she saw a pale ribbon of light. She pointed herself upward, kicking and pushing with all her might. She felt her clothes weighing her down, but she couldn't stop to shed them. Her face burst the surface of the murky pond and the chill moonlight caressed her like a lover's kiss.

For a moment she bobbed there, exhausted, thanking God for her deliverance, and then she heard the blessed wail of police sirens and saw the flash of lights. Erny, she thought. He did it. He got help. Shivering but exultant, she summoned all her remaining strength and began to swim to the shore.

CHAPTER 36

"Something's happening in there," said Kenneth.

Dawn looked up at the front door of the Morris house as a stretcher emerged and the EMTs rushed the patient down the steps toward the waiting ambulance.

"Who is it?" Dawn asked.

Kenneth strained to see. "I can't tell from here."

The ambulance was parked beside Chan Morris's black Mercedes. Dawn peered at the car next to the Mercedes. "Isn't that Mr Ramsey's car?" she asked.

"I don't remember," said Kenneth.

A maroon van pulled up beside where they were standing and a heavyset woman in a tweed coat clambered down from the driver's seat. The van had an acronym on the side: SHARE. Dawn recognized the logo. It was from the center for abused women. The driver walked over to where Dawn, Kenneth, and Erny were standing. "Excuse me," she said. "I heard on our scanner at the center that the police were called here," she said. "Is that Mrs Morris they're carrying out?"

"We don't know who it is," said Dawn. "We heard gunshots inside the house just as we arrived. We're waiting for some word. I'm afraid my daughter might be in there."

"Oh my God," said the woman, shaking her head. "This is just awful. Sally Morris called us today. She wanted to get away from him, but when I came here this afternoon to pick her up, she wouldn't come with me. If only I could have convinced her . . ."

"Here comes another one," said Kenneth, pointing to the front door as another group of rescue workers carried out another stretcher.

Erny watched the stretchers being loaded into the ambulance with a heavy heart. Was his mother on one of them? He had done his best to try to save her. He even got into the car of a stranger — something he knew he should never do — to try to get help. He was afraid to get into that car, but he was more afraid for his mother. So he did it. Luckily, it turned out okay because the man, Ken, knew Dawn and took him right to the inn. He told the cops everything he knew. He was brave and didn't cry, and everybody told him how good he did. But now . . . now it seemed it was all for nothing. There was no sign of his mother. If she was in that house and still okay, she'd be running out of there and down those steps, calling out for him. He told the cops about the shed where the creep had locked him in and the cops were looking for her there and in the barn, but so far she wasn't anywhere that he could see.

Erny leaned against Dawn, who was talking to the woman who had driven up in the van. He tuned out their conversation and looked hopelessly up the driveway, wishing that he and his mother had never come on this trip. If they had stayed home, none of this would have happened and his mother would be with him and would be okay. He stared blankly into the darkness beyond the flashing red lights of emergency vehicles toward the driveway and the pond, which was illuminated by only a silver band of moonlight. What would happen to him now? Would he be alone again?

All of a sudden Erny saw something moving. He frowned and looked harder. There was something out there. Maybe it was an animal, crackling through the leaves and branches, he told himself. Just an animal, like that moose me and Mom saw that day from the canoe, he thought, as a cloud obscured the band of moonlight. Erny's already low spirits sank even further as he remembered that canoe adventure and how excited he had been. Before I found that dead man in the woods. Before that Chan guy took me away. He and his mom were getting ready to make a campfire. It was going to be the best day, and then it turned into the worst day. Erny sighed and slumped against Dawn's side, wondering if he would ever feel good again.

And then, materializing out of the gloom, he saw it again. A figure. At first he thought it was a ghost. It had long stringy hair and clothes that appeared to be melting. But then he realized that it was no ghost. It was a person who was walking down that driveway. Erny's heart beat wildly. He held his breath and waited, hoping against hope, as the bedraggled figure stumbled on the macadam, nearly fell, and let out a mild oath. Hearing that familiar voice, suddenly, he knew.

"Mom," he whispered.

Dawn raised her head and looked around in confusion as Erny pushed away from her and began to run toward the swaying woman. He threw himself at her. Tess saw him coming, streaking toward her like a comet in the darkness. She swept him up in her arms, pressing him against her sopping wet clothes, and let out a sob of relief.

"Ma," he cried and then recoiled from her. "You're all wet."

"I know, I know," said Tess, beaming at him.

Dawn was running toward them, Kenneth following close behind.

"Grandma!" Erny crowed. "I found her."

* * *

Dawn threw her own jacket over Tess's shoulders while Erny told anyone who would listen about how he had spotted her and knew it was her. Tess, still shivering, explained what had happened in snatches to her mother and a policeman whom Kenneth had summoned. Erny stayed glued to Tess's side, refusing to let go of her hand. She rubbed his hair and kissed him on the top of the head.

"What happened?" she asked him. "How did you get away?"

"Ken found me," he said.

Tess looked up at Kenneth Phalen, who was standing very close to Dawn. "Ken?" she said.

"He was looking for me," Erny told her. "And he took me right to Dawn. And the cops."

"Thank you so much," Tess said to Ken sheepishly. "I can never thank you enough. I'm sorry I've been so . . ."

Ken raised a hand to silence her. "I'm so happy that you're okay. I couldn't stand it if your mother had lost you."

The police officer who had taken her statement reappeared. "Chief Bosworth wants to talk to you," he said. "Can you come with me?"

"Now?" Dawn cried. "She's freezing. We need to get her home."

"We won't keep her long," said the cop.

"Okay. Sure," said Tess. She turned to Erny. "I'll be right back. Don't worry."

Pulling Dawn's coat tighter around her, Tess and the policeman started toward the house, the officer parting the crowd of curious reporters and onlookers. As they reached the spot where Chan's Mercedes was parked, Tess stopped in her tracks.

"That's Ben's car parked there," she said. "Ben Ramsey."

"Yeah," said the officer. "He was in there. He got shot."

Tess stopped, swaying on her feet. "No . . ."

"They took him in the ambulance," said the officer. "He'll be okay. Here, let me give you a hand. You look a little shaky."

Tess accepted his offer of an arm. "I am," she admitted. She was full of fear for Ben, but she clung to the officer's hopeful prediction like a life preserver. Together with the officer, they approached Chief Bosworth, who turned and frowned at them.

"This is Miss DeGraff, sir," said the officer.

"Thanks," the chief said gruffly. He looked critically at Tess. "What happened to you? Where were you? I've had teams of men searching for you."

"He tried to kill me. Chan Morris did," said Tess. "He tied me up and sank the car I was in. He tried to drown me. He killed my sister. He admitted it."

"Well, he won't hurt anyone else. He's being read his rights even as we speak."

"How is Ben Ramsey?" Tess asked. "The officer said he was shot."

"He'll pull through," said the chief. "Morris's wife wasn't so lucky."

An excited buzz suddenly arose and a cry among the onlookers as two policemen appeared in the doorway, flanking Channing Morris, who was in handcuffs. Reporters shouted his name and begged for a comment, but Chan did not look anywhere but straight ahead, his handsome face a blank mask.

Tess turned to Rusty Bosworth, who had moved to the open door of the cruiser. "Chief," she said.

"We'll need to talk to you some more at the station," Rusty said grimly. "You'd better get some dry clothes on first."

There was a slight scuffle as Chan resisted being shoved down into the backseat of the waiting police cruiser.

"Can I speak to him for a minute before you take him?" Tess asked.

"That's up to him," said Rusty Bosworth.

Tess looked closely at Chan. At this moment of ultimate defeat, his gray eyes looked indifferent and distant. His gaze flickered slightly when he saw Tess.

"I'm still alive," she said to Chan.

Chan shrugged. "Too bad," he said.

"She wants to talk to you," said Rusty Bosworth.

"I have nothing to say to her," said Chan.

"I want to ask him something," said Tess.

"I guess you'll have to visit him in jail," said Rusty.

Tess looked Chan in the eye. "Please."

Chan looked at her and shook his head. "Why?"

"Please. Give me one minute," said Tess.

Chan shrugged. "Fine."

The officers looked to their chief. Rusty Bosworth held up his index finger. "One minute," he said.

"I want you guys out of earshot," said Chan.

Rusty put his hand on the gun in his holster. "Don't try anything."

The officers stepped back and Chan, still handcuffed, inclined his head so he could hear what Tess was saying.

Tess licked her lips. She didn't want to alienate him with her question. He would turn away and never answer her. And she knew already that he would plead innocent and refuse to answer questions at his trial. But she needed to know. She spoke carefully. "You said you killed my sister out of revenge. But you didn't even know us. How could it have been revenge?" she asked.

Chan laughed scornfully. "Why should I tell you that? So you can get up on the witness stand and testify against me?"

Tess shook her head. "We both know I'm going to testify against you. But nothing I say will matter. The DNA will speak louder than I ever could."

Chan shrugged again. "You're honest," he said. "I like that."

"Then tell me why," Tess pleaded. "Please."

A white van came tearing down the driveway and screeched to a halt in the midst of the crowd of onlookers. Jake and Julie had arrived. Jake rushed over to his mother and Erny. He picked up Erny in his arms, holding him close. Julie followed right behind him, her round face beaming. Chan's disdainful gaze seemed to be fixed on the newcomers.

"I don't remember saying that," said Chan.

"You said you were angry when you saw my sister tied up in that shed," Tess prompted him. "That you wanted revenge."

Chan looked over at Julie, bulky and sensibly coiffed, and shook his head. "It's unbelievable. I didn't even recognize her when I saw her the other day."

"Saw who?" said Tess, confused. "What are you talking about?"

Chan snorted with disgust. "She was pretty then. And had a great body. And she was mine. Until your brother showed up that day at the lake."

"Julie?" Tess asked.

Chan's face was a blank, his eyes faraway, remembering. "When I saw Lazarus coming and going from the gardener's shed, and I found your sister locked up there, I considered letting her go. And then I thought, Forget that. It's payback time."

"Payback," Tess whispered.

"I probably shouldn't have taken it out on Phoebe. I know that now. But you're stupid when you're young. You think your heart will be broken forever." Chan shook his head. "What a waste. Now I wouldn't give that cow the time of day."

Chan turned his head and looked at Tess. "I'm warning you. If you say this at my trial, I will deny it."

Everything inside of Tess shrank from his cruel words. She looked over at her family. Dawn, standing close to Kenneth, was talking on her cell phone, spreading the good news that Tess was safe. Jake looked on indulgently as Julie took her turn tearfully embracing her nephew. Tess looked back at Phoebe's killer. "No. No one will ever hear that from me."

CHAPTER 37

Tess tapped at the wood frame of the screen door. Ben, who was sitting on the porch in a rocker, his feet up on the inner railing, looked over at her, smiled, and gestured for her to come in. He used his good arm, the one that was not taped to his chest.

Tess opened the door and shivered. "How can you sit out here in this weather? It's turned so cold," she said.

Ben got up from the rocker. "You're right. I was just about to go in," he said.

"I'm sorry. I didn't mean to disturb you," said Tess.

Ben leaned down and gave her a lingering kiss. "You could never disturb me," he said. He reached for the knob on the front door. "Come on. Let's go in."

"Thanks," said Tess. She followed him inside and put the bag she was carrying down on the dining table in the great room. "I raided the gourmet deli and brought us some dinner," she said. "And Dawn sent along some apple cake."

"Between your mother's cake and the doc forbidding me to run," said Ben, "I'm gonna be a blimp."

Tess smiled. "You're lucky to get any. Dawn is busy trying to fatten up Kenneth."

"Ah, the way to a man's heart," he said. "So, where's young Erny tonight?"

"He went to the movies. With his uncle. It's an action picture."

Ben chuckled. "They'll both enjoy that."

"You know it," said Tess.

"Here. Come and sit." Ben sank down into the corner of the sofa and indicated the cushion beside him.

Tess sat down beside him and shifted her body so that she was looking directly into his lake blue eyes. The urge to touch him was irresistible. As soon as she did, they moved together, cheek to cheek, their eyes closed, and then they were kissing and kissing. Tess felt like she was floating under the sun in a warm ocean as a wave of desire rose within her, around her. No, she thought. Time is short. We have to talk. Reluctantly, she pulled away from him and more reluctantly, he let her go. For a minute they gazed at each other. "How are you feeling?" she asked.

"Good," he said. "Great. Doc says I can go back to work next week."

Tess nodded. "That's good." She was quiet for a moment. Then she looked away from him and said, "I've got to get back to it, too. Erny needs to get back to school. And my team has been calling me. They're taking turns, calling me in shifts. They got grant money for a new film. It's a documentary about this suburban, junior league-type woman who moved to the inner city to try and do something meaningful with her life."

"This is a true story?"

"Oh yeah. Her husband divorced her and all the kids stayed with him except for her oldest son. He went with his mother and they run a shelter together. It's very bizarre. I think it's going to be an interesting film."

Ben nodded. "It sounds like it."

Tess glanced at him. "Still, I hate to go back," she said.

"Really?" he said. "Why?"

Tess shrugged. "Lots of reasons."

Ben reached for her hand with his free hand and kneaded it. His touch was electric to her and she did not dare to look in his eyes. They sat in silence for a few moments. Then they both spoke at once.

"You know I . . ." he said.

"It's not that . . ." she said.

Then they both stopped. "You first," she said.

"Oh. Well, I was just going to say that I got a call from the county prosecutor this morning," Ben said. "Apparently they've made a deal with Chan Morris."

Tess nodded, disappointed. She thought he was going to say something about their future — if they had one. They had spent a lot of time together since the night of the shooting — some of it in the hospital, some with Erny, and much of it alone, sharing their thoughts, their laughter and their feelings, complicated and passionate. She recognized what was growing between them — she could see it in the way he looked at her and feel it in her own heart — but neither one of them had said a word about what would happen when they had to part. Besides, there had been so many distractions. Like the upcoming trial, which had been very much on her mind, as well. "I know," she said. "They called us, too. I'm kind of glad. I didn't want to have to go through another trial. We know what happened."

"Chan will have to allocute and the judge will require a full recounting. But you know that this means . . ."

Tess looked at him. "What?"

"Well, he'll go to jail for life. The death penalty is definitely off the table."

"I thought Governor Putnam was putting a moratorium on the death penalty in this state," Tess said calmly.

"He's announced it, yes. But it hasn't officially gone into effect yet."

"Why are you bringing up the death penalty?" asked Tess.

Ben avoided her gaze. "I wasn't sure if you knew."

"Is this a test?" she asked coolly.

Ben thought about it for a minute, then he looked at her directly. "I'll tell you something, Tess. Chan Morris was my test. I thought about killing that man myself that night at his house. When he wouldn't tell me where you were, when he implied that you were dead, it did cross my mind. I'd be lying if I said it didn't."

"Well, I know you're saying that for my sake," said Tess. "The old 'solidarity' thing. I feel your pain, et cetera."

Ben looked slightly embarrassed. "Maybe a little," he said. "But it happens to be true. And I've been harsh on this subject. Self-righteous, you might say. So it's only fair to admit it. I did think about killing him. Just to get even. Just to make him pay."

"Payback," she mused, thinking about Chan's rationale for killing Phoebe. "Where does it ever end?"

Ben peered at her. "What does that mean?"

"It means that I hope Chan Morris lives a long and terrible life in prison. And that I never have to see his face again. But that's the only payback I'm interested in. Nothing else makes sense. There's been a lot of killing. And, as far as I can see, there's been no justice in any of it."

Ben nodded and they were silent again for a moment. "So, no trial. I guess that means you can leave at any time."

"Yeah," said Tess. She felt as if something precious was slipping through her fingers and she didn't know how to stop it.

"You know," he said, "this place used to be our summerhouse. When Melanie was alive. And after she died, I moved up here to . . . get away from it all."

"Yes, so you said."

Ben frowned. "I'm not sure it's the right pace for me, though, this rural life. I don't know. It was perfect at first. But then . . . well, I was thinking of maybe starting over again in a more . . . urban area."

Tess nodded. "Back to Philadelphia?"

"I don't know. How do you think I would like Washington, D.C.?" he asked.

Tess looked at him and saw that his face was pink. She felt as if the weight on her heart had turned into a balloon. "Are you thinking of moving there?"

Ben chewed the inside of his mouth. "How would you feel about that?"

Tess's mouth dropped open. "Do you mean it?" She pulled back from him and searched his face for any sign of teasing. "Really?"

"I don't want to crowd you, Tess. I know you have your job, and Erny."

Tess shook her head. Then she put her arms around him and embraced him as tightly as she could until he let out a little groan of pain.

She let him go. "I'm sorry. Are you okay?"

He put his hand on his bandaged chest. "It's just . . . this. Oh baby, wait until I get rid of this."

Tess and Ben smiled into each other's eyes and an unspoken admission passed between them that they were both imagining that day. Living for it, in fact. Tess could feel all her senses tingling at the thought. "I can't believe it," Tess said at last. "I felt so blue coming over here. At the thought of leaving you."

"I can't lose you. I can't afford a mistake like that," he said seriously.

Tess smiled. "Me, neither." She nestled carefully under his good arm, her face against his shoulder.

"I think I'll keep this place, though," he said. "We'll want to visit here."

From the safety of her position in his arms, in his heart, she looked around the room. "I guess it has a lot of good memories for you," she said. "I can understand that."

Ben did not reply.

Tess looked up at the mantel and frowned. "You took down the painting of your . . . of the woman in the woods."

Ben nodded. "Yeah."

"I just want you to know," she said, "that I'm not going to be jealous of your memories. I mean, you lost her and no one can really take her place in your heart."

Ben frowned. "About that . . ." he said.

Tess heard the reservation in his voice and turned to look at him. "Ben?"

Ben sighed. "I need to tell you about that. It's not exactly what you think."

In his eyes she saw him struggle with something secret and painful that was coming to the surface. She was not afraid. "Tell me," she said settling back down beside him. "I want to know everything."

THE END

ACKNOWLEDGMENTS

A writer needs all kinds of help. Special thanks to Anne McKenna for explaining the language of Molière. Thanks to M.J. for finding me that dress. Thanks, always, to Art, who gives me the bad news and forgives me the fallout.

ALSO BY PATRICIA MACDONALD

FROM CRADLE TO GRAVE
SISTERS
MISSING CHILD
I SEE YOU
CAST INTO DOUBT
DON'T BELIEVE A WORD
THE GIRL IN THE WOODS
SAFE HAVEN
MOTHER'S DAY
SECRET ADMIRER
LOST INNOCENTS
LITTLE SISTER
MARRIED TO A STRANGER
STOLEN IN THE NIGHT

Thank you for reading this book.

If you enjoyed it please leave feedback on Amazon or Goodreads, and if there is anything we missed or you have a question about, then please get in touch. We appreciate you choosing our book.

Founded in 2014 in Shoreditch, London, we at Joffe Books pride ourselves on our history of innovative publishing. We've been honoured to be shortlisted for Independent Publisher of the Year at the British Book Awards for the last three years.

www.joffebooks.com

We're very grateful to eagle-eyed readers who take the time to contact us. Please send any errors you find to corrections@joffebooks.com. We'll get them fixed ASAP.

Printed in Great Britain
by Amazon

12637298R00181